# SATORI

# SATORI

## DON WINSLOW

### A Novel Based on
### TREVANIAN'S SHIBUMI

GRAND CENTRAL
PUBLISHING

NEW YORK    BOSTON

Copyright © 2011 by Don Winslow and the Trevanian Beneficiaries

Grand Central Publishing
Hachette Book Group
237 Park Avenue
New York, NY 10017

www.HachetteBookGroup.com

Printed in the United States of America

First Edition: March 2011

10   9   8   7   6   5   4   3   2   1

Grand Central Publishing is a division of Hachette Book Group, Inc.
The Grand Central Publishing name and logo is a trademark of Hachette Book Group, Inc.

Library of Congress Cataloging-in-Publication Data
Winslow, Don, 1953–
    Satori / Don Winslow. — 1st ed.
        p. cm.
    ISBN 978-0-446-56192-1
    1. Assassins — Fiction.   2. Fugitives from justice — Fiction.   3. International business enterprises — Fiction.   I. Trevanian. Shibumi   II. Title.
    PS3573.I5326S38 2010
    813'.54 — dc22

                                                                2010012415

To Richard Pine

# SATORI

*Part One*

# TOKYO, OCTOBER 1951

# 1

NICHOLAI HEL WATCHED the maple leaf drop from the branch, flutter in the slight breeze, then fall gently to the ground.

It was beautiful.

Savoring the first glimpse of nature that he'd had after three years of solitary confinement in an American prison cell, he breathed in the crisp autumn air, let it fill his lungs, and held it for a few moments before he exhaled.

Haverford mistook it for a sigh.

"Glad to be out?" the agent asked.

Nicholai didn't respond. The American was as nothing to him, a mere merchant like the rest of his compatriots, peddling espionage instead of automobiles, shaving cream, or Coca-Cola. Nicholai had no intention of engaging in meaningless conversation, never mind allowing this functionary access to his personal thoughts.

Of course he was glad to be out, he thought as he looked back at the bleak gray walls of Sugamo Prison, but why did Westerners feel a need to voice the obvious, or attempt to give expression to the ineffable? It was the nature of a maple leaf to drop in the autumn. I killed General Kishikawa, as close to a father as I ever had, because it was my filial nature —and duty— to do so. The Americans imprisoned me for it because they could do nothing else, given their nature.

And now they offer me my "freedom" because they need me.

Nicholai resumed his walk along the pebbled path flanked by the maple trees. A bit surprised that he felt a twinge of anxiety at being outside the closed, small space of his cell, he fought off the wave of dizziness brought on by the open sky. This world was large and empty; he had no one left in it except himself. His own adequate company for three years, he was reentering a world that he no longer knew at the age of twenty-six.

Haverford had anticipated this, having consulted a psychologist on the issues that face prisoners going back into society. The classic Freudian, replete with the stereotypical Viennese accent, had advised Haverford that "the subject" would have become used to the limitations of his confinement and feel overwhelmed at first by the sheer space suddenly confronting him in the outside world. It would be prudent, the doctor warned, to transfer the man to a small, windowless room with voluntary access to a yard or garden so that he could gradually acclimate himself. Open spaces, or a crowded city with its bustling population and incessant noise, would be likely to upset the subject.

So Haverford had arranged for a small room in a quiet safe house in the Tokyo suburbs. But from what he could learn from what there *was* to be learned of Nicholai Hel, he couldn't imagine the man being easily overwhelmed or upset. Hel displayed preternatural self-possession, a calm that was almost condescending, confidence that often crossed the line into arrogance. On the surface, Hel appeared to be a perfect blend of his aristocratic Russian mother and his samurai surrogate father, the war criminal Kishikawa, whom he had saved from the shame of a hangman's noose with a single finger-thrust to the trachea.

Despite his blond hair and vibrant green eyes, Haverford thought, Hel is more Asian than Western. He even walks like an Asian — his arms crossed behind his back so as to take up as little space as possible and not cause inconvenience to anyone coming from the other direction, his tall, thin frame slightly stooped in modesty. European in appearance, Haverford decided, Asian in substance. Well, it made sense — he was raised by his émigré mother in Shanghai, and then mentored by Kishikawa when the Japs took the city. After the mother died, Kishikawa moved the boy to Japan to live with and study under a master of the impossibly complicated and nuanced board game Go, a sort of Jap chess, albeit a hundredfold more difficult.

Hel became a master in his own right.

So is it any wonder that Hel thinks like an Asian?

Nicholai sensed the man's thoughts on him. The Americans are incredibly transparent, their thoughts as obvious as stones at the bottom of a clear, still pool. He didn't care what Haverford thought of him — one doesn't solicit the opinions of a grocery clerk — but it did annoy him. Shifting his attention to the sun on his face, he felt it warm his skin.

"What would you like?" Haverford asked.

"In the sense of what?"

Haverford chuckled. Most men emerging from long confinement wanted three things — a drink, a meal, and a woman, not necessarily in that order. But he was not going to indulge Hel's arrogance, so he answered, in Japanese, "In the sense of what would you like?"

Mildly impressed that Haverford spoke Japanese, and interested that he refused to surrender such a small stone on the board, Nicholai responded, "I don't suppose that you could organize an acceptable cup of tea."

"In fact," Haverford said, "I've arranged a modest *cha-kai*. I hope you find it acceptable."

A formal tea ceremony, Nicholai thought.

How interesting.

A car waited at the end of the walk. Haverford opened the back door and ushered Nicholai in.

# 2

THE *CHA-KAI* WAS not only acceptable, it was sublime.

Nicholai savored each sip of the *cha-noyu* as he sat cross-legged on the tatami floor next to the lacquered table. The tea was transcendent, as was the geisha who knelt nearby, discreetly just out of hearing range of the sparse conversation.

To Nicholai's shock, the functionary Haverford knew his way around the tea ceremony and served with impeccable courtesy, his ritual flawless. Upon arrival at the teahouse, Haverford had apologized that there were, by necessity, no other guests, then led Nicholai into the *machiai*, the waiting room, where he introduced Nicholai to an exquisitely lovely geisha.

"This is Kamiko-san," Haverford said. "She will serve as my *hanto* today."

Kamiko bowed and handed Nicholai a kimono to put on, then offered him *sayu*, a cup of the same hot water that would be used to brew the tea. Nicholai took a sip, then, as Haverford excused himself to go prepare the tea, Kamiko took Nicholai outside to the *roji*, the "dew ground," a small garden that held only arrangements of rocks but no flowers. They sat on the stone bench and, without conversation, enjoyed the tranquility.

A few minutes later Haverford, now kimono-clad, walked to a stone basin and ceremonially washed his mouth and hands in the fresh water, then stepped through the middle gate into the *roji*, where he formally welcomed Nicholai with a bow. In turn, Nicholai purified himself at the *tsukubai*.

To enter the *cha-shitsu*, the tearoom, they had to pass through a sliding door that was only three feet high, forcing them to bow, an act that symbolized the divide between the physical world and the spiritual realm of the tearoom.

The *cha-shitsu* was exquisite, elegant in its simplicity, a perfect expression of *shibumi*. As tradition demanded, they first walked to an alcove, on the wall of which hung the *kakemono*, a scroll with painted calligraphy appropriate to the day's occasion. In his role as guest, Nicholai admired the skillful brushwork, which depicted the Japanese symbol for *satori*.

An interesting choice, Nicholai thought. *Satori* was the Zen Buddhist concept of a sudden awakening, a realization of life as it really is. It came not as a result of meditation or conscious thought, but could arrive in the wisp of a breeze, the crackle of a flame, the falling of a leaf.

Nicholai had never known *satori*.

In front of the *kakemono*, on a small wooden stand, was a bowl that held a single small maple branch.

They stepped over to a low table, on which was a charcoal burner and a kettle. As Nicholai and Kamiko knelt on the mat by the table, Haverford bowed and left the room. A few moments later a gong sounded, and he returned carrying the *cha-wan*, a red ceramic bowl that contained a tea whisk, a tea scoop, and a cloth.

As *teishu*, the host, Haverford knelt at his proper place at the table, directly across the hearth from Nicholai. He wiped all the utensils with the cloth, then filled the bowl with hot water, rinsed the whisk, then poured the water into a waste bowl and carefully wiped the tea bowl again.

Nicholai found himself enjoying the old ritual, but did not want to be lulled into complacency. The American had obviously done his research and knew that in the few years of freedom Nicholai had enjoyed in Tokyo before his imprisonment, he had established a formal Japanese household, with retainers, and had observed the old rituals. Surely he knew that Nicholai would find the *cha-kai* both nostalgic and comforting.

And it is both, Nicholai thought, but be cautious.

Haverford presented the tea scoop, then opened a small container and paused to allow his guest to appreciate the aroma. Nicholai realized with surprise that this was *koi-cha*, from plants one hundred years old, grown only in the shade in certain parts of Kyoto. He could not imagine what this *mat-cha* might have cost, then wondered what it might eventually cost him, given that the Americans had not gone to such extravagance for nothing.

Pausing for precisely the correct time, Haverford then dipped a small ladle into the container and scooped out six measures of the finely powdered pale green tea into the *cha-wan*. He used the bamboo ladle to heap hot water into the bowl, then took the whisk and whipped the potion into a thin paste. He examined his work, then, satisfied, passed the bowl across the table to Nicholai.

As ritual demanded, Nicholai bowed, took the *cha-wan* with his right hand, then passed it to his left, holding it only in the palm of his hand. He turned it clockwise three times and then took a long sip. The tea was superb, and Nicholai politely finished his drink with a loud slurp. Then he wiped the rim of the *cha-wan* with his right hand, turned it once clockwise, and handed it back to Haverford, who bowed and took a drink.

Now the *cha-kai* entered a less formal phase, as Haverford wiped the *cha-wan* again and Kamiko added more charcoal to the hearth in preparation for making cups of thinner tea. Still, there were formalities to observe, and Nicholai in his role as guest began a conversation about the utensils used in the ceremony.

"The *cha-wan* is Momoyama Period, yes?" he said to Haverford, recognizing the distinct red tincture. "It is beautiful."

"Momoyama, yes," Haverford answered, "but not the best example."

They both knew that the seventeenth-century bowl was rightfully priceless. The American had gone to immense trouble and expense to arrange this "modest" *cha-kai*, and Nicholai could not help but wonder why.

And the American could not quite contain his satisfaction at pulling off this surprise.

I don't know you, Hel, Haverford thought as he sank back into his own *seiza* position, but you don't know me either.

In fact, Ellis Haverford was something quite different from the Company thugs who had beaten Nicholai to a bloody pulp during three days of brutal interrogation. A native of Manhattan's Upper East Side, he had spurned Yale and Harvard for Columbia, as he couldn't imagine anyone choosing to live anywhere but on the isle of Manhattan. He was majoring in Oriental history and languages when Pearl Harbor was bombed, and was therefore a natural to go into an intelligence desk job.

Haverford refused, joined the Marines instead, and commanded a platoon on Guadalcanal and a company in New Guinea. Purple Heart and Navy Cross on his chest, he finally conceded that his education was being wasted, agreed to go into the covert side of the war, and found himself training local resistance movements against the Japanese in the jungles of French Indochina. Haverford was fluent in French, Japanese, and Vietnamese and could make himself understood in some parts of China. As aristocratic in his own way as Hel—although he came from far more money—Ellis Haverford was one of those rare individuals who seemed comfortable in any setting, including an exclusive Japanese teahouse.

Now Kamiko served thin tea and brought out *mukozuke*, a tray of light snacks — sashimi and pickled vegetables.

"The food is good," Nicholai said in Japanese as Kamiko served.

"It's garbage," Haverford answered, pro forma, "but I'm afraid it's the best I can offer. I am so sorry."

"It's more than enough," Nicholai said, unconsciously slipping into Japanese manners that he had not had the opportunity to use for years.

"You are more than kind," Haverford responded.

Aware of Kamiko's passive attention, Nicholai asked, "Shall we switch languages?"

Haverford already knew that Hel spoke English, French, Russian, German, Chinese, Japanese, and, randomly, Basque — so there was quite a menu from which to choose. He suggested French and Nicholai accepted.

"So," Nicholai said, "you have offered me one hundred thousand dollars, my liberty, a Costa Rican passport, and the home addresses of Major Diamond and his apprentices in exchange for my performing a service that I assume involves a murder."

"'Murder' is an ugly word," Haverford answered, "but you have the basic elements of the deal correct, yes."

"Why me?"

"You have certain unique characteristics," Haverford said, "combined with specific skills required for the assignment."

"Such as?"

"You don't need to know that yet."

"When do I begin?" Nicholai asked.

"More a question of *how*."

"Very well. *How* do I begin?"

"First," Haverford answered, "we repair your face."

"You find it unpalatable?" Nicholai asked, aware that his once handsome countenance was indeed a lopsided, swollen and disjointed mess from the fists and truncheons of Major Diamond and his associates.

Nicholai had worked for the Americans as a translator until he had killed Kishikawa-san; then Diamond and his goons had beaten Nicholai before subjecting him to mind-altering, horrifying experiments with psychotropic drugs. The pain had been bad enough, the disfigurement still worse, but what hurt Nicholai even more was the loss of control, the terrible helplessness, the feeling that Diamond and his disgusting little helpers had somehow stolen his very being and played with it the way a twisted and stupid child might have toyed with a captive animal.

I will deal with them in due time, he thought. Diamond, his thugs, the doctor who administered the injections and observed the results on his "patient" with cold-blooded clinical interest — they will all see me again, albeit briefly, and just before they die.

Right now I must come to terms with Haverford, who is essential to achieving my revenge. At least Haverford is interesting — impeccably dressed, obviously well educated, just as obviously a scion of what passes for the aristocracy in America.

"Not at all," Haverford said. "I just believe that when you damage something, you should repair it. It seems only fair."

Haverford is trying to tell me, Nicholai thought, in a quite un-American subtle way, that *he* is not *them*. But of course you *are*, the clothes and education are but a patina on the same cracked vessel. He asked, "What if I do not choose to be 'repaired'?"

"Then I am afraid we would have to cancel our arrangement,"

Haverford said pleasantly, glad that the French softened what would be a harsh ultimatum in English. "Your current appearance would prompt questions, the answers to which don't match the cover we've taken a lot of trouble creating for you."

" 'Cover'?"

"A new identity," Haverford answered, reminded that while Hel was an efficient killer he was nevertheless a neophyte in the larger world of espionage, "replete with a fictitious personal history."

"Which is what?" Nicholai asked.

Haverford shook his head. "You don't need to know yet."

Deciding to test the board, Nicholai said, "I was quite content in my cell. I could go back."

"You could," Haverford agreed. "And we could decide to bring you to trial for the murder of Kishikawa."

Well played, Nicholai thought, deciding that he needed to be more cautious when dealing with Haverford. Seeing that there was no route of attack there, he retreated like a slowly ebbing tide. "The surgery on my face—I assume we are discussing surgery..."

"Yes."

"I also assume it will be painful."

"Very."

"The recuperation period?"

"Several weeks," Haverford answered. He refilled Nicholai's cup, then his own, and nodded to Kamiko to bring a fresh pot. "They won't be wasted, however. You have a lot of work to do."

Nicholai raised an eyebrow.

"Your French," Haverford said. "Your vocabulary is impressive, but your accent is all wrong."

"My French nanny would be greatly offended."

Haverford switched to Japanese, a better language than French to express polite regret. "*Gomen nosei*, but your new dialect needs to be more southern."

Why would that be? Nicholai wondered. He didn't ask, however, not wanting to appear too curious or, for that matter, interested.

Kamiko waited at their periphery, then, hearing him finish, bowed and served the tea. She was beautifully coiffed, with alabaster skin and sparkling eyes, and Nicholai was annoyed when Haverford noticed him looking and said, "It has already been arranged, Hel-san."

"Thank you, no," Nicholai said, unwilling to give the American the satisfaction of correctly perceiving his physical need. It would show weakness, and give Haverford a victory.

"Really?" Haverford asked. "Are you sure?"

Or else I would not have spoken, Nicholai thought. He didn't answer the question, but instead said, "One more thing."

"Yes?"

"I will not kill an innocent person."

Haverford chuckled. "Small chance of that."

"Then I accept."

Haverford bowed.

# 3

NICHOLAI STRUGGLED against unconsciousness.

Yielding control was anathema to a man who had lived his life on the principle of firm self-possession, and it brought back memories of the pharmacological torture that the Americans had inflicted on him. So he fought to stay conscious, but the anesthesia took its course and put him under.

As a boy he had commonly experienced spontaneous mental states in which he would find himself removed from the moment and lying in a serene meadow of wildflowers. He didn't know how it happened or why, just that it was peaceful and delicious. He called these interludes his "resting times" and could not understand how anyone could live without them.

But the firebombing of Tokyo, the deaths of friends, then Hiroshima, Nagasaki, and the arrest of his surrogate father General Kishikawa as a *war criminal* — that cultured man who had introduced him to Go and to a civilized, disciplined, thoughtful life — had robbed him of his precious "resting times," and, try as he would, he could not seem to recover the serenity that had once been natural to him.

Tranquility was harder to achieve when they put him on an airplane with blackened windows and flew him to the United States, taking him off the flight with bandages around his face as if he had been wounded. He found it harder yet to maintain his equanimity when they rolled his stretcher into the hospital and put the needles into his arm and a mask over his nose and mouth.

He woke panicked because his arms were strapped down to the gurney.

"It's all right," a female American voice said. "We just don't want you rolling around or touching your face."

"I won't."

She chuckled, not believing him.

Nicholai would have argued further, but the pain was acute, like a horribly bright light shimmering in front of his eyes. He blinked, then controlled his breathing and sent the light to the other side of the room where he could observe it dispassionately. The pain still existed, but it was now a detached phenomenon, interesting in its intensity.

"I'll give you a shot," the nurse said.

"It isn't necessary," Nicholai answered.

"Oh," she said, "we can't have you wincing or clenching your jaw. The surgery on your facial bones was very delicate."

"I assure you that I will lie perfectly still," Nicholai answered. Through the slits that were his eyes he could now see her preparing the syringe. She was a Celtic-looking healthy type, all pale skin, freckles, rusty hair, and thick forearms. He exhaled, relaxed his hands, and slipped them through the bonds.

The nurse looked terribly annoyed. "Are you going to make me call the doctor?"

"Do what you think you must."

The doctor came in a few minutes later. He made a show of checking the bandages that covered Nicholai's face, clucked with the satisfaction of a hen that has just laid a splendid egg, and then said, "The surgeries went very well. I expect a successful result."

Nicholai didn't bother with a concurring banality.

"Keep your hands off your face," the doctor said to him.

Turning to the nurse, he added, "If he doesn't want anything for the pain, he doesn't want anything for the pain. When he gets tired of playing the stoic, he'll call you. Take your time getting there if you want a small measure of revenge."

"Yes, Doctor."

"I do good work," the doctor said to Nicholai. "You're going to have to beat the women off with a stick."

It took Nicholai quite a while to work through the idiom.

"There will be some minor paralysis of some small facial muscles, I'm afraid," the doctor added, "but nothing you can't live with. It will help you keep that indifferent front of yours."

Nicholai never did call for the shot.

Nor did he move.

# 4

CAMOUFLAGED BY NIGHT and the monsoon's slashing rain, the one they call the Cobra squatted perfectly still.

The Cobra watched the man's feet plop down in the mud and slosh onto the trail that led toward the bushes where he would do his personal business. It was his routine, so the Cobra was expecting him. The assassin had sat and waited many nights to learn the prey's habits.

The man came closer, just a few feet now from where the Cobra waited in the bamboo beside the narrow footpath. Intent on his destination, the man saw nothing as he wiped a sluice of rain from his face.

The Cobra chose that moment to uncoil and strike. The blade — silver like the rain — shot out and slashed the man's thigh. The victim felt the odd pain, looked down, and pressed his hand to the bloody tear in his pants leg. But it was too late — the femoral artery was severed and the blood poured around his hand and through his fingers. Already in shock, he sat down and watched his life flow into the puddle that quickly formed around him.

The Cobra was already gone.

# 5

If Major Diamond was pleased that Nicholai Hel had accepted the deal, he wasn't overly demonstrative in his enthusiasm.

"Hel's a half-Nippo nut job," Diamond said, "with scrambled brains."

"Yes," Haverford answered, "you had something to do with scrambling them, didn't you?"

"He was a Commie agent." Diamond shrugged. Sure, he'd roughed Hel up a little, used him as a guinea pig for some of the new pharmaceutical techniques. So what? They were at war with the Communist bloc and it was a dirty war. Besides, Hel was an arrogant young shit — that superior, condescending attitude of his just made you want to hurt him.

Diamond thought he'd left him far behind when he transferred to the new CIA and left Japan for the Southeast Asian assignment, but the troubling Hel was like a kite tail. They should have executed him when they had the chance — now they were going to use him as an *asset*?

It was just like that pansy-ass pinko Haverford, another over-educated, know-it-all little prick. Shit, Haverford had fought *with* the Viet Minh during the war, and what the hell kind of name is Ellis, anyway?

Now Haverford said, "Hel was not a Communist agent, a Soviet agent, or an agent of any kind. As your 'interrogation' of him proved, by the way."

Haverford despised Diamond, from his looks to the core of his alleged soul. The man resembled nothing more than an over-strung guitar with a pair of thin lips and drooping eyelids, and the inner man was even uglier. A bourgeois thug who would have been a cheerful Nazi save for the accident of his American birth—more's the pity—Diamond was the sort of intelligence officer that the army seemed to crank out like so many widgets—unimaginative, brutal, his prejudices undisturbed by thought or education.

Haverford hated him, his class, and what they threatened to do to America's relationships in Asia.

John Singleton, head of the CIA's Asia Desk, sat behind his broad desk observing the debate. His white hair lay over his craggy face like snow on a rocky mountain, his pale blue eyes were the color of ice.

He was truly a "cold warrior"; in fact, the coldest man that Haverford had ever known.

Singleton's ruthlessness had made him a legend. The éminence grise of the Washington intelligence community, he was respected—even feared—from Foggy Bottom to Capitol Hill, even to Pennsylvania Avenue itself.

For good reason, Haverford thought. Compared to Singleton, Machiavelli was a naïve choirboy and the Borgias subjects of a Rockwell painting. Standing beside Singleton, the devil himself would appear as the angel Lucifer *before* the fall.

Chief of the OSS Asian Bureau during the war, Singleton was reputed responsible for guerrilla operations in China and Vietnam and was even thought to have been influential in the decision to drop the bombs on Hiroshima and Nagasaki.

After the war he had politically survived the "loss" of China, the surprise invasion of Korea, and even attacks from McCarthy and his cohorts. In fact, Singleton was probably more powerful now than ever, a fact that his many enemies, albeit quietly, attributed to his close relationship to Satan.

Now he looked across his desk at the two rival officers.

"Is Hel unstable?" he asked Haverford.

"To the contrary," Haverford answered. "I've never met a man as self-possessed as Nicholai Hel."

"What are you, in love with the guy or something?" Diamond chimed in, his mouth leering with the crude homophobic implication.

"No, I'm not in love with the guy," Haverford answered tiredly.

"Kill this mission, sir," Diamond said to Singleton. "It's too risky and Hel is a loose cannon. I have much more reliable assassins in southern China that we could send to—"

"Hel is perfect," Haverford said.

"How so?" Singleton asked.

Haverford laid out his reasoning—Hel was fluent in Chinese, Russian, and French. He was a trained martial artist who could not only execute the sanction, but do so in a way that would leave the manner of death ambiguous, a crucial factor in achieving the maximum positive result.

"Why is French important?" Diamond asked, smelling trouble.

"It's why we brought you in for briefing," Singleton said. "Ellis?"

"Hel's cover will be a French arms dealer," Haverford said, anticipating Diamond's discomfiture with great pleasure, "selling weapons to the Viet Minh."

Indeed, Diamond's lips bent into a grimace.

"As that affects your Indochinese bailiwick," Singleton said, "we thought you should know."

Great, Diamond thought. I don't have enough trouble trying to keep the Frogs from punting another war without my own team sending aid to the enemy? "You're not telling me that you're actually going to —"

"Of course not. It's just a cover to get Hel to Beijing," Haverford said. "But we didn't want you overreacting to any radar pings you might pick up."

Diamond glared at Haverford. "Keep your boy the hell away from my turf."

"Don't worry."

But Diamond was worried. If knowledge of Operation X—and his real role in it—ever reached Washington... "X" was an Indochinese op, run by the Frogs, so he thought he had it nicely contained. Now this Hel business threatened contamination.

Diamond turned to Singleton. "Sir, I'd like to be kept current with all phases of the operation, if you don't mind."

"You'll be briefed," Singleton assured him. "Ellis, keep him posted on everything you do."

"Yes, sir."

"And, Ellis, if you could stay for a moment."

Diamond left the meeting. Nicholai Hel free, he thought in the elevator. He felt the involuntary tremor in his leg. Face it, he thought, you're afraid of the guy, and with good reason. He's a trained killer with a grudge against you.

And then there's Operation X.

If there's even the slightest chance of that getting out.

He couldn't allow it to happen.

"Does Hel know the identity of his target?" Singleton asked Haverford.

"I haven't told him yet."

Singleton thought this over for a few moments, then asked, "Is there anything to what Diamond said? About Hel being a loose cannon?"

"I don't think so," Haverford answered. "But I've taken the caution of providing, to mix nautical metaphors, an anchor."

Singleton dismissed Haverford, then checked his schedule with his secretary and saw that he had a few moments for reflection. He went into his private study, sat down at his table, and contemplated the Go board in front of him.

He'd been at this game against himself for some weeks now, and the shapes of the opposing stones were slowly becoming beautiful. They could almost be called graceful in the delicate interplay between the yin and yang of opposites. Only on the *go-kang* did life promise perfect balance.

Diamond would be Diamond and Haverford would be Haverford — they were virtually fixtures on the board.

But Hel...

Singleton moved a black stone.

Hel would soon learn the identity of his target and would be, shall we say, *motivated*.

But to do what?

How would this Go player respond? It was not an exaggeration to say that the immediate future of Asia depended on the complex persona of Nicholai Hel.

An "anchor," Singleton mused.

How interesting.

# 6

SOLANGE WAS as lovely as her name.

Her hair was the color of spun gold swirling with streams of amber, her eyes as blue as a midday sea. An aquiline nose betrayed the Roman colonization of her native Languedoc, but her full lips could only have been French. A light spray of freckles disrupted an otherwise almost monotonously perfect porcelain complexion, and the soft curve of her high cheekbones prevented what might be an unfortunate severity. She was tall, just a head shy of Nicholai's height, longlegged and full-bodied, her breasts stretching taut the simple but elegant blue dress.

But it was her voice that affected Nicholai the most. Low but gentle, with that particular Gallic softness that was simultaneously genteel and sensual. "Welcome to my home, monsieur. I hope you will be comfortable."

"I'm sure I will be."

Solange offered her hand to be kissed, as if most of his face weren't obscured by bandages. He took her hand in his—her fingers were long and thin—and kissed it, the cotton of the bandage touching her skin along with his lips. "*Enchanté.*"

"May I show you to your bedroom?"

"*S'il vous plaît,*" said Nicholai. The long flight from the United States back to Tokyo had tired him.

"*S'il vous* plaît," she said, gently correcting his pronunciation to hold the "a" sound a touch longer.

Nicholai accepted the criticism and repeated the phrase, echoing her enunciation. She rewarded him with a smile of approval. "Your nanny was from Tours, perhaps? The purest accent in France. But we need to give you an *accent du Midi*."

"I understand that's why I'm here."

"I am from the south," she told him. "Montpellier."

"I've never been."

"It is beautiful," she said. "Sunny and warm. And the light..."

His bedroom was simple but tasteful, the walls a yellow that was cheerful without being oppressively chirpy, the spare furniture painted a middle-range blue that perfectly complemented the walls. The large bed—after the cot in his cell it looked massive—was covered with a blue duvet. A single chrysanthemum had been placed in a vase on the bedside table.

"It is a Japanese flower, no?" Solange asked.

"Yes."

"And you have missed them?"

"Yes," he said, feeling oddly touched. "Thank you."

"*Pas de quoi.*"

"I beg your pardon?"

"The proper response would be to say '*je vous en prie,*'" she said, "but the—*comment vous dites*—the 'vernacular' would be '*il n'y a pas de quoi*' or simply '*pas de quoi.*' *Vous voyez?*"

"*Très bien.*"

"Very good," she said. "But roll your 'r' on your tongue, please. *Comme ça.*" She formed her mouth into a shape that Nicholai found rather attractive. "*Très bien.*"

"*Très bien.*"

"And a bit more through the nose, please."

He repeated the words, giving the ending a nasal twang.

"*Formidable,*" she said. "Notice the trace of a 'g' at the end, but just a ghost of one, please. You don't want to sound like a rustic, rather a cultured man of the south. Are you tired or would you like to take lunch now?"

"I am more hungry than tired."

"I have taken the liberty of preparing something."

She led him into a small dining room. The window gave a view onto a *karesansui* Japanese rock garden bordered by a high bamboo wall. The garden had been done with skill, and reminded him of the garden he had so meticulously constructed at his own home in Tokyo. He had found a measure of contentment in that home before making the decision to kill Kishikawa-sama. He asked, "Am I allowed the freedom of the garden?"

"Of course," she said. "This is your home for as long as you are here."

"Which is for how long, please?"

"As long as it takes you to recuperate," she said, effortlessly deflecting the real question. Then, with a smile that was just mischievous, she added, "And to learn proper French."

Solange gestured to a chair at the table.

He sat down as she walked into the kitchen.

The room, like the rest of the house's interior, was completely European, and he wondered where she had acquired the furnishings. She probably hadn't, he decided, it was more likely her American masters who provided the resources to replicate a French country house, albeit with a *karesansui*. Doubtless they'd calculated that he would absorb his French "cover" through some sort of decorative osmosis, just as doubtless after consultation with a "psychologist," one of those priests of the new American civil religion. Nevertheless, the room was pleasant and stimulating to the appetite.

So was the aroma coming from the kitchen. Delicate, with a trace of wine perhaps, and he thought he detected the musty aroma of mushrooms. Solange returned and set a stoneware casserole on the table, removed the lid and announced, "Coq au vin. I hope you like."

The smell was tantalizing.

He said, "I have not had European cuisine in many years."

"I hope it will not upset your stomach," she said. "It is necessary, though, that you eat mostly French food from now on."

"A pleasure, but why?"

Solange pursed her lips into a pretty pout, then answered, "I wish to say this delicately, without giving offense..."

"Please be blunt," he said, although he doubted that bluntness was in her repertoire.

"As it is," she said, "you smell like a Japanese. *Il faut que vous ayez l'odeur d'un vrai français.*"

"I see." It was so, of course. In his prison cell, he could discern the nationality of someone coming down the corridor by his odor. The Americans had that beef smell on them, the Russians the strong scent of potato, the Japanese guards smelled of fish and vegetables. And Solange? All he could smell was her perfume.

"May I serve?" she asked.

"Please."

She ladled out a healthy portion of the rich chicken and wine dish, then took some asparagus spears from another dish and put them on his plate. Then she poured him a glass of rich red wine. "It is good to serve the same wine in which you braised the chicken. Good *French* wine, monsieur."

"Call me Nicholai."

"*Eh bien*, Nicholai," she answered. "Please call me Solange."

"What a lovely name."

She blushed, and it was very pretty. Then she sat down and served herself, but waited for him to taste his food. When he did, she asked, "Do you like?"

"It's extraordinary." He was telling the truth. The flavors, subtle yet distinct, burst in his mouth, and the taste of the wine recalled boyhood meals at home with his mother. Perhaps, he thought, I might take up European wine...if I survive. "My compliments to the chef."

She bowed her head. "*Merci.*"

"You made this?" he asked, surprised.

"I love to cook," she said. "I've had little chance these past few years, so it is a great joy."

Solange took up her fork and ate with a relish that would have been considered unbecoming in a Japanese woman, but in her was quite appealing, a joie de vivre that Nicholai hadn't seen during the long years of war, the hungry occupation, the lonely prison. It was a pleasure to watch her enjoy the meal. After a few minutes he said, "So the man I am meant to imitate, he ate French food even in Asia?"

"I believe so."

"How did he manage that?"

"Money," she answered, as if it were obvious. "Money makes all things possible."

"Is that why you work for the Americans?" he asked, instantly regretting it and wondering why he felt an impulse to offend her.

"*Tout le monde*," Solange said. "Everyone works for the Americans now."

Including you, *mon ami*, she thought, smiling at him. She got up from her chair. "I made a *tarte tatin*. Would you like some?"

"That would be nice."

"Coffee?"

"I would prefer tea, if you have it."

"Coffee for you now, Nicholai," she said. "*Un express avec une cigarette.*"

She left for a minute, then returned with the apple *tarte*, a small pot of espresso, and a pack of Gauloises and set them on the table.

"I apologize for my rudeness," Nicholai said. "I have become unused to conversation."

"*Pas de quoi.*" She liked that he apologized.

The *tarte* was delicious, the coffee, surprisingly more so. Nicholai sat back in his chair and Solange nudged the pack of cigarettes toward him. "Take two," she said, "light them, and give one to me."

"Seriously?"

She laughed. "Didn't you ever go to the cinema?"

"No." It always seemed an odd concept to him, to sit and stare at other people's fantasies projected through a strip of celluloid.

"I love the cinema," Solange said. "I wanted to be an actress."

Nicholai thought to ask what had prevented her — certainly she was attractive enough — but then decided that the answer might cause her sadness, so he refrained. Instead, he shook two cigarettes from the pack, put them both in his mouth, then struck a match and lit them. When the tip of one glowed, he handed it to her.

"*Formidable*," Solange said. "Paul Henreid would be jealous."

Nicholai had no idea what she meant, but he inhaled the smoke and endured a spasm of coughing. It hurt where the stitches were. "It's been a while," he said when he recovered.

"Apparently." She laughed at him but he didn't feel in the least offended or embarrassed. It was more as if they were sharing an amusing moment, and he started to laugh himself. Again, it hurt a little bit, and he realized that it had been a very long time since he'd laughed with another person.

Solange discerned his thought. "It is good, no? We have not lived through laughing times, I think, you and me."

"Nor the world at large," Nicholai said

She refilled his wine glass, then her own, lifted it and said, "To better times."

"To better times."

"You must learn to smoke, Nicholai," she said. "All Frenchmen smoke."

"I sneaked cigarettes when I was a boy in Shanghai," Nicholai answered. "The Chinese smoke like chimneys. Smoke, and spit."

"We can do without the spitting, I think."

After lunch he strolled in the garden.

It had been very well done, indeed. Pathways led around an area of gravel carefully raked to replicate the ripples of the ocean. A small "island," of short grass and stone, in the middle of the "sea," represented the mountains of Japan. Shrubs had been perfectly placed around the path to offer a fresh perspective at every curve.

Like life itself, Nicholai thought.

# 7

THE NEXT FEW WEEKS passed in pleasant routine.

Nicholai woke early and went into the garden to meditate. When he came out, Solange had a café au lait and a croissant ready for him, and while it took him some time to get used to the concept of bread for breakfast, he came to enjoy it. After breakfast they engaged in conversation, during which she corrected his accent and suggested current slang and vernacular. Solange was an exacting taskmistress, which Nicholai appreciated.

For her part, Solange knew that the slightest slip, a careless anachronism or a lapse into a stilted formality, could cost him his life. So she pushed him hard, insisted on perfection, challenged his intellect and considerable talent for languages. He exceeded her expectations — his pride made him a superb student.

They conversed through lunch, and then Nicholai took his customary walk in the garden. Knowing that he needed solitude, she was discreet enough never to accept his polite invitation to join him. Instead, she had a small rest before starting preparations for dinner. When he came back, they would go over maps of Montpellier, photographs of certain cafés, restaurants, and landmarks that a native would know. She quizzed him about the Place Ste.-Anne, the marketplace, who sold the best peaches, where one could get a decent bottle of wine for a price.

Following the afternoon study session, Nicholai repaired to his room to rest, study, and bathe, which he did in a gloriously hot

Japanese tub. He emerged from the near-scalding water delight-
fully refreshed, and then dressed for dinner, which was always
French and always superb. After dinner they had a coffee and a
cognac, conversed casually, perhaps listened to a little radio until
Solange retired to her bedroom.

Then Nicholai changed into a *gi* and went out into the garden for his nightly ritual. At first, Solange peeked through her
window blinds to watch him perform the intricate maneuvers of
the *kata* — the repetitive martial arts routines — of *hoda korosu*,
"naked kill." He appeared to be dancing, but after a few nights of
watching Solange started to perceive that he was fighting numerous imaginary enemies coming at him from all directions, and
that the motions of the "dance" were in fact defensive blocks followed by lethal strikes. If it was a dance, it was a dance of death.

Nicholai enjoyed these sessions very much — it was a joy to
exercise in the garden, it calmed his mind and spirit, and besides,
his instinct told him that he might very well need to polish his
rusty skills to survive the mission, the target of which Haverford
would still not disclose.

So Nicholai exercised with a purpose, glad to find that
his mind and body responded even after the years of relative
inactivity — although he did thousands of press-ups and sit-ups
in his cell — and that the complicated and subtle movements of
the *hoda korosu kata* came back to him.

He had started studying "naked kill" during his second year
in Tokyo. The rarefied form of karate — which itself means
"empty hand" — was taught by an old Japanese master of the
lethal art who at first refused to teach an apparent Westerner the
ancient secrets. But Nicholai persevered, mostly by kneeling in a
painful position at the edge of the mat and watching, night after
night, until finally the master called him over and administered
a beating that was the first of many lessons.

Essential to *hoda korosu* was the mastery of *ki*, the internal life force that came from the proper management of breath. It was *ki*, flowing through the body from the lower abdomen to every vein, muscle, and nerve in the body, that gave the *hoda korosu* strikes their lethal force, especially at close range.

The other necessary element was the ability to calm the mind, to free it for the creativity to find a lethal weapon among common objects that might be at hand in the suddenness of an unexpected attack.

As he resumed his practice now, the first few nights were brutal in their clumsiness and would have been appalling had he not found his ineptitude almost comical. But his quickness and strength developed quickly and it wasn't long before he reacquired some skill and even a measure of grace. His master had taught him — sometimes with a bamboo rod across the back — to train with utter seriousness, to picture his enemies as he dispatched them, and Nicholai did this as he slid back and forth across the garden, repeating the lengthy *kata* dozens of times before he stopped, his *gi* soaked with sweat. Then he treated himself to a quick bath, collapsed into bed, and was soon asleep.

One morning, two weeks into his stay, Solange surprised him by saying, "This is a big day for you, Nicholai."

"How so?"

"The unveiling, so to speak."

"Of…"

"You, of course," she said. "Your face."

He had gone to the doctor's office once a week for the hefty Irish nurse to change his wrappings, none too gently at that. But she had deliberately kept him away from a mirror until the healing process was complete, so this would be the first time that he would see his reconstructed face.

If he was at all nervous or anxious, he didn't betray it. It was as if Solange had told him that they were going to see a photo exhibit or a film. He seemed detached. If it were me, she thought, I would be a mess—he was as cool as a March morning, placid as a still pond.

"The doctor said that I could do it," Solange said.

"Now?" Nicholai asked.

"If you wish."

Nicholai shrugged. It would be nice to have the bandages off, certainly, but he wasn't really all that curious about his face. He had sat in solitary confinement for those years, where it really didn't matter what one looked like—there was no one there to react except the guards.

But suddenly he felt a twinge of anxiety, which surprised and displeased him. Suddenly it did matter to him what he looked like, and he realized that it was because of her.

I care what she thinks, he marveled to himself. I'm afraid of how she'll react when the bandages come off and I am still ugly. He didn't know that such feelings still resided in him.

Remarkable, he thought.

"I'm ready," Nicholai said.

They went into the bathroom. She sat him down on a stool in front of the mirror, stood behind him, and gently unwrapped the bandages.

He was beautiful.

There is no other word for it, Solange thought. He is a beautiful man. His emerald green eyes stood out now against the high, sharp cheekbones. His long jaw was strong, his dimpled chin cute without being at all effeminate. And he was youthful-looking—far younger than his twenty-six years, even with all he'd been through.

"Bravo, Doctor," Solange said. "Are you pleased?"

I'm *relieved*, Nicholai thought, seeing the smile on her face. She would have feigned the smile in any case, but he was relieved that the surgeon's apparent skill had saved them both that indignity. He said, "I'm not sure that I recognize myself."

"You are very handsome."

"You think so?"

"Listen to you, fishing for a compliment," Solange said. "Yes, I think so. You are very handsome. But now you make me feel so old."

"You're beautiful and you know it."

"But fading," she says. "Perhaps I should go see this doctor..."

# 8

HAVERFORD CAME that afternoon.

He inspected Nicholai's face as if it were a product to be test-marketed and then pronounced it satisfactory. "He did a good job."

"I'm pleased that you're pleased," Nicholai answered.

They sat down in the dining room. Haverford spread a file out on the table and without preamble began, "You are Michel Guibert, twenty-six years old, born in Montpellier, France. When you were ten years old your family moved to Hong Kong to pursue your father's import-export business. You survived the Japanese occupation because your family were residents of Vichy France and therefore at peace with the Axis powers. By the time the war ended you were old enough to go into the family business."

"Which was?"

"Arms," Haverford said. "*La famille* Guibert has been in the weapons black market since the ball-and-musket era."

"Is there an actual Guibert family," Nicholai asked, "or is this a total fiction?"

"Papa Guibert is quite real," Haverford answered.

"And does he have a son?"

"He did," Haverford answered.

He spread out photographs of what certainly could have been a young Nicholai happily playing in a Chinese courtyard, helping the cooks, smiling over a birthday cake. "Sadly, Michel was in a terrible car crash. Disfiguring, I'm told. Requiring massive reconstructive surgery. He looks somewhat like his old self."

"Did you arrange for this 'accident'?" Nicholai asked.

"No," answered Haverford. "My God, do you think we're monsters?"

"Mmmmmm ... The mother?"

"She died just recently. You were very torn up about it."

"You amaze and appall me," Nicholai said.

"You've matured quite a bit," Haverford continued. "You used to have quite the reputation as a gambler and ladies' man and Papa banished you back to France for the last three years. You blew a shitload of the family's money at Monaco, repented of your profligate ways, and have returned to redeem yourself."

"How so?" Nicholai asked.

"You don't need to know yet," Haverford answered. "Study the file. Solange will help quiz you on the details. When you're thoroughly conversant with your new past, I'll brief you on your new future."

My "new future," Nicholai thought. What a uniquely American concept, perfect in its naïve optimism. Only the Americans could have a "new" future, as opposed to an "old" one.

"Now we need to take some photos," Haverford said.

"Why?"

Because they were assembling a file on Guibert, explained Haverford. No one in the arms trade would go very long in this day and age without acquiring a jacket in every major intelligence service in the game. The photos would be placed in CIA, Deuxième Bureau, and MI-6 files, then leaked to the Chinese through moles. Photos of Michel Guibert would be inserted into old Kuomintang police files that the Reds were currently sifting through. The "wizards in the lab" would make Guibert appear on streets in Kowloon, casinos in Monaco, and the docks of Marseille.

"By the time we're done," Haverford chirped, "*you'll* believe you're Michel Guibert and that you sat out the war in Hong Kong. As a matter of fact, from now on you answer to 'Michel' and only Michel. Not 'Nicholai.' Got it, Michel?"

"As difficult a concept as that might be," Nicholai answered, "I believe I have a grasp of it, yes."

Solange came back into the room carrying a stack of clothes that she draped over the back of a chair. "Your new wardrobe, Michel. *Très chic.*"

She went back out to get more.

Nicholai examined the clothes, which appeared to be secondhand. Of course they were, he thought. It makes perfect sense — when you step into someone's life, you step into his clothes, and those clothes would be worn, not new. He examined the labels. Some of the older clothes were from a tailor in Kowloon, but most were French, and mostly from expensive-sounding shops in Marseille. A few of the shirts and two of the suits came from Monaco. All of them were expensive and of lightweight fabrics — silk and cotton. There were several pairs of twill khaki trousers, pleated, of course. It seemed that Michel favored white and khaki suits with colorful shirts and no ties.

And the clothes smelled — of sweat, tobacco, and cologne. You have to give the devil his due, Nicholai thought. Haverford had been nothing if not thorough.

Solange returned with more clothes, stood with the tip of her index finger to her lips and contemplated the wardrobe and Nicholai. "Let me see, what shall you wear for the first shot? It is set in Hong Kong, no?" Her serious concentration on this make-believe was quite charming. She selected a shirt, put it back, chose another, and matched it with a suit. "This, yes? *Oui — parfait.*"

She handed the selections to Nicholai and ordered him to go change. When he came back from the bedroom dressed as

Michel, Haverford had a camera ready. They went out in the garden to get a "blurred, outdoor" background. In what became a painfully tedious afternoon for Nicholai, they repeated this process numerous times, Solange having a wonderful time, however, selecting Michel's ensembles.

"That was excruciating," Nicholai said after Haverford finally left.

"It was fun," Solange answered. "I love fashion, and Michel has a sense, no?"

"You chose all those clothes, didn't you?"

"Of course," she said. "You don't think I'd let them dress you out of fashion, do you?"

After a dinner of *suprêmes de poulet à l'estragon* with green beans *à la provençale*, a dessert of *tarte aux poires et à la frangipane*, and the requisite espresso, cognac, and cigarette, Nicholai studied the Guibert file. The fiction was impressive in its volume and detail, but Nicholai had no trouble memorizing apparently important trivia such as which *tabac* Michel favored in Montpellier, his father's choice in whiskey, or his mother's maiden name. His mind crammed with such detail, he changed into his *gi*, went to the garden to perform his *kata*, bathed, and went to bed.

# 9

His PROXIMITY SENSE woke him.

During his years in prison he developed an almost extrasensory awareness of the presence of another living being, a radarlike perception of the intruder's exact distance and angle of approach.

Now someone was in the room.

In the space of a second, his mind ran through the possibilities and he selected the vase on the bedside table as the best, most easily reached weapon. Then he smelled the Chanel No. 5 and felt her presence. Enough moonlight came through the shutters to reveal Solange standing in the doorway, her body more revealed than hidden by the filmy black peignoir.

"Three years is a long time to be without a woman," she said. "Too long, I think, no?"

Her perfume filled his head as she came to the bed and kissed his mouth, his ears, his neck, his chest, and then slid down. He was dizzy with pleasure as she did delicious things with her mouth and long elegant fingers and it wasn't long before he gasped, "Solange, please stop. I'm afraid I'll...and I don't want to...before—"

Solange stopped, laughed gently, and said, "After three years, mon cher, I think you will recover quickly, no?" She resumed her ministrations and soon he felt the unstoppable wave roll through his body, his back arched like the most powerful samurai bow, and she held him tight with her full lips until he sank back onto the bed.

"*Très fort*," she whispered in his ear as she slid up his body.

"Well, after three years…"

She laughed and rested her head on his chest. Her hair felt wonderful on his skin. They rested for a little bit and then he felt himself recovering. "I told you so," she said as her hand reached down to stroke him. "I want you inside me."

"Are you…"

"Wet?" She guided his hand for him to feel for himself. "Oh yes, my darling, for *weeks* now."

She lowered herself onto him.

Nicholai couldn't believe her sheer beauty as he watched her rise and fall on him. Her blue eyes shone with excitement, pinpoints of sweat appeared on her long neck, her rich mouth smiled with pleasure. He reached up and caressed her heavy breasts, so different from the delicate Japanese women he had known, and she moaned her approval. Her loveliness, the wet heat of her, wrapped him in pleasure. He took her by the waist and turned her over so that he was on top of her, then pressed his lips into the crook of her neck and thrust into her, steadily and insistently but without hurry.

Vocal in her arousal, she throatily whispered and then shouted the dirtiest of French obscenities as she encouraged him, dug her long nails into his buttocks, and pushed him harder. His sweat mixed with hers, they slid together, and then she announced her *petite mort*, her hips rose off the bed, she held him inside her and said, "*Vous me faites briller. Vous me faites jouir.* Come with me. Now."

Her voice and words sent him over the edge, there was no holding back, and he poured himself into her, then collapsed on her and felt her breasts flatten beneath him. They lay there for quite a while, then he heard her say, "I suppose it would be cliché to want a cigarette."

Nicholai got up, found a pack, put two cigarettes into his mouth, lit them both, and handed her one.

So lovemaking was added to their daily routine, although the sex was hardly routine.

Solange delighted in dressing up for the boudoir and had a seemingly inexhaustible repertoire of lingerie that she enjoyed modeling for him. Nor was Nicholai loath to be the audience for this erotic fashion show, as she changed her hair, her makeup, and even her scent, to suit the outfit. Her taste was exquisite, daringly erotic without ever crossing the line into the burlesque, always stylish, never obvious. Her tastes in bed were eclectic as well, and she gave Nicholai every part of herself, reveled in his taking her. As genteel as she was at the dining table, she was equally, surprisingly earthy in the bedroom.

"You have the mouth of a sailor," he told her one night without a trace of disapproval.

"But you love my mouth, no?" she answered, and then proceeded to prove to him that he did. Nicholai did love her mouth, her hands, her fingers, *sa cramouille, sa rose*. He was fast coming to the truth that he simply loved *her*. One night after a particularly robust lovemaking session, she inhaled her postcoital cigarette and said, "No offense, Michel, but you make love like a Japanese."

Nicholai was a bit taken aback, but more curious than offended. "Is that bad?"

"No, no, no," she said quickly. "It is not bad, is just different than...a Frenchman. A bit...*comment vous dites*...a bit 'technical,' no? If you are a Frenchman, you must make love *d'une manière plus sensuelle*, a bit more like music than science."

She knew, sadly, that he would soon leave to perform the errand for the Americans. And as a man, he had needs, and would satisfy those needs, perhaps in a brothel. The girls would talk, and if they talked of a Frenchman who made love like a Japanese, it would not do.

"Is this part of my training?" he asked, staring hard at her. He looked hurt. "Are *you* part of my training?"

"For all your boyish looks," she said, refusing to lower her eyes in shame, looking right back at him, "naiveté nevertheless does not become you. Are you asking me if I am a whore for the Americans? My darling, we are *both* whores for the Americans. I fuck for them, you kill for them. Don't look so hurt, I adore making love to you. *Vous me faites briller.* You make me shine, no?"

He heard the formal "*vous*," as opposed to the more intimate "*tu*," and wondered if she perceived their relationship as only business.

In any case, Solange taught him how to make love like a Frenchman.

# 10

Two nights later they tried to kill him.

Nicholai was halfway through a difficult *kata*, "Tiger Burst Through Bamboo," when his proximity sense told him that he was not alone in the garden. The first assassin — clad all in black, a wicked dagger in his right hand — dropped down the wall in front of him. Nicholai saw his would-be killer's eyes focus slightly over his shoulder, so knew that there was another assassin coming up from behind.

The dagger thrust came low where Nicholai expected it. He shifted into a cat stance and swung his right hand in a low, outward crescent, sweeping the knife hand away from his body. Then he stepped in, grabbed the attacker by the collar of his *gi* and pulled him down, pivoted, and slammed his head into the garden wall. He heard the neck break but didn't stop to look as he ducked under the hatchet blade that the second assailant swung at his head. Nicholai came up and jammed his left hand, poised into a tiger's claw, into the man's eyes, the other into his groin. Dropping his left hand, Nicholai locked the elbow of the arm holding the hatchet and lifted himself onto his toes. The arm snapped like dry wood. The hatchet dropped. Nicholai spun so that his back was to the attacker and he drove an elbow into the man's solar plexus. He released the broken arm, spun again, and delivered a *shuto* strike to the carotid artery.

The man dropped to the ground.

Nicholai knelt beside him, felt his pulse, and cursed himself for striking too hard. His skill had not returned to the point where he could precisely calibrate the force of a blow, and the man was dead. This was unfortunate, because he would have liked to question him to find out who had sent him and why.

Clumsy, Nicholai told himself, clumsy and imprecise.

You will have to improve.

He went back into the house and used the telephone to dial the number that Haverford had given him for emergencies. When the American answered, Nicholai said, "There are two corpses in the garden. I imagine you will want to remove them."

"Stay inside. I'll have a cleanup team there right away."

Nicholai hung up. Solange was standing in the doorway, looking at him. She wore a simple white silk robe, held in place by a wide silk belt tied in a bow that begged for tugging. A kitchen knife was clutched in her right hand, held low by her thigh, and her amazing green eyes blazed. She looked to Nicholai as if she were indeed ready to kill someone.

"Are you all right?" she asked.

"I'm fine. A bit more winded than I'd like to be, perhaps." He wondered at his lack of emotion, then decided that the adrenaline surge had yet to recede and was masking whatever he might feel about his close call, and the killing of two men.

Nicholai looked at the knife in her hand and asked, "Were you going to use that?"

"If I had to," she answered. "Are they dead?"

"Yes."

"You are sure."

"Quite sure."

Solange walked into the kitchen and came back with two squat glasses of whiskey. "I don't know about you, but I need one."

Nicholai took the drink and knocked it back in one swallow. Perhaps, he speculated, I feel a bit more than I thought.

"You are trembling a little," she said.

"Perceptions to the contrary," Nicholai answered, "I am not a practiced killer."

It was true. He had killed Kishikawa-san out of love — something a Western mind would struggle to understand. But that act of mercy could not inure him against the professional dispatching of two sentient beings, who, despite the fact that they tried to kill him first, were still human. As the adrenaline faded, he felt an odd, contradictory mix of elation and regret.

Solange nodded her understanding.

The "cleanup" crew arrived before Nicholai and Solange could finish a second drink. Haverford, uncharacteristically dressed in an untucked shirt and blue jeans, came in through the kitchen door. "My God, are you okay?"

"I'm fine," Nicholai answered.

"What the hell happened?" Haverford asked.

Nicholai told him about the assault, omitting the details of his counterattack, only saying that he was sorry to have killed the second man. He could hear the soft sounds of the crew working outside, removing the bodies, wiping up the blood, restoring the pebbled paths to their pristine order. As if, he thought, nothing had ever happened.

The head of the crew came in, whispered something to Haverford, and left.

"They were Japs," Haverford said.

Nicholai shook his head. "Chinese, or at least in the employ of the Chinese."

Haverford looked at him curiously.

"The Japanese don't use hatchets," Nicholai explained. "The Chinese do, and only Chinese tongs, typically. Besides, no

Japanese assassin would have fallen so easily for "The Angry Monk Paints the Wall." Someone in China wants me—or Michel Guibert—dead."

"I'll get on it," Haverford answered. "And I'll increase security around here."

"Don't," Nicholai said. "Security will only draw attention. The interesting question is, How did they know where I was."

Haverford frowned and Nicholai enjoyed his discomfiture, a welcome crack in the wall of his confidence, almost worth a near death to see. The agent said, "We should probably move you."

"Please don't," Nicholai answered. "It's pleasant here and there's really very little danger. If the assassins were Japanese, they would try again and again until they succeeded. But the Chinese think differently, they would never repeat a failed stratagem. I'm safe until I leave here."

Haverford nodded. "Could I have some of that scotch?"

After Haverford and the cleanup crew left, Nicholai and Solange went to bed but did not make love. Neither of them felt particularly sexual after the events of the evening. They lay in silence for a long time until Nicholai said, "I am very sorry. Please accept my apology."

"What for?"

"For bringing bloodshed into your home."

Solange could see the shame on his young face. Truly, it was the end of youth, this killing business. She knew that any decent person who still had a soul felt revulsion at the taking of life. And she knew that she couldn't remove his pain, only share it with him, make him know that he was not a monster, but a flawed human being trying to exist in a flawed world.

"Do you think," she asked, "I have not seen bloodshed before?"

Her head on his chest, his arm around her, she told him her story.

*    *    *

She was a beautiful child, the pride of the *quartier*. Even as a little girl her skin, her eyes, her hair, the perfect bone structure of
her face made her a treasure. As she grew into adolescence, the
men of the neighborhood stole shamed, sidelong glances while
strangers in the city at large were not so polite, verbally express-
ing their desires in graphic terms.

Mama guarded her daughter's virtue zealously. She gave her a
cultured, religious education with the sisters, took her to church
every Sunday and on all days of holy obligation. Most of all, she
went to great lengths to keep from Solange the knowledge of
how her nice clothes and new pairs of shoes were paid for.

There was sometimes a little money left over for Solange to
go to the cinema, and she would sit in the lovely, cool darkness,
watch the silver fantasies play in front of her, and dream of one
day becoming an actress herself.

Everyone said that she was certainly pretty enough.

Her mother disapproved—actresses were little better than
whores.

Solange met Louis at a formal dance held between their two
schools, and she found him distressingly attractive. He was tall
and thin, with wavy brown hair and warm brown eyes, and he
was intelligent and charming. The son of a prominent city doctor,
he was relatively rich but nevertheless a passionate Communist.

He was also passionate about Solange. He truly cared for her,
but could not help but test her virtue as they sat under trees along
the banks of the canal, or in the cinema, or even at his house
at the rare times his parents weren't home, or at her apartment
when her mother was "out."

Mama was terrified at the beauty she had become. Proud,
yes, but fearful, and she began to lecture her incessantly on the

evils of men. "They only want sex," she harangued, "and your precious Louis is no different. But don't give in—only a *salope* sleeps with men without marriage."

One night Louis walked her past a large four-story house.

"What is it?" Solange asked.

"It's a brothel," Louis said, at the very moment the door opened and Solange saw her mother step out to take a smoke. Her black hair was disheveled, her lips were puffy. She lit her cigarette and turned to see Solange staring up at her.

"Go home," she said, her voice breaking. "Please, Solange, go now."

But Solange just stood there in shock.

Finally, Louis took her by the arm and led her away.

The Nazis came to the south of France later that year, after the Allies invaded North Africa. German soldiers occupied the city, the police helped them locate Jews, La Résistance organized, and the Gestapo came in to track them down.

The head of the Gestapo in Montpellier was a certain Colonel Hoeger, and one afternoon he stepped out of his headquarters to enjoy the sunshine and ended up enjoying the sight of Solange as well.

"Look at that creature," he said to his captain. "How old do you think she is?"

"Sixteen? Seventeen?"

"That face," Hoeger said, "and the body. Find out about her."

"She's a child."

"Look at her. She's ripe."

Madame Sette's had become the brothel of choice for the German occupation forces, and Madame was rapidly becoming a wealthy woman.

As for Solange, she had become used to her mother's occupation, having learned the sad lesson that what was once unbear-
able becomes commonplace with time. She and Mama had a
civil if emotionally distant relationship, and Marie even came to
feel somewhat relieved that she no longer had to disguise what
she did. Solange even went to Madame Sette's from time to
time—to bring her mother a meal, or deliver a lipstick she had
forgotten, or some other minor errand. The girls took to calling her Little Miss Prim, but gradually with some affection, and
every time Madame saw her, she would importune her to consider coming in to make some real money.

Solange, of course, always refused.

She turned more and more to Louis. They spent virtually all
their free time together, although Louis was very busy with his
studies at Montpellier's excellent and ancient medical school.

He was busier with the Resistance, even more passionate about
his communism now that he lived cheek by jowl with facism. A
messenger at first, he rode his bicycle around the city with coded
messages hidden inside his medical texts, but it wasn't long before
his intelligence and courage brought him to the attention of the
leaders and they began to give him more responsibility.

With them came greater risk, and it terrified Solange. She
knew of the torture chambers in the basement of Gestapo headquarters, had heard the firing squads, and carefully avoided the
scenes of gallows that had been hastily constructed for captured
Resistance. She begged him to be careful.

Of course he said that he would, but he also found the dangers
exhilarating, and he returned from missions with an already
keen joie de vivre honed to an edge. Louis wanted to live, and
that included making love to this beautiful girl whom he did
love, very much.

But she turned him down.

"I don't want to become my mother."

Solange was bringing her mother a tin of hot soup — Marie had a slight cold — and Colonel Hoeger was sitting in the parlor. His face was flushed with drink as he looked at her with delighted surprise. "Do you work here?"

"No."

"That's a pity." He looked her up and down, slowly and lasciviously, not troubling to disguise his want. "Do you have a name?"

"Yes."

Hoeger's tone sharpened. "What is it?"

"Solange."

"Solange," said Hoeger, tasting it as he wished to taste her. "A lovely name for a lovely girl."

Three days later, Hoeger made a direct approach. He waited outside until he saw Solange coming across the square, and then approached her.

"Bonjour, mademoiselle."

"Bonjour, monsieur."

"Is there something fascinating on the sidewalk, Solange?"

"No, sir."

"Then look at me, please."

She looked up at him.

Apologizing for his rude behavior at the brothel, he now made a direct offer. "Civilized," he called it. She would not be a whore, but his mistress. He would provide her with a suitable apartment, a budget for clothing and some luxuries, and appropriate — really quite generous — gifts from time to time. In exchange, she would . . . well, certainly she knew what she would provide in exchange, certainly they didn't have to go into such details, did they?

Solange slapped him.

Hoeger had not been slapped since he was a boy and he actually glanced around the square to see if anyone had noticed, then remembered himself and said, "You are very rude."

"As opposed to yourself — sir — who has just made an immoral proposition to a seventeen-year-old girl."

"You are free to go."

"Bon après-midi."

"Bon après-midi."

Solange was home before she gave in to her terror. She trembled for a good ten minutes, made a cup of tea, and sat down at the kitchen table to compose herself. Louis came over, but she told him nothing of the encounter, lest he do something foolishly gallant.

Two days later, Louis was arrested.

"It was a week from a Zola novel," Solange told Nicholai now, lying with her head in the crook of his arm. "One of the bad ones."

She said it ironically, dismissing the possibility of self-pity, but Nicholai heard the deeply buried hurt in her voice as she continued her story.

They caught Louis red-handed — stopped him on his bicycle and found the coded messages in his anatomy text. They hauled him to the cellar of Gestapo headquarters, where Hoeger went to work on him. The handsome boy was quickly handsome no longer. Unfortunately for Louis, he was brave, loyal, and committed, and would not reveal names.

Solange heard about it that afternoon. She went to her room and sobbed, then washed her face, combed her hair and put on the prettiest dress she owned, examined her image, and undid the top two buttons to reveal a deep décolletage. Sitting in front of the mirror in her mother's bedroom, she applied makeup the way she had seen the whores do it.

Then she walked to Gestapo headquarters and asked to see Colonel Hoeger.

Shown into his office, she stood in front of his desk, made herself look him in the eyes, and said, "If you release Louis Duchesne, I will give myself to you. Now and anytime that you wish. In any way."

Hoeger looked at her and blinked.

Solange said, "I know that you want me."

He burst into laughter.

Hoeger laughed until tears ran down his fleshy cheeks, and then he took a handkerchief from his pocket, wiped his eyes, and got up. "Get out of my office. The nerve of you. Do you think I would risk my career, betray my country, just for the honor of breaking your cherry for you?"

Solange stood her ground. "Can I see him?"

"Certainly," Hoeger answered. "You can see him hanged. Thursday noon."

In the square around the gallows where five ropes dangled from the crossbeam, a crowd formed and stood in sullen silence until a German army truck pulled up. Soldiers jumped out the back first, then hauled out a group of prisoners, five in all, who had been sentenced to death.

Louis was the last taken out.

There was nothing romantic about it, nothing heroic. Louis looked badly beaten, limp and in shock, his hands tied behind him as they dragged him up to the gallows. Standing there in just a bloodstained white shirt and dirty brown trousers, he peered out at the crowd uncomprehendingly, and Solange wondered if he was looking for her.

I should have given myself to him, she thought. I should have loved him completely. I should have taken him inside me, wrapped myself around him, and never let him loose.

A soldier went down the line. He finally came to Louis, jerked his head back roughly, put the noose around his neck, then bent down and tied his ankles together. At the colonel's orders, they put no hoods over the condemned heads.

Louis looked terrified.

Other soldiers formed a line between the crowd and the gallows, lest anyone try to interfere or run up and pull on the legs of the hanged to break their necks and abbreviate their agony.

Solange forced herself to watch.

An officer shouted an order.

There was a crack of metal and wood and Louis dropped.

His neck jerked and he bounced. Then he hung there twisting — his legs kicking, his eyes bulging, his tongue obscenely thrust out of his mouth — as his face turned red and then blue.

Finally — it seemed like forever — he was still.

Solange walked away through the crowd.

She heard a man's voice say, "He was a hero."

"What?"

It was Patrice Reynaud, a railway conductor who had been a friend of Louis. Patrice kept walking, but repeated, "He was a hero, your Louis."

"Your Louis," Solange thought. If only I had let him be my Louis.


That night she walked over to La Maison de Madame Sette and went into the woman's little office.

"I am ready to begin work," she said.

Madame looked at her skeptically. "Why now, chérie?"

"Why not now, madame?" Solange answered. "Why delay the reality of life?"

"Your mother will not like it."

Marie didn't. She yelled, she lectured, she wept. "I didn't want this kind of life for you. I wanted something better for you."

So did I, Solange thought.

Life decided otherwise.

Madame Sette, of course, was delighted and decided to make an event of it. She spent an entire week promoting the auctioning off of Solange's virginity. The girl would fetch a very high price.

"I will give you half," Madame told her. "That is more than I usually give."

"Half is fine," Solange answered.

Put it away, don't squander it, Madame advised her. Put your savings in the bank, work hard, and someday you can open up a little shop of your own. A woman should have her own money in this world, her own business.

"Yes, madame."

The big night arrived, and the parlor was packed with German officers. Most of the local Frenchmen would have nothing to do with this, and those that would had been intimidated by word from the Resistance that it would not treat gently any man who bid for the virtue of a martyr's girl.

Solange let Madame dress her for the occasion.

A crude mockery of wedding garb, the white diaphanous gown concealed little, her white lace headpiece was set gently on her hair that fell freely and shining down her back, adding to the image of virginity. Her makeup was slight and subtle, a little pencil to widen her already beautiful eyes, and just a shade of blush appropriate to a young bride.

Solange felt disgust.

Disgust when Madame insisted on examining her to verify her purity, disgust when she was being dressed up for the ceremonial travesty, disgust as she sat in the "bridal suite" and prepared herself for the event, disgust when she was led into the room, which fell instantly silent as men swallowed their lust. Disgust when Madame started the bidding high and it quickly went higher as the men were willing to spend small fortunes to have what they saw beneath the wedding gown.

Hoeger sat silent, his position and authority speaking for him. He let the bidding rise to an unprecedented height, then lifted the index finger of his right hand. The bidding stopped right there. No one, certainly not his subordinate officers, had the nerve to outbid the commander of the city's Gestapo.

Madame quickly counted three and closed the bidding.

Hoeger took Solange by the arm and led her down the hall-way to the "bridal suite." He stripped off the dress, threw her down on the bed, and took her.

Solange moaned. She groaned in pleasure, called him her man, told him to do it harder, told him it was wonderful, he was wonderful. Said if she only knew, she would have let him before, let him anytime. She bucked and tensed, screamed as she came.

"You beautiful creature," he panted. "I had no idea."

She sighed. "So much pleasure."

He closed his eyes, went back at it, intent on his own pleasure.

She reached under the mattress for the knife that Reynaud had given her, brought it up, and slashed his throat.


The Resistance got her out of the brothel and hid her in the back of a produce truck, then in a small cellar in the slums of Marseille. She was in the tight, dark space for three weeks and thought she might lose her mind before they finally took her out and up into the air, into the light. She still had nightmares.

There was plenty of work for her there, in the brothels frequented by the Germans. Her job was to listen, to pick up bits and pieces, and as a result trains were derailed, messages intercepted, Resistance fighters escaped just before the Gestapo came for them. And if one of the officers was gunned down at his favorite café or outside of his mistress's place—all the better.

Solange never went home.

In the hungry winter of 1946, she returned to the only work she knew, becoming the mistress of an American officer. When he was rotated home, she found another, then another. This last one begged to marry her and take her back to Texas, but she told him not to be so foolish.

Shortly after, she met an OSS officer who said that they might have use for a woman like her.

With that, Solange finished her story.

Nicholai held her close until she finally fell asleep.

# 11

IN THE MORNING, Nicholai summoned Haverford and demanded to know the identity of the person he was meant to terminate. "As I'm a target now myself," Nicholai said over coffee and croissant, "I think I have the right to know."

Solange left the house earlier to buy groceries.

Haverford listened, seemed to seek a response in the milk swirling around in his cup, then looked up and answered, "You're right. It's time."

"So?"

"The Soviet commissioner to Red China," Haverford said. "Yuri Voroshenin."

The name hit Nicholai like a hard slap, but — and perhaps only thanks to the minor paralysis of his facial muscles — he managed to keep his expression placid as he feigned a lack of recognition and asked, "Why eliminate him?"

"Korea," Haverford answered.

Egged on by the Soviets, the madman Kim had invaded South Korea and the United States was forced to intervene. When MacArthur's counterattack pushed to the Yalu River near the border with China, Mao felt that his hand had been forced and sent three hundred thousand troops into Korea.

The United States and China were at war. Worse, the conflict isolated China from the West and forced it to accept Soviet hegemony, thereby creating a solid Communist bloc from the Elbe to the shores of the Pacific.

"We have to drive a wedge between Beijing and Moscow," Haverford concluded.

"By assassinating this Voroshenin?" Nicholai asked. "What good will that do?"

"We'll hand the Russians sufficient evidence to blame the Chinese," Haverford explained. "The Chinese will, of course, know that they didn't do it, and conclude that the Soviets sacrificed one of their own in order to blame the Chinese and demand further concessions — perhaps permanent bases in Manchuria."

It's a classic Go ploy, Nicholai thought, to sacrifice a line of stones to lure your enemy into a misapprehension of your strategy. Uncharacteristic of Americans, who reveled in the childlike game of checkers. A deeper mind was behind this maneuver. It could be Haverford, but certainly he lacked the position to authorize a killing at this high level.

Who is it, then? Nicholai wondered.

Who is this Go player?

"Tell me about Voroshenin," he said.

# 12

"DISABUSE YOURSELF of the notion that we're sending you to murder some innocent diplomat," Haverford told Nicholai.

Yuri Andreovitch Voroshenin was a high-ranking member of the KGB, a fact that the Chinese knew and deeply resented.

"Above all else," Haverford warned, "our boy Yuri is a survivor."

He laid out what the CIA knew about Yuri Voroshenin.

Born in St. Petersburg in 1898, the son of a schoolteacher, Voroshenin was a committed revolutionary even as a boy. By the time he was fifteen he had spent time in three Tsarist jails, at seventeen he barely escaped a traitor's noose and was exiled to Siberia. The Bolsheviks ordered him to join the army in 1914, and he surfaced as a leader of the 1916 mutiny that sent soldiers streaming home from the front.

Haverford took out a photograph that showed a young Voroshenin in an army greatcoat and soldier's peaked cap. Tall and thin, with the typical wire-rimmed spectacles of the left-wing Russian intellectual, he sported an open, happy grin that was unusual for an earnest revolutionary.

The great year of 1917 found him home, now an agent in the Petrograd division of the All-Russian Extraordinary Commission to Combat Counterrevolution and Sabotage, the VchK, the "Cheka." Violence was rife in the hungry city—demobilized soldiers shot, robbed, and raped. Mobs looted churches, stores, and the homes of the rich. The wives and daughters of bankers, generals, and Tsarist officials sold themselves as prostitutes to feed starving families.

Nicholai knew all about the Petrograd Cheka.

"You needn't enlighten me," Nicholai said. "My mother told me the stories."

The Cheka began the Red Terror, a war of extermination against its "class enemies," shooting dozens, sometimes even hundreds of "White" Russians in any single day, without trial or due process. Voroshenin cheerfully participated in the slaughter. "Why bother with a Commissariat of Justice?" he asked once in a party meeting. "Let's just call it the Commissariat for Social Extermination and get on with it."

They got on with it.

His tortures became the stuff of nightmares. He tied captured White officers to planks and slowly fed them into furnaces, he shoved prisoners into nail-studded barrels and rolled them down hills, he peeled the skin off captives' hands to create "gloves" of flesh. His name became a tool that mothers used to frighten their children.

In 1921 he helped suppress the mutiny at the naval base at Kronstad, accomplished with great bloodshed. Then he turned his attention to striking workers in the starving, freezing city. Through the firing squad, the truncheon, and the torture cell he reestablished order, then began tearing down sections of the city to provide fuel for the rest of it. All this activity brought him to the attention of the rising power in Moscow, Joseph Stalin.

"He next shows up in China," Haverford went on. "In, of all places, Shanghai."

It was, after all, at Stalin's insistence that the Nationalists slaughtered the Communists there in 1927, and Uncle Joe thought Chiang Kai-shek could use an adviser experienced in such matters.

Nicholai was just a small boy when this happened, but he nevertheless remembered it. He used to prowl the streets of Shanghai, knew the "Reds" from the "Greens," and when the shootings, stabbings, and beheadings of thousands of young Reds occurred, it was for him childhood's end.

"We lose track of him for the next fifteen years," Haverford said. "No one knows where he was or what he was doing, but it's a pretty fair bet that he was involved in the Trotsky assassination in Mexico as well as Stalin's staged murder of Sergei Kirov as a pretext for his great purges of the 1930s."

The purge turned on Voroshenin himself. The dictator's paranoia led him to imprison and execute his most gifted and ruthless subordinates, especially those who had stories to tell, and Yuri was tossed into Moscow's dreaded Lubyanka Prison.

Voroshenin's career should have ended there, with a bullet in the back of his head. But, as noted, he was a survivor who used all his craft, guile, and courage to survive his interrogations. He became a source of information too valuable to kill, and he sat in his cell for three long years, listening to the screams of less talented men, hearing their executions, and waiting for a moment of opportunity.

"Prison teaches you patience," Voroshenin later said.

"It does," Nicholai agreed, to Haverford's blush.

Hitler opened the prison door when he invaded Russia. Faced with destruction, Stalin could no longer afford to keep his best people locked up. Voroshenin was quickly rehabilitated and released.

Yuri landed on his feet again.

Rather than be sent to the killing grounds of the war against Germany, he used his former connection to the Kuomintang to be assigned back to China, and found himself reunited with Chiang Kai-shek in Chongqing. His assignment was not to help the Generalissimo fight the Japanese, but to track down Mao and his Communists, whom Stalin accurately viewed as a potential future rival.

Voroshenin had no problem fighting against his brother Marxists. No longer a true believer, he had lost his faith in Lubyanka, and was now a hardened cynic, believing in the advance of nothing except Yuri Voroshenin. To that end, he would ally himself with anyone, and as easily betray them.

Haverford showed Nicholai another photograph of a khaki-clad Voroshenin standing outside a Daoist temple with Chiang. Bareheaded, his hairline receding into a widow's peak, his skin pale and drawn from the years in prison, there was still a vitality about him. His shoulders were wide, if a little stooped, and he had certainly put on no weight since his youth. A handsome man, powerful, he loomed over Chiang as both men pretended to study a map for the benefit of the photographer.

"Our man Yuri stayed with the Nats through the whole war and then some," Haverford said. "When Stalin called all his agents back from China, he was afraid they'd been contaminated by Mao, so he had them purged."

Again Voroshenin's head should have been the first on the block, but he was the first to inform on his comrades and became the supervisor, rather than the prime victim, of the purge. Voroshenin personally conducted the interrogations, directed the torture, supervised the executions, in some cases pulling the trigger himself.

And now he was back in China.

"This is the man," Haverford said, "that Stalin chose to represent him in China."

It was a deliberate slap in the face, but what could Mao do about it? Isolated abroad, struggling to create a government and a viable economy at home, he needed Russian aid. If that meant swallowing his pride, the Chairman was willing to smile and bow and do it.

For the time being.

Nicholai listened to the biographical sketch of the Russian murderer and torturer, but much of it was redundant. From his mother, the Countess Alexandra Ivanovna, he already knew a great deal about Yuri Andreovitch Voroshenin.

The question was how to accomplish the mission.

Beijing at the start of 1952 was perhaps the most tightly guarded city in the world. The Chinese secret police were everywhere, and the "Order Keeping Committees" — volunteer snitches and informers — were on every block and in every factory.

Worse, foreigners were a rarity in the country. Mao used the Korean War as a pretext to deport "spies" and "agents," and the very few Westerners who remained were kept under constant surveillance.

"Why do you think that I — as opposed to another one of your 'assets' — have a chance to succeed at this?"

The question had been much discussed in rooms at Langley, and now Haverford debated with himself how much of the answer he should share with Nicholai Hel.

"The assignment requires someone who is fluent in Chinese," Haverford said, "but who could pass for Russian if the moment demanded it."

"You doubtless have many such people on your payroll," Nicholai observed.

"True," Haverford answered. "But in addition to being multilingual, the man must also be brilliant, unflappable, and a trained killer who can do the job without the benefit of a gun or other standard weapon. At this point the list of available candidates gets very short."

Nicholai understood the thinking. A gun would be very hard

to arrange in a police state, and in any case, Voroshenin wouldn't be likely to let an armed assassin anywhere near him. That made sense, but Nicholai knew that there were other qualifications that narrowed the pool of candidates down to him, and he wondered if Haverford knew of the very personal motivation he had to kill Voroshenin. Certainly Haverford was manipulative enough — he wouldn't blink at it. But Nicholai doubted that he knew — there was really no way that he could. No, Nicholai thought, he chose me for other reasons.

"You also require," he said, "a man desperate enough to accept an assignment that has only a slight chance of success, and almost no chance of escape even if he succeeds in the mission. Isn't that true?"

"Only partially," Haverford answered. "We'll have an extraction team standing by to get you out. But the odds are, yes, slim enough to require a man who otherwise has little to lose."

Well, Nicholai thought, that would be me.

Or "Michel Guibert."

The identity solved the problem of inserting Nicholai into Beijing. There was no "cover" available as a Russian, because he would instantly be spotted as an imposter. Obviously, he couldn't be Chinese. An American or British identity was likewise impossible.

But the Guiberts had been particular darlings of the international left since the days of bomb-throwing anarchists with mustaches, and Papa Guibert had paid particular attention to the French Communists in Vichy during the war. So the Guiberts were exactly the type of capitalists that the Communists would tolerate.

And now the Chinese, Haverford explained, had a particular use for the son.

"It's about Vietnam," he said.

"More precisely?"

Both China and Russia supported Ho Chi Minh and his insurgency against the French colonial regime in Vietnam. Ho's

Viet Minh troops needed weapons—preferably American as the United States supplied the French and the Viet Minh could rearm themselves with captured ammunition. China possessed a large cache of American arms through weapons captured in Korea, and because the Americans had also armed the Kuomintang, from whom the Communist victors had seized mountains of American weaponry.

"Why can't the Chinese simply send the guns to the Viet Minh?" Nicholai asked.

China shared a border with Vietnam and the Viet Minh controlled the mountainous area on the frontier. It should have been a simple matter to bring the armaments through the remote terrain to the Viet Minh strongholds.

"They can and do," Haverford answered. "But it all comes down to money."

Of course, Nicholai thought.

"The Chinese are cash poor," Haverford explained. "They'd like to make some dough—especially in foreign currency—from the deal. At the same time, they don't want to be seen making a profit off the backs of their revolutionary Asian comrades. So you provide a convenient excuse. 'Gee, we'd love to give you the weaponry, but those slimy Guiberts got to them first. But we can make them sell the guns to you at a price.'"

So that was the plan. Nicholai, under the cover of "Michel Guibert," would be inserted into Beijing to conclude an arms deal with the Chinese, under the pretext of then turning around and selling the guns to the Viet Minh.

"That gets me into Beijing," Nicholai said, "but how does it get me into, shall we say, 'operational proximity' to Voroshenin?"

Haverford shrugged. "You're the Go master."

# 13

JOHN SINGLETON RECEIVED word of the failed attempt on the asset Nicholai Hel with little surprise and measured satisfaction.

After all, if Hel could be killed so easily he was not the man for the job after all — Yuri Voroshenin would be no easy prey. The fact that Hel had dispatched his would-be killers with apparent ease boded well for the mission.

But Diamond, Singleton thought as he moved a white stone into its new position, is so predictable, and disappointingly so. That, combined with his seeming lack of creativity, created some concern about his suitability for the Indochinese posting.

However, the old Go maxim, "Defeat a straight line with a circle, a circle with a straight line," held a great deal of truth. Diamond, for all his many shortcomings, was certainly a straightforward type, who at least would not trip himself up by overthinking a situation.

Then there was the "circle," Haverford, nuanced to a flaw. Singleton was reminded of the old saying that "a liberal is a man who will not take his own side in an argument," and that certainly described Ellis Haverford. But would he have the courage to choose a course of action and take it?

We shall see, Singleton thought as he turned the *go-kang* around.

That is the wonderful thing about playing both sides of the board.

You never lose.

# 14

DIAMOND SMASHED the wall with his fist.

It hurt.

Examining his scraped knuckles, he cursed again. Two on one, a surprise attack, and the goddamn Chinese screw it up. At least they had the decency to get themselves killed in the process.

A jolt of fear sickened his stomach.

Hel is the real deal. You'll have to find a better way to get to him.

# 15

SOLANGE CAME through the door.

Nicholai got up and helped her put the groceries away.

Haverford noticed the little domestic tableau and it worried him. Due to the previous night's attempted assassination, they had accelerated the schedule for Hel's departure. He'd mastered the French dialect, absorbed everything they'd given him in an amazingly short time, and recovered his fitness. It was time to move, and he didn't want his agent balking now because he'd found love. Although, he admitted, what man wouldn't fall in love with Solange?

"Did I interrupt something?" she asked.

"No," Nicholai answered quickly. "Haverford is just dropping off a file for me to read."

He stressed the "read" to let the American know that he didn't want to be "briefed" anymore and was capable of digesting the file himself.

Haverford smiled. There was always a power struggle between an operative and his handler; it was to be expected and even encouraged. He was glad to see Hel's emerging assertiveness — confidence was a good thing in an operative. To a point. But the wise handler knew when to negotiate, when to insist, and when to yield.

"I was just leaving," Haverford said, getting up from the table. "The croissants were, as always, *très délicieux*."

"*Merci.*"

After Haverford left, Solange turned to Nicholai and asked, "Does it bother you?"

"What?"

"That I was a prostitute."

The question surprised him. "It is an honorable profession in Japan."

"It isn't in France."

"I'm not French," Nicholai said. "There's nothing about you that I find to be anything but a delight, a joy, and an honor."

Solange came into his arms, kissed him lightly on the neck, and said softly, "I think I'm falling in love with you."

"And I with you." His words surprised him as much as the actual emotion, something he had not felt for years, something he had taught himself never to feel again. It had been his experience that anyone he loved went away, usually through the portal of death.

"*Je t'aime; je t'aime; je t'aime.*"

"*Je t'aime aussi,*" Nicholai said, delighted to hear the "*tu.*" "But what are we going to do about it?"

"Nothing." She sighed, her breath warm and moist on his skin. "There is nothing *to* do about it except to love each other while we have each other."

They went into the bedroom to do just that.


Nicholai got up while she was still sleeping, went into the kitchen, and found a can of green tea hidden in the back of a cupboard. There is no reason, he thought as the water heated, that Michel Guibert could not have developed a taste for excellent green tea during his years in Hong Kong.

When the water boiled he poured it into the pot, waited a minute, then stepped outside and poured it onto the ground. He repeated the process, then poured the water in for the third time and let it sit, recalling the old and wise Chinese adage regarding the steeping of tea: *The first time, it's water; the second time, it's garbage; the third time, it's tea.*

Nicholai waited impatiently, then poured the tea into a small cup and sipped. Excellent, he thought. Refreshing in a way that coffee, no matter how good, could never be. He took the tea out into the garden, sat on one of the stone benches, and listened to the water gurgle down the rocks.

Just last night, he thought, I killed two men here and now there is not a trace, as if it never happened. And in a sense it didn't, in a true Buddhist sense this life is just a dream, a samsara of false perceptions that we are somehow separate from any other being or entities. In killing those men I died myself; in my surviving they live in me. I fulfilled their karma, and they mine. It will be the same with Voroshenin.

The Russian's karmic consequence had been a long time coming.

Over thirty years.

Nicholai wondered if Voroshenin even remembered, or if he did, even cared. Probably not, Nicholai decided.

Do you even want to go through with this? he asked himself.

True, the Americans are offering me a vast sum of money, a passport, and my freedom, but the temptation is to go in and wake Solange, pack a few things, and run where they cannot find us.

But where, he asked himself, would that be?

You have no passport, no papers, no money. Where and how far could you run if you couldn't get out of Japan? And in this closed, tight society, where could two round-eyes hide? And for how long? A few weeks, at the most optimistic assessment. And then what? Now that you know the identity of the target, the Americans would have to terminate you.

And Solange, too.

They'll believe you talked to her, told her everything. While it is usually true that what you don't know can kill you, in the topsy-turvy world in which I now exist, what you *do* know can kill you just as easily. If Solange knew the identity of my target, she could be in serious danger.

So there you are, he thought. She is a hostage to your actions.

I cannot allow another person I love to die.

I couldn't bear it.

But can you do it all? he asked himself. Assassinate Voroshenin and still have a life with Solange? Is it too much to ask in this world?

Perhaps, he thought.

But he decided to try.

Solange came out of the bedroom and into the garden. Her hair was charmingly tousled, her eyes heavy and still sleepy.

Nicholai put the file on his lap and closed it.

"We are keeping secrets?" she asked. "Don't worry, I don't want to know."

She lit cigarettes and handed him one. "I don't care about whatever men's business you and Haverford are cooking up. In the end, there is only food, wine, sex, and babies. That's all anyone really cares about. The rest of it? Silly male games. Go play. Come back and give me a baby."

"I would like that," Nicholai said. "Very much."

"Good. I want to get dinner ready."

She kissed him on the forehead and went inside.

Nicholai went back to studying the file. He couldn't have cared less about Voroshenin as a human being, assuming a fact not in evidence, but was deeply interested in him as a target. As such, it was necessary to know how his mind worked—his likes, dislikes, his habits.

In addition to a predilection for sadism, the man also drank, perhaps to excess. But all Russians drank. Nicholai doubted there was a vulnerability there.

The file suggested that he also liked his women — no surprise to Nicholai. Could that present an opening? Possibly, but the "new" Beijing was famously puritanical. The Communists had closed the brothels, and most of the professional mistresses had fled with the Kuomintang. If Voroshenin had a woman in the city, he would keep her well hidden — which suggested possibilities — but would also keep the arrangement very secure.

What else?

Voroshenin played chess — again, most Russians did — but apparently quite advanced, as one would expect. He liked to eat well, he knew his wines, and had developed in his years in China a taste for Beijing opera.

That was about it.

Nicholai closed the file.

# 16

Solange was awake when Nicholai came into the bedroom.

"I'm leaving in the morning," he said.

"I know," Solange said. "I felt it."

He lay down beside her. She rolled over, laid her head on his chest, and he put his arm around her. "I'll come back for you."

"I hope so."

"I will."

When he went out the door in the morning, she had only one word for him.

*Survive.*

Outside, a maple leaf detached from its branch, flickered beautifully in the sunlight, and then fell.

*Part Two*

# BEIJING, JANUARY 1952

# 17

BEIJING WAS freezing.

The north winds swept down from the vast Manchurian plains and coated the willows, their branches already bending under snow, with a sheen of silver ice. The sun was a pale yellow, a thin disk in a pearl sky.

Nicholai stepped out of the train station and took a breath of the freezing air, which bit into his lungs with a burning sensation. He pulled the collar of his Russian coat up around his neck and wrapped the scarf around his neck.

The street was virtually devoid of traffic save for a few military vehicles — Soviet trucks and American Jeeps liberated from the Kuomintang. Most people were on foot, the luckier few struggled to hold bicycles steady on the snow as they bent low over the handlebars to escape the wind. A few rickshaw drivers picked up arriving passengers and pedaled off with them, the back wheels slipping in the snow.

Then a long black sedan, its front fenders festooned with small red flags, emerged out of the snow and pulled up on the curb. A stocky Chinese man in a padded wool overcoat and a PLA cap with a red star on the front got out and walked up to Nicholai.

"Comrade Guibert?"

"Yes."

"I am Comrade Chen," the man said. "Welcome to Beijing. Long live the People's Republic."

"*Wan swei.*"

"Yes, we were told you speak fluent Cantonese." Chen smiled. He gave the slightest emphasis on "Cantonese," just to let Nicholai know that it was inferior to Mandarin, the preferred dialect of government. "You lived in Guangzhou, was it?"

"Hong Kong."

"Ah, yes."

Silly games, Nicholai thought.

Endless, silly games.

"I will be your escort in Beijing," Chen said.

"Escort," Nicholai thought, meaning "spy," "watchdog," and "informer." "I'm appreciative."

"Shall we get out of the cold?" Chen gave a curt nod back toward the car and the driver got out, took Nicholai's suitcase, and loaded it into the trunk. Chen opened the back passenger door for Nicholai. "Please."

Nicholai slid into the back of the sedan and Chen came around and got in on the other side. The car heater was working manfully, if futilely, against the intense cold, and Chen stomped his booted feet on the car floor. "Cold."

"A bastard."

"Do you mind if I smoke?" Nicholai asked, knowing that the answer would be "no," and also knowing that Chen would appreciate a cigarette. He took a pack of Gauloises from his inside coat pocket and held it out to Chen. "Please."

"Most kind."

Chen took the proffered cigarette and then Nicholai leaned over the seat and offered one to the driver. He could see Chen's annoyed look from the corner of his eye. Even in the "classless" society, there are classes, Nicholai thought.

The driver took the cigarette and, gloating, smiled at Chen in the rearview mirror, so Nicholai knew now that he was not terribly subordinate. A watcher to watch the watcher, he thought. He took out his French lighter, lit both men's cigarettes, then his own. The car quickly filled with blue smoke.

"Good," Chen said.

"Take the pack."

"I couldn't."

"I have more."

Chen took the pack.

Five minutes in the incorruptible People's Republic, Nicholai thought, and the first bribe had been accepted.

Actually, Mao's "Three Antis" Campaign to root out corruption among party officials was in full swing, and hundreds of bureaucrats had been summarily executed, shot in public displays, while thousands more had been shipped off to die slow deaths from exhaustion in work camps.

Nicholai noticed that Chen took four cigarettes from the pack and put them on the front seat for the driver. Prudent, he thought.

This was Nicholai's first time in Beijing. He had been a boy in Shanghai, and that cosmopolitan city had seemed the world to him. The old imperial capital was so different, with its broad boulevards intended for military parades, its vast public spaces so open to the winds that it seemed almost meant as a warning of how quickly and completely things can change and how vulnerable one is to shifts in the wind.

Chen seemed a bit ahead of him. "You have never been to Beijing before?"

"No," Nicholai said, peering out the window as the car pulled out onto Jianguomen Avenue. "And you, are you a native?"

"Oh, yes," Chen said, as if surprised by the question. "I'm a Beijingren, born and bred. Outer City."

In two blocks the street became Chang'an Avenue, the city's

main east-west arterial that flanked the southern edge of the Forbidden City, with its distinctive red walls. Nicholai could see the Gate of Heavenly Peace, where Mao had stood a little over two years ago and declared the People's Republic of China. He recalled from his briefing that Yuri Voroshenin was there with him that day.

Enormous plaques on either side of the gate read, respectively, "Long Live the People's Republic of China!" and "Long Live the Unity of the Peoples of the World!"

"A small detour?" Chen asked.

"Please."

Chen ordered the driver to take them around Tiananmen Square, which was a mess of construction work as it was being widened for even larger public demonstrations. Buildings were being torn down, the rubble removed or leveled.

"When it is done," Chen said proudly, "it will hold over a million people."

Many of whose homes had been torn down, Nicholai thought, to create space for them to publicly gather.

Beijing was an impressive, imposing city, created for the exercise of power. Nicholai preferred Shanghai, although he was sure it had changed as well. The China he had known was a motley of color and style — Shanghai was a center of high fashion — but the residents of Beijing in this time seemed almost cookie-cutter in their uniformity, most of them wearing the standard blue, green, or gray padded coats with baggy trousers and the same "Mao" caps.

Having negotiated Tiananmen, the driver turned north onto Wangfujing Street and pulled up in front of the Beijing Hotel, a turn-of-the-century European-style building, seven stories high, with three arched doorways and a colonnade on the top floor. The driver scurried out, retrieved Nicholai's bag, and handed it to a hotel porter. The small middle-aged man struggled to heft the bag to the lobby, but spurned Nicholai's proffered hand.

"He was the deputy mayor," Chen grunted, ushering Nicholai past the porter. "Lucky to be alive."

The lobby seemed a house of ghosts. Nicholai knew this had once been the European center of power in Beijing, where the Western barons of commerce lorded it over the Asians, and Chinese waiters scurried with trays of gin and tonics, whiskey and sodas as they endured the careless racism of the French, Germans, English, and Americans. It had been the same in Shanghai, but here — just a short walk from the Imperial Palace — it must have seemed even more insulting.

He was surprised that the Communists hadn't simply demolished the building, leaving its painful associations in rubble, but he realized that the new regime needed a place to house its foreign guests. The lobby was clean but lifeless, scrubbed of any trace of decadence, devoid of the sense of luxury and privilege that it doubtless once possessed.

As life under capitalism was aggressively gauche, Nicholai thought, life under communism was deliberately drab.

The desk clerk, a young woman clad in the ubiquitous "Lenin suit" — a gray, double-breasted jacket with a sash belt — asked for his passport and was surprised when Nicholai produced it with a greeting in Chinese, "Have you eaten today?"

"I have, Comrade. And you?"

"Yes, thank you."

"Room 502. The porter will—"

"I'll take my own bag, thank you," Nicholai said. He reached into his pocket for a yuan note to give the porter, but Chen stopped him.

"Tipping is not permitted in the People's Republic," Chen said.

"Of course not," Nicholai said.

"Patronizing imperialist anachronism," Chen added.

Quite a burden to carry, Nicholai thought, for a small gratuity.

The elevator ride was frightening, and Nicholai wondered when was the last time that the creaky lift had seen maintenance. But they made it to the fifth floor alive and Chen led him down the long hallway to his room.

The room was basic but clean. A bed, a wardrobe, two chairs, a side table with a radio, and a thermos of hot water for making tea. The attached bathroom had a toilet and a bathtub, but no shower. French doors in the main room opened onto a small balcony, and Nicholai stepped out and looked down on the front of the hotel and East Chang Street. To his right he could see Tiananmen Square.

"These rooms are reserved for very special guests," Chen said when Nicholai stepped back inside.

I'll bet they are, Nicholai thought. He would further bet that these rooms were also wired for sound to record every conversation of said special guests. He took off his coat, gestured for Chen to do the same, and hung both coats up in the wardrobe.

"May I offer you tea?" Nicholai asked.

"Very kind."

Nicholai took two large pinches of green tea from a canister and put them into the pot. Then he poured the hot water in, waited for a few moments, and then poured the tea into two cups. Normally he would not have served tea made in the first steep, but he knew that fuel for heating water was at a premium and that waste would be considered offensive. He handed Chen the tea and both men sat down in the chairs.

After a sufficiently awkward silence, Chen said, "This is very good. Warming. Thank you."

"I can hardly accept gratitude for your hospitality."

Chen was disconcerted at the thought that the visitor might be under the misapprehension that the hotel stay was complimentary. He got right to it. "But you are paying for your room."

"Still," Nicholai said, remembering now how blunt the Chinese could be about business matters. So unlike the Japanese, who would have engaged in ten minutes of circumlocution to subtly inform the guest that he was, after all, a *paying* guest.

Chen looked relieved. "There is a dinner tonight in your honor."

"You needn't go to the trouble and expense."

"It is already organized."

"I look forward to it."

Chen nodded. "Colonel Yu, aide to General Liu himself, will be your host."

General Liu Dehuai was a national hero, one of the key generals on the Long March and the founder of the legendary 8th Route Army. Until recently the commander of Chinese forces in Korea, he was now minister of defense. Liu would have to approve the deal for the sale of the weapons through "Guibert" to the Viet Minh. The fact that he was sending an apparently key aide to evaluate Guibert on his very first night in the country was significant.

And uncharacteristic of what Nicholai knew of the Chinese way of doing business. Typically, they would let a foreign guest cool his heels — easy to do in Beijing in January — for days if not weeks, occupying him with low-level subordinates and endless sightseeing, before getting down to business.

Liu was in a hurry to do this deal.

"I'm honored," Nicholai said.

Chen stood up. "I am sure you are tired and would like to rest."

Nicholai saw him to the door.

He waited five minutes, then put his coat and hat on again and went back out into the cold.

# 18

ALTHOUGH NICHOLAI HAD PORED over maps and aerial photographs, they could not substitute for on-the-ground knowledge, and he wanted to orient himself to the city. His survival might depend on an immediate decision as to what alley to turn into, what street to avoid, and there would be no time for indecision or hesitation.

Beijing in the early days of 1952 was a city of contradictions, divided between spacious governmental sections and the narrow alleys — *hutongs* — on which most of the people lived. The heart of Beijing was the Forbidden City — as its name indicated, closed off to the general public for most of its thousand-year existence. Now that the Communist government had moved in and turned many of its buildings into offices and residences, most of it was still "forbidden" most of the time.

The "other" Beijing that surrounded the Forbidden City was — or used to be — a vibrant, active, cosmopolitan city of some two million people, with open-air markets, streets of fashionable shops, small parks and squares where jugglers, magicians, and other buskers performed.

The Beijingren, the natives, had the same tough, jaded, superior attitude of the residents of all major cities. To them, Beijing was its own universe, and they were not entirely wrong. Everyone had come to the imperial city — not only all manners of Chinese, but, for good or ill, the rest of the world as well. So the sophisticated Beijing citizens knew all the varied cultures of China, Japan, and Europe. A well-heeled Beijingren might well have eaten in French restaurants, bought suits from Italian tailors, watches from German craftsmen. Most of the modern Beijingren had worn British suits or French dresses and danced to American music.

Still, any good Beijingren, from the impoverished night-soil collectors to the richest merchant, would proudly proclaim the superiority of Beijing culture itself — its fabled imperial buildings, its bridges and parks and gardens, centuries-old restaurants and teahouses, its theaters and opera houses, its circuses and acrobats, its poets and writers.

Beijing was a sophisticated imperial capital when London and Paris were little more than insect-infested swamps. Of all the European capitals, only Rome could rival Beijing in terms of antiquity, sophistication, and power.

The Beijingren had seen it all. Within the living memory of many of its citizens, Beijing had survived invasions from the French, the Germans, the Nationalists, the Japanese, and now the Communists. It had adjusted, evolved, and survived.

Many observers were surprised that Mao chose the city, with all its imperial associations, for his capital. Nicholai thought he chose Beijing for exactly those associations. No ruler could claim power in China without those trappings — without possession of the Temple of Heaven, no emperor could claim the Mandate of Heaven, and Nicholai knew that Mao, for all his Communist propaganda, saw himself as the new emperor. Indeed, he had quickly shut himself up in the Forbidden City, and was rarely seen outside it.

The Beijingren knew this. They had known many emperors, had seen dynasties rise and fall, watched them build monuments to themselves and then watched them crumble, and they knew that the Communist Dynasty was but one in a long line. Its time would come and its time would pass, but the city would endure.

But in what form, Nicholai wondered as he walked out the front entrance, up the street, and then turned right onto Chang'an. Mao had plans for the city and announced that he was going to transform it from "a city of consumption to a city of production." Already blocks of old houses had been torn down to make room for new factories, narrow streets were being broadened to allow tanks to roll up and down, and Soviet architects — a perfectly oxymoronic phrase, in Nicholai's opinion — were now busily designing sterile concrete housing units to replace the old courtyard houses that were the center of Beijing domestic life.

The courtyard walls lined the residential streets and *hutongs*, with only small doors opening onto the street. The doors opened onto another wall, and a visitor would have to go to the right or the left — a device that outfoxed evil spirits, which can only move in straight lines. Once around that wall, the space opened onto an interior courtyard, usually of pebbles or, in the richer homes, flagstone. The courtyard usually had a shade tree or two, and an open charcoal brazier for cooking during warmer weather. Depending on the wealth or poverty of the family, there was a single dwelling structure of one or two stories, perhaps with separate wings for the families of the sons. The Beijingren lived privately, quietly, and with great autonomy in these extended family units behind the walls.

This would never do for the control-obsessed Mao, who quickly condemned the desire for privacy as an "individualist" antisocial attitude. While waiting for the Soviets to complete their architectural atrocities, he attacked the courtyard houses on an organizational level, establishing "safety-keeping committees," in which neighbors were encouraged to snoop on neighbors. Black-clad squads of "night people" — mostly erstwhile burglars — used their former skills to prowl around rooftops and listen for the sounds of "bourgeois activities" such as the click of mah-jongg tiles, the trilling of a pet songbird, or for antirevolutionary whisperings and conspiracies.

The assault on urban life was also conducted on public spaces. Theaters and teahouses were closed, street performers harassed for licenses, snack vendors increasingly forced into state-run collectives. Even the rickshaw drivers who once jammed the city's avenues were being gradually phased out as "imperial relics," symbolic of "human slavery." It didn't happen all at once, but it was happening, and the bustle that gave the city so much of its charm was being muted into fearful stillness, in which every activity was watched and heard.

Indeed, Nicholai discerned the man who instantly fell in behind him before he even left the hotel lobby. China was poor in most resources save population, so the intelligence service could easily afford to leave a man at the hotel with the sole responsibility of keeping an eye on "Guibert."

It was good to know.

Nicholai wanted to ascertain the amount of surveillance that he would encounter, so in that sense he was "trolling for tails," as Haverford would put it. Nicholai thought of it differently, of course, and in terms of Go. A basic principle of the game was that motion attracts motion. The movement of a single stone on an area of the board generally provokes a move from the opponent. So it was, he discovered, in the espionage game, at which he realized he was a neophyte.

Pretending not to notice the surveillance, he crossed Chang'an into the old Legation Quarter, past the old Russian Legation building, which the current Soviet delegation had reoccupied. Using only his peripheral vision, he scanned the front of the building, where the security, sitting in Russian sedans, was clearly visible.

He kept his pace up, as if bored with the Legation Quarter and intent on heading west to Tiananmen Square.

He walked around the vast square, chaotic with construction — his watchdog doing a good job of staying with him without getting too close — and then turned north toward the great tiled roofs of the Forbidden City.

His tail backed off then and turned him over to a second man, so Nicholai knew that the surveillance of Guibert was something of a priority. The tall roofline of the Imperial Palace, easily recognizable from a hundred photographs, loomed in front of him as he looked for a place to kill Voroshenin that would offer the requisite time and space as well as offer an avenue of escape.

Nicholai had hoped that the walls of the Forbidden City might offer such a location, but then he realized that the area was of course far too heavily guarded now that Mao had taken up residence there and many of the buildings had been turned into housing for high officials or government offices.

Nicholai went into the palace, now a museum, to get warm and firm up his tourist credentials, and lingered on the grounds (if one could be said to "linger" on this bitterly cold afternoon) before leaving the Forbidden City. Observing that he had now acquired an additional tail, he turned east and walked across a lovely bridge over the southern reaches of Beihai Lake, frozen and silver against the white willow trees along its banks.

It would not do to walk too confidently, so Nicholai assumed the gait and pace of a man who is slightly, albeit unconcernedly, lost. He paused at the corner of Xidan Street, pretended to consider his route, and then "decided" to turn north. His tails switched off, one lingering as he fussed with his scarf, the other coming ahead to pick up the trail.

It was enough for Nicholai to get a good look at their faces without being noticed. He dubbed one of them the Greyhound for his tall, slim build and foot speed, and the other Xiao Smiley, an ironic reference to his dour expression. To be fair, Nicholai thought, no one would be very happy to be pulled from a nice warm hotel lobby onto the freezing streets.

Nicholai upped his pace to see if the Greyhound would keep up with him, or whether there was another agent to turn him over to. The Greyhound quickened his steps, although he was careful to stay far behind Nicholai as he went through the South Gate into Beihai Park.

The park was lovely, Nicholai thought, and represented the very best of Asian landscaping art. Built around the oval of Beihai Lake, its walkways wended through graceful rows of willow trees, impeccable placements of stones, and perfectly located pavilions. Every curve offered a new perspective, and the whole thing came close to achieving the elusive quality that the Japanese called *shibumi* — understated elegance.

In fact, in winter the park resembled a distinguished elderly lady, spare and yet beautiful, who preserves her posture and dignity even in the knowledge of cold death. A man more verbally talented than I, Nicholai thought, might compose a poem about her.

Walking northward along the eastern edge of the lake, he came to a bridge that spanned the lake onto an island. Nicholai read the small sign that pointed toward the Jade Isle and stepped onto the gracefully arched bridge.

He paused at the apex to look over the lake and see if the Greyhound followed him. The Greyhound was smart and strode right past him, never even glancing as he continued onto the island. It was the smart move, Nicholai thought, anticipating that I will keep going onto the Jade Isle, but still allowing him to double back if I change my mind. Lazily scanning the scenery, he saw Xiao Smiley stop and linger in a pavilion near the base of the bridge.

Nicholai turned and crossed the bridge onto the Jade Isle, which was dominated by a tall white tower on a small rise in the center of the thickly wooded island. A narrow footpath flanked by trees and shrubs led up to the tower, identified by a plaque as, not surprisingly, the White Pagoda, built in 1651 to honor the visit of the Dalai Lama.

Ironic, Nicholai thought, considering that the Chinese had just invaded Tibet.

The tower itself was closed. Nicholai strolled around the base of the tower, which, with its curved lines and additional "steeple" with a gold Buddhist symbol on top, more resembled Tibetan than Chinese architecture.

He finished his circuit of the tower and then took a narrow curving path down through the trees to the southern edge of the Jade Isle, where the Bridge of Perfect Wisdom crossed back onto the main part of the park. From the bridge he noticed small docks on the islands, and others across the pond, and realized that on less inclement days one could hire a boat to access the island.

The Jade Isle has possibilities, Nicholai thought, particularly at night, but luring Voroshenin there would be a problem. Schooled in paranoia by the Stalinist purges, the Russian would not easily be lured anywhere, and if he is the chess player he is reputed to be, he will be quick to sniff out a ploy.

But it was a location to keep in mind, and at least Nicholai had fulfilled the immediate task of allowing himself to be spotted by Haverford's spies in the White Pagoda.

# 19

Haverford sat and watched Solange pack.

It didn't take long — she actually owned very few things. The rest of it — the books, the art, the fine kitchen equipment, even most of her wardrobe — had been bought and paid for by the Company and would be sold.

The bottom line was, after all, the bottom line.

She'd taken her eviction stoically, only putting up a small argument.

"But where will I go?" she asked when Haverford came to shut down the house.

He shrugged his lack of an answer. The gesture evoked what they both knew — she'd been hired for a certain job, for a certain period of time. The job was over and the time was up, and she should have thought of her future earlier.

And her concern was a bit disingenuous. Certainly she knew that a woman of her beauty, charm, and doubtless sexual talent would always find a man willing to pay for them. She had done it before and would do it again, and the money he had paid would be more than sufficient to tide her over.

"And how will Nicholai find me?"

As a piece of acting it was beautiful. I was almost convinced for a second there, Haverford thought, smiling at himself and recalling what his father had said after rescuing him from a youthful entanglement with a Broadway dolly that he thought he was in love with.

"All actresses are whores," Haverford Senior had pronounced, "and all whores are actresses."

This one certainly is, Haverford thought, watching Solange dab at her eyes with a handkerchief. "How will Nicholai find me?" He didn't enlighten her that, in the unlikely case that her emotions were genuine, she needn't trouble herself over them.

Now she folded a negligee into her suitcase, paused, and trained her remarkable eyes on Haverford. "Perhaps you and I, we could make an arrangement?"

He had to admit that he was tempted. What man wouldn't be? She was incredibly beautiful and would no doubt be a revelation in bed, but there was no way that he could justify her continued presence in the house to the cold-blooded Company number-crunchers.

"We have an arrangement, my darling," he answered. "You performed a service—brilliantly—and I paid you."

"You treat me like a whore," Solange said, snapping the suitcase shut.

Haverford saw no need for a response. In any case, he had just received word from his sources in Beijing that Hel had made his rendezvous on the Jade Isle and been duly spotted from the White Pagoda.

# 20

MEN ARE FOOLS, Solange thought as she left the house in Tokyo.

A few tears, the sparkle of an eye, the twitch of a hip, and their brains are as easily turned off as an electrical switch.

Haverford was smarter than most, but just as blind.

Like the rest, he sees what he wants to see and nothing more.

Nicholai, on the other hand...

*Dommage.*

What a shame.

# 21

THE PROBLEM WITH the "new" China, Yuri Voroshenin thought as he sipped a vodka and looked out his window at the Legation Quarter, is that there are no more prostitutes.

Which was damn inconvenient.

The "old" China threw no such obstacles between a man and his needs, to put it mildly. Shanghai, for instance, had some marvelous brothels. But the People's Republic was ferociously bluestocking when it came to sexual matters, and all the pleasure girls had been swept off to factories or farms.

This was a damn poor allocation of resources and a gross violation of the economic precept of "highest and best use."

Voroshenin remembered a different Beijing, the halcyon days of the 1920s and '30s when the Bada Hutongs of Tiangao, just south of Tiananmen Square, blossomed with "flowers and willows" and the old Xuanwu District's narrow alleys teemed with teahouses, opium dens, opera theaters, and, of course, brothels.

Those were the nights when a man could go out and get a good dinner and a few drinks, take in an opera, and then attend to his less aesthetic tastes afterward, sometimes with one of the actresses he had seen onstage, or with an expensive courtesan who would serve tea, then sing an aria, and only later get down to business.

He'd even enjoyed the negotiations with the madams, who would have considered it a gross violation of decorum to offer her girls like menu items—instead, she would ask the customer for a "loan" to pay for household maintenance or some particular repair. It was all done with subtlety and style at places like the House of the Golden Flower or Little Fengxian's.

But that was before the damn "reformers" came along—first the persnickety Chiang and then Mao, and now Beijing was a city as desexualized as the eunuchs who once ran it. Sure, there were a few "black gate women," independent prostitutes who risked arrest on the street, but a man would have to have access to far better pharmacists than were available in present-day Beijing to resort to that.

The only person getting any illicit sex in the new China was the chief puritan himself, the Chairman. Soviet intelligence had confirmed that Mao had a personal battalion of "actresses" from the National People's Opera at his beck and call. But it was just like that son of a bitch to feast while everyone else starved.

Even by Stalinist standards, Mao's China was a cloud-cuckoo land of epic proportions. It would be easy to say that the lunatic was in charge of the asylum, but Mao was crazy like the proverbial fox. All of his mad proclamations were ultimately self-serving and brought him yet more power and control.

The Three Antis Campaign was rapidly stripping the country of its bourgeois middle management, and the recently launched Five Antis Campaign (I'll see your Three Antis and raise you two, Voroshenin thought with a chuckle)—tax evasion, larceny, cheating, bribery, and stealing economic information—would soon rid China of most of its private businessmen.

And Mao had used the Korean War to conduct a witch hunt for "spies" and "foreign agents" that was reminiscent of the Red Terror in Russia thirty years ago. Neighbor was encouraged to inform on neighbor, suicides and executions were daily events, and the atmosphere of suspicion, fear, and paranoia in the city was palpable.

No wonder Uncle Joe was jealous.

Voroshenin tipped back the rest of his vodka and then heard Leotov's distinctive knock. The man taps on a door like a mouse, Voroshenin thought—timid and tentative. As the months in this frigid open-air prison went by, Voroshenin found his chief assistant more and more annoying.

Then again, he thought, Beijing is making us all crazy.

"Come in."

Leotov opened the door and stuck only his head through, as if making doubly sure he'd received permission to enter. "It's time for the three o'clock briefing."

"Yes, it's three o'clock."

Leotov minced his slight frame over to the desk and stood there until Voroshenin said, "Sit down."

We do this every afternoon, Voroshenin thought. Every damn afternoon at three o'clock you stand in front of my desk and every damn afternoon at three o'clock I tell you to sit down. Could you not just once come in and plant your skinny ass down in the chair without an invitation?

I'm going stir crazy, he thought.

I need a woman.

"So, what's new in the asylum today?" he asked.

Leotov blinked, then hesitated. Was this some sort of rhetorical trap that would get him denounced and then purged?

"The briefing?" Voroshenin prodded.

Leotov sighed with relief. He ran down the usual goings-on, the reports from moles in the endless Chinese committee meetings, the Chinese Defense Ministry's thoughts on the stalemate in Korea, the latest round of executions of corrupt officials and counterrevolutionaries, then added, "And a new Westerner arrived in the city."

Voroshenin was bored out of his mind. "Indeed. Who?"

"One Michel Guibert."

"Only one?"

"Yes."

Leotov was devoid of humor. A literal-minded drone of the sort we seem to crank out like tractor gears, Voroshenin thought. And completely useless as a chess opponent—plodding, unimaginative, and tediously predictable. Maybe I should have him arrested and interrogated just for amusement. "Go on."

"A French national. The son of an arms dealer with ties to the French Communist Party. The father was apparently quite useful to the Resistance."

"Weren't they all, after the fact?" Voroshenin said. "That was a rhetorical question, Leotov, it doesn't call for you to come up with a correct response. I couldn't bear watching you attempt it. What's this Guibert doing in Beijing?"

"We don't exactly know," Leotov answered. "But we do know he's having dinner with General Liu's aide, a certain Colonel Yu, tonight."

Well, that's interesting, Voroshenin thought. A French fellow-traveler, an arms dealer, being received by a high-ranking officer in the Defense Ministry. Surely the Chinese aren't looking to buy weapons from the French. But it must be a matter of some urgency, otherwise the Chinese would make this Guibert sit on his hands for weeks, just to improve their bargaining position. They would make him work his way up through multiple levels of bureaucracy before getting to an important general like Liu, if he ever got there at all. So, for a high-level officer like Yu to host Guibert on the first day . . .

"Where is this dinner?" Voroshenin asked.

"In the banquet room of the Beijing Hotel."

"A banquet, is it?"

"Apparently."

Voroshenin stared at him. "Do I detect irony, Vasili?"

"Certainly not."

Voroshenin frowned until little dots of sweat emerged on Leotov's upper lip. Satisfied, he said, "Get on the phone to Liu's secretary and tell him that my invitation was apparently lost and I need to know what time I should show up."

"Do you think he will—"

"We pay him enough, don't we?" Voroshenin snapped. "He can come up with an invitation to a lousy dinner. Just tell him to strangle another chicken or press another duck, or whatever the hell it is these people do."

"Yes, Comrade."

"Oh, stop it. Get out, Vasili. Go see if the phones are working." He watched as Leotov jumped up, crossed the room, then slowly closed the door so as to make the least possible noise and not give offense. It was profoundly aggravating.

As was the sudden appearance of a new player, this Guibert. The game was at a critical juncture—the move of a knight or even a pawn would achieve checkmate—and what a pleasure it would be to take this particular king off the board.

He'd had to deal with the obnoxious Chairman for twenty years—tolerate his boundless ego, his sexual voracity, his hypochondria and hypocrisy, his endless treachery and relentless ambition, but soon he would able to view Mao's severed head in a bamboo cage hanging from the Gate of Heaven.

They'd already chosen his successor—Gao Gang was the Chinese party boss in Manchuria, and he was ready to step in. Just waiting for the word to be delivered via Voroshenin from the puppet-masters in Moscow.

If all goes as planned over the next few months, we will replace the troublesome Mao with the pliable Gao.

So this was not the time for an additional complication,

especially one involving Liu. The general was too smart, too tough, and his own man. He'd already rebuffed numerous offers to buy him. And now what's he up to with this gunrunning Frog?

Voroshenin opened his desk drawer and took out the vodka bottle. He'd promised himself that he would only take one drink in the afternoon, but Beijing was really getting to him and the alcohol might quell his sexual frustrations. Perhaps they would have actresses at the banquet tonight, maybe even whores.

As if there's a difference.

As if there's a chance, he admitted.

He knocked back the drink in one throw, looked at his watch, and decided that there was time to go and visit Kang Sheng, the head of the Chinese secret police. Another broken promise, he thought sadly. The better part of him didn't want to go see the man, despised himself for it, and yet he was drawn.

# 22

Kang Sheng dressed all in black.

At this moment, the head of the Chinese secret police wore a black lounging robe and black pajama pants over black slippers, but he was known to go about in public in black padded coats, black suits, and black fur-lined hats. On a lesser person, this sartorial eccentricity would have been labeled counterrevolutionary decadence and had potentially disastrous consequences, but no one in Beijing had the nerve to think, much less utter, such an opinion.

Kang Sheng had been Mao's chief torturer since 1930. He had personally tormented thousands of Mao's rivals back in Jiangxi, and survivors whispered that they had heard the howling of his victims during the long nights in the caves of Yenan. What he didn't know about *xun-ban*, torture, had yet to be discovered; although, to give him his due, Kang Sheng was ceaseless in his efforts to discover new methods of inflicting agony.

In fact, at this very moment Comrade Kang was diligently conducting research.

His new home near the old Bell and Drum Towers in the north-central district of the city was the former mansion of a recently deceased capitalist. More of a small palace, it had guest houses where Kang's armed guards now resided, as well as courtyards, walled gardens, and pebbled pathways. Kang had done nothing to change it, except for the construction of a concrete-lined "cave" far in the back garden.

Now, teacup in hand, he sat back in a deep chair in the cave and enjoyed the screams of his latest subject.

She was the wife of a former general in the northwest district who had been accused of being a spy for the Kuomintang regime in Taiwan. A beautiful young lady — sable hair, alabaster skin, and a body that was a sensual pleasure to behold — she bravely refused to supply incriminating confirmation of her husband's treachery.

Kang was grateful for her uxorial loyalty. It prolonged his pleasure. "Your husband is an imperialist spy."

"No."

"Tell me what he said to you," Kang demanded. "Tell me what he whispered to you in bed."

"Nothing."

A knock on the door interrupted his enjoyment.

"What is it?" he snapped.

"A visitor," came the answer. "Comrade Voroshenin."

Kang smiled. There were so many ways of achieving power and influence. "Send him in."

# 23

THE KEY TO THE CURRENT condition of Chinese plumbing, Nicholai decided, was never to take no for an answer.

He tried three times to get hot water from the taps of the bathtub before he succeeded, and when it finally came, it did so with a scalding vengeance, an all-or-nothing-at-all response to his repeated entreaties.

Gently lowering himself into the water, Nicholai was reminded of the tub he'd enjoyed at his Tokyo home in what seemed like a lifetime ago, but was barely four years. They had been happy, albeit short days, with Watanabe-san and the Tanake sisters in the garden he had carefully constructed with the goal of *shibumi*.

He might have lived his whole life there quite happily, had it not been for the honor-bound necessity to kill General Kishikawa that caused his subsequent arrest, torture, and imprisonment at the hands of the Americans.

And then the offer of freedom in exchange for this little errand.

To terminate Yuri Voroshenin.

Moreover, Nicholai despised nothing more than a torturer. A sadist who inflicts pain on the helpless deserves death.

But Voroshenin was only the first torturer on Nicholai's list.

Next would come Diamond and his two minions who had shattered Nicholai's body and mind and come close to destroying his spirit. He knew that the Americans didn't expect him to survive the Voroshenin mission, but he would surprise them, and then he would surprise Diamond and the two others.

It would mean leaving Asia, probably forever, and that thought saddened him and caused him some anxiety about what life would be like in the West. A European by ethnicity, he had never even been there. His entire life had been spent in China or Japan, and he felt more Asian than Western. Where would he live? Not in the United States, certainly, but where?

Perhaps in France, he decided. That would please Solange. He could envision a life with her, in some quiet place.

Nicholai pushed the thought of her out of his mind to focus on the present. Picturing a Go board in his head, he played the black stones and placed them in their current position. The point now was to push forward to gain proximity to Voroshenin. To create a position from which to get Voroshenin in a vulnerable place.

Given the close surveillance, he couldn't simply track the target down and find an opportune moment. No, he would have to find a way to lure Voroshenin to an isolated spot, while at the same time losing his Chinese tails.

He studied the imaginary board to find that opportunity, but couldn't find it. That didn't worry him—like life, the *go-kang* was neither static nor unilateral. The opponent was also thinking and moving, and very often it was the opponent's move that provided opportunity.

Be patient, he told himself, recalling the lessons his Go master Otake-san had taught him. If your opponent is of a choleric nature, he will be unable to restrain himself. He will seek you out, and show you the open gate to his vulnerability.

Let your enemy come to you.

Nicholai sank deeper into the tub and enjoyed the hot water.

# 24

HAVING MADE a life's study of human weakness, Kang noticed the Russian's fascination with the torture. It emanated from him as strongly as his body odor, which stank of stale sweat and alcohol.

Kang didn't judge. He was a sadist himself, it was simply his nature, and if the Russian joined him in deriving pleasure from other people's pain, it was merely a sexual preference. The odor, however, was offensive. A man could not change his nature, but he could bathe.

Voroshenin tore his eyes off the woman and said, "Actually, I came on business."

Kang smiled. You came on the pretext of business, he thought, but very well. We shall humor your self-delusion.

"The Vixen Yips an Opera," he said to his assistant, naming a relatively mild yet exquisite torture that he knew Voroshenin would find compelling, both from his taste for pain and his passion for Beijing opera.

"*Manban*," he added, meaning that he wanted the beating conducted at a slow tempo. Kang knew that Voroshenin would appreciate it. "We can go to my study."

Voroshenin followed him into an adjoining room, where he noticed that Kang left the door ajar.

"You mentioned something about business," Kang said, enjoying the Russian's discomfiture.

"This Frenchman who arrived today," Voroshenin said. Of course Kang would already know about him. Nothing of note occurred in Beijing without its being reported to the head of the Chinese secret police.

Voroshenin heard the high-pitched yelp, which did indeed sound like a vixen yipping for her mate.

Kang smiled in acknowledgment, then said, "Guibert?"

"I believe that's his name."

"And what of him?"

"What's he doing here?" Voroshenin asked.

"Something to do with arms to our revolutionary little brothers in Vietnam," Kang answered.

"Guns to the Viet Minh?"

"Apparently."

"He's French," Voroshenin said, "and he's selling weapons to be used against his own people?"

"Since when do gunrunners know nationality?" Kang asked. "Or capitalists morality?"

The woman's cry was perfectly in tune with the overall composition.

Voroshenin objected, "Vietnam is in the Soviet sphere."

"A glance at the globe would indicate differently."

"You've never given a damn about Vietnamese independence," Voroshenin grumbled, listening to the woman's moans.

Kang heard them too. The whimpers were now an underlying theme. "I am offended. We care deeply about the plight of all peoples suffering under the imperialist lash."

"This is Liu's operation?"

"It would seem so."

"And you trust him?"

"I trust no one."

It was an open secret among the higher echelons of the

intelligence communities that Liu loathed Mao and was always searching for an opportunity to displace him. It was only the general's personal power and popularity among the army that kept him alive and out of this very cave.

As much as Voroshenin shared Liu's distaste for the Chairman, Liu's success would be a disaster for the Kremlin. They already had their man waiting in Manchuria. A complete puppet, unlike Liu, who would be independent and might very well edge China toward an alliance with the West.

It couldn't be allowed.

The woman hit a high note of crystalline purity.

Voroshenin stood up. "I should be going."

Ten years, Kang thought. It was absolutely essential to preserve the Soviet alliance for ten more years. The ultra-secret military-industrial development was already under way in the southwest and would be completed in a decade. And by that time, China would have the atomic bomb, would be an economic power-house as well, and they would have completed the transformation of the society. Then there would be a reckoning with the condescending, patriarchal, neo-imperialist Soviets.

But they would need ten more years of Russian economic aid and military protection to realize their plans, and nothing must be allowed to interfere with that. So he stood up, took Voroshenin by the elbow, ushered him back into the torture room, and asked, "Do you want her?"

The Russian didn't answer, and Kang took his silence as assent. He walked over to the woman and asked, "Do you want to save your husband?"

"Yes."

"There is something you can do."

"Anything."

Kang drew Voroshenin aside.

"Take her," he said. "Any way you want. My gift to you. But for added pleasure? When you are about to climax, whisper into her ear the truth that her husband is already dead. It will be exquisite, I promise you."

He left Voroshenin alone with the woman, but lingered outside the cave to savor the subtle change in the tone of her screams, what in the opera they would call *wawa diao*, an aria of highest emotion.

# 25

THE FOOD WAS exquisite.

A native of Shanghai, Nicholai was something of a snob when it came to the superiority of southern cuisine over its northern — somewhat barbarian — counterpart, but he had to admit that these Mandarin dishes were as superb as they were surprising.

"*Yushangfang*," Colonel Yu explained when Nicholai praised the food. " 'The Emperor's Kitchen.' It makes sense when you think about it — the emperor could command the best chefs in all of China. They all came here to cook, and their legacy lingers."

Indeed, Nicholai thought.

The banquet started with hot-and-sour soup, then proceeded with spareribs in sweetened Chinkiang vinegar and *zha xiao wan zi*, small fried meatballs made with prime ground pork, and, of course, *jiaozi*, the distinctive Beijing dumplings. Yu had sat Nicholai directly to his left at the circular table, a place of honor, and personally used his chopsticks to select the best pieces and place them on Nicholai's plate.

Another high honor.

Now the colonel perused the platter of cold pig's ear, chose one, and put it on Nicholai's plate. Then he took one for himself, tasted it, and nodded in approval. "I'm a southerner," he said to

Nicholai, "a Sichuan mountain ape, and it took me some time to get used to this northern food. But it's all right, huh?"

"It's very good," Nicholai answered. And Yu was anything but simian. Surprisingly young for a man who was General Liu's right hand, he was hardly a country bumpkin but a sharp, sophisticated staff officer. He was dressed tonight in civilian garb, his Mao jacket pressed, the corners of the large pockets sharply creased. His full black hair was cut short in the current style.

"Of course I miss my rice," Yu said to the table at large. "All these noodles you eat…"

The other diners responded with the expected polite laughter.

Voroshenin said, "Surely, Colonel, a man of your position could have pearl rice brought up from the south."

Nicholai was impressed with Voroshenin's fluent Mandarin, and took further note of his tone of easy familiarity with the colonel. Perhaps it was the three *mao-tais* the man had consumed during the round of toasts that preceded dinner. Nicholai had politely downed three rounds as well, and had to admit that he was feeling them.

"But I am not an emperor," Yu said pleasantly, although everyone at the table heard the subtle reference to Mao, who had the best rice brought into the city and hand-peeled to leave the husks on.

Nicholai found the remark significant — it indicated that Yu felt secure enough in his position to make a jibe at the Chairman.

Voroshenin leaned across the table and speared a pig's foot. He used the moment to ask Nicholai, "Is this your first time in Beijing?"

"It is."

"First time in China?"

"Not really," Nicholai answered. "I was partially raised in Hong Kong."

"That's part of Great Britain, isn't it?" Voroshenin asked. It was rude, a sly dig at his Chinese hosts.

"So think the British," Nicholai answered. "But in reality Hong Kong is no more British than, say, Mongolia is Russian."

Yu guffawed.

"No offense," Nicholai said, looking directly at Voroshenin.

"None taken," Voroshenin replied, although both men knew that offense had been intended and received. He kept his eyes locked on Nicholai's.

The other diners noticed the very Western, very un-Chinese, directness of this standoff, and Chen, seated to Nicholai's left, was relieved when the waiters broke the tension by arriving with a platter of fried pig's livers wrapped in iris blossoms.

But Voroshenin would not let it go. "The French have some colonies in Asia, I'm given to understand."

Nicholai agreed. "French Indochina, to be precise."

"Well, precision is important."

"Precisely."

"Although," Voroshenin said, testing the waters, "I don't know how much longer the French can hold on to, say, Vietnam. Ho Chi Minh is kicking the traces, isn't he?"

"It's a matter of time," Yu said.

"And arms," Voroshenin opined. "Wouldn't you say, as a military man, that the Viet Minh insurgency can't progress to the next phase of the struggle without a reliable supply of modern weaponry? I mean, they really can't stand up to French firepower with what they have now, especially with the Americans arming the French."

"To succeed," Yu answered as he looked over the platter, "every insurgency must make the transition from guerrilla to conventional warfare. Our beloved Chairman taught us that."

He pinched a piece of the liver and transferred it to Nicholai's plate.

"But," Voroshenin pressed, "it can't be done without guns."

"No," Yu said simply. "It can't."

"And what brings you to Beijing?" Voroshenin asked Nicholai, supposedly switching subjects but fully aware of what he was doing.

"Business," Nicholai answered.

"Agricultural equipment?" Voroshenin asked with faux innocence. "Irrigation systems, that sort of thing? In the face of the American embargo? Good for you, Comrade. But, damn, you look familiar, Michel. Something in the eyes. Have you ever been to Russia?"

Nicholai saw the man's eyes scanning for a reaction. He knew that he was being baited, knew that Voroshenin was trying to assess him. But why? Nicholai wondered. Could he have an inkling, could there have been a leak? Could Voroshenin know the real reason for my being in Beijing?

"No," Nicholai answered. "Have you ever been to Montpellier?"

"The one in France?"

"That's the one."

"Yes, but it wasn't there," Voroshenin answered. He rudely stared at Nicholai for another moment, then said, "No offense, but I once knew a woman, in Leningrad, with eyes like yours. She... well, we're all comrades here, right? Friends?"

He was met with silence, Nicholai noted, but despite the well-known Chinese reticence about public discussions of sexuality, Voroshenin continued. "She was a tiger in the sheets. I had her every which way, if you know what I mean."

The slight laughter was forced, the moment horribly awkward. Voroshenin must be very confident in his power, Nicholai thought, to so brazenly offend his hosts' sensibilities. Certainly he knew better — he just didn't seem to care, as evidenced by the self-satisfied leer that lingered on his face.

And his vulgar reference to my mother? Nicholai wondered. A shot in the dark, or does he know? And is testing me?

A part of Nicholai wanted to do it now. It would be easy, a simple matter of thrusting a chopstick through his eye and into his brain. Done in a flash, before Voroshenin's thugs, lurking like dogs along the wall, could do anything but confirm their boss's death.

But that would be suicide.

So he met Voroshenin's gaze, smiled, and asked, "Can you keep a secret, Comrade Voroshenin?"

Voroshenin smiled in return. "I was born for it."

Nicholai leaned slightly toward him and held his eye as he said, "I'm here to do a killing."

Chen gasped.

Nicholai laughed and said, "I'm sorry. My Mandarin, it's rusty. What I meant to say, of course, is that I'm here to *make* a killing."

The diners laughed, then Voroshenin, his face reddening, said, "That's still a brave remark to make at a table full of Communists, *mon ami*."

"I am what I believe you call a 'useful capitalist,'" Nicholai answered. Voroshenin's eyes had provided no answer as to the state of the man's knowledge. Certainly he had been insulted, and flushed with anger, but then he seemed equally relieved when Nicholai explained his grammatical "error."

"That's the expression," Yu said. "Now, enough talk of business at the table. We are being terrible hosts, interrogating our guest. We should show brotherly hospitality. So, what in Beijing would you like to see, Comrade Guibert?"

Nicholai named the expected — the Temple of Heaven, the

Forbidden City, perhaps an excursion to the Great Wall. Then he decided it was time to push a line of stones forward, into Voroshenin's part of the board. After all, the Russian had come this far toward him, it was only polite to return the gesture.

"And opera," Nicholai added, careful to look at Yu and not Voroshenin. "I would very much like, if possible, to attend a real Beijing opera."

"Are you a devotee of *jingju*?" Voroshenin asked, his interest piqued.

"I try," Nicholai answered, in his mind's eye seeing the opponent's white stones moving into place. I studied the file on you, you total bastard. I know who you are. "It's difficult in Hong Kong, as you know. Impossible in France, as you might guess. But yes, I'm a fan."

"I'm going this week," Voroshenin said. "I'd be honored if you would accompany me."

"Really?" Nicholai asked. "That's very kind. If it's not too much trouble."

"None at all," Voroshenin assured him. "I'm going anyway — *The Dream of the West Chamber* at the Zhengyici. And Xun Huisheng himself is singing the *huadan*, the 'Red Maid' role."

"I've always wanted to hear him," Nicholai said.

Yu said, "Catch him while you can. The party doesn't approve of men playing women on the stage. It is effete and unnatural. We shall soon be putting an end to this anachronistic practice."

"But Xun is sublime," Voroshenin argued.

"These old operas are a waste of time," Yu sniffed. "Ancient fairy tales and romantic fables of the old ruling class. The *jingju* should be utilized for social purposes, for propaganda and education."

"Madame Mao is an enthusiast," Voroshenin argued.

"Of course," Yu countered, "and we are given to understand that she is even now writing new operas that will instruct the people in socialist principles."

"Sounds wonderful," Voroshenin said dryly. He turned back to Nicholai. "If you'd like to attend, I have a private box."

*If your opponent is of a choleric nature, he will be unable to restrain himself. He will seek you out, and show you the open gate to his vulnerability.*

*Let your enemy come to you.*

"I accept," Nicholai answered. "With pleasure."

It's a date, a rendezvous, he thought.

The waiters brought out a new platter, set it in the middle of the table, and Nicholai saw that Chen was looking at him for a reaction. Not to disappoint, Nicholai asked, "What is this?"

"*Yang shuang chang,*" Chen said, then clarified, "goat's intestine filled with blood. A delicacy."

Yu and Chen watched for his response.

Nicholai knew that the dinner was not only a ritual, but a test—of his manners, his language skills, his temperament. It was also a time-honored ploy, to lull a business associate with massive amounts of food and drink to dull his mind, move the blood from his brain into digesting the food.

He was also aware that the selection of dishes was also a measure of his attitudes. For so long insulted by Western condescension and cultural arrogance, the Chinese wanted to see if he would meet them on their own terms. If not, it could very well end the business deal that was the cover for his mission.

Nicholai was somewhat satisfied to see that Voroshenin's face had turned slightly green. Not waiting for Yu, Nicholai speared a piece with his chopstick, leaned across the table, and put it on Voroshenin's plate. Then he took a piece for himself and put it directly into his mouth.

"Exquisite," Nicholai said, to his hosts' apparent delight. Then he looked at Voroshenin and asked, "You don't like it?"

The Russian pinched the chunk of bloody intestine and popped it into his mouth but was unable to keep the expression of distaste off his face.

Small victories, Nicholai thought, are nevertheless to be savored.

The *yang shuang* was followed by a dessert course, to please the Western guests, although it consisted of Mandarin-style delicacies such as glazed yams, small honeycomb cakes, and jellied bean curd.

Nicholai was full to the point of bursting.

Yu leaned back in his chair and said, "Now we can *really* drink."

In honor of their respective nationalities, they switched between *mao-tai*, vodka, and Pernod, a dusty bottle of which the bartender found in the back of a cabinet.

Toasts were proposed and drunk.

"Our French guest."

"Our Chinese hosts."

"The eternal friendship between our three countries."

It was another test, Nicholai knew, an effort to loosen his tongue with alcohol, to see if he was who he said he was. And a dangerous test, for getting into a drinking match with Voroshenin was no mean feat—the Russian was big, a practiced drinker who could hold his liquor. So could Yu, for a small man, and the toasts went on.

"Our beloved Chairman, the Great Pilot."

"Comrade Stalin, who shows the way."

"Jean Jaurès."

Between toasts, Nicholai struggled to keep his head and recall his briefings as Voroshenin pushed the conversation toward Guibert's background.

"There is a café in Montpellier," Voroshenin said casually, "renowned among the locals for its *pain au chocolat* —"

"Le Rochefort."

"On the Square of St. Martin."

"On the Place Ste.-Anne, actually."

"That's right."

Through his thickening head, Nicholai thanked Solange for her attention to detail and incessant drills, even as his head began to swim. But that was the point of drill, after all — just as in the martial arts, repetition trained one to go beyond thought into pure reflex.

Voroshenin kept at it. The Russian invited him to share memories — some true, others false — about restaurants, regional dishes, even the local football side.

Nicholai fended off each probe.

Then Chen started in about Hong Kong. He had been there as a young man, when he had fled the Nationalist police for a while. He waxed on about Victoria Peak, the Peninsula Hotel, the street markets of Kowloon.

"Where did you live?" he asked.

"On the Hill," Nicholai answered casually, recalling Haverford's briefing and the fact that staged photographs had been created of him outside Guibert's home in Hong Kong, pictures that were doubtless in Chen's file.

Chen then proceeded to ask him about a tea merchant on the Hill that didn't exist and Nicholai admitted to ignorance of any such place. It would have been a childishly easy trap to avoid had Nicholai been anywhere near sober, but with three brands of strong liquor swirling around his stomach and brain, nothing was easy.

He realized that they had been at the table for nigh unto four hours, and not a jot of business had been discussed.

But I have been vetted, he thought, and now I must wait to see if I've passed the tests.

Voroshenin rose unsteadily to his feet. "Back to the office for me, I'm afraid. You know the Kremlin — night owls."

"It is the same with us," Yu said, pushing back his chair. Chen steadied him as he got up.

"A pleasure," Voroshenin said to Nicholai. "Those eyes... I wish I could remember...A countess, would you believe...I will see you at the opera, then? Thursday night?"

"It's a date," Nicholai answered.

I will kill you during *The Dream of the West Chamber.*

Sleep well, Comrade Voroshenin.

# 26

Voroshenin chose to walk home from the banquet, to let the cold air attempt to clear the alcohol-induced fog from his head.

One bodyguard walked ahead, the other two kept a pace or so behind him, their hands in their coats, on the butts of their pistols. Idiots, Voroshenin thought. Beijing — especially this quarter — is perhaps the safest city in the world. The criminal class had been mostly exterminated in public executions, and an assassination attempt was highly unlikely. The only people who might try are the Chinese themselves, and if they want to kill me, these three aren't going to stop them.

But Mao still needs to maintain his crouching posture and suck Stalin's balls, so we are all pretty safe in China. The greatest risk is being bored to death. Or the related danger of cirrhosis of the liver.

But this Guibert, if that's his name.

If he's a French gunrunner, I'm a Japanese sumo wrestler.

The man is a Frenchman, all right, down to the stench of his cologne, but an arms merchant? He's far too...aristocratic...for that bourgeois occupation. He possesses the slightly remote and superior air of a Russian —

Those damn green eyes.

Was it possible?

Back in his legation quarters, Voroshenin picked up the phone and dialed Leotov's rooms.

"Get down here."

"It's two o'clock in the—"

"I own a watch. I said to bring your skinny ass down here."

Five minutes later, a sleepy and slightly resentful-looking Leotov appeared in Voroshenin's office.

"Get on a secure line to Moscow," Voroshenin ordered. "I want everything on this Michel Guibert and his family."

Leotov glanced at his watch.

"Don't say it," Voroshenin ordered. "Beria's men rather famously work nights, or would you like to find that out for yourself? Also, I want everything on an old White, the Countess Alexandra Ivanovna. I believe she might have left Petrograd sometime in '22."

"That's thirty years ago."

"Is it? Well done, Vasili. See, you've already got a start on it."

A soon as Leotov left, Voroshenin opened the desk drawer and pulled out the bottle. Despite himself, he poured a stiff drink and knocked it back.

Those damn green eyes...

# 27

GENERAL LIU ZHU DE was small of stature.

His iron-gray hair was cut short, and his browned, lined face showed both his southern roots and every step he had taken on the long journey from guerrilla leader in Sichuan, through the Long March and creation of the 8th Route Army, to the hideous losses he had suffered in command of the Korean venture.

It was said that Liu felt the death of every soldier. He had opposed the Korea invasion, hadn't wanted the command, but took it as a matter of duty. Now, almost two years later, each of the three hundred thousand casualties showed in his eyes, and rumor had it that he blamed Mao for every one of them.

Colonel Yu knocked on his door, received permission to enter, and sat down in the gray metal chair across from the general's desk.

He admired Liu more than any man alive. A fellow native of Sichuan, the general was a true Communist and a patriot, unlike the would-be emperor Mao. General Liu worked for China and the people, Mao worked for Mao and Mao.

"How was dinner?" Liu asked. His voice sounded tired.

"Voroshenin showed up."

"Didn't we think that he would?"

"He knows about the weapons to the Viet Minh."

Liu nodded. "Kang tipped him off. He has spies in our department, I'm sure."

"Shall I send Guibert away?"

"Not necessarily," Liu said. "Tell me about him."

Yu related the events of the dinner—Guibert's knowledge of Chinese, his manners, his intelligence, his little victories over Voroshenin.

"So you think he could be our man?" Liu asked.

"Possibly."

Liu sat back in his chair to think.

Yu knew the issues.

The Russians were keen to prevent Chinese influence in Vietnam. As such, they wanted to interfere with arms shipments that might earn China just that influence.

Mao was a fool. He had already let Stalin trick him into the Korean disaster, and now he was falling even deeper into the Soviets' arms. But a quick look at the map showed the danger—the Russians already controlled North Korea, and with it the long northeast border and the strategic Yellow Sea. They retained bases in Manchuria to the northeast and "Outer Mongolia" to the northwest. To the west, they threatened Xinjiang, its Muslim population eager to join their brethren in Kazakhstan, Kyrgyzstan and Tajikistan.

Let the Russians gain control of Vietnam as well, and they would have the southern border too. The French were walking ghosts in all of Southeast Asia; it was only a matter of time. The Russians would scoop up Cambodia, then move on to the weak sister in Siam and Burma. Soviet agents were already busy in India.

The Soviets could soon have China surrounded, and then they would gobble up Manchuria and the rest of Mongolia, and Xinjiang.

But for now, Vietnam was the key. The Korean stalemate was all but over, the Soviets would control the North, the Americans the South.

Vietnam was the next front.

The problem was that the Americans were going to move in to replace the French. That would be a terrible mistake for the United States and a huge problem for China. An American move against the Viet Minh would derail any possible détente between Beijing and Washington, and drive China toward Moscow.

The Americans were busy making their own worst nightmare come true—a Communist monolith.

But the future of China—General Liu knew it and Yu believed it—was not with Russia but with the United States. Only America could provide a counterweight against the Soviets, only an alliance—or at least a working relationship—with Washington could bring China the economic prosperity it needed to develop.

Approaches, indirect and tentative, had been made, but had been rebuffed by antiprogressive elements in the American intelligence and diplomatic communities. The diplomats in Washington were as afraid of their right-wing radicals as the Chinese were of their own left-wing extremists. Yet approaches had been made, people were at least talking, and if General Liu could count on Washington's support, he might feel strong enough to make a move against the faux-Communist dictator who now terrorized China.

But Yu knew they were in a race against the clock.

The Viet Minh were going to win in Vietnam.

The Americans were also sending aid, money, and weapons to the French and had the CIA crawling all over the country, laying the foundation for the eventual takeover. Only a quick and decisive victory against the French might dissuade Washington from a disastrous intervention that would keep America and China apart for decades.

And such a quick victory would require weapons.

Rocket launchers, for instance.

But, Liu thought, we cannot afford to be seen doing it just yet.

We need middlemen.

We need the Michel Guiberts.

# 28

Nicholai knelt over the toilet and vomited *mao-tai*, vodka, Pernod, and most of the contents of what had been a superb feast.

It is as the Buddhists say, he thought, resting between retches — everything changes and at the end of the day the most pleasurable food turns a disgusting mess. He vomited again, then splashed some cold water on his face and brushed his teeth.

Not bothering to undress, he just flopped face first on the bed for a few hours' sleep. He awoke early, just before dawn, got dressed, then jotted a quick note in code, which when Haverford transliterated it would read, *Zhengyici Opera, Thursday night*. He rolled the thin paper into a tight cylinder and put it in the left pocket of his jacket.

On the street just as a fragile sun was coming up over the city, he made a show of stretching just as a sleepy and very grouchy-looking Xiao Smiley emerged, his arms wrapped around his chest against the cold.

Nicholai took off jogging.

The air burned his lungs and the wind stung his face, but the exercise felt good and the acceleration of his heartbeat quickly warmed him as he ran north toward Beihai Park. Workers were already out, sweeping last night's light dusting of snow off the sidewalks, and the night-soil collectors were coming back from delivering containers of human waste out to the countryside.

On the *hutongs* of Xidan Market, the vendors were setting up their stands and lighting small fires in braziers, stopping from moment to moment to warm their hands over the flames. The smell of charcoal was in the air.

Nicholai kept running, aware that he was leaving the chugging Smiley far behind. It wouldn't be long, though, before the Greyhound joined the chase and caught up with him. He sped up, barely avoided a spill on a sheen of black ice, regained his balance, and kept running until he reached Beihai Park.

He slowed to a jog again and trotted along the edge of the lake.

Even in winter, the early-morning tai chi players were out, moving slowly and gracefully against the silver sky, and Nicholai was suddenly, serenely happy to be back in China again. He ran along the lakeside and then turned left on the arched bridge to the Jade Isle.

He stopped at the apex of the bridge, put his hands on the tiled rail, and stretched his legs. Looking under his arm, he saw the Greyhound running along the lake, headed toward him. Nicholai reached into his left pocket, his hand screened by his body, took out the note, and slipped it under the loose tile.

Then he finished his stretch and resumed his run, making a circuit around the White Pagoda and then heading down toward the South Gate. Smiley stood on the south bridge, cupping a cigarette in his gloved hands. Nicholai ran past him and headed back toward the hotel.

The air in the lobby felt hot and close.

Nicholai went straight to his room, coaxed some lukewarm water from the tap, and took a quick bath. He made a single cup of tea from the water in his thermos, got dressed again, and went down to the dining room, where he got more tea, a *baozi*, and some pickled vegetables. He enjoyed the moist, chewy warmth of the steamed bun as he thought about the "dead drop" he had made on the bridge.

Fairly confident that he had done it cleanly, he had to acknowledge the possibility that he had been caught at it, in which case he knew that the note was now in the possession of code-breakers, and that he would soon be back in a prison cell, a torture chamber, or both.

He couldn't read Chen's face as his handler came through the door and approached him.

"How are you this morning?" Chen asked.

"A little the worse for wear," Nicholai answered. "And you?"

"Very good," Chen said. "Colonel Yu would like to see you now. Are you ready to go?"

Nicholai was ready.

# 29

THE MONK, HIS HANDS FOLDED in front of him, stepped out of the White Pagoda.

Earlier, just after dawn, the monk known as Xue Xin had meditated in the tower and stared out the window onto the Jade Isle bridge and seen the man lean against the railing.

Now he walked slowly toward the bridge. Slowly because he did not want to appear to be in a hurry, but also because his legs were oddly bowed and he had little choice but to walk slowly.

He knew that he was risking his life, knew that there was a strong possibility that any of the other strollers in the park, or one of the tai chi players, or a street hawker, even one of the other monks might be a police spy waiting to see who came to pick up the message.

Then one of two things would happen. Either they would arrest him immediately, or they would lay back and follow him, hoping that he would lead them to the entire cell. But he knew that he wouldn't let that happen—he was experienced enough to spot surveillance, and skilled enough to dispatch himself with his own hand should it come to that.

Xue Xin would not allow himself to be captured.

He had been captured before.

Tortured, he had learned what no man should have to learn—the sounds of his own screams—and when they returned him to the cage it was only the kindness of his cellmate that kept him alive, gave him hope when he wished to die, shared the meager handfuls of rice that were their starvation diet.

Now, ten years later, he still limped.

He knew that he shouldn't be alive at all. His captors had decided to kill them all before the Japanese took over, so they marched them to a field outside the prison, handed them sharpened sticks, and made them dig a long trench.

When the common grave was finished, they were lined up in front of it, and Xue Xin was eager for the bullet that would end this life. But the commandant explained that they were not worthy of expensive bullets, and would be slashed and stabbed to death instead.

Then it started, a blur of silver blades and spraying blood, and Xue Xin felt himself fall backward into the trench and was glad for death. It seemed days later when he felt the dirt falling on him, and he wanted to scream that he was still alive but he swallowed his fear and pain with the dirt.

The monks came that night.

Like ghosts they padded through the fog and dug with their hands, literally pulling him from the grave. Weeks later he could stand, weeks after that he could walk, if you could call it walking. He had bad dreams every night, waking in that grave.

Now Xue Xin walked past the loosened tile in the bridge, deftly snatched the message, and tucked it into his robe. In his other hand he clutched a slim sharp blade, meant for his belly if they came for him or if he detected anyone following him.

But no one did.

He walked undetected out of the north gate into a *hutong* in the north-central district. Five minutes later he was in the back of a small house, squatting by the dim glow of a small radio transmitter, into which he read the coded message.

He left the house reciting, *"On mani padme hung."*

The jewel is in the lotus.

# 30

THE BLADE PLUNGED deep into the victim's belly.

The man gasped and then tried to stuff his innards back into his stomach as he staggered through the alley near Luang Prabang's crowded marketplace, but it was far too late.

The Cobra jerked the knife back, turned away, and walked quickly out the dark alley into the streets of the northern Laotian town.

It all had to do with something called "Operation X," but the Cobra didn't really care. All that mattered was the money, and the payments from this client were always prompt and reliable.

The Cobra fingered a small medallion and could feel the outline of the embossed face and the script—

*Per tu amicu.*

For your friendship.

# 31

A LARGE CROWD had formed in Tiananmen Square.

Traffic stopped, and Nicholai looked out his window to see a military caravan — Soviet trucks and American Jeeps — come past as the crowd hooted and jeered.

Nicholai spotted the objects of their derision.

Two men, one Western and one Asian, stood in the back of an open Jeep, propped up by PLA soldiers holding their legs, their arms bound to their sides by ropes. In an open truck behind them, a squad of soldiers sat, their rifles held barrel up. Members of the mob threw garbage and old vegetables, shouted insults, rushed at the Jeep and spat at the prisoners.

"Spies," Chen explained, watching for Nicholai's reaction. "An Italian and a Japanese. They were plotting to assassinate the Chairman."

"Truly?"

"They confessed."

Chen's car fell in behind the military caravan as it slowly made its way past Tiananmen Square toward the Temple of Heaven. The parade halted at the Bridge of Heaven and the crowd swarmed around it like an amoeba. Soldiers jumped out of the truck and roughly pulled the prisoners from the Jeep and shoved them to an open space at the base of the bridge. Other soldiers used the rifles to push people back, as an officer formed other soldiers into a file.

"You execute them in public?" Nicholai asked.

"It teaches a lesson."

In a reversal of ethnic stereotypes, the Italian stood silent and stoic while the Japanese prisoner's legs gave out and he dropped to his knees, sobbing. A soldier yanked him back and then Nicholai saw a man dressed in a long black coat and black hat emerge from the back of a car and walk toward the prisoners.

He held sheaves of paper in his left hand.

"Kang Sheng," said Chen, a tremor of fear in his voice.

Nicholai watched Kang strut in front of the crowd, stand beside the prisoners, and shout the proclamation that recited their crimes and condemned them to the people's righteous rage. The Chairman in his mercy had allowed them to be shot instead of strangled, beheaded, or simply beaten to death by the mob.

Kang finished the speech, posed for a moment, and then stepped offstage.

The officer shouted an order and the rifles were lifted with a metallic clatter that echoed through the crisp air. The Italian braced himself, but Nicholai could see the stain of urine darken his trousers. The crowd saw it too, and made much fun of it.

"Look! He pisses himself!"

"He drank too much wine last night!"

The Japanese dropped to his knees again. A soldier started for him, but the annoyed officer shook his head, barked another order, and three soldiers adjusted their aim. The officer had a feel for the moment, and he lifted his arm but paused for dramatic effect until the crowd quieted.

There was a moment of silence, and then the officer dropped his hand and shouted. The rifles roared and Nicholai saw the two prisoners crumple to the ground.

The Temple of Heaven, its famous blue-tiled roof glistening in the sun, loomed over them.

"Spies," Chen concluded.

# 32

NICHOLAI'S MESSAGE was relayed five times before it reached Haverford in Tokyo. Still, it arrived accurately, and Haverford decoded it instantly.

*Zhengyici Opera, Thursday night.*

The staff at the CIA station in Tokyo rushed into action. Within minutes, Haverford had a map of Beijing and several aerial photographs in front of him, and he drew a red circle around the Zhengyici Opera House.

Minutes after that, a Chinese refugee, a Beijing native, was in the room and identified the building as being in the Xuanwu District, southwest of the Old City, not far from the Temple of Heaven. One of the oldest parts of the city, it was a rabbit warren of narrow *hutongs* and old tenement houses. Before the Communist takeover, the area was host to the Bada Hutongs, the red-light district.

Haverford thanked and dismissed him, then got on a secure line to Bill Benton, chief of station Beijing, now working out of Macau.

"I need photos and plans of something called the Zhengyici Opera House," Haverford said, "and an asset check in the Xuanwu District."

Normally a request like this would take weeks, if it was answered at all, but Benton had been told in no uncertain terms that Haverford had Immediate Access Status. The requested pics and plans were on the wire within fifteen minutes, and an hour later Benton was back on the horn.

"What do we have in Xuanwu?" Haverford asked.

"You're in luck. The Temple of the Green Truth is right down the street."

"And what, pray tell, is the Temple of the Green Truth?" Haverford said as he scanned for it and then found the building on the map.

"The oldest mosque in Beijing," Benton answered.

A photo of the temple appeared under Haverford's nose. It looked like any old Chinese temple — Buddhist or Daoist — with blue-and-red columns and a sloping roof. But then Haverford noticed that the roof tiles were not the usual blue, but green. "The Commies left it standing?"

"No choice — it's in the middle of a Hui neighborhood."

Haverford knew that Benton was playing the "I know more than you know" game. But it was typical of the old China hands, always defensive about the fact that they "lost" the country to the Communists, and ever resentful at now being subordinate to the Asia Desk and Johnny-come-latelies like Haverford. But he was sympathetic — most of their assets had been rolled up, and now an entirely new network had to be built, slowly and painfully.

"Chinese-speaking Muslim minority," Benton explained. "Been in Beijing for a thousand years. They call their brand of Islam *qing zhen* — 'the Green Truth.'"

"Do we own a few of these Huis?" Haverford asked.

"More than a few," Benton answered. "They hate the fucking Reds, see them as godless infidels trying to suppress their religion. Also, they're hooked into the Muslim minority out in Xinjiang who are looking to secede."

It has possibilities, Haverford thought. "I'll need an extraction team."

"We can do that."

"And a dead drop location for an asset in Beijing," Haverford added.

"Can you toss a few guns to Xinjiang?"

"Sure."

"I'll get back to you with details," Benton said.

"I'll come to Hong Kong to work out the details." He didn't want Benton fucking this up and he didn't have much time to finalize a plan and get it to Hel.

# 33

THE WEAPON LOOKED as ugly as it was lethal.

There is no honor and hence no beauty in it, Nicholai thought. A sword is beautiful for the care and craft that goes into its creation, and honorable for the courage it takes to wield in personal combat.

But a "rocket launcher"?

It is ugly in proportion to its destructive power. Anonymously produced by soulless drones on an assembly line in some American factory, it brings no distinction to its owner, just the ability to kill and destroy from a distance.

Still, Nicholai had to admit as Yu recited the weapon's particulars, its power was impressive.

The M20 rocket launcher—a.k.a. the "Super Bazooka"— weighed a mere fifteen pounds and was a little over sixty inches long, half of that being barrel. It fired an eight-pound HEAT rocket that, at a velocity of 340 feet per second, could penetrate eleven inches of armor plating at an effective range of a hundred yards. It could take out a heavy tank, an armored personnel carrier, a half-track, or a fortified pillbox.

The weapon, basically a tube with an electric firing device and a reflecting sight attached, could be broken down into two pieces for easy carrying by two men. It could be fired from a standing, sitting, or—critically for its intended purpose—prone position. That is, a man could lie in a rice paddy or stand of elephant grass and get off an accurate shot. A well-trained team of two men could fire six rounds inside of a minute, while an elite team could fire as many as sixteen shots in the same period of time.

"Could one man operate it if he had to?" Nicholai asked.

"Once it's on its tripod."

"And they are included?"

"Of course, Comrade Guibert."

Nicholai made him open each of the fifty cases and inspected each rocket launcher. He was no expert on these weapons, but a failure to do so would have aroused Yu's suspicions. No serious arms dealer — as Guibert certainly was — would have gambled on buying five cases of rocket launchers and forty-five cases of mud bricks.

The weapons were packed in a thin layer of grease to prevent fungus damage to the gunsights.

"You provide the solvent to clean them?" Nicholai asked.

"Of course."

Fifty of these weapons, Nicholai contemplated, each of them capable of taking out a French tank, half-track, or pillbox, could make an enormous difference to the Viet Minh.

Perhaps a decisive difference.

The Viet Minh had prematurely launched a conventional offensive against the French troops on the Day River. Gunned down en masse by superior French firepower and armor, the Viet Minh lost eleven thousand men in just twenty-six days of fighting. Even so, they had almost prevailed and might have done so, had the Americans not intervened with yet another new weapon.

They called it "napalm," liquid fire dropped from airplanes, and the Viet Minh were incinerated where they stood.

Does the American genius for mass destruction know no bounds? Nicholai wondered, recalling the firebombing of Tokyo, and of course the atomic weapons that annihilated Hiroshima and Nagasaki.

"I'll take them," he said, "depending, of course, on the price."

Not that he really needed to drive a bargain — Haverford had supplied him with more than enough money — but, again, what kind of arms merchant wouldn't try to drive the price down?

Not Michel Guibert.

"I am authorized to negotiate for the Defense Ministry," Yu said. "Perhaps over lunch?"

They repaired to an enclosed pavilion overlooking Longtan Lake.

The food was quite good. A whole boiled fish in a sweet brown sauce, followed by greens in garlic and then *zha jiang ma*, thick wheat noodles with ground pork in yellow soybean sauce.

Nicholai asked, "So what is your price?"

"What is your offer?" Yu asked, refusing to take the bait of making the first bid.

Nicholai stated a ridiculously low figure.

"Perhaps you misunderstand," Yu replied. "You are not purchasing just the crates, but the contents as well." He quadrupled Nicholai's offer.

"Perhaps I misspoke," Nicholai responded. "I wish to buy fifty, not five hundred." But he raised his offer a bit.

"We have expenses," Yu said. He gave his new figure.

"Apparently heavy ones," Nicholai answered. But now he knew Yu's real price, for the colonel had shifted in mere arithmetic proportion toward his goal. An unimaginative Go player lacking in subtlety or flair. But Nicholai was eager to conclude this distasteful bargaining, so he raised his offer to a figure just below Yu's desired one. He was surprised when Yu accepted. It raised Nicholai's hackles and he wondered why.

Yu quickly provided the answer. "Now we must discuss transportation."

Nicholai feigned interest. Of course he had no intention of actually buying these arms, much less shipping them anywhere. By the time the weapons were ready to go, he would have killed Voroshenin and hopefully made his escape. Still, the game must be played, so he said, "Of course I will pay reasonable shipping charges to some location near the Vietnamese border."

Yu nodded. "You will deposit the funds into an account in Lausanne. When we have received the payment, we will give you a location in Yunnan Province. The appropriate army unit will help you to transport the merchandise to the Vietnamese border. Beyond that, it is up to you and your ultimate client."

"I will deposit half the money into the Swiss account," Nicholai replied, "and the other half when the merchandise and myself arrive safely at the border."

"Your lack of trust is unsettling."

"I am told," Nicholai responded, "that despite the doubtless heroic efforts of the PLA, the mountains of Yunnan are rife with bandits."

"There are a few, very minor counterrevolutionary elements clinging to survival," Yu answered. "We will wipe these *tu fei* out soon."

"In the meantime," Nicholai said, "I should not wish my merchandise to be taken from me until I can deliver it to my client. Pardon my rudeness, but I cannot help but think that the local army unit of which you spoke would be even more diligent if it had, shall we say, a rooting interest."

Yu set down his chopsticks. "Capitalists always assume that everyone is motivated by money."

"And Communists are not," Nicholai answered. "Hence the

bank account in Lausanne. And why do you assume that I am a capitalist?"

"You are certainly not a Communist."

"I'm a Guibertist," Nicholai responded.

Yu chuckled. "Two-thirds and one-third."

"Done."

Nicholai picked up his chopsticks and went back to eating.

# 34

"THE DEAL IS MADE?" Liu asked.

"Yes," answered Yu.

"Good," Liu said. "And is he still pretending to be this Frenchman, Guibert?"

"And doing it very well, as a matter of fact."

Liu laughed.

# 35

DIAMOND PICKED UP the phone. "Yeah?"

"It's me," the voice said. "Benton. Haverford asked me to bring you up to date."

"I'm listening," Diamond said.

He chuckled to himself.

Benton liked his job, was lucky to still have it, and wanted to keep it.

# 36

"You ARE A..." Chen searched for the word in Chinese, then decided on French. "...gourmet."

Nicholai shrugged. "I'm French."

When he'd returned from his meeting with Yu, a pretty desk clerk at the hotel handed him his key and asked if he needed a suggestion as to a restaurant for the evening.

"Please," Nicholai said.

"May I recommend Hong Binlou?" she asked.

Chen was quite pleased that Guibert wanted to go to the distinguished old establishment to sample its distinctive Muslim cuisine. One of the perquisites of being an escort to a foreign visitor was the opportunity to dine in restaurants that he otherwise couldn't afford. Or, even if he had the money, frequent custom of the finer establishments could expose him to accusations of decadence.

Of course there was no pork, but that was more than made up for by the succulent lamb on wooden skewers, the Mongolian hotpot, and especially the sliced sautéed eel.

The waiters, all of the Hui people who had migrated from the western provinces generations ago, wore short white jackets, black trousers, and, as Muslims, white pillbox caps. The few women in the place, mostly relatives of the owners, were veiled or wore shawls to cover their heads.

"Religious superstition," Chen felt obligated to say, in order to cover himself in political orthodoxy. "You are a Catholic, I suppose?"

"By birth," Nicholai replied.

Halfway through the meal, Nicholai excused himself to go to the toilet. The waiter gave him only the slightest glance as he passed by him near the kitchen and eased through the narrow hallway to the toilet.

Locking the door behind him, Nicholai relieved himself to satisfy any listening ears, and turned on the tap to wash his hands and cover the sound of lifting the lid of the old water tank. The message, written on cigarette paper, was stuck to the inside of the tank by a piece of gum.

Nicholai translated the code, committed it to memory, then tore the paper into small shreds, dropped them into the toilet, and flushed.

"You feel all right?" Chen asked him when he returned to the table.

"Splendid," Nicholai answered. "Why?"

"I was worried that the eel might have upset your stomach," Chen said.

"It's a common dish in my part of France," Nicholai said.

"Ah."

The waiter was a young man, handsome, with high cheekbones and startling blue eyes. His hand trembled just a little as he handed Nicholai the bill. "Was everything as you hoped, Comrade?"

"It was everything I'd been told," Nicholai said, glad that Chen was busy mopping up the last of the red sauce with a steamed bun and didn't notice the waiter's anxiety.

"I am so pleased. I will tell the chef."

"Please do."

The car and driver were waiting out front.

"Shall we walk instead?" Nicholai suggested.

"It is very cold."

"We're well fortified," Nicholai said, patting his stomach, "inside and out."

Chen agreed but was not pleased. A car and driver were major privileges, and now the foreign guest wanted to walk like a peasant. Still, he must be humored — the whisperings were that he had just concluded an important piece of business with the Ministry of Defense.

Shoes crunching on the snow, Nicholai listened to the rhythm of his footfalls as he reviewed Haverford's instructions in his head.

*Complete the termination. Run out of the theater, through the market, and into the Temple of the Green Truth. The extraction team, anti-Communist Hui Muslims, will be waiting for you. They will take you by truck to the port of Qinhuangdao, where a fishing boat will take you out to an American submarine in the Yellow Sea. Good luck.*

Good luck indeed, Nicholai thought. It would take insanely good luck even to get out of the opera house, never mind make it through the narrow streets to the mosque. And then would the "extraction team" be able to get him through the multiple checkpoints all the way out to Qinhuangdao?

Doubtful.

But there was little point in dwelling on the unlikelihood.

# 37

NICHOLAI GOT UP for his morning run.

This time Smiley and the Greyhound were ready for him, and Nicholai wryly noted that they were now wearing running shoes, at least the PLA version of them.

Nicholai didn't really like running—it seemed a dull, repetitive exercise, lacking the excitement of cave exploration or the demands of "naked kill" *kata*, but he supposed that it served a cardiovascular purpose.

Hitting a stride, he turned his mind to the challenge of killing Voroshenin. The Russian had a box at the theater, which provided the necessary privacy but would be easily secured. Doubtless his three bodyguards would be present, as would the usual Chinese security, both plainclothes and regular police.

Voroshenin's guards will doubtless search me, Nicholai thought, before allowing me into the box next to their master, so I can have no kind of weapon on me. That's not particularly a problem, he told himself; in fact, it's the precise reason you were selected for this assignment and are now jogging through the brisk Beijing air instead of rotting in your Sugamo prison cell.

The killing itself would be relatively easy—at some point Voroshenin would lean toward the performance on the stage, thereby exposing his neck or throat to a lethal strike. If this were a suicide mission in the Japanese style, there would be nothing further to consider. Nicholai would simply prepare himself for death and that would be that.

But given that you do not prefer to die, he thought as he turned north toward Beihai Park, you must then consider how you are going to dispatch Voroshenin and get out of that box, never mind the building.

The theater will be dark, with the bright lights focused on the stage, so that was an advantage. Then there is the noise. Beijing Opera, with its drums, gongs, and shrill vocalizations, seemed to the uninitiated a migraine-inducing cacophony that would easily drown out the sound of Voroshenin's dying. (Although Nicholai hoped to reduce that anyway with an efficient strike.)

He entered the park and then decided to give his followers the gift of a little variety by taking the west instead of the east path around the lake. It's the least that I can do, he thought, for getting them up so early, and there is no scheduled dead drop on the bridge anyway.

But, he thought, what if I can kill Voroshenin without anyone noticing at all? Then I could simply get up and walk out, followed only by my Chinese handlers, whom I could then leave behind in the *hutongs* of Xuanwu before disappearing into the mosque.

Is it possible? he asked himself as he jogged along the lake's edge.

Of course it is, he thought, hearing the voice of General Kishikawa. *Never consider the possibility of success — consider only the impossibility of failure.*

*Hai*, Kishikawa-sama.

He reviewed the dozens of methods that naked kill offered to dispatch an opponent from close range without undue fuss. Then he sorted them into categories based on his potential situation — sitting to the right of Voroshenin, to the left, behind him, or, a bit more difficult, if he were separated by a seat with a guard or another guest between him and his target.

Difficult, yes, but not impossible.

Only failure is impossible.

Unthinkable.

As he rounded the northern edge of the lake, Nicholai broke into a sprint to break up the boredom but mostly to see what sort of speed the Greyhound really had. It might come to that—a footrace to create space and time to lose the man in Xuanwu.

The Greyhound lived up his moniker. He accepted Nicholai's challenge and stayed with him for the first minute or so, but then Nicholai took it up another notch, gained ground again, and noted that the Greyhound couldn't catch up.

So it is possible, Nicholai thought as he slowed down so as not to cause his followers any undue alarm.

It is possible to do this thing and live.

Back at the hotel, he stripped off his sweaty clothes, took a quick bath in water that could only achieve tepid, dressed, and went downstairs for a spare breakfast of warm soy milk and pickled vegetables. He had been eating too much and too richly, his body felt consequently dull and slow.

Chen arrived a few minutes later. He sat down, barked an order for tea, and looked at Nicholai unhappily.

"You like to exercise," he accused, dropping all pretense that his guest was not under constant surveillance.

"Is that a problem?"

"It is self-indulgent."

"I had thought quite the opposite."

Chen's mug of tea arrived at the table. "It is self-indulgent," he explained, "in the sense that it uses up the people's resources that could be better spent elsewhere."

"Such as lounging around the lobby?" Nicholai asked, wondering why it was so much fun to bait Chen.

"My men are very busy," Chen said. "They have a lot to do."

"Comrade Chen, I agree with you completely," Nicholai said. "It is a total waste of precious time and resources for your men to follow me about—"

"They are not 'following' you," Chen huffed, "they are 'protecting' you."

"Certainly it is a waste of resources to offer protection in the new people's society," Nicholai observed blandly, "where crime is an anachronism that has been relegated to the imperialist past."

"They protect you," Chen insisted, growing more agitated, "against counterrevolutionary agents."

"Ah," Nicholai said. He bowed slightly. "I now realize the mistake in my thinking. Please accept my apologies for my thoughtlessness. I shall cease my morning run."

"No," Chen said, softening. "I just wanted to make you aware . . . Is that all you're having for breakfast?"

"It was," Nicholai answered, "but now I am thinking perhaps some steamed buns? With red bean paste?"

"Only if you want."

"Only if you will share them with me."

"Only to be a congenial host."

That settled, they ordered the buns, and, friends again, ate and discussed safely mundane topics such as the weather.

Then they got up and went to the bank.


Although they deeply resented these symbols of capitalism, the Communists nevertheless needed banks to conduct business, so several survived in Beijing, their staffs vaguely shamed and tinged with guilt by association.

"Which bank?" Chen asked when they got into the car.

"Banque de l'Indochine," Nicholai answered.

"Of course." Chen's response was colored with mild irony. There were banks and there were banks—some kept a close eye on the transactions of their depositors, others were more famous for blinking. Banque de l'Indochine had a well-earned reputation for the latter, its censorial eyesight as stringently selective as that of Southeast Asia itself—cheerfully and self-consciously corrupt.

If a French arms dealer was going to conduct shady monetary business in Asia, Banque de l'Indochine was the place to do it.

Nicholai took a pack of cigarettes from his coat and offered one to Chen and the other to the driver, then lit all three.

"*Xie xie*," the driver said, the first words he had spoken to Nicholai.

It took only a few minutes to get to the bank. The driver waited in the car while Chen took Nicholai inside and asked to see the manager.

All bank managers are the same, Nicholai thought as the man emerged from his office, looking slightly startled at having been interrupted for business this close to opening time. This one quickly affected the standard attitude that any transaction with a depositor was an interruption.

Nicholai had intended to speak Chinese, but now he used French instead.

"Do you speak French, Comrade?"

"Yes, of course," the manager said, jutting his chin toward the window, into which the French "Banque de l'Indochine" was etched.

Nicholai thought the manager looked a little uncomfortable in his Mao jacket. Certainly he would have preferred the standard charcoal gray suit that was uniform for bankers back in the good old days.

"I wish to make a wire transfer and I wish to make it privately," Nicholai said, deliberately rude so that the banker would instantly understand the difference in their social status, behave obediently, and want him to conduct his business quickly and leave. He didn't want the manager to check too many papers or perform too much due diligence.

"You have an account with us, I assume?"

"Yes, of course," Nicholai said. He handed the manager his passbook, created by the CIA's forgers.

The manager glanced at it. "And your passport?"

Nicholai gave him the passport, and the manager looked from the photo to Nicholai and then back again. "Very well, Mon — Comrade Guibert. Please come with me."

When Chen started to come with them, the manager snapped, "Not you."

Nicholai followed the manager down a hallway to a glassed cubicle that contained a desk and a single chair. He gestured for Nicholai to sit down and then said, "Please complete these forms."

Nicholai sat and filled out the complex paperwork as the manager discreetly turned his back. He handed the papers over and the manager asked him to make himself comfortable and wait.

As he waited, Nicholai hoped that Haverford had indeed deposited the necessary funds. The Chinese were serious about business and wouldn't tolerate a deadbeat. If the funds are not in the account, Nicholai thought, I will be swiftly shown the door and just as quickly given the bum's rush out of the country.

That was the best scenario. The worst possibility would be that the paperwork would trigger an internal alert of some kind, that there had been a leak from CIA, and that it would be the Chinese police, not the cowed manager, who returned to the room.

\* \* \*

The phone rang in Haverford's room at the Peninsula Hotel in Hong Kong.

"Monsieur Cartier?" the voice asked, speaking French with a heavy Vietnamese accent.

"Yes?"

"A large transfer of funds request has just come through our Vientiane branch," the speaker said, "and triggered an internal notice that you were to be notified."

"Yes?"

"From a Monsieur Guibert?"

"Routed to what destination, please?"

The speaker rattled off an account number in Lausanne.

"That's fine, yes."

"Thank you. Good morning."

"Good morning."

Twenty long minutes later, the manager returned with the happy news that everything seemed to be in order, and escorted Nicholai to a different room where a wire operator sat behind a broad wooden table. The manager handed the operator the papers and told him to effect the transfer.

"The funds will be available at opening of business in Switzerland," the manager said, nonverbally according Nicholai more respect. It had been a very large sum indeed.

"Thank you," Nicholai said.

"Thank you for banking with us," the manager replied. Then, needing to let Nicholai know that he was a busy man, he added, "If there is nothing else?"

"That will be all, thank you."

Nicholai met the insulted Chen back in the lobby.

"Finished?" Chen asked brusquely.

"The man is an officious fool," Nicholai said.

"It doesn't matter."

"I would like to see some of the sights now," Nicholai said, "if you would be kind enough to escort me."

"With pleasure."

They got back in the car and headed for the Great Wall.

# 38

THE PLAN, HAVERFORD THOUGHT as he stood at the Star Ferry landing in Kowloon, is coming together.

Hel had received the message sent through the Muslim restaurant. He knew where to go and how to get there. The members of the extraction team, composed of Hui, were making their way to the Temple of the Green Truth.

"We'll need some talent," Haverford warned. "Things could get tough."

Benton answered, "The whole team is trained in a Muslim Chinese martial art—*bajiquan*. Very good for close-range work in confined spaces. Same art used by Mao's personal bodyguard. The team leader is a master."

"He'll need to be," Haverford said.

"Don't worry," Benton answered. "He's quick and clean."

Quick, maybe, Haverford thought, but nothing about what we do is ever clean.

It would be good to get out of Hong Kong. Haverford never really liked the city, and the British were ridiculously sensitive about the "cousins" poaching on their turf. Just this morning, his British counterpart, Wooten, had accosted him at the breakfast table at the Peninsula before Haverford could even get down a cup of the less than mediocre coffee.

"Good morning, Adrian," Haverford said. "A little early for you, isn't it?"

"A Bloody Mary's on the way over," Wooten answered. A large, bluff man with, if Haverford recalled correctly, a rugby background, Wooten looked out of place in China. Looks were deceptive — Wooten was a noted Sinologist, a first at Cambridge and a lifetime in Asia attesting to the fact. "What brings you onto my patch, Ellis?"

"It isn't the coffee, I'll tell you that."

"Then what is it?"

"Awfully direct, Adrian."

"It's early and I'm hungover." The waiter arrived with the Bloody Mary. Wooten took a grateful sip.

"Just passing through," Haverford said, "on my way back from Macau, checking in with some of the tea-leaf readers there."

"Anything my king should know about?"

"Not unless he's awfully bored," Haverford said. "It's the usual unusual — the Chairman is winnowing his enemies, what opposition he has are keeping their heads low, anti-this and anti-that campaigns are going on."

"My boys reported a Benton sighting yesterday."

"Everybody gotta be someplace," Haverford answered, echoing the old Myron Cohen joke. He'd have to catch him the next time he was back in New York. But damn Benton and his leadfootedness.

Wooten nodded. "But a Benton sighting *and* a Haverford sighting. Raises the hackles, you must admit."

Haverford shrugged.

Wooten's red face turned unusually serious as he said, "I don't want you mucking around on my pitch, Ellis. You, or Benton, or the both of you. Do I make myself clear?"

"I'm just back to Tokyo, Adrian."

"Didn't mean to be inhospitable," Wooten said. "How are you getting to the airport?"

"Taxi."

"No need," Wooten said. "I'll get one of my boys to drive you. Otherwise they just sit around all day quaffing beer."

So I'm being escorted out of the colony, Haverford thought.

All right by me, the planning here is about done anyway.

# 39

Wu Zhong smashed his elbow into the wooden post.

A bolt of pain shot up from his forearm, through his wrist, and into his hand, still open in the distinctive "rake" posture that gave *bajiquan* its name, but Wu exhaled it away and looked back at the splintered wood. His elbow had put a hole three inches deep into the post.

That was *bajiquan* — it relied on quick, single, devastating strikes. Its great master Li Wu Shen once said, "I do not know what it feels like to hit a man twice." Had this post been a man, the explosive force of the blow would have shattered his throat or his forehead, or simply stopped his heart. Wu would have continued practicing, but heard the call for prayer from the minaret just a block away.

He slipped into a white kaftan, put on his cap, and stepped out of the dojo onto Nelson Street. The mosque was the largest in Hong Kong, servicing the island's small but devout Muslim community. The ulama had grown in recent years, as refugees fled from the mainland and found a more congenial home in cosmopolitan Hong Kong than in Chiang Kai-shek's Taiwan.

As he walked toward the mosque, Wu was glad to be going to prayer. Tonight he would be infiltrated through the New Territories across the border into his homeland. The assignment itself should be nothing, the danger lay in getting in and getting out. A *wushu* instructor with the KMT Army for years before he retired to civilian life, he would find rough handling if he fell into Communist hands.

Now thirty-five years old, Wu had a wife and three young children who needed him. Still, he could not refuse an assignment like this. It paid well; moreover, it allowed him to strike a blow against the hated Communists, godless Kaffirs who oppressed his people. Not only would he bring home a year's worth of income, but the American agent promised to provide a shipment of rifles to the nascent rebel movement in Xinjiang.

A tall man with impressively broad shoulders, he had to turn sideways to get through the old doorway of the mosque. He shucked off his slippers, found the prayer mat in its accustomed place, walked into the sanctuary, and knelt. Several other men, all friends from the neighborhood, were already there and had begun prostrating themselves.

Stretching his forehead to the floor, Wu could not get the assignment out of his mind. Killing was as nothing. He had used his mastery of *bajiquan* to kill many times before — Communists in Shanghai, Japanese in Hunan, and then the Reds again until Chiang gave up the fight and left so many of them to flee for their lives.

Now he was in a new war — a jihad to save his people. If killing helped to achieve that, then so be it. He would do it and if it was God's will that he survive and come home to his family, then *inshallah*. If not, at least he knew that the ulama would not let his family starve. A brother would marry his widow and take care of his children.

Comforted by that thought, Wu gave himself over to prayer, and the ritual, as always, felt good to him. Old, solid, and reliable. There was joy in pure worship, peace in the repetition of the ancient words as he chanted, "There is no God but Allah, and Muhammad is His prophet."

# 40

A BLEARY-EYED LEOTOV stood in front of Voroshenin's desk.

He had worked all night and now Voroshenin didn't as much as offer him a glass of tea, although he sipped his own, the white sugar sitting at the bottom of the glass like sand under a lake at one of the vacation dachas that Voroshenin could use but Leotov couldn't.

"So?" Voroshenin asked.

Leotov started with Guibert.

It all seemed to check out. The Guiberts were indeed a Languedoc family of arms merchants with loose ties to the French Communist Party. Papa Guibert opened a Hong Kong office to take advantage of the business opportunities presented by the incessant warfare between Chinese warlords following the 1911 Revolution. He appeared to have ceased operations during the Japanese occupation, owing his survival to that discretion and to the Vichy French status as noncombatants. There were rumors, however, that he continued to work, with American collusion, with Vietnamese rebels fighting against the Japanese, especially but not exclusively Ho Chi Minh and that lot.

His leftist ideology appeared to be somewhat flexible, as, after the war, he dealt with both Nationalists and Communists in China, as well as with independence movements in French Indochina.

"Connections with L' Union Corse?" Voroshenin asked, citing

the Corsican mafia that controlled the drugs and arms between France and its Southeast Asian colonies.

"Naturally," Leotov answered, "although Guibert isn't Corsican, so the relationship is strictly business. Certainly he dealt with La Corse during the war."

"What about the son?" Voroshenin asked.

"Michel?"

Voroshenin sighed. "Yes."

Again, all appeared to be as it seemed. Leotov laid some grainy photographs on the desk. The son was born in Montpellier but raised in Hong Kong, hence his fluent Cantonese. He had the reputation of a gambler, womanizer, and ne'er-do-well, out of his father's favor until after the war and the auto accident.

"The what?"

"There was a car crash in" —Leotov checked his notes — "the summer of '50, in Monaco. Michel had apparently dropped a bundle at the casino, drowned his sorrows, and crashed the car halfway through a wicked S-curve."

Apparently it was touch and go for a while, and Guibert fils needed extensive surgery to repair his face. The surgeries seemed to have accomplished a character transplant of a sort—the son emerged a changed, more serious man, eager to take his place in the family business.

"That's interesting," Voroshenin said.

Leotov shrugged. He really didn't see what was so interesting about it.

Voroshenin did. He hadn't survived the Stalinist purges by being tone deaf, and this auto accident struck a discordant note. Reconstructive facial surgery followed by a moral metamorphosis?

"Where is the father now?" he asked. "Do we know?"

"I suppose in Hong Kong."

"You suppose? Find out."

"Yes, Comrade."

"All right, what about Ivanovna?"

"I have a full report." Leotov started to recite his findings.

"Leave it."

"But there are—"

"I said to leave it."

Leotov set the file on the desk and left.

Voroshenin opened the desk drawer. He had a feeling he would need a stiff drink to read this file.

# 41

THE GREAT WALL certainly is, Nicholai thought.

A monumental, as it were, achievement of architecture and organization. But, like a static Go defense, it never fulfilled its function of keeping out an invader. There is no point building a wall when the gatekeepers can be purchased.

Still, the wall was a marvel to see, as it stretched along the rises and falls of the ridges and hills, flexible as a giant snake, its stones resembling the scales of a reptile. Or a dragon, perhaps, Nicholai thought, in the Chinese zoological cosmology.

No, he decided, the Go analogy is more apt. The wall was like a thin long line of stones, vulnerable by its very length, unsupported by defensive depth.

A lesson to be had there, certainly.

Chen fell asleep on the drive back to Beijing, sparing Nicholai the necessity to make small talk. Instead he began to prepare his mind for the task at hand, and as he thought about it, he realized that he was soon to become a professional assassin.

He had killed three men in his young life—nothing by the standards of his generation, which had endured the slaughters of the war.

His first had been Kishikawa, his father figure, and he had done it to spare his mentor shame. So it was a matter of filial duty, almost as if he had assisted the general in committing seppuku.

The next two had tried to kill him first, so they were acts of self-defense.

But this would be an intentional act of murder for profit. He could rationalize it by thinking that he was reclaiming his own life, and Solange's, but the fact remained that he was about to take another's life to benefit his own, and moral evasions were as useful as the towers of the Great Wall.

Yet the monetary compensation from the Americans was almost irrelevant.

This was a matter of honor.

Voroshenin was not just another man, another human life.

Shortly before she died, Nicholai's mother had told him the story of what happened between her and Yuri Voroshenin.

Petrograd was frozen and fast running out of fuel.

The winter of 1922 was unusually harsh, the small supply of coal had already dwindled, and the Communists were tearing down private homes for firewood. The famed lindens of Taurichesky Gardens had been stripped of the branches for firewood, and the trees looked like execution stakes.

It was a miracle—no, not a miracle but a testament to her iron will—that the Countess Alexandra Ivanovna's family house, occupying half a block on Kirochnaya Street, still stood, although the Soviet Petrograd had forced her to turn most of it into a *kommunalka*, housing several dozen workers' families.

Well, workers in theory, anyway—the lack of fuel and materials and the hyperinflation brought on by Western financial assaults on the ruble had closed many of Petrograd's factories. The workers were freezing and starving.

It was on a February afternoon that Yuri Voroshenin, then the head of the Petrograd Cheka, climbed the steps to the huge wooden doors and kicked the snow off his shoes. He entered without knocking.

The enormous foyer was full of people, shuddering in coats and blankets, and yet she had prevented them from chopping up the expensive wooden furniture that filled the house. Voroshenin walked past them onto the sweeping curved staircase and went up to the rooms where she retained her "apartment."

She was thin, her cheeks a little sunken, her skin pale with hunger. Even the upper classes were hard-pressed to find or pay for food. Nevertheless she regarded him with the haughty look of the ruling class, as if to ask what he was doing disturbing her at such an early hour of the afternoon.

Clearly he was not used to insolence. He wanted her to be afraid, as well she might have been, for this creature was responsible for countless executions and hideous tortures and she was at his mercy. But she showed no fear.

"Good day, Comrade Ivanovna."

"I am not, nor never will be, your 'comrade.'"

"You know that such an attitude could get you shot."

She closed the book. "Now? Shall we go? Should I bring a wrap or are you going to shoot me here?"

"I am not amused."

"Nor amusing."

She reached to her bed table for a square of colored paper and unwrapped it to reveal a piece of chocolate and then noticed the Bolshevik's hungry stare. Despite the fact that she had saved this little bit for weeks, she said, "How rude of me. Would you care for a bite?" Snapping the chocolate in half, she held it out to him.

He accepted it. "I haven't seen chocolate since..."

"I believe 'since before the Revolution' is the phrase you're searching for," Alexandra said pleasantly. "Yes, St. Petersburg was a city of large and small pleasures then."

"It's Petrograd now."

"As you wish," she said.

She watched him savor the chocolate, and then he said, "You will be required to move out."

What was she to do? she asked Nicholai as she told him the story. Her family had all been killed in the war or executed by the Reds. More than death, she was terrified by the thought of being out in the street, without her attachments, her belongings, her things. There were few places to live in Petrograd, fewer still where a notorious "White" would find a welcome. She had seen her peers on the streets carting human waste, selling apples, renting their bodies.

"And where will I go?" she asked.

"That is not my concern."

Alone and helpless, the only power she retained was the only power a woman had in those days. She looked at him for several moments and then said, "It could be. Your concern, that is."

"Whatever would make you think that?"

"The way you look at me," she answered. "But am I wrong? Perhaps I am mistaken."

"No, you are not wrong."

Releasing her hand from his grip, she walked over to the huge bed.

She kept her apartments.

He joined her there many afternoons and most nights, his position in the Cheka protecting him, at least for the time being, against the "social contamination" of an affair with a member of the "possessing classes."

One night he told her that he loved her. She laughed. "Certainly a good Bolshevik such as yourself doesn't believe in romantic love."

"Perhaps I do."

"Perhaps you shouldn't," she said. "Romance is dead in this world, my dear. You should know, you helped to kill it. We have an arrangement, Voroshenin, nothing more."

An arrangement indeed, he thought. She gave him herself, he protected her from himself. The symmetry was mind-boggling.

The next afternoon he walked into her apartment, his face white with concern. "Alexandra, you have to go. Now."

She looked startled. "I thought that—"

"The Cheka knows about Rizhsky Prospect."

Since the Revolution she had carefully, secretly, bit by bit hidden the Ivanov family fortune—millions of rubles—away in the safekeeping of an old accounting firm on Rizhsky Prospect. For a fee, the men there were slowly smuggling it out of the country, little by little, into banks in France and Switzerland. It was an act of incredible daring—Whites had been tortured to death for hoarding a watch, a ring, some loaves of bread, and she conspired to hide millions. And the discipline—feigning poverty, going hungry, starving herself, allowing herself only the odd little square of chocolate.

"It's only a matter of time before they come for you," he said. "Me too. You have to go. Get out. Leave the country."

"But my things, my furniture—"

"A train east out of Finland Station tomorrow morning at seven," Voroshenin said. "I've arranged space for you and all your things. A heavy bribe, but apparently you have money, no? I've drawn up travel papers that will take you safely to Vladivostok. After that..."

Thousands of Whites had taken this route—to Vladivostok,

then across the porous border into China, where most had sought the relatively cosmopolitan refuge of Shanghai. It was not a pleasant choice, but the only choice she had.

"Where is your money?" he asked. "I'll need some of it for bribes. The rest, carry with you in cash."

"I'll go get it."

He shook his head. "Too dangerous. You would be arrested and then...I could no longer protect you. And you would tell them everything, Alexandra. Trust me on this, you would tell them everything they want to know and more."

She told him where the money was. "But most of it is still there?" he asked.

She nodded.

They made plans.

Cheka agents would storm her house that night, "confiscate" and cart off all her furniture and belongings, and take them to a waiting rail agent at the station, where they would be loaded onto a special Cheka car.

"No one will have the nerve to inspect it," Voroshenin assured her.

She would be "arrested" before dawn and taken to the station for removal to some hellhole in Siberia. Instead, she would ride in relative comfort to Vladivostok with the papers asserting her new identity.

"And my money?" she asked.

"I will deliver it to the train myself," he said.

"And what about you?" she asked. "Aren't you in danger?"

"I will be on the next train," he said, "with my new papers. In Vladivostok, we can decide what to do next about our arrangement. But we have to act quickly," he urged. "There is much to do and little time to do it, and the Cheka is on the hunt."

Ivanovna gave him the address of the accountants in Rizhsky

and then started to gather her personal belongings — jewelry, china, crystal, treasured family heirlooms, all the things she had protected against the mob for the past five long years.

Voroshenin went to Rizhsky Prospect.

His Chekan subordinates, suitably bribed and cowed, arrested her in the morning and took her to the train.

Voroshenin, of course, never turned up.

She knew that she had been outsmarted and was lucky he had let her take her belongings into exile.

This was the story that the Countess Alexandra Ivanovna told her son.

How Yuri Voroshenin had taken her honor and his inheritance.

# 42

VOROSHENIN SET DOWN the file.

Staring out the window, he forced himself to focus on the current applications and not drift into the realm of memory.

The reports, many of them copies of old and handwritten documents, were unanimous in the opinion that the Countess Alexandra Ivanovna had fled Russia in 1922, but that much Voroshenin already knew. Apparently she took the quite common eastern route, through Manchuria and into then wide-open China, where she was reputed to have settled in Shanghai. Although she had all her household possessions, she was otherwise penniless—but, again, Voroshenin knew that—and survived by using her wit, beauty, and seductive skills to charm a series of wealthy expatriates and adventurers.

Voroshenin had no doubt about her seductive powers, having experienced them himself. The memory of her lush body, satin skin, and...

According to the reports, Ivanovna had seduced a German nobleman, become pregnant by him, and then refused the pro forma offer of marriage from the young Keitel zum Hel. Sometime around 1925 or '26, she gave birth to a son, whom, unreconstructed aristocrat that she was, she christened Nicholai.

Nicholai Hel, Voroshenin noted, was almost precisely the same age as Michel Guibert. It was a coincidence, but the men Voroshenin knew who believed in coincidence were all dead men.

Such as zum Hel, who had died at Stalingrad.

Ivanovna disappeared from intelligence reports until 1937, when the Japanese occupied Shanghai and her house was commandeered, literally, by the Japanese general, Kishikawa. The cited informants salaciously repeated gossip that the relationship became something a bit more than hostess and hosted, and Voroshenin felt an unexpected twinge of jealousy, remembering afternoons in…

The countess might very well have made herself vulnerable to charges of collaboration had she survived the war, but she died of natural causes.

But what of the son? Voroshenin wondered.

On the subject of Nicholai Hel, the files had nothing more to offer. The boy simply disappeared from the record, which was not unusual, Voroshenin reassured himself. In the chaos that was wartime Asia, hundreds of thousands of people simply disappeared.

Now, as Voroshenin sat in his office at the Russian Legation, he wished that he *had* ordered Ivanovna to be executed — or done it himself — before the bitch could spawn.

But is it possible?

Is it possible that this Guibert is Hel, come for his vengeance?

Just when I am on the verge of making my escape?

# 43

THEY TOURED ALL the major sights.

Tiananmen Square, the Temple of Heaven, the Forbidden City, the Bell and Drum Towers, and Beihai Park.

"Which you've already seen," Chen remarked.

He was relieved when Nicholai suggested that they go to Xidan Market to sample the street vendors' wares. It was bitterly cold now, in the gloaming dark of late afternoon, and they paused by the open braziers and trash-can fires to warm their feet and hands as they wandered through the *hutongs* of Xidan. During one such hiatus Nicholai finally learned that the driver's name was Liang Qishao and that he was a Beijing native, as he treated both men to fried dough cakes, mugs of hot green tea, scorched sausages, roasted chestnuts, and bowls of sweet porridge.

Nicholai enjoyed the outing, a colder and somewhat tamer version of his youthful forays into the seedier parts of Shanghai, and the common food was as delicious as anything served in the finer restaurants.

Sated, he said to Chen, "Now I would like to go to church."

"To church?"

"A Catholic church," Nicholai clarified. "I am French, after all. Do any survive in Beijing?"

Liang nodded. "Dongjiaomin. 'St. Michael's.' In the Legation Quarter."

"Could you take me there?" Nicholai asked.

Liang looked to his boss.

Chen hesitated, then nodded.

"All right."

The church was lovely.

Nicholai was not a devotee of religious architecture, but St. Michael's had an undeniable charm, its twin Gothic spires rising above the otherwise low skyline. A statue of the Archangel Michael stood above the two arched doorways.

Chen had him dropped off on the east side of the building, off the main street, and neither he nor Liang accompanied him through the iron gate into the courtyard. Nicholai enjoyed the rare moment of privacy before going inside.

The interior was relatively dark, lit only by candlelight and the dim glow of a few low-wattage wall lamps behind sconces. But the fading afternoon sun lit the stained-glass windows with a subtle grace, and the atmosphere was quiet and peaceful.

As Solange had tutored him, Nicholai dipped his fingers in the small well of holy water and touched his forehead and shoulders, making the sign of the cross. He walked down to the altar, knelt in front of the votive candles, and said a prayer. Then he retreated to the pews and waited for someone to come out of the confessional booth.

She was a Chinese woman, her head covered in a black scarf, and she looked at Nicholai and hurried out, frightened. He waited for a moment, remembering the words Solange taught him, and then went in and knelt in the confessional and said in French, "Forgive me, Father, for I have sinned."

He could barely make out the priest's face through the screen in the darkened booth, but it looked Asian.

"What is your name, son?"

"Michel."

"How long has it been since your last confession?"

Nicholai recalled the number called for. "Forty-eight days."

"Go on."

Nicholai confessed a precise list of "sins," in precise order — lust, gluttony, dishonesty, and lust again — Haverford's small joke. When he had finished, there was a short silence and the priest's face was replaced with a piece of paper.

"Can you see?" the priest asked. He turned up the lamp a bit.

"Yes," Nicholai said, studying the floor plan of the Zhengyici Opera House. A certain box was circled in red.

He memorized the plan — the doorways, stairs, the halls — then said, "I have it."

The priest's face came back into view. "Your sins are forgiven you. Ten Hail Marys, five Apostles' Creeds, and an Act of Contrition. Try to curb your lust. God be with you, son."

Nicholai left the confessional, returned to the altar, knelt, and said his prayers.

# 44

VOROSHENIN SAT and thought.

There was something about the name Kishikawa.

A few minutes later, he thought he recalled something and got on the phone. Half an hour later, he was on the line to Moscow, in touch with an old colleague, Colonel — now General — Gorbatov.

"Yuri, how are you?"

"In Beijing, if that answers the question."

"Ah. To what do I owe—"

"Does the name Kishikawa mean anything to you?"

"I was the Soviet part of the joint Allied prosecution of Japanese war criminals outside of Tokyo back in '48," Gorbatov answered. "Kishikawa was my biggest fish. Why do you ask?"

"Did you execute him?"

"We were going to," Gorbatov said. "Didn't get the chance."

"Why not?"

"It was extraordinary, actually," Gorbatov said. "Quite the story. There was this young man who worked as a translator for the Americans and was somehow a friend to Kishikawa. Actually he was the son of a Russian aristocrat...hold on...it's coming to me...Ivanovna. A countess, no less."

"Do you remember his name? The young man's?"

"He was quite a memorable chap. Very self-possessed—"

"His name, Piotr?"

"Hel. Nicholai Hel."

Voroshenin actually felt the hairs on the back of his neck rise. "What happened to the general?"

"That's the extraordinary part," Gorbatov answered. "Young Hel killed him. In his cell. Right in front of the guards, some sort of Japanese strike to the throat. Apparently he wanted to save him the shame of hanging."

Voroshenin felt his own throat tighten. "Is this Hel in our custody?"

"No, the Americans took him. We were happy to see him go, believe me."

"Do we know what happened to him?"

"I don't," Gorbatov said. "Glad to wash my hands of it. Very spooky, the whole thing, if you ask me. On which subject, why are you asking, Yuri?"

"A favor, Piotr?" Voroshenin asked. "Forget I called?"

He hung up the phone.

# 45

Nicholai pushed a chair against the wall to create some space in his room, then he stripped down to his shorts and did twenty repetitions of the demanding *hoda korosu* "Caged Leopard" *kata*.

He selected this particular form because it stressed close-in fighting — precise strikes that demanded the buildup of force at short range. Starting with the entire room, he performed the *kata* in increasingly smaller circles, until by the end he barely moved his feet as he fought in the tightening bamboo cage of his imagination.

Although the form included brutal elbow and knee strikes, its principal feature was its unique "leopard paw" hand posture, the fingers bent at the second knuckle but not closed to make a complete fist. The striking surface was therefore thin, just the second knuckles, intended to penetrate a narrow space.

Precision was key.

That, and the concentration of force, and Nicholai practiced until he could generate explosive power in a strike that traveled just two inches before striking its target. He thought he might have as much as six inches to two feet in the actual situation, but didn't want to allow himself the mental leisure of that luxury.

Physically exhausted but mentally invigorated when he finished, Nicholai sat on the floor, pulled himself into a rigid meditation posture, and envisioned the plan of the Zhengyici Opera House.

He had the floor plan perfectly in mind, and now he worked from the box Voroshenin had reserved, out the hallway, and down a set of stairs. A left turn would take him into the main part of the theater, then into the lobby and out the main doors. But a right turn at the bottom of the stairs led to another short corridor and a door that would lead to the backstage area.

At that point, he could turn right to go backstage or left into the alley behind the theater.

So there it was, and he mentally walked through the escape route. Out of the box, left down the hallway, down the stairs, right down the hallway, left out of the building. He "walked" it twenty times in his mind before adding the next mental level.

Obstacles.

First would be Voroshenin's guards, but if he performed the strike properly, they would not know anything was wrong for another crucial minute. But he had to consider the possibility of having to fight his way out. There was no way to know how the guards would be positioned, so that would have to be improvised on the spot. But that was the purpose of *kata*, to train the body to react instantly to any threat, without the fatal necessity of thought.

So he dismissed the guards from his mind.

The hallway outside the boxes should pose no problems. There might be Chinese police, but if the killing of Voroshenin raised no outcry, he should simply be able to walk past them on his "way to the toilet."

But he mentally slowed his pace, "walking" casually, not as a man who has just killed, but as one who simply needed to empty his bladder.

He walked down the stairs and took a right. At the end of the hallway was a door to the backstage, and there would almost certainly be an employee of the theater, a doorman, to bar the way of adoring fans.

Killing the man would be easy.

But killing the innocent doorman would be a shameful dishonor, out of the question, so now Nicholai mentally rehearsed a nonlethal blow to the side of the neck, to the carotid artery, to disable but not kill. He threw the strike, lowered the man to the floor, and opened the door.

The next door was just to his left, and he stepped out into the cold night air.

Simple, he thought, then chuckled at his self-delusion.

Simple, *if* you get within lethal proximity to Voroshenin.

*If* you perform the perfect strike that renders him quietly dead while still sitting up in his seat.

*If* the guards notice nothing amiss.

*If* you don't have to kill three more men and then fight your way through the Chinese police.

If all of it goes your way, it's simple and easy, but those are a lot of *ifs*. Small wonder Haverford had given him a one in a hundred chance of success and survival.

And if *not?* he asked himself.

If not, then that is your karma, your "joss" as the Chinese would have it, and you will be killed.

Are you prepared for that?

Yes.

Kishikawa's words came back to him. *When one is prepared to die, that is settled. There is then only the action to consider. Think then only of success, because failure will take care of itself.*

Nicholai sat for another hour and envisioned the entire operation, step by step, going perfectly. He got up, coaxed hot water from the taps, and bathed. Then he dressed and went down into the lobby, where Chen was waiting to inflict more hospitality on him.

# 46

THE ACROBATS WERE wonderful.

Superb athletes, they performed amazing feats of strength, balance, and courage. It all brought back to Nicholai happier childhood days in Shanghai, going to the street circuses and marveling at the performers.

The show tonight was held under a huge tent, dangerously warmed with gas heaters. The floor was pounded dirt and the audience — even the important officials and foreign guests such as Nicholai — sat on rough wooden benches, ate peanuts and tossed the shells on the ground, but it all added to the ambiance.

The other difference was in terms of theme — the acrobats of Nicholai's childhood had been colorfully dressed as kings, generals, courtesans, monkeys, dragons, and tigers and performed their tricks to ancient folktales. The performers tonight were clad in PLA uniforms and arranged their tricks around heavy-handed political tableaus such as "The PLA Liberates the People from the Evil Imperialists," or "The Peasants Successfully Struggle Against the Landlord," or the ever piquant, oh-so-whimsical "Dijuan Factory #10 Produces a Record Annual Output of Ball Bearings."

Still, the acrobatics were fantastic and entertaining, even wedged into the relentless propaganda. If the costumes lacked color, the performers did not, and Nicholai found himself absorbed in admiration of their skill. They tumbled, did double somersaults, swung from the tops of bamboo poles, balanced on wires, created impossibly high human towers.

"Amazing, aren't they?" Voroshenin said in French as he stepped over the bench and squeezed between Chen and Nicholai. "Sorry."

A somewhat sorry-looking man stood behind Voroshenin, and Nicholai noticed that the Russian didn't bother to offer him a seat. He was clearly an underling of some sort, but not, judging by his spindly frame, a bodyguard.

Nicholai turned and introduced himself. "Michel Guibert."

"Vasili Leotov."

"'Dijuan Factory #10' is one of my all-time favorites," Voroshenin observed, ignoring the introductions, and Nicholai couldn't tell if he discerned irony in his tone. Certainly he could discern the vodka on his breath.

"It's superb," Nicholai said.

The circus ring became a sea of red, as some of the performers unfurled enormous flags, then turned them flat as other acrobats used them to leap from one flag to a higher one to a higher one, as if they were climbing the sky on the red clouds of dawn. The audience gasped as the final performer reached the pinnacle. Steadying himself with one hand on a skinny bamboo pole, he used the other to pull a final flag from inside his jacket, and waved it as all the actors sang "We Rise Ever Higher on the Wings of Chairman Mao."

"Soon," Voroshenin said, "there will be no art, no grace or charm in this country. Only 'Mao thought.' It will be a wasteland."

"Surely you're having a joke on me."

"It will be dull as the proverbial dishwater," Voroshenin added. He tilted his head toward Leotov, still standing over his shoulder. "Dull as this one, if that's possible."

Nicholai felt embarrassed for Leotov, slid over on the bench as far as he could, and asked, "Wouldn't you care to sit down?"

"He wouldn't," Voroshenin interjected. "He is as you see him, a post. Besides, if you aren't bored enough already, you soon would be with him as a companion. His conversation is as vapid as his face, which strains credulity, I understand. I mean, look at the fellow."

Leotov's humiliation was palpable, but he said nothing. Then Voroshenin leaned in toward Nicholai and whispered, in Russian, "Your mother was my whore, Nicholai. I rode her like a sled."

Nicholai felt the insult burn, but he didn't flinch. "I'm sorry?"

"*I'm* sorry," Voroshenin said. "I lapsed into Russian there for a second. One forgets sometimes what country one is in."

But had there been the slightest blink? Voroshenin asked himself. The slightest glimmer of self-consciousness in the eye?

Nicholai wondered the same thing. He fought to keep the fury off his face as he asked, "But what did you say?"

Peering back into those green eyes, Voroshenin switched to French. "Just that I'm looking forward to the opera tomorrow night."

"No more than I."

"I hope you can still come."

"Why wouldn't I?"

Cymbals and gongs clashed as the voices rose to a climax.

The two men held their gaze.

# 47

HE KNOWS, Nicholai thought.

Chen droned on in his enthusiasm about the acrobatic troupe.

Voroshenin knows.

The car slowed to negotiate a patch of black ice.

He knows my real identity.

Or does he? Certainly, he suspects. *Your mother was my whore, Nicholai. I rode her like a sled.* Did I react? To the language, the name, the insult? Even for a second? If even for a fraction of a second, Voroshenin would have picked it up.

Assume the worst, he told himself. Assume that Voroshenin now thinks he knows that you are Nicholai Hel. What does that mean? It doesn't necessarily mean that he knows you are here to assassinate him. It only means that he knows you are not who you claim to be.

Bad enough, but not necessarily fatal.

But why, Nicholai pondered, is Voroshenin keeping the appointment at the opera?

Because he doesn't know. He only suspects, which is why he was probing, why he stretched a line of stones deep into my defense. A risky move, because he's given so much of his thinking away. But Voroshenin is no fool, he must have thought it worth the risk. And was it?

Face it, you don't know. He's a chess player, not a Go player, Nicholai thought, cursing himself for not knowing more about the Western game. It was linear, though, he knew that, and geometrical—rich in forward, machinelike thinking, poor in subtlety and nuance. Voroshenin believes that he sacrificed a minor piece—a "pawn," I believe—to expose a more important piece of mine, and now he invites my countermove.

*I'm looking forward to the opera tomorrow night.*

*No more than I.*

*I hope you can still come.*

*Why wouldn't I?*

A lot of reasons, Nicholai thought, including the very real possibility that my purpose here has been discovered, "compromised," in Haverford's jargon.

By rights, he knew that he should use one of the dead drops to report this development to the American, but he also knew that he wouldn't. Haverford might call the mission off—"abort"— and Nicholai didn't want that.

He wanted to kill Yuri Voroshenin.

Fine, he thought, envisioning the Russian's florid face as he delivered his adolescent insult.

You play your chess game, I will play Go.

We shall see who wins.

# 48

Voroshenin was furious.

Livid with himself.

Clumsy, ham-handed, and stupid, he thought as he pushed open the door of the Russian Legation. How could I have thought he would fall for such an elementary trick?

But was there a glimmer? Just a trace?

He walked up the stairs to his office and immediately went for the vodka bottle. It's improbable, he told himself. Improbable, unlikely, and so anachronistic, the offended son coming to settle a score older than he is, to redeem his mother's honor. No one kills for honor anymore, that died with the Romanovs.

And assuming that Guibert *is* Hel, he doesn't necessarily know who I am, or that I had any relationship to his mother.

So, if Guibert is Hel, what the hell is he doing here?

In the guise of a French arms dealer.

His paranoia rising, Voroshenin pulled the shades on the window. He sat down, but soon found himself pacing back and forth in the room.

Assume he is Hel, he told himself.

What of it?

Why is he here?

To know that, you must first answer the question of who he's working for. Well, you know that he was last in the control of the Americans. Did they simply turn him loose after a few years?

He killed a Jap general whom they were going to hang anyway, so easy come, easy go?

Highly unlikely.

In the first place, the rigid Americans don't possess that level of moral flexibility. In the second place, Hel couldn't obtain a "cover" without professional help and backing. The Guibert cover — if that's what it is — is both sophisticated and deep. Someone went to a lot of trouble and expense to place Guibert in Beijing, and no intelligence service of any government would do that so some young man with a grudge can pursue his romantic notion of revenge.

For what, then?

Voroshenin walked to the window, edged the bottom corner of the curtain open, and peeked out onto the street. It was empty, quiet, a gentle snow falling.

He let the curtain fall back.

Hel was in American control, but he appears now as a French national.

Is this a French operation? Doubtful — the French were still supine from the war, and more than had their hands full in Vietnam. They were not about to do anything that would bring China into that mess.

All right, so Hel was in American control, appears as a French national, albeit with a Chinese background. Is this a Nationalist operation? Is Hel on loan from the Americans to the Nats, and if so, for what purpose? It didn't make sense — why would the Nats use a Westerner when they had thousands of disaffected Chinese available?

So that leaves the Americans, Voroshenin concluded.

Don't dismiss the obvious just because it's obvious.

Hel was in American control and still is. Quite a useful tool, really — familiar with China, speaks the language. Has Russian and French as well. *Born* to be a spy, when you think about it. You'd have recruited him yourself, and it's a pity that Gorbatov didn't when he had the chance.

So assume Hel is working for Washington.

What's his task?

His cover as an arms dealer puts him in touch with the Ministry of Defense and he was hosted at dinner by —

Liu.

General Liu.

Mao's chief and only rival.

Could the Americans be using Hel to make overtures to Liu? Or has he already accepted them? His smile genuine for the first time that night, at last Voroshenin saw the entire board, his next move, and its potential result.

I'm sorry, Alexandra, he thought, your son will have to die under exquisite torture, but that is the cost of allowing oneself to become a pawn in someone else's game.

He looked at his watch.

It was only midnight.

Kang Sheng would still be up.

# 49

NICHOLAI SLIPPED OUT of the hotel.

He simply took the elevator down to the basement, had a pleasant chat, and shared a few cigarettes with the men in the kitchen and then went out the delivery entrance at the back of the hotel.

Then he walked briskly into the Legation Quarter. The streets were almost empty now, this late at night, with most of the Beijingren securely tucked away inside their living units. Lights were on, of course, in the Russian Legation, and Nicholai stood across the street under an elm tree and watched the front door.

A car pulled up and waited, its tailpipe smoking in the cold.

Voroshenin, trailed by his faithful hounds, came out a few minutes later and got into the car, which quickly pulled out.

A nice piece of luck, Nicholai thought, for the move he contemplated was a terrible risk. But Otake-san had taught him that very often not taking a risk was more dangerous than taking one.

Cupping his hands against the bitter wind, he lit a cigarette, moved to a spot under the glow of a streetlight, and waited.

It took twenty long minutes for Vasili Leotov to work up enough nerve to come out. Chin tucked into his collar, hands jammed into his coat pockets, his head on a swivel looking nervously about, he crossed the street.

Nicholai walked slowly away, out of range of the listening

devices that doubtless studded the Soviet building. He could hear Leotov's footsteps crunch on the snow, following him. He shortened his step and slowed his gait, allowing the smaller man to catch up with him.

If I have guessed right, Nicholai thought, I might become a wealthy man.

If I have guessed wrong, I will certainly be a dead one.

# 50

Kang sat back and savored his Dragon Well tea — the finest in China, supplied only to Mao and himself — as he regarded the Tang Dynasty painting on the wall. The overall effect was sublime, so Kang was more than annoyed by the interruption.

What was that *mao-tzi* Voroshenin doing here after midnight?

Kang sighed and gave permission to allow him in. Then he put a smile on his face and walked out to greet his unwanted and uninvited guest.

"An unexpected pleasure," Kang said.

Voroshenin caught the tone. "It's urgent."

"Apparently," Kang said. "Please come in."

Kang walked him into the large sitting room, which was filled not only with paintings but also with bronzes, rare ceramics, and ancient seals, all liberated from the former possessing classes. His collection of fine art was worth many thousands of yuan; his assemblage of erotica only slightly less valuable in terms of money, far more precious in the influence it purchased with Mao, a fellow enthusiast.

Had Voroshenin, the poor lonely fellow, come on some pretext to see if there was new pornography? The Russian looked at the Tang painting, a classically formed depiction of a southern mountain.

"New?" he asked.

"Do you like it?"

"It's good."

The *mao-tzi* wouldn't know good from garbage, Kang thought. That being the case, he didn't offer him tea—which anyway wouldn't be appreciated—but some rice wine instead. The Russian was an incipient drunkard, it would sooner or later kill him, and Kang hoped it was sooner.

The drink having been offered and accepted, the Russian said rudely, "Quite an art collection you have here."

Kang didn't like the smirk on his face. "I do what I can to preserve our cultural treasures," he said, "at least the ones not already stolen by Europeans."

They both knew that the best collections of Chinese art were to be found in the Hermitage and the Louvre. One day, Kang thought, we shall get them all back. "You said something about an urgent matter."

"What if," Voroshenin said, "Liu could be linked to the Americans?"

"What if shit were gold?" Kang responded.

"What if," Voroshenin countered, "Guibert were made to say that this arms shipment to the Viet Minh was a sham, to cover up something else?"

"Such as?"

"What if he were to confess," Voroshenin asked, carefully selecting his words, "that the weapons were not for the Viet Minh, but were to be diverted to counterrevolutionaries in Yunnan instead?"

"Then I am very much afraid," Kang said, "that would implicate General Liu in an imperialist plot to overthrow the People's Republic. The Chairman would be shocked and heartbroken, of course."

It was a delightful thought. Kang had been searching for

years for a pretext to arrest Liu, one that the army and public would accept, and this dissolute Russian might just have handed it to him.

"But why would Guibert confess to something like that?" Kang asked, his eyes alight with wry amusement. Actually, he could think of a dozen reasons — "Toads Drinking," "Monkeys Holding a Rope," "Angel Plucking a Zither," or perhaps some new technique that had yet to be discovered or named. "And how are the Americans involved in this?"

"Guibert," Voroshenin answered, "is actually an American agent named Nicholai Hel."

He told Kang what he knew of the Guiberts and of Nicholai Hel, omitting, of course, his own past with Alexandra Ivanovna.

"Do we know this for a fact?" Kang asked.

"No," Voroshenin admitted. "But I'm reasonably sure."

" 'Reasonably sure' is not good enough," Kang said. "I can't arrest a foreign national on 'reasonably sure,' torture him, and then find out that he really is this Michel Guibert. Even the French might object to that."

It is tempting though, Kang thought, so tempting. The thought of parading an American spy down to the Bridge of Heaven and having him shot... The titillating image of that bastard Liu following him a few days later... It would solve so many problems. But this "Guibert-Hel" connection — it was tenuous at best.

"What would you need?" Voroshenin asked.

Kang leaned back and thought about it for a few moments. "Perhaps if the father were to tell us this is not his son..."

# 51

NICHOLAI ROSE BEFORE DAWN, performed ten "Caged Leopards," and then got dressed to go out for his morning run.

The very real prospect that this might be his last morning sharpened the air, brightened the colors, and lifted the mundane sounds of the city's waking to the level of a symphony. The rumbling of a truck engine, the jingling of a bicycle bell, the clatter of a trash can being dragged across the pavement all had a clear, crystalline beauty that Nicholai appreciated for the first time.

The trees, then, took on a startling fresh beauty, artful compositions of silver, white, and black, delicately and perfectly balanced, changing tones with the gathering light. The ice on the lake reflected their images back to themselves as a friend reveals to a friend his best qualities.

The morning was truly beautiful, the tai chi players truly beautiful, China itself was truly beautiful and Nicholai realized with some sorrow that he would miss it all if he should, as was probable, die tonight.

But that is tonight, he thought, and this is this morning, and I am going to enjoy every moment of it.

As he ran onto the arched bridge to the Jade Isle, another jogger fell in behind him.

This was new, and Nicholai was aware of the interloper's footfall behind him. He flexed his hands, preparing them for the leopard paw, if necessary. The runner was catching up with him, and Smiley and the Greyhound were a good twenty yards behind.

"*The Dream of the West Chamber,*" he heard the runner puff.

"What about it?"

"Be quiet and listen."

In short bursts, the runner gave him the bones of the story, then said, "Near the end, the *sheng* and the *dan* find each other again..."

The runner sang:

*I have helped the lovers come together*
*Although I have suffered hard words and beatings*
*The moon is rising in its silvery glow*
*I am the happy Red Maid.*

"There will be much noise — gongs, drums, cymbals, then a moment of darkness..."

"Yes?'

"That is your moment."

The runner picked up his pace and sprinted past Nicholai onto the island, then disappeared around a curve. Nicholai held his own pace and then saw an odd sight.

A lone monk walked toward him on the bridge.

He had a strange gait, as if walking were painful or he had some old injury that still troubled him. He came in small, delicate steps, as an old man would who feared that the bridge was slippery with ice, but as he came closer Nicholai saw that he wasn't really old.

His eyes were old, though. They stared straight at Nicholai's as if searching for something, and Nicholai recognized that those eyes had seen much, too much, things that no eyes should be made to see. Eyes that held knowledge that no man should be forced to know.

Nicholai stopped in his tracks.

The monk said softly, "*Satori*."

"What?"

"*Satori.* To see things as they really are."

The monk turned around and limped back toward the Jade Isle.

Nicholai hesitated and then followed him. "What am I not seeing?"

"The trap," the monk answered. "And the way out of it."

The vegetables were delicious, the steamed bun delicious, even the ordinary tea outdid itself.

I should "die" more often, Nicholai thought, if this is what the possibility of imminent death does for the senses. He could only imagine how making love to Solange today might feel. One might die from just the heightened pleasure.

A silly thought, he chided himself. You won't die from pleasure—you'll die in the trap, unless you find the way out. But, like all traps—in Go or life itself—the way out is never back the way you came.

Once in, you can only get out of the trap by going through the trap.

Chen arrived to take him to the Ministry of Defense.

"That acrobatic troupe was good last night, eh?" Chen asked, sitting down at the table. Sharing breakfast with Guibert had become a habitual perquisite.

"Superb. Thank you for taking me."

"Too bad that Russian had to show up." Chen looked around, leaned across the table, and muttered, "Tell you something?"

"Please."

"I hate those *mao-tzi* bastards."

"I'm not overly fond myself."

Chen smiled with satisfaction at the shared intimacy. "Good buns."

"Quite good."

"I'm sorry you'll be leaving soon," Chen said, looking down at his plate.

"Am I leaving soon?"

"Tomorrow."

"Ah."

"We should be going."

The day was now bright and sunny. A warming front had come in — jackets were left unbuttoned, scarves hung loosely around necks, people tilted their faces to catch the warmth of the sun. Nicholai insisted they take a detour into Xidan to buy some roasted chestnuts.

"You're cheerful today," Chen observed as they munched on the treats.

"I love China."

They got back into the car and drove to the Ministry of Defense.

"The payment went through," Colonel Yu said.

"Of course."

Yu handed Nicholai a sheaf of travel papers. "Your train to Chongqing leaves tomorrow morning at nine. Please be on time. Rail tickets are difficult to acquire."

"What do I do when I get to Chongqing?"

"You will be contacted."

Nicholai looked skeptical. In truth, he couldn't care less, but the role had to be played out to the end. "You told me you would give me an exact location."

"I'm afraid that is not possible at the moment," Yu said. "Don't worry. We wouldn't cheat you."

"It's a long train trip to Chongqing," Nicholai answered. "I don't want to run into some accident. Or find myself wandering about the city and not hearing from you."

"I give you my word."

"I gave you my money."

Yu smiled. "Again, it always comes back to money."

"I didn't hear that you declined the payment."

"What will you do on your last night in Beijing?" Yu asked.

"I'm going to the opera."

"An imperial relic."

"If you say so." Nicholai stood up. "If I get to Chongqing and do not hear from you within twenty-four hours, I will go to the Viet Minh and explain that they were cheated by the revolutionary comrades in Beijing."

"Comrade Guibert, you are an arms merchant..."

"I am."

"So you will sell these weapons to our Vietnamese comrades."

"Yes."

"For a profit."

"That's the idea, yes."

Yu frowned. Torn between candor and courtesy, he finally said, "I do not understand how a man can live without ideals."

"It's easy when you get used to it," Nicholai answered.

"And it does not bother you," the young colonel said, "that these weapons might be used to kill your own countrymen?"

"I have no country," Nicholai said, realizing that this was a rare statement of truth.

"The *people* are my country," Yu said with practiced conviction.

Nicholai looked at his fresh face, aglow with idealism. With any luck, he thought, he'll have time to grow out of that.

He walked out of the office and the building.

# 52

EMILE GUIBERT LEFT his mistress's flat in Hong Kong's Western District.

In a nice part of town, the flat was expensive — *merde, la femme* was expensive — but both well worth it. A man comes to a certain age and success, he deserves a little comfort, not a tawdry assignation in some "blue hotel" over in Kowloon.

He decided to walk to his club for his afternoon pastis. It was a pleasant day, not overly humid, and he thought that he could use the exercise, although Winifred had given him quite the workout.

A lovely girl.

A Chinese pearl, Winifred, delightful in every aspect. Always beautifully dressed, beautifully coiffed, always patient and eager to please. And not some foulmouthed *salope*, either, but a young lady of refinement and some education. You could have a conversation with her, before or after, you could take her to a gallery, to a party, and know that she wouldn't embarrass herself or you.

Winifred was the new love of his life, in fact, a new lease on life itself, the very renewal of his youth.

Lost in this reverie, he didn't notice the three men come in. One stepped around him toward the elevator, the other went to check his mail at the boxes along the opposite wall. The third barred the doorway.

"Excuse me," Guibert said.

He felt a forearm come around his throat and a cloth held against his face.

# 53

HAVERFORD SAT in the "situation room" in the Tokyo station and finished his coded cable to Singleton in Langley.

ALL IN PLACE. + 6 HRS. ADVISE PROCEED OR
ABORT.

Part of him still hoped that Singleton would call the whole thing off. It was so risky from so many angles. Fail or succeed, Hel could be captured. If captured, he might talk. If he talked, Kang would quickly wrap up the whole Beijing network, from the White Pagoda to St. Michael's to the Muslims in Xuanwu. Liu could be terminally weakened and China forced even deeper into the Soviet orbit.

"Great rewards demand great risks," Singleton had said.

Fine, Haverford thought.

In fact, everything was in place.

The extraction team was embedded in the mosque, its leader had successfully been infiltrated into the country. A string of "sleeper alerts" about a Chinese attempt on Voroshenin's life had been successfully planted into the Soviet intelligence services through double agents and would be triggered after his assassination. A similar string — indicating that the killing was a disinformation plot by the Soviets and laying the blame on an apparatchik named Leotov — had been laid with the Chinese.

As for the assassination itself, Hel had done a brilliant job of luring Voroshenin onto the killing ground. Hel was fully briefed on the site, the opportune moment of the opera, and his "escape route."

Haverford looked at his watch, a graduation gift from his old man. Five hours and fifty minutes until the opera commenced. An hour or so after that, the termination.

The train was in motion.

Nothing could stop it now, unless Hel backed out — which he wouldn't — or Singleton called it off, which was unlikely.

Still, Haverford hoped he would and sat waiting for the "abort" cable.

# 54

VOROSHENIN SAT by the phone.

The damn thing was quiescent and the clock not his friend. Barely three hours now until his appointment with Hel.

The more he thought about it, the more convinced he was that "Guibert" was Hel and the more concerned he became that whatever Hel's assignment with the Americans, he had really come on a mission of vengeance.

If this were Russia or one of the Eastern European satellites, he would simply have the young man killed. Or if it were a city in Western Europe, he could arrange for his quiet disappearance. Even in China, just a few years ago, a few coins and a whisper in the right ear and the young Hel would be fish food by now.

But not in China these days. Even with the Soviets' enormous influence, Beijing wouldn't easily tolerate an unsanctioned killing on its territory. There would be an incident, and an incident could very well send him back to a cell in Lubyanka.

Better there than dead, though, he thought, fingering the pistol he had slipped into his belt that morning before leaving his quarters. If it is Hel, and if he does intend to kill me for some fancied transgression against his slut of a mother, I do not have to play the sacrificial lamb.

They say he killed that Jappo general with a single strike to the throat.

Well, let him try.

I have three bodyguards, all trained in judo, all armed. And if somehow he gets through them... Voroshenin touched the gun butt again and felt reassured.

But why is my hand shaking? He took another sip of vodka. When this is over I shall have to do something about the drinking, he thought. Perhaps go off to one of those spas in the mountains. Clean air, exercise, and all that.

Hopefully it won't come to my shooting Hel, he thought. Hopefully they will have picked up the elder Guibert, sweated him, and made him admit that his real son died in that car crash. Then I will not have to worry about it at all. I can enjoy the opera knowing that young Hel will be singing a different kind of aria, to a tune of Kang's composition.

But ring, damn phone.

# 55

THE OLD MAN WAS tougher than he looked.

"I have met the Sûreté," he told them, "the Gestapo, L'Union Corse, the Green Gang. What do you *bande d'enfoirés* have to show me that I haven't already seen?"

They threatened to kill him.

He shrugged. "I'm old. I take one decent shit every three or four days, get one good hard-on a week, if I'm lucky. I sleep three hours a night. Be my friends, kill me."

They threatened to hurt him.

"What can I tell you that I haven't told you?" Guibert answered. "You show me pictures, I've told you, yes, that is my worthless son. The one who thinks that money squirts out of chickens' asses and that you should always hit on sixteen. Hurt me."

He was a tough old bird, and one that didn't sing.

"'Is Michel in Beijing'?" he parroted after they had wrenched his thin shoulders almost out of their sockets. "What can I say except that he's supposed to be. Does that mean he really is? You tell me."

"What's he doing there?"

"Supposed to be buying guns," Guibert said, "but if I know my boy, he's chasing pussy. Is there still pussy in Beijing? If you're looking for him, look there. If you don't find him, look for a pair of loaded dice. He'll be betting against them."

"Your real son died in a car accident," they told him. "This man is an imposter."

"I don't know my own son? Why do you bother to ask questions of a man who doesn't know his own child? How stupid must you be?" Then the old man got aggressive. "This is Hong Kong. There are laws here, not like the shitholes you must come from. I know every cop and every gangster. The tongs call me 'sir.' You let me go right now, I'll forget about this, call it a mistake. You don't, I'll be tickling your feet while you're hanging from meathooks. Now untie me, I have to take a piss."

They untied him and walked him into the toilet.

The phone rang.

Voroshenin had the receiver in his hand before the ringing stopped. "Yes?"

"He's tough."

"So?"

"We think he's telling the truth."

Voroshenin didn't. He looked up at the wall clock. Three hours and fifteen minutes. "Have one more go."

"I don't know what to—"

"I'll tell you what to do," Voroshenin said.

When Guibert came out of the toilet, Winifred was on her knees in front of the chair, her eyes wide with terror, her mouth wrapped around the pistol barrel that his interrogator held in his hand, his finger on the trigger.

The interrogator looked at Guibert and said, "Three, two..."

# 56

Nicholai eased into the steaming bath.

Karma's gift to him, he thought as he lowered himself into the near-scalding water, took a deep breath, and then exhaled, relaxing away the slight pain. Then he lay back and let the hot water soothe his muscles and his mind.

As a boy he would spontaneously slip into a state of total mental relaxation, his mind taking him to lie down in a serene mountain meadow. But the vicissitudes and sorrows of the war had stolen that tranquility from him and he mourned that loss deeply, as he also regretted the loss of his freedom and control over his own life.

The best that he could do now was to control his breathing and clarify his thoughts.

That this was in all likelihood his last night in the trap of life saddened him only because of Solange. Recalling the Buddhist tenet that all suffering comes from attachment, he acknowledged that he was in love with her, in a very Western, romantic way, and that the thought of leaving her was painful.

The thought that Diamond and his minions would escape justice also saddened him, but he comforted himself with the idea that karma was perfect.

So if I live, he thought, I will avenge myself; if I die, let them be reborn as maggots on a dung heap.

He turned his mind to his mission.

Envisioning it step by step, he walked himself through the evening. Chen would pick him up at the hotel and drop him at the theater. He would go to Voroshenin's box, sit down, and enjoy the opera. At precisely the right moment—as the drums pounded and the gongs clanged—he would strike his mother's tormentor with a single, explosive blow to the heart. Then he would simply walk out of the theater, elude his watchers, and make his way to refuge at the mosque.

Suddenly, something about it troubled him.

He reenvisioned it, and the same troubling feeling lingered, but he could not discover its source.

Switching paradigms, he envisioned the scenario as the Go board, set his black stones down, and played the game. It had its expected challenges, but nothing more. If, Nicholai thought, Voroshenin knows my real identity and recalls his treatment of the Countess Alexandra Ivanovna, then I might well be moving into a trap, but I already know that and am prepared.

There is something else.

He switched mental models again and decided to play the white stones against his own black.

It was a revelation.

Oddly, he found that he counted among the white stones not only the Russians and the "Red" Chinese, but the Americans as well. His mind lined them up as white stones and, examining the board as he would if he were playing that side, he saw it.

*Satori.*

# 57

NINETY MINUTES from operational status.

Unable to contain his nervous energy, Haverford paced the situation room. In thirty minutes they would go "dark," all substantive cable and telephonic traffic would cease. Some "flak" would be thrown up—run-of-the-mill crap to let the Soviets and Chinese think that it was just business as usual, but there would be no communication between Langley and the situation room.

Singleton would go off to some affair at the White House. Diamond was going hunting with his buddies.

If this went south, it would all be on the Tokyo station.

"Do a final status check."

"We just did—"

"Did I ask you what you just did?"

They ran another check.

Alpha Tiger: In place.

Bravo Team: In place.

The Monk: In place.

Go Player: In place.

Papa Bear...

Papa Bear.

"Papa Bear's off the radar."

"What?"

"Papa Bear," the nervous young agent said. "He's off the radar."

"Run it down."

Frantic phone calls to Hong Kong turned up nothing. Emile Guibert wasn't at his house on Victoria Peak, not at his office downtown, his club in Western. Not at his mistress's pad. Off the radar.

They were thin on the ground in HK because of British hypersensitivity. In fact, Haverford briefly considered reaching out to Wooten for help. The MI-6 man had the Hong Kong police on his payroll and could scour the island quicker than the small American contingent.

But he decided that he couldn't answer the questions that Wooten would ask, and that the payback would be too ferocious, so he had to leave it to Benton's people.

The search took twenty-eight endless minutes.

Haverford jumped on the cable.

P-BEAR OFF GRID. ABORT? ADVISE.


John Singleton took his wool overcoat off the coat rack and put it on. His left shoulder suffered from bursitis, so it took a few seconds. He wrapped his scarf tightly around his neck, put on his hat, and headed out the door of his office.

For most people, going to the White House was a thrill; for Singleton, it was a chore. He was halfway down the hall when his assistant scurried up behind him.

"Yes?"

"An urgent cable from Tokyo."

He glanced at it and said, "Not now."

"You don't want to res—"

"I can't very well respond to something that you didn't give to me, can I?" he said. "I had already left the building. I'll look at it when I come back."

The elevator doors slid open.

\*     \*     \*

"We're dark," the young agent said.

That is *not* good, Haverford thought.

Singleton had hung him out to dry. The old spymaster would take credit for the success, but dump blame for the failure on Haverford.

"It's your call."

"Just find Emile Guibert," Haverford snapped, "and spare me your observations of the obvious."

"Sorry."

Fifty-nine minutes out.

Once operational, Haverford had the authority to abort the mission at his discretion. He could flip the "kill switch," which would trigger an alert that Hel knew to look for. In that case, Hel would simply walk out of his hotel, a preplanned diversion would occupy his surveillance, and he would go straight to the Niujie Mosque.

"Keep trying on Papa Bear."

"Yes, sir."

Assume the worst-case scenario, Haverford told himself.

Assume that Voroshenin has Guibert and is sweating him.

Assume that Guibert has given it up.

Given that scenario, Voroshenin knows that Guibert is a cover, but Guibert couldn't have given him Hel's real identity. All Voroshenin knows is that "Michel Guibert" is a cover under British control, which is what Guibert believes. Voroshenin will take the next logical mental step, though — he'll believe that the British were subbing in for us. He'll know it's an American operation.

So what does he do?

He gives it to the Chinese, to his buddy Kang.

What does Kang do?

Either he lets Hel stay operational to see where it leads him, or he picks Hel up and tortures the truth out of him. Everything they knew about Kang indicated the latter course of action.

"You confirmed that Go Player is in place?" Haverford asked.

"He signaled."

Their watchers outside the hotel had seen Hel go in but not come out, and they observed the correct arrangement of the window curtains. Only ten minutes ago, Hel had called room service to request a fresh thermos of water for his tea, so there was every reason to believe that he was safely in his room and not in Kang's hands.

But for how long? Haverford wondered.

Abort, he told himself.

Get a signal to the Monk, hit the kill switch now.

# 58

Nicholai stepped out on the little balcony.

Across the boulevard, lit by the amber streetlamp, the monk still stood under the tree, facing south.

The mission was a "go."

Nicholai started to pull a cigarette out to light it and acknowledge.

Then the monk moved.

# 59

"We have Papa Bear."

"Kill the abort signal," Haverford said. "Where the hell was he?"

It turns out that Papa Guibert found himself a new honey and took her to her place. He was surprised and a little indignant to find out that handlers were looking for him.

"So I wanted a little variety," he told the Brit who was under Haverford's employ. "So what, I am French." He didn't really expect a Brit to comprehend a man's sexual needs. The British were about as sensual as their food.

"Keep him on ice," Haverford ordered. "Did you signal the Monk back?"

"Confirmed."

Haverford sat down and looked at the illuminated wall clock. Twelve minutes out.

# 60

Voroshenin was on the phone.

The old man had broken — no Frenchman of his generation would let a beautiful woman have her brains spattered all over the walls — and confirmed that his son had died in the car crash, and "Michel Guibert" was the cover of an agent working for the British.

The British my liver, Voroshenin thought. The British are ass-clenching happy just to hold on to Hong Kong, they're not going to wake the dragon by messing about in China. Besides, it wasn't London that had control of Nicholai Hel, it was Washington.

Kang finally came on the line.

"*Wei*," he asked blandly, as if nothing out of the ordinary was going on.

"The father confirmed my hypothesis," Voroshenin said.

There was a long pause, then Kang said, "Enjoy the opera."

I will, actually, Voroshenin thought.

# 61

NICHOLAI SAW THE MONK start to turn to the north, then change his mind and face south again.

The mission had been aborted, then just as quickly revived. That didn't trouble Nicholai — the *go-kang* was a kinetic field that required fluid thought and action.

But then the monk did something unexpected. He turned to face the hotel and looked directly up at Nicholai. Even from that distance — five floors down and across the street — Nicholai could feel the monk's eyes, almost as he had once sensed the intensity of Kishikawa-sama and Otake-san.

Nicholai nodded.

Cupping one hand around his cigarette, he lit it — the signal that he was ready to proceed. He took a long drag, then stepped back into the room and shut the doors behind him.

Then he left the room and went downstairs.

# 62

"Go PLAYER acknowledged."

"Roger that."

Now all Haverford could do was sit and wait.

Worst part of the job.

# 63

DIAMOND MADE A POINT not to be in, or even near, the office. But he left word where he could be reached and an order that he be immediately briefed on any developments coming out of Beijing.

Waiting around is the shits, he thought.

# 64

THE NORTH WIND had picked up again and Nicholai wrapped his scarf around his neck as he stepped out into the cold night air and waited for Chen and the car. Where were they? Chen was usually pathologically prompt.

Across the boulevard the monk walked away, toward the south.

The last check, Nicholai thought with a twinge of sorrow. The last chance to stop this thing literally just walked away.

The car came up the street, its red flags snapping in the stiff breeze. It pulled up in front of the hotel, the back door opened, and Chen got out.

"Sorry to be late," he said. "Traffic."

He looked afraid.

Chen ushered Nicholai into the backseat and got in beside him.

Nicholai started to greet Liang, but saw that it was a different driver.

"Where is Liang?" Nicholai asked.

"Sick," Chen said. The smell of fear came off him. A sheen of greasy sweat shone on his cheeks.

Nicholai took two cigarettes from his pack and offered one to Chen. The escort took it, but his hands shook as Nicholai held the lighter up to the cigarette. He steadied Chen's wrist and said, "Perhaps it was catching."

"Maybe."

"You should go home and take care of yourself." Nicholai looked into his eyes. "It's all right."

"I'm so sorry," Chen answered, "that I was . . . late."

"Truly, it doesn't matter." He let go of Chen's wrist.

Nicholai sat back in his seat, smoked, looked out the window, and pretended not to notice when the car turned not for Xuanwu, but toward the Bell and Drum Towers.

# 65

Kang readied the stage.

He wanted it perfect, a flawless setting for the drama that he was about to enact, the play that he had already written.

This Nicholai Hel person would speak his intended lines. Maybe not at first, when his masculine pride would force him to resist; but eventually he would give in and pronounce the words. He would come in as a man but leave as a eunuch, enter the stage as a *sheng* but exit as a *dan*, shamed and pleading to die.

But the dignity of a private death was not on the page for this Hel. Kang would save what was left of him for another performance, his humiliation played before an audience of thousands at the Bridge of Heaven. Hel would have a placard on his back instead of an embroidered robe, he would be bound with heavy ropes, and he would take a final bow to the bark of rifles and the roar of the crowd.

Kang fingered the exquisitely thin, stiff wire — sharpened at one end, looped at the other — with which he intended to skewer Hel's masculinity.

"Drawing the Jinghu Bow Across the Strings" is what Kang had titled this new technique, and he could already imagine the notes that Hel would achieve as the wire was pushed and pulled back and forth through his testicles.

Kang had dressed for the occasion — a black jacket with black brocade over black silk pajamas and black slippers. He had slicked his hair back carefully, trimmed his eyebrows, and applied the most subtle, indistinguishable layer of rouge on his cheeks.

He looked forward to matching the rhythms of the mental torture along with the physical—show Hel the agony that was inevitable, then offer to rescind the sentence, and then apply it anyway. Draw the strings back and forth between despair and hope, terror and relief, anguish and cessation, building to a climax in which there was only pain.

As in any worthy opera, the music would be punctuated by passages of speech, as Hel recited his monologues. Yes, he was an American agent, yes he had been sent to pull the strings of the puppet, the traitor Liu, yes they conspired to deliver guns to antirevolutionary elements in Yunnan, yes, they hoped to murder Chairman Mao.

He heard car doors close, and then footsteps on the pebbled walkway.

The opera was about to begin.

# 66

THE LIGHTS IN THE HOUSE dimmed as the stage lamps came up.

Voroshenin, comfortable in his private box, leaned forward and looked down at the black square stage, traditionally placed to the north of the audience. He loved this old theater, with its red gilded columns framing the stage, its old wooden floor, the vendors milling around selling peanuts and steamy hot towels, the chatter, the laughter.

The chair beside him was empty.

Hel had not arrived.

Voroshenin knew that the foolish young man was attending an opera of his own, one in which he would unwillingly sing the lead role.

After a moment of anticipatory silence, the orchestra struck its first notes, and the audience hushed as Xun Huisheng stepped onto the stage. Dressed as a *huadan* — a saucy young woman — Xun wore a long scarlet Ming-era robe with flowers brocaded on the shoulders and wide "water" sleeves. He stood center stage and gave his *shangching*, the opening speech, identifying himself as the Red Maid.

Then, waving his hand with a grace born from decades of practice, he produced a scroll from the sleeve, paused, and began the famous first aria.

*This letter is the evidence of the affair.*
*Commanded by my lady, I am on my way to the West Chamber.*
*In the early morning silence reigns supreme.*
*Let me, the Red Maid, have a little cough to warn him.*

Voroshenin was delighted.

## 67

"Go Player is off the radar."

Haverford felt his blood go cold and his stomach flip. "What?"

"He didn't arrive at Point Zero."

"Didn't or hasn't?" Haverford asked.

The young agent shrugged. A few seconds later he asked, "Do you want to give the scramble code?"

A scramble code would do just that—send the extraction team in the Niujie Mosque scrambling for cover before they could be rounded up, send the Monk, the Hui agents, all of them, running for the border.

He considered the possibilities:

The mundane—Hel was simply delayed, tied up in traffic.

The treacherous—Hel had chickened out and was running on his own.

The catastrophic—Hel was in Kang Sheng's hands.

The last scenario would definitely trigger a scramble code.

"No," Haverford said. "Let's give it a while longer."

Where are you, Nicholai?

# 68

THREE POLICE AGENTS hauled Nicholai from the car, pushed him over the hood, and handcuffed him behind his back.

He didn't resist. This wasn't the moment.

They straightened him back up, and an agent held him by either elbow.

"Spy!" Chen yelled at him, his eyes begging forgiveness. Flicks of spit hit Nicholai in the face as Chen screamed, "Now you will feel the people's righteous fury! Now you will know the anger of the workers and peasants!

Chen turned to get back into the car, but the driver was out of the car, pulled a pistol, and held it at Chen's head. "Li Ar Chen, I arrest you for treason against the People's Republic."

The third policeman grabbed his arms, twisted them behind him, and cuffed him.

"No!" Chen yelled. "Not me! Him! Not me! I did everything you said!"

The driver holstered his pistol, slapped him hard across the face, then ordered, "Take him."

The policeman pushed Chen in front of Nicholai.

Without a word, they frog-marched him through a stone garden to what looked improbably like a cave. One of the cops knocked on the thick wooden door and a moment later Nicholai heard a muffled, "Come."

The door opened and the agents pushed Nicholai inside.

It was indeed a cave, or at least an effort to replicate one in concrete. Communists, Nicholai thought, they do love their concrete. The ceilings were curved and the walls painted with streaks to imitate geological striations.

This "cave" was beautifully furnished with rosewood tables and chairs, a lounging sofa, and the machinery of torture. There was a bench of sorts, obviously used for beatings and perhaps sodomy, a staggering variety of whips and flails hung neatly from assigned hooks, and two straight-backed chairs, the seats of which had been removed, bolted to the floor.

The cops shoved Nicholai down onto one of the chairs, removed the cuffs, and used heavy leather straps to tightly fasten his wrists to the arms of the chair. Nicholai watched as they took Chen, roughly stripped off his clothes, and then hung him by the handcuffs from a steel rail that ran across the ceiling. Then they tied his ankles down to bolts in the floor, so that he was spread-eagled.

His chin on his chest, Chen hung, quietly weeping.

An interior door opened and Kang Sheng made his entrance.

Nicholai had to admit that it was dramatic — the lighting perfect, the moment correct, and he held an ominous prop that glistened in the lamplight.

A wire, perhaps a foot long, needle-sharp on one end.

"Good evening, Mr. Hel, I believe it is?"

"Guibert."

"If you insist." Kang smiled.

Nicholai fought the terror that he felt rising in his throat and forced himself to keep his mind clear. Kang has already made the first mistake, he thought. He has shown his opening position on the board by revealing his knowledge of my real identity.

"Perhaps," Kang said, "when I have shown you what I have planned for you, you might decide to be more cooperative."

"There's always that chance," Nicholai answered.

"There is always that chance," Kang agreed pleasantly. Hel's bravado was delightful, so very *sheng*. And how thoughtful of him to play his role so beautifully—the fall of a falcon is so much more dramatic than the fall of a sparrow. He turned his attention to Chen, who would play the perfect *chou*, the clown. "Counterrevolutionary dog."

"No," Chen blubbered. "I'm a loyal—"

"Liar!" Kang screamed. "You were part of this conspiracy! You helped him every step of the way!"

"No."

"Yes!" Kang yelled. "You took him to the church, didn't you?"

"Yes, but—"

Nicholai said, "He had nothing to do with—"

"Be quiet," Kang snapped. "It will be your turn soon enough, I promise you that. Just now it is the fat pig's. How many yuan do you eat a day, *pang ju*? Is that why you like entertaining foreign guests, so that you can fatten yourself on the backs of the people?"

"No..."

"No, it is because you are a spy."

"No!"

"'No,'" Kang said. "I will give you one chance to confess."

This was the boring part of the play. The *shangching*, the preamble. Prisoners never confessed at this point, knowing that they would be signing their own death warrants. They knew the pain they were about to suffer, knew that they would eventually confess to the capital charge, but human nature is such that they must first struggle to survive.

Chen was silent.

"Very well," Kang said.

Nicholai saw Chen's eyes almost bulge out of their sockets as Kang approached him with the needle. Kang giggled. "I have never done this before, so it might take a little experimentation."

Chen jerked as Kang touched the point of the wire to one of his balls.

"The problem is the flexibility," Kang said.

He pulled the wire back a couple of inches and then pushed.

# 69

Xun Huisheng hit a marvelous note, rich in tone, pitch-perfect, rising in an oblique *ze*.

*Look, my poor mistress frowns every day*
*And the young man is sick and skinny.*
*Despite the punishments imposed by the Old Lady*
*I, the Little Red Maid, will help their dreams come true.*

Voroshenin clapped as the audience below shouted, *"Hao! Hao!"* in approbation of the superb performance.

## 70

COLONEL YU SAT in his office and worried.

The so-called Michel Guibert had not arrived at the opera, nor was he in his room, and none of the watchers knew his location. All they could say was that they had seen him get into the car outside the Beijing Hotel.

Was he in Voroshenin's hands?

Or in Kang's?

Either way it was a desperate situation. Who knew what Kang would make him say? If Mao was ready to make a move against General Liu, this could be the prime moment. "Guibert" would confess to the murder plot against the Russian commissioner, and Kang would make him implicate General Liu.

Escape routes had been set up through the south.

Was it time for the general to flee?

Activate "Southern Wind"?

Perhaps, Yu cursed himself, it had been too bold a move—premature perhaps—for them to have allowed the American plot to move forward. Perhaps they should have tossed Guibert out of the country five seconds after he stepped in. But it had been so tempting to set Stalin and Mao back at each other's throats. The Russians would move Gao Gang into place prematurely. Mao would respond but lack the strength to succeed. General Liu would move in to fill the power vacuum.

So tempting, so rich with possibilities...

And the idea to kill Voroshenin at the opera was lovely in its irony. Very un-Western, but then again, this "Guibert"...

Should I go and tell the general? Yu asked himself. Actualize the escape plan and demand that he leave immediately? Years of long work would be wasted, hopes squandered, dreams of a truly Communist country indefinitely delayed, perhaps destroyed... But can you take the chance of the general being arrested, tortured, shot?

Where is this man "Guibert"?

# 71

NICHOLAI STRUGGLED not to vomit.

Chen screamed and screamed, his body tossed against the chains as Kang sawed the wire back and forth through his testicles, all the time offering advice on how to better vocalize.

"*Hum qi,*" he coached, using operatic terms. "'Exchange breath'—slow in, slow out. Now 'steal breath'—a sharp intake, please, sudden, fierce. That's it...very good..."

Nicholai made himself focus on his own breathing. In deep through the nose, force it down into the lower abdomen, hold and store, release...deep through the nose, force it down into the lower abdomen, hold and store, release...hold and store, hold and store, deeply in the abdomen until you can feel it in all your muscles...

He tuned out the sound of Chen's agony.

"I confess, I confess I confess!" Chen screamed.

But Kang appeared not to hear him and continued "Drawing the Jinghu Bow Across the Strings" until Chen shrieked at a pitch that was scarcely human. He would not stop until Chen demonstrated all the mouth shapes of a proper opera singer: *kaikou*—open mouth; *qichi*—level-teeth; *houkou*—closed mouth; and, finally, *cuochun*—scooped lips.

Kang pulled the wire out and Chen's neck dropped. His body went limp. Sweat dripped off his skin onto the concrete floor.

"I am a spy," Chen said between sobs. "I was part of the conspiracy. I helped him every step of the way."

"To send arms to rebels in Yunnan?"

"Yes."

"To murder Chairman Mao?"

"Yes."

"Who gave you your orders?" Kang asked. "Was it General Liu?"

"Yes, it was General Liu."

Nicholai knew that Chen would say anything now, agree to anything, to prevent Kang from resuming the torture.

And Kang had revealed more of his strategy.

*Remain calm* — Kishikawa-sama came to him — *and keep your thoughts as clear as a pool. Breathe and store your* ki.

Liu is the target, he realized, and you are only a string of stones on the way to that target.

Very well.

Kang turned to him and said, "Now, Mr. Hel, it is your turn."

He held up the wire.

# 72

"It really isn't necessary," Nicholai said. "I'll tell you anything you want to know."

Kang smiled. "Admit that you are not 'Michel Guibert.'"

"I admit that I am not Michel Guibert."

"Admit that you are Nicholai Hel."

"I admit to being Nicholai Hel."

"Why did you come to Beijing, Nicholai Hel?"

Nicholai leaned forward in his chair as far as the straps would allow. He looked straight into Kang's eyes and answered, "I came to Beijing to kill Yuri Voroshenin."

Kang turned pale.

# 73

"GET THAT PIG out of here," Kang ordered. "Wait outside."

Position on the board changed, Nicholai thought. Not wanting underlings to hear anything that sensitive, Kang has removed those stones for me. *Breathe and store your* ki. *Breathe and store your* ki.

The agents unhooked Chen and dragged him out of the room. When the door closed, Kang asked, "You admit that you came to assassinate Voroshenin?"

"Admit it?" Nicholai said. "I proclaim it."

"Why?"

Nicholai jutted his chin toward the wire in Kang's hand. "I wish to spare myself needless pain. And I wish to make a deal."

"You are in no position to make any deal."

"How do you know?"

Kang waved the wire in front of his face. "I will make you tell me without any 'deal.'"

"Probably," Nicholai agreed. "But possibly not. You know that I was raised as a Japanese. What is your experience with Japanese under torture? And what if you make a mistake? What if you miscalculate and I die under your ministrations? Then you will never know."

This is delightful, Kang thought. Exciting. A different script, a departure from the usual. He asked, "Know what?"

"How you can get power over Voroshenin."

He saw it in Kang's eye. It was fleeting, but it was there. Power over Voroshenin was a very desirable prize. Kang was desperate to get out from under the Soviet thumb.

Stone moved.

*Breathe and store your* ki. *Breathe and store your* ki.

Kang laughed, but the scoff was unconvincing. "And you can tell me how to get Voroshenin under my power."

Nicholai nodded.

"How?"

"Put down that wire."

Kang set the wire down. "How?"

"Blackmail."

"Specifically?"

Nicholai shook his head. "If I tell you, how do I know I walk out of here alive? How do I know I leave China alive?"

"You'll have my word."

"You think me a fool."

Kang nodded toward the wire. "If you make me perform 'Drawing the Jinghu Bow Across the Strings,' I promise that you will tell me. As you said, spare yourself that agony. As for your life…"

*Breathe and store your* ki. *Breathe and store your* ki. Do not waste effort negotiating over lies. Lull him now, lure him into overconfidence, draw his stones into the trap.

"Yuri Voroshenin," Nicholai said, "extorted my mother into handing over a considerable fortune, which he placed into various bank accounts and investments. It was quite some time ago, but interest accrues, and Yuri is now an extremely wealthy man. I am sure that he wouldn't want Beria to hear of it, much less Uncle Joe. Do you have a tape recorder?"

"Of course."

"Get it," Nicholai said. "I will relate the whole story, and Voroshenin will be yours."

*Breathe and store your* ki. *Breathe and store your* ki.

Kang got the tape recorder and Nicholai passed on to him the whole story that his mother had told him about what happened in Petrograd thirty years ago.

# 74

"How long has it been?" Haverford asked.

"Thirty-one minutes."

The "traffic" scenario was out. Either Hel had taken off or he was under adverse control.

Give the scramble order, he thought.

*Sauve qui peut* — every man for himself.

But if you pull the extraction team and Hel is alive . . .

# 75

Colonel Yu got up from his chair, left his office, and walked down the hallway.

The general was at his desk. He heard the door open, looked up from his work and quietly said, "Yes?"

"I'm afraid it's time, sir."

"For?"

"Southern Wind."

He explained the situation. When he had finished, General Liu said, "Make some tea, please."

"General, I really think that—"

"Make tea," Liu repeated softly. "And steep it three times."

## 76

Nicholai finished his speech.

Kang said, "So that is why you wish to kill Voroshenin."

"Wouldn't you?"

"No," Kang said. "I hated my mother."

"I'm sorry."

Kang shrugged.

"But certainly the Americans didn't sponsor you to come on a matter of personal revenge," Kang said. "Why did they send you?"

"To kill Voroshenin," Nicholai answered.

"Why?"

Nicholai told him all of it—the whole plot to drive a wedge between Beijing and Moscow.

Because it didn't matter now.

All he needed now was for Kang to make the anticipated move. There was a chance that he wouldn't, but Nicholai discounted it. A man's nature is his nature—Kang had revealed his—and he would act according to that nature.

Kang did. "You have told me everything now?"

"Everything."

"Very well," Kang said. He picked up the wire. "It is time to resume the opera."

*Breathe and store your* ki. *Breathe and store your* ki. Nicholai allowed fear to seep into his throat as he said, "But why? I told you everything!"

"Exactly."

"But there is no point now!"

"The point is," Kang said as he squatted in front of Nicholai, "that I will enjoy it."

Stones in place.

Nicholai forced all the energy into his legs, felt it course through the veins and muscles as Kang reached up to unbuckle his belt and pull down his trousers.

*Store and* —

*—release.*

The energy exploded from Nicholai's feet and through his legs as he surged upward with all the *ki* he had stored in his body. The chair shattered from its bolts. Kang sprawled back, then got to his feet. Nicholai spun twice to develop momentum and then whirled into him and struck him with the legs of the chair, sending Kang spinning toward the wall. Then Nicholai threw himself into Kang, smashed him into the wall, and heard the air come out of Kang's lungs.

Nicholai backed off and did it again, then again, then pinned the shocked and rattled Kang against the wall and pressed all his weight against the smaller man, trapping his hands.

Kang still clutched the wire, and Nicholai counted on his next move.

Desperate, Kang pressed the point of the wire to Nicholai's throat.

Nicholai let it come, felt it bite into his throat, felt the blood start to come and saw Kang smile in triumph.

Then he craned his neck down, grabbed the wire with his teeth, jerked his neck back, and yanked the wire from Kang's grasp.

Kang's eyes went wide with surprise.

Nicholai stretched his neck as far back as it would go, then jammed it forward.

The wire went into Kang's eye. He screamed in agony, wriggled against Nicholai, trying to escape.

Nicholai held the wire just there for a moment…then said, "For Chen."

He pushed and sent the point through Kang's eye and into his brain.

Kang stiffened.

Groaned.

And died.

Nicholai let his body crumple to the floor. Then he lowered himself down and started on the buckles of the leather strap with his teeth. It took five long minutes to free one wrist, then he unbuckled his other hand. He took a few deep breaths, gathered his energy, got up, and then took the tape out of the machine and put it in his pocket.

Looking at his watch, he saw that there was still time to go kill Voroshenin.

# 77

THE THREE AGENTS were tormenting Chen in the outer room.

One looked up in surprise as Nicholai came through the door, the more so as Nicholai killed him with a kick to the head. The second went to pull his gun but was dispatched with an elbow to the throat. The third tried to escape, but Nicholai grabbed him by the back of the neck and slammed his head into the door, crushing his skull against the heavy wood.

All of this took no more than five seconds, and then Nicholai knelt over Chen, who lay quivering on the cold concrete floor.

"Did you kill him?" Chen asked, his voice rattling.

"Painfully," Nicholai answered. He placed his index and middle fingers on Chen's neck, along the carotid artery. "Xiao Chen, think of bowls overflowing with pure white pearl rice, and dishes of pork in hot brown sauce. Do you have those things in mind?"

Chen nodded.

"Good," Nicholai said. He pressed until he felt Chen's life slip away.

Nicholai found the corpse of the largest agent, took off his coat, slipped it on, and then put on the dead man's hat. He walked out of the "cave," through the beautiful garden, and outside, where he saw the glow of a cigarette inside the car. The engine was running, the heater on.

Nicholai walked over and rapped on the window. "Open up."

The driver rolled down the window. "What do you want? It's fucking cold, brother."

"Let me in," Nicholai said in Chinese. "The bastard wants us to go for some hot noodles and pork."

The locks unclicked and Nicholai slid in the back.

He pressed the agent's pistol into the guard's neck. "Zhengyici Opera House. And I know the route, brother, so don't fuck me around."

"Kang will kill me."

"Actually, he won't."

The driver put the car in gear and pulled out.


The drive took twenty minutes.

Nicholai used the time to try to restore his energy. He was exhausted — the exertion it had required to break the chair from the floor had drained his *ki*, and now he was uncertain if he had sufficient energy left to perform the perfect strike required to silently kill Voroshenin, much less make his escape.

He also realized that emotion had sapped his energy. The terror of the torture chamber, the effort to maintain his self-control, the horror of Chen's agony, the genuine sorrow over the man's death — all had taken a toll. Over the killing of Kang and his three minions, Nicholai felt not a jot of remorse.

If the Buddhists were right, Kang would spend long ages in *bardo*, the limbo-like stage between death and rebirth, before returning to the earth for a lifetime of suffering.

Now Nicholai concentrated on his breathing, on attempting to recuperate his strength. He felt it slowly coming back, but whether it would be enough, and in time, was a real question.

The car arrived at the opera house.

"Go another block," Nicholai said.

The driver went up a block and pulled over. Nicholai set the pistol down and then hit the driver with a *shuto* strike to the base of the brain. As the driver fell dead over the steering wheel, Nicholai got out of the backseat and walked to the Zhengyici.

A guard at the front door stopped him.

"My name is Guibert," Nicholai said. "I am guest of Comrade Voroshenin."

"The opera is almost over," the guard complained.

"I was…otherwised engaged," Nicholai answered, sliding his index finger back and forth through a "V" he made with his other hand.

The guard chuckled. "Go in."

Nicholai stepped into the lobby, which was almost empty. Recalling the plan of the theater, he quickly found the stairs, bounded up, and walked down the corridor. Two of Voroshenin's guards leaned against the wall outside his box. They straightened as they saw Nicholai, and one reached his hand inside his jacket.

Now, Nicholai thought, either Voroshenin has played his cards very close to his chest, or I am dead. He strode toward the guards and put his hands up in a "What are you going to do?" shrug.

The guard without the pistol was sullen. He patted Nicholai down from his armpits to his ankles, found nothing, and opened the door to the box.

The encroaching light caused Yuri Voroshenin to turn around.

Even in the dim light, Nicholai could see the surprise in his eyes. That's right, he thought, I'm supposed to be dead. He edged past the guard standing inside the door and sat down next to Voroshenin.

"I'm so sorry I'm late," he whispered.

In Russian.

On the stage below, the *sheng*, lit by a vermilion lamp, his face vertically divided into a white-and-black design, delivered a speech bemoaning the loss of a battle. It was beautifully performed, every syllable perfectly in place.

Before Voroshenin could respond, Nicholai added, "I was unavoidably detained."

# 78

Xue Xin saw Nicholai go into the theater.

He turned to a small boy huddled against the flaming trash can and said, "Run. Tell your *sifu* that the performance has not ended."

The boy ran.

Xue Xin waited until he saw Nicholai get into the theater, and then he ambled off, slowly working his way to the alley in back.

## 79

"Go Player is on the screen."

"Jesus Christ." Haverford felt limp. Sweaty and exhausted. Hel was a roller-coaster ride. "Where?"

"At Point Zero."

"No shit."

"No shit, sir."

# 80

Colonel Yu ran down the hall and burst into Liu's office.

"He's at Zhengyici."

Liu considered the development. It was one thing for the American agent to have made it to the opera house, quite another for him to complete his mission there. But if he did kill Voroshenin . . . then there was something to consider.

"Good tea," said Liu.

# 81

DRUMS BOOMED and gongs clanged as the handsome *sheng* came back onstage.

The *dan*, beautifully garbed in a silk brocade robe, crossed the stage in tiny steps as delicate and light as falling cherry blossoms. She waved her fan, saw her lover, then looked up to the "moon"—a solitary white spotlight—and began her aria.

It was beautiful.

Her voice was a revelation, a seamless blend of form and emotion. As she built to her high note, Nicholai saw Voroshenin's right hand slowly ease into his jacket at his waist.

Knife or gun? Nicholai asked himself.

Gun, he decided.

And what is he waiting for?

The same thing that you are—darkness and more noise. If he waits for the climactic moment, he can shoot you and have your body hustled out of here before anyone can notice, avoiding a public incident. Very smart of him, very disciplined.

The music began its rise.

Nicholai leaned over toward Voroshenin.

"I relate greetings" he said, whispering into Voroshenin's ear, "from the Countess Alexandra Ivanovna. My mother."

He felt Voroshenin's body tense, his hand inch toward the pistol.

"Nicholai Hel."

"I'm going to kill you in a moment," Nicholai said, "and there's not a single thing you can do about it."

Xun Huisheng warbled:

*I have helped the lovers come together*
*Although I have suffered hard words and beatings*
*The moon is rising in its silvery glow*
*I am the happy Red Maid.*

The drums rattled.

The gongs clanged.

The theater went dark.

Voroshenin went for the pistol.

Nicholai trapped his hand, breathed deeply, and released all the *ki* he had left into a single leopard paw strike to Voroshenin's chest.

He heard the Russian grunt.

Then Voroshenin slumped back in his seat, his mouth a frozen oval.

The guard started forward.

"Too much vodka," Nicholai said as he got up. Down in the orchestra, the audience was applauding wildly.

Nicholai walked out the door of the box.

"Your boss is sick," Nicholai said.

They rushed inside.

Nicholai let his mind take over and walk him through the escape. Down the stairs and to the right. Down the hallway toward the interior stage door, where an old man sat on a stool.

"You can't go in here," the old man said.

"I'm sorry, *liao*," Nicholai said as he swung his right hand in a lazy arc and struck him as gently as possible on the side of the neck. He caught the old man and lowered him gently to the floor, opened the door, found the next door to his left, and stepped out into the alley.

It was only as he walked out the back end of the alley that he felt something warm running down his left leg, then a jolt of burning pain, and realized that Voroshenin's gun had gone off, and that he was shot.

Then he saw the monk standing at the end of the alley.

"*Satori*," Nicholai said.

"Yes?"

"Yes."

The monk limped off in one direction, Nicholai in the other.

He saw it clearly now.

What would happen in the Temple of the Green Truth.

*Satori.*

The way out of the trap.

# 82

"SIGNAL."

"What?" Haverford asked. He stubbed out his thirteenth cigarette of the night and rolled his chair over to the young agent who sat by the cable.

"Go Player is on the move toward Point One."

"I'll be goddamned," Haverford said, half in surprise, half in admiration.

Nicholai fucking Hel.

# 83

The blood froze on his skin, forming a bandage of sorts.

It didn't hold up, as Nicholai walked quickly through the *hutongs* of Xuanwu, his heart beating strongly, pumping blood into his leg and breaking the intermittent clotting. But the cold slowed the blood loss and eased the pain.

Nicholai wasn't thinking about his leg.

He placed a map of the district in his head, remembered Haverford's instructions, and moved swiftly past the few people out on the streets in the winter night. Some watched him, most had their faces wrapped against the cold and were indifferent to this tall *kweilo* as he strode past them. None of them noticed when he dropped the crumpled tape recording into a trash-can fire.

Police sirens started to wail, headed toward Zhengyici Opera House.

Voroshenin's body had been discovered.

Nicholai put the Go board in front of his eyes and scanned the new situation. The Kang stones had been removed, the Voroshenin stones captured. But Voroshenin's corpse had been revealed, and soon — if it hadn't already happened — the Chinese National Police would discover that their master Kang was also dead.

Murdered, if you care to call it that.

They would be coming for him, and the move now was to get to other black stones on the board.

He had an appointment in the Temple of the Green Truth.

# 84

Wu Zhong waited in the sanctuary.

A team member, a Muslim brother, had relayed the signal that "Go Player" was on the way.

*Inshallah.*

He got to his feet, stretched, and prepared his muscles for the task at hand.

The American had told him what to do.

# 85

NICHOLAI TURNED onto Niujie Street and saw the mosque, its three sections roofed in green tile, a small minaret with a crescent rising above the center section. A white-capped Hui Chinese waited by the iron gate.

"Go Player?"

"The opera is over."

The Hui took Nicholai by the elbow, looked around, and quickly ushered him through the small courtyard and into the door of the section farthest to the right.

It was dark inside, lit only by oil lanterns, and Nicholai blinked to adjust his eyes as the door shut behind him. His escort led him through the foyer to a narrow set of stairs, then showed him into the basement and closed the door.

A tall, wide-shouldered man stood in front of him.

"Welcome, Go Player," the man said in heavily accented Mandarin.

"Thank you," Nicholai answered.

The man glanced down at Nicholai's leg and then observed, "You are hurt."

"Shot, I'm afraid."

"The target?"

"Terminated."

"You are certain?"

"Terminated," Nicholai repeated. His leg started to throb and, worse, felt weak underneath him. This was very bad, because the Chinese man in front of him, struggling with his English, carefully pronounced, "Haverford sends his regrets."

# 86

Wᴜ Zʜᴏɴɢ ᴍᴏᴠᴇᴅ with unbelievable speed for such a large man, and Nicholai just managed to slip the elbow strike that would have crushed his throat. The blow missed by a thread as Nicholai turned sideways and raised his forearm to block. He pivoted to throw a punch of his own at the man's exposed temple, but his leg gave from under him and he toppled to the floor.

Wu Zhong turned, saw Nicholai on the floor, and raised his leg into an axe kick to cave in his opponent's chest.

The leg came down, Nicholai rolled away, and Wu Zhong's heel left a hole in the wooden plank. Wu followed with a low front kick to the head. Nicholai got his arm up in time and took the force of the blow on the shoulder, but his arm went numb. He rolled onto his back just as Wu Zhong reached down to grab him, slipped his kicking leg between Wu's arms, and struck him full on the chin with the ball of his foot.

Wu Zhong flew backward. The kick should have killed him, or at least knocked him out, but Nicholai hadn't fully recovered from the ordeal in Kang's cave, was weak with loss of blood and the blow he had just sustained, so the lethal power wasn't there.

But it gave him time to jump back to his feet and set himself as Wu Zhong came in, throwing powerful left and right punches to drive Nicholai back toward the wall. Blood flowed freely from his wounded leg now, he felt lightheaded, and knew that if he allowed the larger, stronger man to pin him against the wall, he was finished.

He ducked under the next two punches and drove into Wu's midsection, his leg sending a fierce jolt of pain through him as he pushed off the floor and drove Wu to the floor. Wu tried to wrap his forearm around Nicholai's neck to snap it, but Nicholai jerked his head out of the trap as they fell to the floor. Wu did wrap his own leg around Nicholai's right leg, trapping it, so Nicholai had no choice but to use his wounded leg to pry Wu's legs apart. Then, despite the pain, he drove three successive knee strikes straight into Wu's exposed groin.

The man groaned but didn't yell, and he didn't change his position. Instead, he brought his big arms up behind Nicholai and pounded his fists into the back of his neck and head.

Nicholai felt the fog gather around him.

First would come fog, then darkness.

He raised himself up to avoid the fists, and that's what Wu needed. He bucked his hips and threw Nicholai off. Sprawling backward, Nicholai struggled to get up, but his wounded leg wouldn't let him.

Wu struggled to his feet as Nicholai pulled himself backward along the floor, now seeking the wall so that he could ball himself up against it and try to weather the storm he knew was about to break on him.

The first kick came to the kidney, the next to the small of the back, the next to his wounded leg.

Nicholai heard himself howl in pain.

He pulled himself back, but his arms were too weak now and his feet could find no purchase on the floor.

He wanted to die standing.

He tried to push himself up, but his arms collapsed and he

fell flat. All he could do was roll over so that he could at least die facing his opponent. In the clarity before death, he saw the Go board and knew the answer to why Haverford would leave the black stone in place.

He wouldn't.

He didn't.

Wu Zhong chambered his leg for the lethal axe kick.

"*Salaama*," he said.

Peace.

The bullet struck Wu Zhong square in his broad forehead and he fell backward.

Nicholai turned his head in the direction of the shot.

Colonel Yu lowered his pistol.

The monk, standing behind Yu, squatted beside Nicholai and said, "*Satori*."

"You're late," Nicholai said.

Then he blacked out.

*Part Three*

# WULIANG MOUNTAINS, YUNNAN PROVINCE, CHINA

# 87

THE SOUND OF A FLUTE woke him.

At first Nicholai thought it was a bird singing, but then he heard the deliberate repetition of a particular phrase and realized that he was listening to someone play a *lusheng*.

But there was birdsong in the background.

Birdsong and clean fresh air, and then he knew that he was no longer in the city, or in the tight, fume-choked back of an army truck, but somewhere in the countryside, perhaps even in the wilderness.

He turned toward the slight breeze he felt on the back of his head, but movement was still painful and difficult, and it took him over a minute to roll over and feel the cool air dry the sweat on his face.

His leg throbbed in protest of the motion.

A voice snapped an order in a language that Nicholai did not understand, and then he heard footsteps quickly shuffling across a wooden floor.

He didn't know where he was, but then it seemed like a long time since he *had* known. The last thing that he clearly remembered was his fight with the formidable *bajiquan* practitioner and his rescue by Yu and the monk. He remembered waking up briefly in the back of what must have been a truck — because its rattling forced him to suppress a scream of pain before he blacked out again. He recalled being given a shot of what was probably morphine, and the deep, painless slumber that followed, and he had a vague memory of being lifted out of the truck and placed in another, soft worried voices, and a nightmare in which he heard concerned whispers and hushed discussions about amputating his leg.

Now he reached down in alarm and felt with intense relief that both limbs were still attached to his body. But his left leg was hot and swollen, and now he recalled the fevers and the shaking, his head being lifted to receive sips of bitter tea, and the horrible pain as the truck bounced over rough roads as it first climbed and then descended hills.

Indeed, Nicholai saw that he was in the hills now. Outside the window he saw a lush forest of firs, pines, camphor, and *nanmu* trees in a series of rolling ridges below him. The landscape seemed impossibly green, after the white and silver of Beijing, and the blackness of the journey to this place, wherever it was.

Maybe I'm dead, Nicholai speculated without alarm. Perhaps this is *chin t'u*, the paradise promised by the *amida* Buddha. But the "pure land" was not for killers, and he had killed Yuri Voroshenin with a single leopard strike to the heart.

At first he thought this might have been part of his morphine-induced dreams — crazy, twisted images of Solange, Haverford, *shengs* and *dans* and sharp wires and men dressed all in black. But then he realized that the memory of killing Voroshenin was just that — a recollection of an actual event, and he felt some satisfaction at completing his mission, even though the Americans had betrayed him.

Nicholai blamed himself as much as them.

I should have seen it earlier, he thought as he lay in what he now realized was a hammock. I should have known that Haverford never intended to honor his part of the deal.

Even this small mental exertion exhausted him and he sank

deeper into the hammock, feeling only now that his clothes were soaked with sweat. His leg hurt and his body still ached from the beating he had absorbed in the Temple of the Green Truth.

Then Nicholai heard footsteps and felt the palm of a hand on his forehead. The hand lingered for just a moment and then he heard a voice he recognized as the monk's say, "The fever has broken. Good. For a while we thought we were still going to lose you."

"So I am alive."

"But shouldn't be," the monk answered. "By all rights, you should be in *bardo*, awaiting rebirth."

"Perhaps I am."

"Perhaps we all are," the monk said. "Who knows? My name is Xue Xin."

"Michel Guibert."

"If you wish," Xue Xin said, a trace of amusement in his voice. "We need to turn you back over now, and change your clothes. It will hurt."

Nicholai felt two pairs of firm hands on his shoulder and then they turned him onto his back. A jolt of pain shot up from his leg to the top of his head and he swallowed a grunt of pain.

Xue Xin looked down on him, and Nicholai recognized the man from the bridge to the Jade Isle, the alley outside the opera, and the Temple of the Green Truth. His close-cropped hair was jet black, but what seized Nicholai's attention were his eyes — they looked through you, albeit not unkindly.

If Xue Xin was eaten up with sympathy, it didn't show on his face. "You will have tea."

"No, thank you."

"You will have tea," Xue Xin said.

The "tea," Nicholai decided, tasted like wet grass, but Xue Xin insisted that the brew of herbs was healing his infection.

"If you want to live, drink," Xue Xin shrugged. "If you don't, don't."

Nicholai drank.

Colonel Yu was relieved to see the American agent looking better.

At first they thought he was going to die. He'd lost a great deal of blood from the bullet wound and had taken a severe beating as well. The internal damage from the *bajiquan* blows alone would have killed a man with less *ki*, and the leg quickly became infected.

Nor did they have the leisure to give him adequate medical care. They'd had to get the American out of Beijing, and quickly. Yu's own PLA staff carried him to a waiting army truck that quickly drove out to the Ring Road, where they transferred the unconscious man to a military convoy headed south. An army medic dug the bullet out of his leg in the moving truck. Then they managed to hook up a blood transfusion and started to administer morphine for the pain.

It might have been easier to let him die, Yu thought—dispose of the body and simply shrug at the mystery that swept across official Beijing like the north wind.

The government was rattled, to say the least.

The Russian commissioner Voroshenin was dead—officially from a heart attack suffered while watching the opera, but no one in the intelligence or military communities believed that, not along with the "coincidental" murder of Kang Sheng, found with a wire thrust through his eyeball and into his brain.

The American plot had worked perfectly.

Moscow and Beijing were busy blaming each other, Mao dug a hole and pulled it closed over himself—especially with his dog

Kang no longer there to protect him. General Liu remained the calm and stable figure, ready to step in to end the chaos.

The only problem, Yu thought now as he looked at Nicholai, was the "disappearance" of a French citizen, Michel Guibert.

He had been seen going to the opera. Voroshenin's guards, quickly summoned home to Moscow, had reportedly claimed that Guibert was sitting beside Voroshenin in his private box at the time of his death but got up suddenly and left.

Then disappeared.

Was he dead?

Was he involved in Voroshenin's death?

In Kang's?

Beijing and Moscow buzzed with rumors. Some had it that Guibert had killed Voroshenin, others that it was his assistant Leotov, who had also disappeared shortly after his boss's death.

The Russians claimed that Guibert was a Chinese agent, the Chinese countered that he was Russian. Each accused the other of hiding him at the same time that each accused the other of killing him to stop him from talking. To quote the Chairman himself, "All is chaos under the heavens and the situation is excellent."

"Guibert" opened his eyes.

"Where are we?" Nicholai asked.

"You don't need to know," Yu answered.

The air, while cool, was still warm for winter, and the *nanmu* tree Nicholai could see through the window didn't grow up north. The brief dialogue he had overheard as the attendants came in and out was unintelligible to him, not Han Chinese at all, so he guessed that it was some southern tribal dialect.

"Sichuan or Yunnan," he said.

"Yunnan," admitted Yu. "In the Wuliang hills."

"Why?"

"Beijing was unhealthy for you."

Nicholai remembered his manners. "Thank you for saving my life."

"Gratitude is misplaced," Yu answered. "I was doing my duty, Mr. Hel."

# 88

"How long have you known my real identity?" he asked Yu.

"Since before you entered Beijing," Yu answered. He recited Nicholai's history to him — his birth in Shanghai, his removal to Japan, his killing of Kishikawa, his torture and imprisonment by the Americans.

The Chinese seemed to know it all. Nicholai could only hope that they did not realize the depth of his connection to the late Yuri Voroshenin.

"Am I a prisoner?" Nicholai asked.

"I would prefer to call you a guest."

"Can the guest get up and leave?"

"The question is academic in any case," Yu answered. "The reality is that you cannot get up, much less walk. And, even if you could, you have no place to go. They are hunting for you everywhere, Mr. Hel. This might be the only place in the world where you are safe."

A sadly accurate summation of the reality, Nicholai thought, since the moment I killed Kishikawa-sama. The locations and circumstances change, but the fact does not.

I am a prisoner.

He heard Kishikawa's voice. *If you have no options, then it is honorable to accept your imprisonment, although you might consider seppuku. But you have options.*

*What are they?*

*Nikko, you must find them yourself. Examine the* go-kang. *When you are trapped and can find no escape route, you must create one.*

*Again, please, how?*

*It is your* kang, *Nikko. No one else can play it for you.*

"You wanted Voroshenin dead," Nicholai said, probing.

"Obviously."

"To create a rift with the Soviets."

Yu nodded.

"And you rescued me from the American ambush because..."

"How often would we get a chance to obtain an American agent so motivated to cooperate?" Yu asked. "I'm sure you can tell us names, places, methods of operations. After all, you agreed to be rescued."

Hel had understood the monk's warning and signaled in turn that he understood, the act of a drowning man reaching out for the rope. Surely he knew it would come with a price.

Nicholai said, "I will tell you nothing."

"The Americans betrayed you," Yu answered. "Why would you hesitate to betray them in turn?"

"Their dishonor is their own," Nicholai responded. "Mine would be mine."

"How Japanese."

"I accept the compliment," Nicholai said. He tried to sit up, but the effort was painful and enervating. "I will not become an informer, but I will force the Americans to honor the arrangement they made with me."

"And how will you do that?" Yu asked, amused at this wounded man who could barely support his own weight.

Yet there was something in Hel's eyes that made Yu believe him.

# 89

"Where is he?" Singleton demanded.

"I don't know," admitted Haverford.

"Is he dead?"

"I don't know."

"Alive?"

"Again…"

Diamond didn't bother to conceal his smirk. Singleton frowned at him and then turned his attention back to Haverford. "You don't know much."

"I'm trying to find out."

"Try harder."

Haverford thought briefly of defending himself. Voroshenin was dead, apparently at Hel's hands, and the Chinese and Russians were snapping at each other's throats. And while Hel had possibly escaped, he hadn't been found—not by Moscow or Beijing anyway—because there had been no blowback at all. Apparently no one had connected Voroshenin's assassination to the Company.

"I want him found," Singleton said. "Do you understand?"

"*I* do," Diamond said, stressing the first-person pronoun and sounding like a sycophantic schoolboy.

"What's that supposed to mean?" Haverford asked.

"Hel's gone over to the other side, and you know it," Diamond said. "And I'm not so sure you're not happy about it."

"That's a goddamn lie."

"You calling me a liar?" Diamond jumped up from his chair.

Haverford stood up. "A liar, a torturer—"

They started for each other.

"This is not your sixth-grade schoolyard. Sit down, both of you." Singleton waited until both men took their chairs.

My straight line and my circle, Singleton thought. We shall see which one wins. It is a basic law of Go and of life—the side that wins is the side that deserves to win.

Haverford thought of resigning on the spot. He could probably find a job in academia, or in one of the new "think tanks"—there's a concept—now sprouting like mushrooms in the damp intellectual soil of the greater Washington metropolitan area. The place had, after all, once been a swamp.

But there was unfinished business, so he clamped his jaw tight and listened.

"Assume Hel is out there," Singleton said. "Lure him in."

"How?"

"You're clever young men," Singleton answered. "You'll think of something."

The meeting was concluded.

# 90

THINK LIKE NICHOLAI HEL, Haverford told himself as he left the building for his hotel in Dupont Circle. No easy task, he admitted, as it was probably true that no one else in the world thought like Nicholai Hel.

Well, try anyway.

He ran his thoughts through Nicholai's options.

Would Hel...

*Could* Hel...

Yes, he decided.

Both.

## 91

"I'M GOING TO DELIVER the weapons," Nicholai said.

It was a bold, even risky move. A breakout maneuver on the *go-kang* that had small chance of success and could only place him in great danger. Still, when one is surrounded there are few choices other than to surrender, die, or break out.

"Please don't be ridiculous," Yu answered. "Your cover as an arms merchant was just that, a cover. Not a reality."

"I saw the rocket launchers," Nicholai said. "They looked quite real."

"Props," Yu answered, "for your little opera. The play is over, Mr. Hel."

"And yet here you are in Yunnan," Nicholai answered, "for weeks now, near the Vietnamese border. Perhaps that is mere coincidence, or perhaps you are overly solicitous of my recuperation, but more likely it's because you intend to take the rocket launchers across the border into Vietnam."

"Even if that were true," Yu said, "it hardly concerns you."

"Let me tell you why it does," Nicholai said. "I have demonstrated skills that might be very useful. I'm fluent in French, have an established cover as an arms merchant, and I'm a *kweilo*, which would give me certain advantages in the French colonies. So much for my utility, here is my offer: I will deliver the weapons to the Viet Minh and retain the payment as my recompense for services rendered. Once the weapons have been safely delivered, you will provide me with a new identity and documentation. Then we are quit of each other."

It seemed the perfect solution, Nicholai thought. The Americans, through the gift of the rocket launchers, would unintentionally honor their deal with him, and it would have the added effect of harming their interests.

"You think a lot of your value, Mr. Hel."

"It is simply an objective evaluation."

Yu stared at him. "If you reemerge anywhere in Indochina, the Americans will find you."

"Just so."

Yu agreed to consider his offer.

The Americans will find me, Nicholai thought when Yu left the room. No, we will find each other, and I will hold Haverford accountable for his treachery.

And then I will find Solange.

## 92

DIAMOND PORED over the Hel file.

God*damn*it, he thought. How could Hel have escaped the trap in the Beijing temple and that Chinese kung-fu son of a bitch who was supposed to have been so good? Yeah, so goddamn good that he let Hel put a bullet in his head and kill the rest of his men as well.

Two swings at Hel, he thought, two misses. First he dispatches the two would-be killers in Tokyo, then the massacre in Beijing.

Three strikes and you're out, Diamond told himself.

The next try has to connect.

But you have to *find* Hel before you can kill him.

"Lure him," Singleton had said.

Easy for the old fart to say, a little harder to do. Lure him with what? What bait can you set that would bring Hel in?

Diamond went back to studying the file that Singleton had forced Haverford to turn over. Start at the beginning, he told himself.

Start in Tokyo.

Find the bait that will bring that arrogant half-Jap bastard waltzing in.

# 93

Nicholai's room was pleasant.

Large, airy, made entirely of poles, it sat on stilts, the space below housing chickens and a pig. Nicholai learned that it sat on the edge of a remote Buddhist monastery in the hills of Wulian, high above the Lekang River, and that the nearby villagers were Puman people, an ethnic minority that spoke a Dai dialect but little Han Chinese. He could see the people through the window — the men wore black turbans, the women colorful headscarves with pieces of silver sewn into them.

It was all so different from drab Beijing.

As a further comfort, Yu had acquired all of Guibert's clothing and personal effects and had them brought to Yunnan. Nicholai particularly appreciated the razor and small travel mirror, and one morning asked for a bowl of hot water so he could shave.

His image in the mirror was a bit of a shock. His skin was pale, his face drawn, the beard gave him the look of a prison camp survivor. Shaving made him look and feel better, but he realized that he would have to start eating regularly to regain his health.

"I want to get up," he said.

The young monk who had brought the water looked nervous. "Xue Xin says not for five more days."

"Is Xue Xin here at the moment?"

The young monk comically looked around the room. "No."

"Then help me get up, please."

"I will go ask —"

"If you go ask," Nicholai said, "I will try to get up on my own while you are gone, and probably fall and die as a result. What would Xue Xin say to you then?"

"He would hit me with a stick."

"So."

The monk helped him out of the bed. Nicholai tentatively put some weight on the wounded leg. The pain was ferocious, and it started to buckle beneath him, but the monk steadied him and they walked across the room.

Then back again.

After three trips, Nicholai was exhausted and the monk helped him back into the bed.

The next morning he walked outside.

Painful and slow at first, his walk from the village to the monastery became part of a thrice-daily routine as he rebuilt his physical and mental stamina. Making his unsteady way along the narrow, stone-laid paths, he focused on details — unraveling individual birdsong from the cacophony of a score of species, identifying types of monkeys from their incessant chatter and warning screeches, distinguishing plants and vines from among thousands in the verdant forest.

The jungle was reclaiming the monastery.

Its vines cracked the old stones, swallowed columns and stiles, crept over flagstone pavilions like a patient, persistent tide of Go stones on a board. Yet statues of Buddha peeped through the vegetation, his eyes content with the knowledge that all things change and all physical matter inevitably decays.

The discipline of the walk was good for Nicholai's mind, and every day the pain lessened and his strength returned until he could walk with strength and confidence. His spirit recovered as well, and soon he began to think about the future.

He almost tripped over the monk.

Xue Xin was on his hands and knees with a small blade, carefully trimming vines away from a stone path that led to a modest stupa. The monk wore a simple brown robe tied at the waist with a belt that had faded almost to white.

He looked up and asked, "Are you feeling better?"

"Yes. Thank you."

Xue Xin slowly got to his feet and bowed. Nicholai bowed deeply in return.

"You don't bow like a Frenchman," Xue Xin said.

"I was raised in China," Nicholai answered. "Later in Japan."

Xue Xin laughed. "That explains it. The Japanese, they like to bow."

"Yes, they do," Nicholai agreed.

"Would you like to help?" Xue Xin asked.

"Forgive me," Nicholai said, "but it seems an impossible task."

"Not at all. Every day I clean each day's growth away."

"But it grows back," Nicholai said. "Then you just have to do it again the next day."

"Exactly."

So Nicholai took to helping Xue Xin with the repetitive task of trying to keep the path clear. They met every morning and worked for hours, then stopped and took tea when the afternoon rain slashed down. Nicholai learned that Xue Xin was an honored guest at the monastery.

"They put up with me," Xue Xin said. "I work. And you?"

"I don't know if I am a guest here or a prisoner," Nicholai answered truthfully, although he left it at that.

"As in life itself." Xue Xin chuckled. "Are we its guest, or its prisoner?"

"As life dictates, I suppose."

"Not at all," Xue Xin answered.

"What do you mean?"

"It has stopped raining," Xue Xin observed in response. They went back to work on the path.

The next day Xue Xin observed, "You attack the vines as if they are your enemy."

"Are they not?"

"No, they are your allies," Xue Xin answered. "Without them, you would not have a useful task to perform."

"I would then have another useful task," Nicholai answered, annoyed.

"With another set of ally-enemies," Xue Xin said. "It is always the same, my Eastern-Western friend. But, by all means, if it makes you feel better, attack, attack."

That night, lying in his *kang*, lonely and missing Solange, Nicholai had a crisis of the mind and soul. Raised as he was, he was familiar with basic Buddhist philosophy—only the unfamiliar would call it a religion, or the Buddha a god—that all suffering comes from attachment, that we are prisoners of our longings and desires that keep us bound to the endless cycle of life, death, and rebirth. He knew the Buddhist belief that these longings make us take negative actions—sins, if you must—that create and accumulate bad karma that must be ameliorated through the lifetimes, and that only enlightenment can free us from this trap.

He got up, took his flashlight, and made his way to Xue Xin's cell. The monk was in full lotus position, meditating.

"You wish to trim vines by moonlight?" Xue Xin asked. "Very well, but do it without me, please."

"I want my freedom."

"Then trim vines."

"That is glib," Nicholai answered. "I expect more from you than Zen riddles."

"You are suffering?"

Nicholai nodded.

Xue Xin opened his eyes, exhaled a long breath as if to reluctantly end his meditation, and then said, "Sit down. You cannot find enlightenment, you can only be open to it finding you. That's *satori*."

"And why you chose it as a code word," Nicholai said. "Back in Beijing."

"You needed to see things as they really were," Xue Xin answered. "Until then, there was no helping you."

"If you cannot find *satori*, how —"

"It might come in a drop of rain," Xue Xin continued, ignoring the question, "a note from a faraway flute, the fall of a leaf. Of course, you have to be ready for it or it will pass unnoticed. But if you are ready, and your eyes are open, you will see it and suddenly understand everything. Then you will know who you are and what you must do."

"*Satori*."

"*Satori*," Xue Xin repeated. Then he added, "If our thoughts imprison us, it stands to reason that they can also set us free."

Yu came to see him the next morning.

The Chinese had accepted his offer.

# 94

THE NORMAL ROUTE of arms shipments from China to Vietnam, Yu explained, was through Lang Son, across the border, and directly into the north of Vietnam, where the Viet Minh had secure sanctuaries in the mountainous jungles.

But they were not going to take that route.

The rocket launchers were needed in the south, not the north.

"That is information that our enemies would pay dearly to obtain," Yu said.

Indeed it is, Nicholai thought. Since its last disastrous effort in the south, the Viet Minh had confined their activities to the north. But now it appeared that, if armed with the new weaponry, they were planning to launch a new southern front.

The northern Viet Minh were dominated by the Soviets, the southern were more independent or allied with China. A successful southern offensive would shuffle the geopolitical deck in Asia.

Yu was playing a deep game.

Given the fact that the weapons had to go to the southern Viet Minh units, there was only one possible route, down the Lekang River into Laos.

It would be no easy feat, he explained. The Lekang ran through deep gorges with boiling rapids and sharp rocks that could pierce the hulls of boats like eggshells. The river was not easily navigable until south of the town of Luang Prabang, deep into Laos.

Luang Prabang itself would present problems. They would have to switch boats there for the rest of the journey, and the area was rife with spies and French special forces.

And then there was the Binh Xuyen.

"What's the Binh Xuyen?" Nicholai asked.

"Pirates," Yu answered.

"Pirates?" Nicholai asked. It seemed a tad anachronistic.

Originally river pirates from the vast Rung Sat marshes south of Saigon, the Binh Xuyen, now opium merchants, virtually controlled that city. Their leader, a former convict named Bay Vien, supported the Viet Minh, but had changed sides and was now a close ally of the puppet emperor Bao Dai and his French masters. As a reward, Bay Vien controlled drugs, gambling, and prostitution in Saigon, and used the resulting vast wealth to acquire modern arms and equipment.

"That's Saigon," Nicholai said. "What does Bay Vien have to do with Laos?"

"It's where the opium comes from," Yu answered.

The Viet Minh used to buy raw opium in the mountains east of Luang Prabang and sell it to buy weapons, but through bribery, intimidation, and assassinations, the Binh Xuyen had virtually taken control of the Laotian opium trade.

Luang Prabang swarmed with Binh Xuyen. Yu went on, "A Viet Minh agent will meet you there and escort you into Vietnam."

Nicholai noted the shift to the second-person singular and mentioned it.

"This is why we require your services," Yu said. "My superiors have decided that they cannot take the risk of my getting captured in French territory."

He told Nicholai how he would be contacted in Luang Pra-bang and later in Saigon, and then resumed his briefing.

In Laos, the Lekang changed its name to the Mekong as it flowed through Cambodia into the Mekong Delta of Vietnam. The delta would be a challenge — not only would they have to evade the patrols of the French army and the Foreign Legion, but they would have to make their way through a network of blockhouses and forts.

Worse still, the Mekong Delta was patrolled by well-armed militias allied to the French occupiers.

"Where do I deliver the weapons?" Nicholai asked.

"We don't know."

"That would make it difficult."

Yu explained, "In Saigon you will be told where to rendezvous with a Viet Minh agent code-named Ai Quoc, to whom we will deliver the weapons. Quoc is one of the most wanted men in the country, in hiding even now. He's survived a score of assassination attempts and the French have a huge reward on him. You won't be told his location until the last possible moment."

Nicholai mentally reviewed the obstacles — the river, the Binh Xuyen, the French, their Vietnamese militias, and then locating the elusive Ai Quoc.

"So basically," he said, "this is a suicide mission."

"It does have that aspect," Yu answered. "If you want to change your mind, now is the time."

"I don't."

"Very well."

"We have an arrangement, then?" Nicholai asked.

Yu shook his hand.


Nicholai found Xue Xin at his usual task of trimming vines.

"I came to say goodbye," Nicholai said.

"Where are you going?"

"I'm not sure," Nicholai answered, then decided that he owed a better answer. "To find my *satori*."

"And if you don't?"

"Then I will keep my eyes open," Nicholai answered.

"We will meet again," Xue Xin said. "In this life or another."

Nicholai felt an emotion welling up inside him, something he had not felt since the death of General Kishikawa. "I cannot tell you how much you have meant to me."

"You don't need to," Xue Xin said. "I know."

Nicholai knelt and bowed, touching his forehead to the ground. "Thank you. You are my teacher."

"And you mine," Xue Xin said.

Then the monk knelt back down and resumed his work, serene in the knowledge that Nicholai Hel had determined his destiny.

We will meet again, he thought.

# 95

Yu had left the crates of weaponry in the care of a local battalion commander.

Colonel Ki's belly hung out over his belt, an indication that life was good for a commander in the remote hills of Yunnan. He treated Yu and Nicholai to a very good lunch of fish, vegetables, and mounds of rice, served by an orderly who virtually salivated as he presented each dish.

"I'll take command of a squad of your soldiers," Yu said to Colonel Ki, "and we'll need some of the local Puman as porters."

"To Lang Son?"

"To the river," Yu answered. "We will take them from there."

"Perhaps," Ki said, "you have misunderstood what 'Lekang' really means in Chinese."

"It means Unruly Waters," Nicholai answered.

"Unruly to say the least," Ki commented with the expression of mild sympathy that one gives to an acquaintance who has just embarrassingly revealed that he is terminally ill. But there was money to be made. "For a nominal fee, I can provide boats."

"I have already arranged for the boats."

Ki inwardly cursed the rivermen who had sold their services without gaining his permission or giving him his cut, and worried how such a transaction could occur without his knowledge. "An escort, then? You are four days' march from the river, and despite the party's heroic efforts, there are still bandits in these mountains."

"Bandits?"

"Bad people," Ki said, shaking his head. "Very bad people."

The porters shouldered the heavy crates on bamboo poles down the steep mountain trail, slippery with mud from the recent rains. The short legs and long trunks of these Puman tribesmen gave them an advantage that Nicholai did not possess as each step jarred his already sore knees and ankles. While the climb up from the last valley had been grueling, the descent down into the next was simply painful, and Nicholai thought that the route more than lived up to its sobriquet, "the Dragon's Tail."

They'd been on it for three days now, with another day yet to go before they reached the river and the boats.

The soldiers that Yu commandeered went out ahead and along the flanks. Some had Chinese "burp guns" slung over their shoulders, others carried captured American M1 rifles. At each pause in the day, and at their camps for the night, Yu gathered the soldiers and conducted study sessions on Marxist theory and Maoist thought.

Communism, Nicholai thought. It promises to make everyone equally rich and instead makes everyone equally poor.

During a break in the march one day, Nicholai took out a pack of cigarettes, shook out two, and offered one to Yu.

"French," Yu observed. "They are very good, I think."

"Take one," Nicholai said. "You're allowed the occasional bourgeois indulgence."

A man needs a whiff of sin now and then, Nicholai thought, or he becomes something not quite a man. Yu took the proffered cigarette with an expression of delicious guilt. Nicholai lit it for him and Yu took a long drag. "It is very good. Thank you."

"Not at all."

Yu took two more short, disciplined puffs, carefully snuffed the cigarette out on the ground, put the butt in his shirt pocket, and buttoned it.

Nicholai thought of Solange, and missed her.

"Is there a girl at home?" he asked Yu.

"As a revolutionary," Yu answered, "I have no time for bourgeois concepts such as romantic love."

"So there is."

Yu allowed himself a shy smile. "She is also a revolutionary. But perhaps someday, when the revolution has been established . . . You?"

"Yes. A French girl."

"And you think about her."

"Yes."

After three years in prison, Nicholai thought he had come to terms with loneliness. Its return to his internal life was a mixed blessing. But, yes, he thought about Solange.

Too often and not often enough.

He took the next painful step down the mountain.


They stopped for the night at a Daoist monastery built on a small knoll along the side of the trail. The view was magnificent, the food somewhat less so, composed as it was of congee with small bits of vegetables and fish. But Nicholai ate ravenously and then stood on the periphery of a rectangular stone pavilion and watched the monks perform their kung-fu *kata*, which he recognized as the classic southern *hung-gar* form of "Tiger and Crane."

Beautiful and doubtless deadly, he thought, although not as efficient as *hoda korosu*. But that was the main distinction between Chinese and Japanese martial arts—the former used many elaborate and circular moves while the latter emphasized one quick, direct, fatal strike.

Nicholai contemplated which was superior and decided that it was the Chinese for beauty, the Japanese for killing.

On the far side of the pavilion, Yu inflicted Communist doctrine on his students. One of the victims, a thick country lad named Liang, stared wistfully off into the bamboo thickets, doubtless wishing that he could find sanctuary there. But Liang was something of a special pet of Yu's and so good-naturedly sat through the lecture as if genuinely interested. Yu had great, if misplaced, hopes for him.

One more day on the Dragon's Tail, Nicholai thought. They would reach the river late the next afternoon and load their cargo onto the waiting boats. It would be a nice change to be on the water and off the arduous trail.

He walked back to the chamber that had been assigned to him. It was a small room with a single *kang*, the classic Chinese raised bed, which was draped with thin mosquito netting. Someone had already come in, lit a lantern, and left a thermos of hot water and an old porcelain cup with which to make tea.

But Nicholai craved rest more than the stimulation of the strong southern green tea, so he stripped off his clothes, climbed into the *kang*, and stretched out. He closed his eyes and told his mind to allow him five hours of sleep. He wanted to wake up well before dawn to make sure that the caravan got an early start.

Nicholai's proximity sense woke him before his internal alarm did.

The two men smelled of cheap Chinese tobacco. Their heavy steps made clear that they were bandits and not professional assassins — they tried to walk quietly but were clumsy and obvious. Amateurs assume that to step slowly is to step softly, while professionals know that the opposite is true and are both quick and light.

Willing himself to remain still, Nicholai measured the slow heavy footsteps of the lead bandit as they creaked on the wooden floor. If they were going to use guns they would have done it already, but they apparently didn't want to make noise and spring the main attack prematurely, before they had eliminated the leadership. So it would be a sword, a knife or an axe, maybe a garrote, but more likely an edged weapon that could slice through the mosquito netting, sparing the extra second to open it.

So there would be time for *hoda korosu*.

He edged his hand along the *kang*, felt for the teacup, and slid it beside him under the thin sheet. Silently he crushed the cup in his hand until he felt blood running from his palm, and then pinched the sharp shard of glass between his thumb and forefinger.

Then he waited.

The footsteps stopped and Nicholai felt the bandit pause as he lifted his arm to strike.

Nicholai swung the shard in a horizontal backhand that sliced the bandit's throat. The knife arm came down in a limp, useless arc and then the bandit, his left arm futilely clutching his throat, pitched forward onto the *kang*.

The second bandit made the fatal error of backing up and reaching for the pistol at his belt as Nicholai launched off the *kang*, grabbed the heavy metal thermos, and swung it like a club. The man's skull fractured with a sickening crack. Nicholai bent over his body, took the pistol, and stepped outside.

Red muzzle flashes tore the black silk fabric of the night.

Yu, clad only in trousers, stood with a pistol in his hand, trying to form the startled men into some kind of order.

Nicholai heard the *zip-zip* of gunfire and felt the little pockets of air concuss as the bullets flew past him. He had experienced bombings, beatings, and hand-to-hand combat, but this was his first firefight and he found it chaotic. The bandits had chosen a good time to strike, the hours of deepest sleep before dawn, and the fight had the surreal quality of a waking dream.

The bullets were real, however, and Nicholai heard the hollow thunk of a round strike the soldier beside him. The boy reached down to the hole in his stomach and looked at Nicholai with an expression of hurt surprise, as if to ask if this were really happening, then howled with pain. Nicholai eased him to the ground as gently as he could. The boy would die and there was nothing he could do.

He could only try to save the cargo.

Nicholai exchanged his pistol for the soldier's rifle and moved out.

Yu was already rallying the men he had left toward the crates stacked in the monastery's central pavilion. A few of the sentries guarding the crates had already fled, two others lay slumped dead at their posts, while three crouched behind the boxes and returned the shots that were coming from the bamboo thicket on the far side of the pavilion. But they were under heavy fire and it was obvious that they couldn't hold out for long.

Yu started across the pavilion for the pile of crates but Nicholai held him back. It was brave but useless to join the three soldiers in their isolated post. We would just become additional targets, Nicholai thought, a few more sacrificed stones in a soon-to-be eliminated position on the board. Better to create a new position and give the bandits something new to think about.

So Nicholai squatted behind a stone bench set at the edge of the pavilion. He waited until he saw a muzzle flash come from the bamboo and fired at it, then heard a man scream in pain. Yu did the same with the same result.

The shooting from the bamboo stopped as the bandits considered how to handle the new situation.

Nicholai used the pause to belly-crawl across that side of the pavilion to a bench on the perpendicular side. It would be better, he thought, if the bandits formed a tactic to deal with a situation that had already changed.

Go is a fluid game.

It was quiet for a moment longer and then a spray of bullets hit the stone bench that Nicholai had vacated. Yu pressed himself flat on the stones and survived the blast, but the bullets kept him down as a group of a dozen or more bandits sprang out of the bamboo and rushed the crates.

Nicholai, on the flank of the attack, easily picked the lead bandit off with his first shot but missed the second one and had to fire again. He dropped the next man, but the bandits in the bamboo adjusted quickly and turned their guns on him. Nicholai flattened out and the bullets passed over him.

Then he pushed himself up on his hands and the balls of his feet, took a deep breath, and vaulted over the bench.

Lit only by muzzle flashes, the scene before him played like cinema in a bad old theater with a creaky projector. Nicholai saw flickers of the melee at the crates — a bayonet thrust, a pistol fired at close range, a wounded man's mouth agape. He plunged in, firing his rifle until the clip was empty. Then he used it like an ancient Chinese weapon — a sharp blade on one end, a blunt object on the other. He swung and thrust, ducked and dodged, beyond thought in the realm of instinct that came from constant training.

But the bandits were simply too many. The most skillful Go player will lose his few isolated white stones against a tide of black ones.

It was inevitable.

Die with honor.

*Hai*, Kishikawa-sama.

The cherry blossoms of Kajikawa floated in front of his eyes as he recalled his walk, so long ago, with the general. Kishikawa had focused on the beautiful blossoms to prepare himself for his death.

Then through the flashes of light Nicholai saw a row of brown-robed monks, bamboo staffs in their hands, advance onto the pavilion.

The fight became a whirling blur of bamboo, a *tai-fung*, but the rain pellets were wood striking flesh and bone, and then it was over, like a sudden squall. The surviving bandits fled back into the forest.

Without the precious cargo.

But six soldiers and one monk lay dead, and others were wounded.

Nicholai squatted beside the body of one of the bandits. Yu held up a lantern and they examined the dead man's face. It took a moment, but then Nicholai recognized him...the orderly who had served lunch for Colonel Ki.

You have been careless and stupid, Nicholai told himself. "Michel Guibert" did not see the obvious ploy. Whereas Nicholai Hel would have. He resolved to retain a piece of his authentic self regardless of any situational guise.

The monks mopped up blood under lantern light.

Nicholai found the abbot, bowed deeply, and apologized for fouling the monastery with violence.

"You did not," the abbot responded. "They did."

"Still, I was the cause of it."

"And so I will ask that you leave at first light and never return."

Nicholai bowed again. "May I risk a possibly impertinent question?" When the abbot nodded, Nicholai asked, "I thought that you were pacifists. Why——"

"Buddhists are pacifists," the abbot answered. "We are Daoists. We eschew violence except when necessary. But it is the mission of our order to offer hospitality. So we were forced to choose between two competing values—our desire not to harm our fellow creatures and our vow of sanctuary to our guests. In this case, we chose the latter."

"You fight well."

"When one chooses to fight," the abbot replied, "it is one's responsibility to fight well."

Nicholai found Yu in his chamber, angrily stuffing his small gear into his haversack.

"They were your own men," Nicholai said.

"I know that."

His face already showed a loss of innocence. Nicholai felt some sympathy, but it did not prevent him from pressing the necessary question. "How am I supposed to trust you now?"

Yu led him out of the monastery to a wide spot on the trail, where a soldier was bound around the chest to the trunk of a tree.

It was Liang. Blood ran down his nose and a purple welt swelled under his eye. He had been beaten.

"He was one of the sentries," Yu said disgustedly. "The one who survived. He claims he fell asleep, but I suspect that he deliberately let the bandits pass. Either way he is guilty. The monks would not let me execute him at the monastery so I brought him here."

"You should not execute him at all."

"At the very least, he failed in his duty."

"So did we," Nicholai said. "We should have been better pre-pared."

"He caused the deaths of comrades," Yu insisted.

"Again, as did we," Nicholai argued. "Men aren't perfect."

"The new man must be," Yu responded. "Perfect, at least, in his duty."

Nicholai looked at Liang, who trembled with cold and fear. While we debate philosophy, Nicholai thought. It's cruel. He tried again. "Perhaps he was performing his duty to Ki."

"His duty is to the people."

"He *is* the people, Yu."

In response, Yu pulled his pistol from its holster and held the barrel to Liang's head. His hand trembled as the boy cried and begged for his life.

Yu pulled the trigger.

"And that is how you know," he said, "that you can trust me."

# 96

DIAMOND FOUND HER in Vientiane, in the square outside the Patousay.

The monument, even with its Laotian spires, reminded him a little of an *arc de triomphe*. Indeed, Solange thought so too.

"It reminds me a little of home," she said. "In Montpellier we have something similar."

"What are you doing in Laos?" Diamond asked.

"Looking for work, monsieur," she answered. "What are *you* doing in Laos?"

"Looking for you."

"Ah, well. *Your* task, at least, is finished."

"Yours too, maybe," Diamond said. He was instantly jealous of Nicholai Hel. The thought that the arrogant bastard had slept with this gorgeous creature was infuriating.

"How so?" she asked.

"We might have something for you," he said.

"'We'?" she inquired, her tone slightly sarcastic and tantalizing at the same time. "You mean 'we Americans'?"

"Yes."

"I usually deal with Monsieur Haverford," she said.

She pronounced it "Averfor," which Diamond found stimulating beyond belief. "He's on another assignment. He sent me. I'm Mr. Gold."

Her smile was sensuous, ironic, and infuriating. "Really?"

"No."

They walked out of the park onto Lane Xang.

"What do you have in mind, Monsieur Gold?" she asked.

Diamond told her, then added, "I think you'll like it. It could be very lucrative, and Saigon is a lot like France, isn't it?"

"In some aspects, yes."

"So your answer?"

"*Pourquoi pas?*"

"What does that mean?"

She trained the full force of her green eyes on him and smiled. "Why not?"

"Good," Diamond said, his throat tight. "Good. Uhh, do you need a taxi? Where are you staying?"

"At the Manoly," she answered. "I can walk, thank you."

"I could walk with you."

She stopped walking and looked at him. "What are you asking now, Monsieur Gold?"

"I think you know," Diamond answered, summoning up his nerve with the thought that the woman was, after all, a glorified whore. "I mean, you said you were looking for work."

She laughed. "But not *that* desperately."

They quickly made the necessary arrangements for her trip to Saigon and he walked away hating her.

But the whore will serve her purpose, he thought. The file said that Hel had fallen in love with her and intended to return to her. Good — if the son of a bitch is alive, he'll come find her in Saigon.

And I have connections in Saigon.

Solange made sure that the disgusting American wasn't following her, and then returned to her hotel and had a mint tea in the quiet of the shady garden.

Saigon, she thought.

Very well, Saigon.

Nicholai had yet to surface and she had to face the probability that he never would. Men die and men disappear, and a woman must take care of herself. The abhorrent "Gold" was right that Saigon was a congenial city, French in many ways.

# 97

THEY REACHED THE RIVER late that afternoon.

Nicholai had to admit it was something of a shock.

Early in winter, he had expected the Lekang to be at its lowest flow. Still, beyond the long eddy where the waiting rafts were beached on the pebbled shore, the river ran fast, full, and angry.

The roar of water running shallowly over rock was impressive, even intimidating, but there was no time for trepidation. Nicholai worried that Ki might take another shot here where they would be pinned down without cover on the narrow strip of beach. He was glad to see that Yu had posted two of his "true believers" to cover the trail.

"We need to get loaded," he said to Yu.

Yu shouted some orders and his soldiers helped the porters carry the crates onto the rafts, where the boatmen lashed them down. The head boatman, a squat middle-aged Tibetan with a cigarette in his mouth, approached Nicholai.

"Are you Guibert?" he asked in American-accented English that Nicholai knew too well from his years in his cell, listening to the American guards converse in what passed for their native tongue.

"That's me."

"I lost two men just getting down here."

"They'll be reborn well."

The boatman shrugged his indifference at the concept of

reincarnation. This life was plenty to deal with at the moment. "I'm Tasser."

He didn't offer his hand.

"Michel Guibert."

"I know that. Did you bring the money?"

"Yes."

"Give."

"Half now," Nicholai said, "half when we get to Luang Pra-bang."

Tasser scoffed and looked at the roaring river. "Give me the whole megillah now. In case we don't make it to Luang."

"It's your job to see that we do make it," Nicholai said. He counted out half the money and handed a wad of bills to Tasser. "By the way, where did you learn your English?"

Tasser pressed the fingers of his right hand together and made a swooping arc. "American flyboys. They'd crash their crates into the mountains and I'd get what was left of them down. War had gone a couple of more years, I'd be sitting pretty."

"Could we speak in Chinese instead?"

"I don't pollute my mouth with that foreign tongue," Tasser said in Chinese. He switched back to English. "You got any decent smokes?"

"Gauloises."

"Frenchie shit? No thanks."

"Suit yourself."

"I will," Tasser said. "So what's in the crates?"

"None of your business."

Tasser laughed, then crumpled up one of the bills and tossed it into the water. "You gotta grease the river gods," he explained. But one of his men scrambled downstream, retrieved the bill, and brought it back to Tasser.

Nicholai raised an eyebrow.

"They're gods," Tasser said. "What are they gonna do with cash?"

Nicholai walked away and found Yu nervously peering back up the trail. He took out a cigarette and handed it to the colonel.

"Back at the monastery," Yu said, "you didn't fight like a man motivated just by profit."

"Yes, I did."

"Do not fool yourself," Yu said. "You believe in a cause, even if you don't yet know what it is."

"I believe in my own freedom."

"Individual freedom is bourgeois illusion," Yu answered. "You should give it up."

"I won't, if you don't mind."

"Just get the weapons to their destination," Yu said.

"You have my word."

They shook hands.

Nicholai walked back to the rafts. "Let's get going!" he yelled, and the boatmen pushed off.

The river quickly swept them away.

The river slowed and flattened.

For a distance that Nicholai judged to be a couple of miles, the water ran fast but evenly, and he had a chance to peruse the rafts and their crews.

The rafts were about fifteen feet wide and made of buoyant logs tightly lashed together, although with enough give to allow some flexibility. They had hardly any draft and seemed to roll easily over the shallows. Long oars were laid on the sides, although the crew didn't need them in this current. A canopy had been stretched over poles at the aft, with a charcoal stove just in front. The crates were stacked in the middle of the raft and tightly lashed to boltholes that had been drilled in the sides.

The crewmen, four to each raft, were all Tibetan, with squat bodies, full faces, and skins darkened by the sun. They sat cross-legged at the sides, near the oars, and enjoyed the respite given by this relatively benign stretch of river.

"I never pictured Tibet as having much of a river trade," Nicholai said to Tasser.

"You got that right."

"How did you learn to do this?"

"Crazy Brits," Tasser answered. "They're always going up or down something. Up mountains, down rivers. As long as it's crazy and dangerous. Before the war, a bunch of wiseguys from Oxford wanted to be the first to go down the Lekang. They needed a 'river sherpa.' I was a kid, needed the moola, and thought, 'What the hell.'"

"Did they make it down?"

"Most of 'em."

"All the way to Luang Prabang?"

"I dunno," Tasser said.

"What do you mean?" Nicholai asked.

Tasser looked at him and smiled. "I've never been down this stretch of the river."

Nicholai felt the water quicken beneath him and looked downriver, where a cloud of mist suddenly appeared.

"What's that?" he asked.

Tasser took a map from his pocket and spread it out. Nicholai looked over his shoulder and the map appeared to be more of a picture, a cartoon, really, of the river, with drawings of tall peaks and midstream boulders. Tasser considered for a moment, and then hollered over the increasing rush of water, "That would be the Dragon's Throat!"

"The Dragon's Tail?"

"The Dragon's *Throat*!" Tasser shouted, pointing at his

Adam's apple. He looked at the "map" again and asked, "What the hell does 'Level 5' mean, ya think?"

A few seconds later, he answered his own question.

"Holy shit!"

The first fall was only twenty feet but it crashed onto a broad shelf of rock that would certainly smash the rafts to pieces.

Nicholai felt the bow pitch forward, grabbed on to a line, and held on. There was nothing else to do.

Then they went over the edge.

They landed with a heavy impact and Nicholai was sure that he would feel the raft break up beneath him; the logs bounced and rolled but held together and the current swept them over the rock into a chute where the water was whirling in a violent circle just upstream of a second waterfall.

"Get to the oars!" Tasser yelled, and his men abandoned the relative safety of the line and scampered to man the oars.

Nicholai could see why. The circular current was pulling the raft sideways, and if it went into the falls broadside it would surely capsize as it went over. They had to right it so it entered the next fall bow first.

But the raft was spinning like a leaf in the wind.

"Where are the lifejackets?" Nicholai hollered to Tasser.

"The what?" Tasser hollered back.

The current spat them out, but sideways — the starboard side facing the waterfall — and Nicholai saw a large backcurrent, a small wall of water coming toward them.

"Look out!" he yelled.

The backcurrent lifted the raft and pitched one of the aft oarsmen off the starboard side. Nicholai, one hand on the line, crawled back and tried to pull him out of the water, but Tasser yelled, "The oar! Get the oar, goddamnit!"

Nicholai grabbed the oar just before it slipped into the water.

The crewman was pulled back into the circular current and Nicholai saw him try to stay above water as the current spun him around and around like some malevolent funhouse ride.

"Pull!" Tasser yelled.

Nicholai sat down and pulled on the oar, straining every muscle and sinew to try to pull the raft around. They were almost straight when the bow went over the edge. This fall was not as high. They landed in a deep pool and the raft bobbed once before it was pulled into the next chute of water.

The flume raced to a narrow fall between two towers of rock. The raft scraped the edge of the rock to the left, bounced off, and then slid over the low fall onto a shallow stretch that rushed over rocks that banged against the bottom.

Downriver he saw a large column of what looked like smoke.

It wasn't smoke, though. Nicholai knew that could only be mist from a large volume of water crashing over a very high waterfall.

"Pull to the side!" Tasser yelled.

Nicholai looked to his right, where Tasser was pointing toward a long eddy. But the current was pulling them away, and they had little time or space to make it over into the eddy, and the crews were already exhausted.

He lifted his oar from the water as the crew on the port side pulled. When the raft was pointed starboard, both sides would row as hard as they could, for their lives. He took a few deep gulps of air and then, at Tasser's order, started to stroke.

It was only a small bump, but it was enough. Nicholai had pulled himself up on the end of his stroke, and the bump hit before he could settle back down and lifted him up and off the side of the raft.

The first thing he felt was the shock of the cold water as he went under. He pulled himself to the surface, then felt the mental shock of knowing that he was in the river and inexorably headed for the waterfall.

He had been in bad situations before, while exploring narrow passages in caves during his happy years with friends in Japan. Then, the chambers had closed in and seemed to offer no way out. Or he'd been trapped by underground streams, the water hissing below him in the pitch black, and he'd enjoyed the danger, so now he forced his mind to dismiss the terror and focus on survival.

The first thing to do was get turned around, so he struggled successfully to get feet-first into the current. He didn't know what waited at the bottom of the fall, but it was certainly better to encounter it with his feet instead of his head, smashing his legs, perhaps, instead of his neck or skull. He knew that he was dead anyway if the fall landed shallowly on rock, but honor demanded that he do his best.

Then he pressed his arms tightly to his sides and closed his legs to create as compact a vessel of himself as he could, so his limbs wouldn't create levers that might tip him sideways and roll him, akimbo, over the falls.

He held his neck and head up out of the water until the last possible moment, then took a deep breath (his last? he wondered) and went over the edge.

The fall was long and violent, the water battering him to try to knock him out of his posture, but he held firm, waiting for the "landing" that would shatter his body, maim him, or offer the next challenge.

Then he felt the stillness of a pool and realized that he'd survived the fall.

He looked back up and realized that he'd plunged at least forty feet. Treading water to catch his breath, he looked downstream and saw, on the right edge, both rafts pulled up on the shore.

They were in bad shape.

The canopy of the first raft was stoved in, and several oars were broken. The second raft looked little better, its bow jagged like a broken tooth. But both had made it through the Dragon's Throat and, miraculously, the crates sat in the middle like cows lying down in the face of bad weather.

One of the crew standing on the edge saw him and started to point and yell as Nicholai, exhausted, swam for the shore, where he just lay on the rough stones, unable to move.

"Thought you were a goner," Tasser said, standing over him.

"So did I."

"Glad you made it."

"Thank you."

"Yeah, you have the rest of my dough."

On that sentimental note, he pulled Nicholai to his feet.

They spent the next three days resting, repairing the damaged rafts and oars, and perusing the rough map of the next stretch of the river.

"This so-called map is useless," Nicholai said.

So Tasser and Nicholai walked downstream, climbed a steep cliff on the right bank, and confirmed their worst fear: an enormous fall, higher than the one that nearly killed them, loomed just downstream.

"We can't run that," Nicholai said.

"Nope."

They would have to go around it. With only nine men, a portage would be long and arduous, but they had no choice. So they went back and began the long task of disassembling the rafts and hewing poles with which to heft the crates. This took two more days—making an unplanned delay of five days—so dwindling supplies became a concern. With no villages in the wilderness of

SATORI 305

the Lekang River gorges in which to buy food, they would have to cut rations, a serious problem with the increase in labor that the portage would extract.

But no one complained about these hardships, when weighed against the terror of another run down worse rapids. The men worked steadily, and in two days they were ready to set out.

For three days they worked in relay teams, hefting, pulling, dragging, and pushing the rafts' logs up the slope beside the massive waterfall, then lowering them down using ropes wrapped around trees as counterweights. Then, while two of the crewmen reassembled the rafts, the other six men carried the heavy crates with their lethal cargo over the same route.

To the extent that one can enjoy grueling physical labor, Nicholai did so. The battle against the physics of hauling heavy material up and down a mountain and the struggle against the limitations of his own body and spirit seemed simple and clean as opposed to the more underhanded conflicts of his mission.

No deception was involved in this, just the direct application of muscle and sweat, determination and brains. Nicholai found it to be a cleansing process — even the sharp edge of hunger that came on the second day seemed only to sharpen his senses and purge the malaise that he only now realized had set in after leaving Solange.

And the Tibetan crewmen were a marvel of cheerfulness and stamina. Having begun their working lives as sherpas, lugging heavy baggage on the slopes of the Himalayas, they were not daunted by this task and seemed to find the complexities of maneuvering the loads to be a pleasant intellectual as well as physical challenge. They loved to solve the problems of weight and counterweight using complicated arrangements of ropes and knots that fascinated Nicholai.

He resolved that, if he survived this mission, he would spend

more time in the mountains and master the techniques of technical climbing.

At night the Tibetans would build a fire, brew strong pots of
tea from the dwindling supply, and make soup that got thinner
each night. Still it was a good time, resting sore muscles and listening to the tales of ghosts and spirits, sage holy men and brave
warriors that the crewmen would tell while Tasser translated
into colloquial American English.

Then Nicholai would sleep the sleep of the dead, waking only
just before dawn, when the day's good and hard work would
begin again. He was almost disappointed when, after three days,
the portage was accomplished, the rafts reassembled, and the
journey downriver could begin again.

The river was gentler below these falls. Jagged rocks and
shallows, with the occasional rapids, still caused problems, but
in only two days, Tasser checked the cartoon-map and happily
announced, "We're out of goddamn China."

They were in the French colony of Laos, and the river changed
its name from the Lekang to the Mekong.

In an almost mystical way, the river itself seemed to recognize the change. It broadened, slowed, and darkened with the
collected silt brought all the way down from the Himalayan
foothills.

"Like us," Tasser observed. "Brown and down from Tibet."

The mountains that flanked the river became greener, verdant
with jungle vegetation, and here and there a bamboo village, its
houses on stilts against the seasonal floods, appeared suddenly
around a bend of the twisting river.

They put in at one of these villages to buy food, and Nicholai
realized that Tasser knew a little more than he let on.

"I don't know what you got in those goddamn crates," Tasser
said, "and I don't want to know. But if you're taking them where

I think you're taking them, keep your lips zipped. These are Hmong people, and they don't much like Commies. So don't give them any of that "Comrade" shit, or they might take one of them curvy knives and lop off your head. Got it?"

"Got it."

"Another thing," Tasser warned as he piloted the raft onto a sandy spot along the right side of the river. "Turn a blind eye to what you see here."

He pointed across the river. "That's Siam over there. Land of the Thais. Also land of the poppy. This here is prime opium-growing country, and the river downstream from here is a highway for dope. The Hmong grow it, so do the Thais. It's how they feed their kids."

"I understand."

"You'd better," Tasser said. "We smile, we buy our groceries, we get back on the water pronto."

Nicholai stayed on the raft while Tasser took two men and went to buy supplies. Naked Hmong children happily dove off a rickety bamboo pier into the water. The women, in their unique black caps, sat nearby, kept a watchful eye, and sneaked shy glances at the tall European sitting on the raft. Nicholai heard dogs barking in the village and the ubiquitous bleating of goats and cackling of chickens.

Barely half an hour later Tasser returned with mesh nets full of bananas and other fruits, greens, rice, and smoked fish. Nicholai felt ashamed of his suspicions as Tasser gave the order to shove off and the raft swirled back into the gentle current. Then the captain handed Nicholai a bottle of clear liquid.

"Take a belt," Tasser said.

Nicholai took a swallow and felt like his stomach, lungs, and brain were on fire. "Good God, man, what is it?"

"*Lao-lao*," Tasser answered. "Hmong moonshine."

Nicholai helped one of the crew build a fire in the charcoal stove and soon they had a delicious meal of rice, fish, and bananas. Then he took his turn at an oar, and when relieved sat on the edge and enjoyed the beautiful, verdant countryside, the green mountains and limestone cliffs.

Two days later they came into Luang Prabang.

## 98

Nicholai cut an odd figure checking in to the small guesthouse.

His clothes were torn and mud-stained, his hair long and disheveled, his face brown as a nut and weatherworn. He ignored the desk clerk's stare with an aristocratic insouciance and asked for the best room available, preferably with a view of the river.

"Does Monsieur have luggage?"

"Monsieur does not."

"Will it be arriving from the airport, perhaps?"

"Probably not," Nicholai said. He produced a handful of bills from his pants pocket and laid them on the counter.

"Passport?"

Nicholai handed over the passport indentifying him as Michel Guibert. It was a calculated risk, one that might send teletypes singing in Beijing, Moscow, and Washington, but Nicholai doubted it. Luang Prabang was a backwater even in Indochina, and there were probably no alarm bells here to be rung. Still, French intelligence would no doubt have a presence here, but Nicholai was counting on that.

The clerk copied down the passport information and handed it back to Nicholai with a key. "Room 203 has a charming view of the river. Would Monsieur like a razor sent up?"

"Yes, please," Nicholai answered. "And coffee, croissant, and the most recent newspaper available, if you will."

The clerk nodded with satisfaction.

\*       \*       \*

Clean and shaven, Nicholai sat on his small balcony and enjoyed the excellent croissant.

The pastry seemed at odds with the intense heat that was building in the late morning, but nevertheless tasted good along with the cup of strong espresso. It was all very French — even as the file of saffron-robed young monks walked by on their way back from the ritual morning alms solicitations.

A main thoroughfare of the old Laotian royal capital, Khem Kong Road ran along the riverbank and was lined with shops, restaurants, and French cafés. A blend of odors — steamed fish and crepes — spoke redolently of the town's mixed culture. Ancient Buddhist temples stood beside elegant French colonial manor houses, the red-tiled roofs of which would not have been out of place along the Mediterranean Sea instead of the banks of the Mekong. Beautiful emerald green mountains rose across the brown, muddy river. It was a scene of great tranquility, in sharp contrast to the shipment of lethal weapons waiting on the rafts just a few hundred yards upriver.

Nicholai took another bite of the croissant and read his newspaper, a week-old copy of the *Journal d'Extrême-Orient*. He hadn't seen the news in several months, but was not surprised to see that little had changed. Negotiations to end the Korean conflict dragged on, the Viet Minh had defeated the French at a battle near Hoa Binh in the north, a Cambodian nationalist demanded that French forces leave the country, then was forced to flee and was branded both a Communist and an agent of the CIA by the editorialist. In Saigon, the puppet emperor Bao Dai welcomed a delegation from the French film industry and —

He almost missed it at first, in the dull list naming the delegation: Françoise Ariend, Michel Cournoyer, Anise Maurent...

Solange Picard.

Solange was not in Tokyo but in Saigon. As a member of a French film delegation. Interesting.

Saigon, he thought.

How interesting, how coincidental.

Haverford must think me a fool.

Nicholai walked up the street to a clothier.

The heat of afternoon was on — the air was moist with the promise of rain. The dry season in Southeast Asia would soon be over, the monsoons would be coming on. With the temperature at least a hundred degrees and humid, Nicholai's shirt was soaked with sweat by the time he went into the shop. He bought three cotton shirts, two pairs of linen trousers, a white linen suit, a pair of oxford shoes, and a panama hat and had them sent back to his hotel. Then he found another shop and bought a decent suitcase. Now he could simply pack, walk away from the suicide mission to take the weapons into the south of Vietnam, and go to Saigon into the trap that the Americans were setting with Solange as bait.

He could see the *go-kang*, and the stones moving, and he saw his way through.

But he couldn't and knew that he couldn't.

He had given his word to Yu, and he had to go and make contact with the Viet Minh agent.

## 99

NICHOLAI SAT in the back of a pedicab as it wound its way down Sisavangvong Road.

The cab dropped him off at the edge of an old Luang Prabang institution, the "Night Market," an open-air bazaar with hundreds of small stands selling balls of sweet sticky rice, bits of fried fish, steaming cups of tea, and a few dozen delicacies that Nicholai didn't recognize. Other stands offered delicate parasols, brightly colored paper lanterns, cotton shirts, trousers, sandals, candles, and little statues of Buddha.

The rich smells, sights, and sounds were a heady contrast to the austerity of the long river journey. The merchants loudly proclaimed the virtues of their wares or haggled with buyers, the acrid smell of charcoal fires competed with the aromas of sizzling chili sauces in open woks, and, even under lantern light in the dark alleys, the various merchandise combined to make a riotous panoply.

Nicholai easily edged his way through the crowd. At least a head taller than most of the shoppers, he was nevertheless inconspicuous. The Laotians were used to the French colonials and Nicholai looked and acted like one.

He came to a stand selling live birds. The birds were pretty and much too small to eat. Choosing a bird with electric blue and green feathers, he untied it and the bird flew into the night, albeit without the Buddhist prayer that freed birds were usually meant to convey.

Nicholai strolled farther into the market, drank a hot green tea, made a few small purchases, and then tried some fried fish in hot chili oil and coriander. He'd not quite finished it when a man sidled up and quietly said in French, "Follow me."

They left the market through a narrow alley and Nicholai's nerves tingled in this potential trap. But it was not unlike working through a tight chamber in a cave, and he calmed his mind and let his senses guard for danger.

They emerged from the alley into a tight dirt street. Nicholai smelled the distinct aroma of opium as he followed the man into a ramshackle building. It was dark inside, the front room lit only by the glow of the pipes. The smokers, sitting or lying around the walls, lost in their opium dreams, didn't even look up, but Nicholai's proximity sense alerted him.

The third opium smoker along the wall, in the stained black shirt, was there to kill him, if need be. Nicholai grasped the small ivory letter opener with the carved elephant handle he'd bought at the Night Market.

"*Wangbadan*," Nicholai said in Cantonese.

Son of a bitch.

He saw the flicker of recognition in the alleged Viet Minh's eyes before the man quickly recovered and asked in French, "What?"

The ivory blade flashed out of Nicholai's sleeve and pressed against the neck of the supposed Viet Minh agent. He said in Cantonese, "If that man moves, I'll kill you."

The agent understood. He looked at the "opium smoker" and slowly shook his head. Then he said to Nicholai, "I didn't see you buy that."

"That's right," Nicholai said. "Where is the man that I was supposed to meet?"

"I am the man you—"

Nicholai pressed the point against his carotid artery. "I won't ask again."

"Dead."

Nicholai felt more than saw the gun come out from under the "opium smoker's" black shirt and he flicked the letter opener. The blade went straight into the gunman's throat and he slumped to the floor.

The other Binh Xuyen took the chance and launched a knee strike at Nicholai's solar plexus. He turned to deflect the blow, then crossed his hands, grabbed the man's head, and jerked in both directions. The neck snapped and the man went limp in his hands.

Nicholai let him drop just as three men with machine pistols burst through the back door.

"I'm impressed, Monsieur Guibert."

The boss of the Binh Xuyen gang was physically unimpressive.

Short and slight, with a receding line of nevertheless jet black hair, his left eye went off at an odd forty-five-degree angle, and it looked like the orbital bone around it had been smashed. He wore a plain khaki linen shirt, light khaki trousers, and sandals over white socks.

Now he contemplated Nicholai for a moment and asked, "Would you prefer to speak in French or Chinese?"

"As you wish," Nicholai said in French.

"Do you know who I am?" the man asked in Cantonese.

"I imagine," Nicholai answered, "that you're with the Binh Xuyen."

"I am not *with* the Binh Xuyen," the small man said. "I *am* the Binh Xuyen."

"Bay Vien."

Bay nodded. "You should be flattered by my personal attention. I usually delegate these errands, but I was in town on business anyway, so... You appear to have killed two of my men, Monsieur Guibert."

Nicholai knew that this was not the time to attempt a retreat. To back off would be to die. "Generally speaking, I do kill people who try to kill me first."

"They disobeyed instructions, then," Bay said. "I had hoped to accomplish this without violence. Simply have you sell your wares to what you thought were Viet Minh, pay you your money, and let you go on your way. But now..."

Bay shook his head with what appeared to be regret. "Please understand it's only business."

Nicholai knew that this development had rearranged the stones on the *go-kang*. His promise to Colonel Yu to deliver the weapons to the Viet Minh now seemed impossible to redeem, and his own death wouldn't change the outcome.

He could almost hear Otake-sama's gentle counsel. *When the immediate situation is untenable, Nikko, what do you play for?*

*Time, Otake-sama.*

*Play for the long game.*

"Yes, poor business," Nicholai answered.

"How so?"

"Fifty rocket launchers will make the Binh Xuyen very powerful," Nicholai said. "So what would a hundred make you? Or two hundred?"

Bay Vien scoffed, "You can't get that many."

"Not if I'm dead," Nicholai agreed.

He could virtually see Bay Vien thinking, as well he might. The Binh Xuyen would eventually have to fight the militias, other gangs, and perhaps the Viet Minh. They might even have to go up against their current ally Bao Dai and his regular Vietnamese troops in the future. These weapons could decide the outcome of a battle fought in the streets of Saigon.

And Bay Vien's thinking, Nicholai contemplated, will determine if I live or die.

# 100

Ellis Haverford always liked Saigon.

In the guise of an employee at the United States Information Service, he had been in and out of the city quite often over the years, and considered it a second home. To him it was the ideal blend of the best of Paris and the best of Asia—the food, the architecture, the wine, the fashion, the women—all without the gray winters and accompanying existential angst that often plagued the city on the Seine. Saigon was a sophisticated town with an easy tolerance for vice—its casinos were honest and well-run, its brothels cheerful, hospitable, and famed for the staggering variety of their courtesans.

And he liked the city's bars. Saigon was a great town for booze and boozy conversations. The escalating war brought reporters from all over the world, always good for a laugh and a little inside information, always available for late-night card games and early-morning Bloody Marys.

Besides, Haverford liked the Vietnamese. He loved their kind demeanor, respected their long struggle for independence, admired how they had adopted the best of Western culture and adapted the worst.

Still, he hoped to spend as little time as possible there, praying that the "cold warriors" back in Washington would not step into the shoes of the French. He had fought in Vietnam before, and he didn't want to fight there ever again.

Now he waited for Nicholai Hel, hoping that he would arrive with the spring rains.

# 101

Nicholai took a separate pedicab down to the river, got off a half mile from where the rafts were docked, and walked the rest of the way.

Tasser shone a bright lamp on him as he approached.

"That you, Mike?"

"And if it wasn't?" Nicholai stepped onto the raft. "A truck will be pulling up anytime now. We'll transfer the cargo."

"Not a minute too soon for me," Tasser said. "These fucking Hmong give me the heebie-jeebies."

"What will you do now?"

"Back to the high mountains," Tasser answered. "See if any more crazy Brits, Yanks, or Frogs want to climb to the top of the world. Look for me in the photos—I'll be the guy they don't name."

A pair of headlights came down the road. Tasser's men offloaded the cargo onto the shore. Nicholai shook Tasser's hand. "Thank you for everything. It's been a genuine pleasure."

"Same here."

Tasser gathered his crew and disappeared into the darkness.

Nicholai walked toward the truck.

Bay Vien sat in the front passenger seat.

# 102

THE TRUCK ROLLED OUT of town in the morning, Nicholai in the front seat beside Bay Vien.

"Where are we going?" Nicholai asked.

Bay pointed east, across the river, up toward the mountains.

"Why?"

"You ask too many questions," Bay answered, sucking on a cigarette. He was irritable, unused to the early hour and the jostling of the truck. Besides, the Binh Xuyen boss wasn't thrilled that Nicholai insisted on coming along with the weapons instead of just meeting him in Saigon.

"Until I get my money," Nicholai had said, "I stay with my merchandise."

"I don't pay," Bay answered, "until your merchandise is safely delivered."

"So I guess you're stuck with me."

Now Nicholai lit a cigarette of his own and sat back, enjoying the relative cool of the early morning and the streaking red shafts of daylight coming over the hills. Young boys were already herding buffalo down to the river for a drink and a bath, and women were collecting buckets of the muddy water to bring back to their village.

They waited twenty minutes for the ferry to return from the other side of the river, then the heavy truck carefully drove onto the floating platform. Thick ropes on the ferry ran through large eyebolts and then out to the harnesses of elephants, one on each side. A young Lao mahout kicked his elephant in the flank and the two animals started across the river, pulling the ferry along with them.

The ferry came to a shuddering halt on the opposite bank. Two large sheets of corrugated tin were thrown down for traction, and the truck rumbled up the slope and onto a dirt road that cut up through the forest.

They climbed for five hours, slowly making their way up the switchbacks into the mountains, where limestone cliffs punctuated the otherwise green hills. Fields of dry mountain rice broke up the jungle, while other scorched patches told of primitive slash-and-burn agriculture. Men, women, and children — most of them wearing loose-fitting black jerseys, baggy black trousers, and black turbans — were out on the burned fields, hoeing away the debris and getting the rich red soil ready for planting. Small, shaggy ponies grazed the edges of the burned fields.

"Who lives here?" Nicholai asked, risking conversation.

More awake, Bay was a little more gregarious. "The Meo. They came down from Sichuan two thousand years ago."

Nicholai saw the rice fields, and small patches of potatoes and other vegetables. Then, as they climbed higher, he noticed a different crop.

Poppies.

"The Meo are also florists?" Nicholai asked dryly.

Bay chuckled. "The Viet Minh used to control the opium crop, now we do. I guess it's caused some resentment."

An hour later the road leveled onto a valley and then a broad plateau that led into a town — mostly wooden shacks and a few shops clustered around a few brick-and-tile buildings and an enormous colonial structure that looked as if it had been some kind of administrative center.

"The old French governor's palace," Bay said.

"Where are we?" Nicholai asked.

"Xieng Khouang," Bay answered. "It's about the only town up here. The French built it back in the 1880s, then the Japs took it. When they got chased out, the Pathet Lao had it for a while, until the Meo helped the French take it back."

"Why did they do that?"

"Money," Bay answered. "Why does anyone do anything?"

They drove through town without stopping. A mile outside of town they came to a large airstrip that had recently been bull-dozed out of the terrain. An American-made DC-3 with French military markings sat on the strip, guarded by French paratroopers. Other soldiers, along with Meo men, loaded crates from trucks and carts into the cargo hold.

"This you didn't see," Bay warned.

He got out of the truck. Nicholai slid out behind him and followed him across the dirt landing strip to where a paratroop captain stood, supervising the loading. The captain saw Bay Vien, walked toward him, held him by the shoulders, and kissed him on both cheeks.

Then he noticed Nicholai. "Captain Antoine Signavi."

"Michel Guibert."

They shook hands.

Signavi stood just a shade shorter than Nicholai. He wore crisp camouflage gear, jump boots, and the vermilion beret of a paratrooper. "I have some beer on ice. About the best I can do up here."

He led them just off the airstrip to a canvas canopy with a portable table and three stools. An orderly reached into an ice chest, came out with three bottles of Tiger beer, opened them, and set them on the table.

Signavi held up his bottle. "*Santé.*"

"*Santé*," Nicholai echoed.

"Three more weeks," Signavi said, "and this runway will be a river of mud. Unusable. The road up here too. Very difficult. I'll be glad to be back in Saigon."

He removed his beret, exposing a thick head of black hair.

"I have some cargo," Bay said, "to put on this flight. It's okay?"

"Sure," Signavi answered. "We're light this trip."

"And two additional passengers?"

"You and you?" Signavi asked.

Bay nodded.

Signavi looked hesitant.

"In my area of business," Nicholai said, "discretion is of the utmost importance. I see nothing and I say less."

"I'll vouch for him," Bay said.

"You can understand," Signavi said, "that this is all...sensitive. We're fighting a war, someone has to pay for it, and the Reds in Paris are unwilling to do it. So one holds one's nose and does what is necessary." He jutted his chin toward the opium being loaded onto the plane.

Nicholai shrugged. "Who am I to judge?"

"Indeed," Signavi said, his nuanced tone leaving no doubt that while he was going to tolerate this gunrunner for practical purposes, he nevertheless found it distasteful.

Nicholai wasn't willing to allow the implied insult to pass. He asked, "Signavi, is that a Corsican name?"

"Guilty," Signavi said. "Napoleon and I, we both sought our futures in the French army. We take off first thing in the morning. I'll arrange beds for tonight. I hope you will both join me for dinner."

Nicholai never ceased to marvel at the French ability to dine well under any circumstances. Here, at a secret airstrip in the middle of the Laotian highlands, emerged a lunch of vichyssoise, cold roasted guinea fowl, and a very acceptable salad made from local greens, all washed down with a decent white wine.

Dining accomplished, Signavi led them to a large barracks tent surrounded by concertina wire.

His proximity sense woke him.

He lay still and listened to the sharp *click-click* as the wire-cutters snipped the fence, then to the sound of a man crawling.

Bay Vien was sound asleep on his bed by the tent wall.

Nicholai dove just as the blade slashed through the tent. He knocked Bay off the bed onto the floor, then got up and went through the tent door.

The would-be assassin was already running back toward the fence.

A klaxon sounded and a searchlight swept the ground. Nicholai heard Alsatian dogs bark and then one burst across the stockade ground after the man. The man leapt for the fence and became entangled in the concertina wire. He twisted in the wire, a grotesque acrobatic act, as the machine-gun bullets hit him.

Signavi, clad in satin pajamas, a pistol in his hand, ran out, and a moment later Bay Vien came out of the tent and looked at the corpse hanging from the fence.

"Viet Minh," Bay said. He turned to Nicholai. "You saved my life, Guibert."

"Just looking out after my interests," Nicholai answered. He walked back into the tent and lay back down.

Bay came in. "I'm in your debt," he said.

"Forget it."

"I won't," Bay said. "It's a matter of honor."

Nicholai understood.

# 103

COLONEL YU KNOCKED on the door of Liu's office and received permission to enter.

Liu looked up from the stack of papers on his desk. "Yes?"

"The Viet Minh agent who was supposed to meet Hel was killed."

"Ah."

"So Hel didn't make the rendezvous."

"Obviously."

"There's a report," Yu said, "unverified, that he went with the Binh Xuyen."

"Stay on top of it," Liu ordered.

Yu left the room deeply troubled. If Hel was with the Binh Xuyen, he was either a prisoner or had willingly betrayed him.

# 104

THE PLANE FOLLOWED the Mekong south.

Nicholai watched out the window as the broad brown river flowed out of the mountains down into the plains of Cambodia, then broke into multiple tributaries as it entered the delta in southern Vietnam.

Looking down at the endless stretch of green rice paddies, cross-stitched with irrigation canals and dotted with innumerable villages, Nicholai knew that he had made the right decision to deal with Bay Vien.

Blockhouses and guard towers rose every two or three kilometers above the paddies, and Nicholai could spot military convoys patrolling the main roads. Not only was the Foreign Legion thick on the ground, but also the well-armed militias whose arms the French purchased from the proceeds of the opium in the plane's cargo hold.

The French army bought the opium from the Meo, purchasing their loyalty as well. Then the army sold the crop to the Binh Xuyen, who monopolized the opium traffic in Saigon. The French used the profits to pay the militias and mountain tribes to fight a guerrilla war in the countryside, while the Binh Xuyen held Saigon for them.

We would never have made it through all this, Nicholai thought, with the shipment of arms.

It was the right thing to do.

He had a dull headache that throbbed with the pulse of the engines and was exacerbated by the engine fumes. The propellers were noisy and the plane rattled and bumped, and he was glad when he saw the sprawling metropolis of greater Saigon appear below.

But the plane banked southeast, away from the city and down the coast, and Nicholai saw what looked like a military base.

"Vung Tau!" Signavi shouted over the noise. "'Cap St.-Jacques'!"

The plane made a rapid descent and landed on the military airstrip. Trucks were waiting, and Binh Xuyen troopers in green paramilitary uniforms hopped out and quickly loaded the crates of opium and rocket launchers.

"I'm off to a bath and a decent drink," Signavi said. He shook Nicholai's hand. "Perhaps I'll see you in Saigon?"

"I would enjoy that."

"Good. See you there."

A black limousine pulled up. Two troopers armed with machine pistols got out and escorted Bay and Nicholai into the back of the car and it quickly drove off the airstrip.

"Where is the cargo going?" Nicholai asked.

"The opium, to our processing plant in Cholon," Bay answered. "The weapons, somewhere safe."

"Until I've been paid," Nicholai said, "the rocket launchers are still my property, and as such, I have a right to know where they are."

Bay nodded. "Fair enough. They're going to the Rung Sat—'the Swamp of the Assassins.'"

"Colorful."

"It's the base of the Binh Xuyen," Bay said, smiling. "Remember, we started as 'river pirates.' Your property will be quite safe there."

"When do I get paid?" Nicholai asked.

"Do you have an account in Saigon?"

"I prefer cash."

"As you wish," Bay said. "It's nothing to me. I'll arrange for payment tomorrow. Meet me at my casino, Le Grand Monde."

"What do I have as security?"

Bay turned and glared at him. "My word."

# 105

SAIGON WAS beautiful.

Nicholai thought the city's sobriquet as "the Pearl of the Orient" was perfectly justified as he rode in a blue Renault taxi down the Rue Catinat.

The broad boulevard—lined with plane trees, studded with sidewalk cafés, bars, restaurants, expensive shops, and exclusive hotels—seemed a perfect blend of French and Asian culture, as if someone had chosen the best of both and placed them in happy harmony, side by side.

Vietnamese police, in their distinctive white uniforms, stoically struggled to manage the swirling Citroën and Renault autos, *cyclo-pousses*, Vespa scooters, and swarms of bicycles that competed for the right-of-way in a chaos that was a true mixture of the French and Asian styles of driving. Honking horns, jingling bells, and shouts of good-natured abuse in French, Vietnamese, and Chinese contributed to an urban cacophony.

Child street vendors darted and dodged through the traffic to sell newspapers, bottles of orange soda, or cigarettes to customers momentarily stuck in a jam, or sitting at a café table, or just walking down the busy sidewalks.

The women were magnificent, Nicholai thought—slim, tiny Vietnamese in tight silk *ao dais* stopped to window shop, while the elegant French *colons*, dressed in fashion only a year removed from Paris runways, strode in their slow, long-legged gait to the unabashed, admiring stares of the café denizens.

The cab pulled up to the Continental Hotel, a broad white colonial building in the Beaux-Arts style, with its arched windows and pedimented doors. It was the *apero* hour, that time in the late afternoon when the privileged classes sought refuge from the heat and the day's work, and all the smarter types gathered on the Continental's broad café terrace that flanked the boulevard. Just across Catinat from the USIS office, the Continental was a convenient place to have a drink, exchange information and intelligence (to such an extent that the café was nicknamed "Radio Catinat"), or perhaps to find a companion to share a table now or a bed later.

Ellis Haverford looked through the anti-grenade netting to observe the new arrival as Nicholai unfolded himself from the backseat of the small car. He was dressed like a classic Southeast Asian *colon*, in the clothes that he had bought in Luang Prabang. Vietnamese bellboys in short white jackets and black trousers ran out to take his luggage and take it into the lobby.

I'm glad to see you, Nicholai, Haverford thought.

He had been reasonably sure that Hel would come to Saigon, but it was good to know he was right.

Nicholai walked past a rather surprising bronze statue of Napoleon to the reception desk.

"Monsieur Guibert?" The *métis* clerk smiled. He had received a call from Bay Vien himself and was appropriately obsequious. "Welcome to the Continental. It is our pleasure to have you."

"Thank you."

"Your room is ready," the clerk said. "And Monsieur Mancini invites you to have a drink with him, if it is convenient for you. In the bar? Six o'clock?"

"Please relay my honored acceptance," Nicholai said. Signavi had apparently wasted no time informing his Corsican colleagues of his arrival in the city.

Mathieu Mancini had come to Saigon after World War I, married a wealthy Vietnamese woman, and bought the Continental. Reputed to be the head of L'Union Corse, the Corsican mafia, in Saigon he was a confidant of Bao Dai's.

And a friend to Bay Vien.

A bellhop took Nicholai to his room on the fourth and top floor. It was large and high-ceilinged, with whitewashed walls and simple but elegant wooden furniture. French doors opened onto a small, private balcony behind iron grillwork. A ceiling fan circulated the humid air, providing some relief.

Nicholai tipped the bellboy and then was glad for some privacy and solitude. He called room service for an iced beer, drew a steaming hot bath, and luxuriated in it for half an hour.

It was good to be in a city again and experience some luxury and sophistication that he hadn't known since Shanghai. The contrast between the near-scalding water and the cold beer was a sharp delight, and Nicholai allowed himself to give in to the realm of the senses for a few minutes.

Then he evaluated the Go board.

He had advanced his position. I'm safely out of China, he thought, have funds—or will have tomorrow—and am in Saigon with Bay Vien as a patron and protector.

Good and good.

And Solange is likely somewhere in the city.

Better.

But my position is nevertheless precarious.

Haverford is sitting in the bar across the street, apparently unconcerned with being discovered. He knows I'm alive and where I am. Beijing and Moscow will soon know, if they don't already, and might well send people to kill or kidnap me. Of the two, the Chinese are the greater threat as the Russians will have a problem getting agents into Saigon.

The "Guibert" cover has a short life. I need a new identity, and quickly, if I'm ever to get out of Saigon. And before I leave, I have things to accomplish.

But all that is several moves off, he reminded himself. The next part of the game is to see what Mancini wants.

The Corsican greeted him warmly.

"Monsieur Guibert," Mancini said. He kissed Nicholai on both checks, patted him on the shoulders, and continued, "Welcome, welcome."

Mancini smelled of cologne and tobacco.

"Thank you, Monsieur Mancini."

"Call me Mathieu, please."

"I'm Michel."

The Continental's owner was short but looked immensely powerful, barrel-chested with the big, sloping shoulders of a former boxer. A few strands of silver glistened at the temples of thick black hair that was slicked straight back. His off-white cotton suit and monogrammed white shirt were beautifully cut, and he saw that Nicholai noticed.

"I'll introduce you to my tailor," Mancini said. "Vietnamese guy at the 'Botany' shop, just down Catinat."

"I would appreciate that."

"You're new to Saigon?"

"First time here."

"You're in for a treat," Mancini said. "It's a beautiful city, beautiful. So many pleasures on offer."

And which, Nicholai wondered, are you going to offer me?

"*Pastaga?*" Mancini asked, using Marseille slang for pastis. He searched Nicholai's eyes for any blink of incomprehension.

"I could do with a pastis," Nicholai answered. Solange had covered the word with him many times and familiarized him with the thick yellow liqueur, a close cousin of absinthe.

"Ah, you're from the south," Mancini said.

"Montpellier," Nicholai said, deciding to end the honeymoon. "But you knew that already."

"I know everything, young man," Mancini said amiably. "Come on, then. I won't insult you with the crap we serve the *colons*. The real stuff is out here."

As he led Nicholai out of the bar into a private garden, Mancini said, "Me, I'm from Corsica originally. But you already knew that. Did you also know that Corsicans make the best assassins in the world?"

"Is that right?" Nicholai answered. He wondered what the ninja might have to say about it.

"Take it as a fact."

And a warning, Nicholai thought.

They walked into a narrow strip of garden where several older men sat around two white wrought-iron tables. The men all wore white short-sleeved shirts and either white or light khaki loose-fitting trousers. A couple of them sported broad-brimmed hats for protection against the sun.

Nicholai knew that he was looking at L'Union Corse.

Mancini took off his jacket, draped it on the back of a chair, sat down, and gestured for Nicholai to do likewise.

"This is my newest guest," Mancini said as Nicholai took a chair. "Michel Guibert."

He introduced each of the five men — Antonucci, Guarini, Ribieri, Sarti, Luciani — each of whom offered a hand with a gruff nod. Mancini filled Nicholai's glass with pastis. The men looked on as Nicholai took the carafe of water set on the table and poured some in to dilute his drink. Then he raised the glass, said, "*Salut*," and sipped. His familiarity with the *pastaga* seemed to relax the group, who sat back in the chairs, drank, and took the sun.

"So," Mancini said, "what brings you to Saigon?"

"Business," Nicholai answered.

"How is your father?" asked Antonucci.

Antonucci looked to be in his early fifties, and was as skinny as Mancini was stout. But the deeply tanned forearms under his rolled-up sleeves looked like iron, and despite his casual but expensive clothes, the man looked like he could be a day laborer.

"He's well," Nicholai responded. "You know him?"

"We've done business," Antonucci said. "In the past."

"Well," Nicholai said, raising his glass, "here's to the future."

They drank a round. Then Antonucci raised his glass toward Mancini and said, "To my new neighbor."

Mancini explained to Nicholai. "After years of trying, I just managed to acquire the Majestic Hotel, next door to Antonucci's nightclub."

"Your nightclub?" Nicholai asked.

"La Croix du Sud," Antonucci said, then added pointedly, "In the Corsican quarter, on the harbor. Where all the imports and exports come and go."

"You'd like his club," Mancini said to Nicholai. "One of those pleasures we talked about."

"Come tonight," Antonucci said.

"Tonight?" Nicholai asked.

Antonucci leaned across the table and looked Nicholai full in the face. "Tonight."

*    *    *

A little while later, Mancini and Antonucci went out the back gate and strolled across the broad Opera Square. On the other side, the Saigon Opera House loomed in all its French colonial glory. The other Corsicans had drifted home. It was that hour, "the hour of the pipe," and these longtime residents of Saigon had acquired many local habits.

"What do you think?" Mancini asked.

"Smart young man," Antonucci said, pausing for a moment to relight his cigar. "Maybe we can make some money with him."

They walked across the square, quiet now in the torpid hour before the cool of evening would bring out young lovers, old strollers, people looking for relaxation and those searching for excitement.

In his lifetime Antonucci had seen many things. He had started life as a shoeless shepherd, but soon decided that a life of barefoot labor and drudgery was not for him. So he hopped a freighter to Indochina, jumped ship in Saigon, and within two years turned the gaggle of girls he pimped into a prosperous brothel. He used those proceeds to buy the Croix du Sud, the Southern Cross, which turned a profit of its own but really served to launder the money he made with Mancini smuggling heroin and gold into Marseille.

They bought the heroin directly from the French army. Bay Vien bought the bulk of it, but La Corse purchased the surplus. The profits were enormous, even after the hefty cut that went to Bao Dai. They used the money to buy yet more clubs, restaurants, and hotels. Mancini had the Continental and now the Majestic, Luciani owned the Palace. It wouldn't be long before the Corsicans had a monopoly on Saigon's hosting business. Their children, or at least their grandchildren, would be restaurateurs and hoteliers instead of dope and currency smugglers.

It was a good life, and he had survived the French, then the Japanese, briefly the British (who were fools anyway), and then the French again. Now the French, desperate for allies, turned a blind eye to the heroin, and the Corsicans had forged a working relationship with the Binh Xuyen and Bao Dai.

All this could end if the Communists won and took over the country, but still Antonucci thought he could work out an accommodation with them. Asia was Asia, and life would go on as usual. Communist or no, men would still want women and money.

Corsica had been conquered by everybody — Greeks, Romans, Arabs, Turks, Normans, French, Germans — and the Corsicans were used to working out a way of living with all of them. It was a national trait, an innate talent.

But now the Americans were edging out the French, and that was a different story. *Les amerloques*, the "crazy Americans," were impractical, puritanical, and moralistic. They would seek to dump Bao Dai and put in their own man, sweep the carpet clean.

And now this young Guibert had turned up and the rumor was that he had sold a shipment of stolen American arms to Bay Vien. "We should find out more about this Guibert. Use the Belgian dwarf, I can't think of his name…"

"De Lhandes," Mancini said. "Odd little fellow. But he seems to sniff out everything."

"Useful."

"Very useful."

Guibert might be just what he claims to be, the heir to his family's gunrunning business. But then again, perhaps he is an agent of French intelligence. The Deuxième Bureau, SDECE, or perhaps the Sûreté. Or does he serve the Americans, as so much of the world seems to do these days? Maybe he is simply a young man on the make. In which case we can make some money together.

"I already did," Mancini answered. "Even before he arrived. The dwarf says that he appears to be who he says he is. Bay Vien's people say the same thing. I had his room searched while we were having *pastaga*."

We shall see, Antonucci thought. He looked at Mancini and uttered the ancient words. "*Per tu amicu*."

"*Per tu amicu*," Mancini ritually responded.

For your friendship.

# 106

His room had been tossed.

Carefully and professionally, Nicholai observed, but tossed nevertheless. Before leaving the room he had plucked a hair from his head and placed it across two drawers on his bureau, and now the hair was gone.

It didn't matter — they would find nothing they weren't supposed to find.

Had Mancini ordered it? Probably, although it could have been the French, who had a veritable alphabet soup of police and intelligence services in Saigon, none of whom were known to be overly respectful of privacy.

And the Corsican mob expects my presence at La Croix du Sud tonight. For what purpose? To be grilled, seduced, observed, threatened, perhaps assassinated? Again, it didn't matter — to complete his assignment he would have to do business in Saigon, and the Corsicans had made it very clear that he couldn't do business in Saigon without doing business with them.

Leave it to later, he told himself. You have something else to do now.

He splashed some water on his face to wipe off the sweat and the slightly dizzying effect of the pastis, then went downstairs and out onto the street.

Rue Catinat was amber in the late dusk as the streetlights came on. Nicholai took a moment to orient himself. On one end of the boulevard was the harbor, on the other end the distinctive twin spires of the Cathedral de Notre Dame.

A five-block walk took him to a shop called International Philately. The man behind the counter was a turbaned Sikh. The three shelves of the glass counter held frames of postage stamps, most of them rare, many of them expensive.

"How may I help you, sir?"

"I was hoping," Nicholai said, using the code that Yu had given him to contact the Viet Minh, "that you might have a 1914 'Mythen'?"

"Blue or green, sir?"

"Green."

"Green" meant that he was under no immediate danger and that it was safe to proceed.

"I will need to check in the back, please."

"Thank you."

The man was gone for less than a minute and returned with a thin glassine envelope. He carefully opened it and showed Nicholai the block of stamps. Nicholai held it up to the desk lamp for inspection and said, "Yes, I'll have them."

"Five hundred and forty piastres, please."

Nicholai paid him.

The Sikh returned the stamps to the glassine envelope, sealed it, and then slipped it into a larger, padded envelope that he handed to Nicholai. Nicholai put the envelope into his jacket pocket and left. He stopped at a newspaper kiosk, bought that day's edition of the *Journal d'Extrême-Orient* and a packet of Cigarettes Nationales, then went farther down the street, found a table at a café called La Pagode, and ordered a beer.

He opened his paper, read for a moment until the beer—wonderfully cold—arrived. Then he took out the envelope and, using the paper to shield his hands from view, opened it and read what was written on the inside flap of the larger envelope:

*One o'clock tomorrow, go to Sarreau's Pharmacie. Buy two packets of enterovioform, then walk to the Neptuna Swimming Pool and wait.*

Vietnamese women, stunningly elegant wrapped in silk, strolled slowly by, shy but fully aware of their effect. Then there were the *métis*— the mixed heritage of Asia and Europe— impossibly beautiful with their golden complexions and almond eyes, which in their glint seemed to say that East and West can definitely meet and that it is indeed possible to have the best of both worlds. And the occasional *colon* woman with blonde hair like Solange.

Nicholai felt a tinge of guilt along with the physical stirring.

But if the coming of night signaled a certain sexual excitement, it also meant danger, and the Vietnamese police and French army patrols also came out, a prosaic reminder that this beautiful city was also a city at war. The restaurants on the boulevard sported anti-grenade screens, and the eyes of the police showed not the usual boredom of merely walking the beat but an alertness to genuine threat. The Binh Xuyen rode up and down the street in their green Jeeps, a few with machine guns mounted on the back.

Nicholai finished his beer, left a few piastres, and headed out.

# 107

Bernard De Lhandes found the Saigon chief of SDECE in his office.

Service de Documentation Extérieure et de Contre-Espionage. Only the French bureaucracy, De Lhandes thought, could come up with that title.

*Sans prélude*, De Lhandes took the bottle of cassis from the desktop, helped himself to a glass, and folded his thin frame into a chair. The air around the desk was thick with smoke, and Colonel Raynal's ashtray was already overflowing.

Raynal was a fat man with dark, heavy rings under his eyes. De Lhandes thought that both conditions came from his spending countless hours behind his desk, smoking cigarettes and eating bad food as he went over the stacks of reports that came through every day. If you were charged with keeping up with all the espionage in Saigon, you were charged with a lot.

"There's a new player in town," De Lhandes said. The Corsicans had asked him to find out what he could about this Guibert, and De Lhandes was in the business of buying and selling information. If he could do both at the same time, all the better.

Raynal sighed. There were already too many *old* players in town, a new one was the last thing he needed. "And who would that be?"

"Something called a 'Michel Guibert,'" De Lhandes said. "He turned up at the Continental."

Raynal resisted the bait. "Probably just some businessman."

"Probably," De Lhandes agreed as he helped himself to another drink and one of Raynal's cigarettes. "But he joined the Corsicans for their afternoon pastis."

Raynal sighed again. A true Parisian, he despised Corsicans as a matter of social duty, and resented that his job forced him to at least tolerate, if not actively cooperate with, them here in Saigon. "What do they want with this . . . Guibert, was it?"

"It was," De Lhandes said. "And who knows?"

Who does know, De Lhandes pondered, what L'Union Corse is ever up to? It has its greasy fingers into every pie. He slumped a little more into the chair and contemplated the slow circulation of the ceiling fan.

Raynal had a fondness for the Belgian dwarf, and he was useful. A few piastres here and there, a few chips at the casinos, a girl tossed in occasionally, it was little enough. And Raynal needed assets just now, especially the sort that warned him of newcomers.

"Operation X" — could we have come up with a less creative name? — was running smoothly and nothing must be allowed to interfere with that, he thought. If "X" failed, we could very well lose the war, with it Indochina, and with that any vestiges of a French Empire.

Personally he didn't give a damn — he would much rather be drinking at a civilized *boîte* in Montparnasse, but professionally it mattered to him a great deal. His job was to defeat the Viet Minh insurgency in the south, and if that meant distasteful operations like the certainly distasteful "X," then *c'est la guerre*.

And De Lhandes brought old news. Signavi had already called to report that this Guibert had apparently sold weapons to Bay Vien and had witnessed X's operation in Laos. Raynal had questioned Signavi's judgment in allowing Guibert to actually fly in with the opium shipment, but Signavi answered that Bay Vien had given him little choice.

"De Lhandes?"

"Yes?"

"Would you mind going around and having a drink or something with this Guibert?" Raynal asked. "Sound him out?"

"If you'd like, Patrice."

"Please."

"Of course."

Raynal opened a desk drawer, pulled out a used envelope, and slid it across the desk. "For your expenses."

De Lhandes took the money.

# 108

Xue Xin clipped a vine away from the stone and looked up to see a novice monk approaching.

"What is it?" he asked, unhappy to be interrupted.

"I have a message for you."

"Well, what is it?"

"I am instructed to tell you," the boy said, looking puzzled, "that 'the Go stones are pearls.'"

"Thank you."

The boy stood there.

"You may go," Xue Xin said.

He returned to his work and smiled.

Nicholai Hel was in Saigon.

# 109

DIAMOND RECEIVED THE CABLE and went straight to Single-ton's office. He cooled his heels in the waiting room for a good forty minutes until the receptionist told him he could go in.

The old man didn't look up from the briefing book that he was reading. "Yes?"

"Hel is in Saigon."

Now Singleton looked up. "Really?"

The boss was in one of his moods, in which every response came in the form of a single-word interrogative. Diamond continued, "Sir, he seems to have arrived on a French military flight with a shipment of weapons, rumored to be rocket launchers."

That information made Singleton somewhat more expansive. "Where did the flight originate?"

"X.K."

"Would that be an initialization of 'Xieng Khouang'?"

"Yes, sir."

Singleton thought for a moment. "Well, that's not good."

"No, it isn't."

It was especially not good, Diamond thought, as he hadn't received this information from Haverford but from Signavi, who had phoned him shortly after Hel left Cap St.-Jacques. The Frenchman had asked him to find out everything he could about this Michel Guibert. Signavi was worried about Guibert's alleged prior relationship with the Viet Minh, especially with the agent

Ai Quoc. Signavi's Vietnamese special forces troops had been hunting Ai Quoc for months, to no avail.

"Who is in possession of the weapons now?" Singleton asked.

"The BX," Diamond answered. Seeing Singleton's annoyed look he added, "The Binh Xuyen."

"Hel is creative."

"That's one word for it."

"Do you have a better word in mind?"

"No, sir."

Singleton sat back and thought. This Hel person is really quite remarkable, he decided.

Remarkable, unpredictable, and dangerous.

"Take care of it," Singleton said.

"What should I tell Haverford?"

Singleton pondered Hel's remarkable escape from Beijing. "Why tell him anything?"

He went back to reading the briefing book.

Diamond stood there for a couple of seconds before figuring out that he'd been dismissed. Feeling the receptionist's contemptuous look on his back, he hurried out of the office and into the elevator, discovered that he was in a sweat, and wiped his forehead with the back of his hand.

Then he realized that it was all working out. Hel would finally be terminated and...

But what if Hel talked to Haverford about what he had seen in Laos.

And what if Singleton ever found out that...

He left the office and booked himself on a military flight to Saigon.

The supposedly brilliant Hel had walked right into his trap.

# 110

Cities, Nicholai pondered as he walked along Boulevard Bonard, are like women of a certain age.

The evening masks the signs of aging, smoothes over lines, shades decay, replicates the golden glow of young years. So it was in Saigon, which at night became a lady in a basic black dress, with diamonds around her neck.

Haverford was doubtless a fine intelligence agent, but he made a damn poor street operative, and his clumsy efforts to follow Nicholai were almost comical. Nicholai quickly grew bored of the game, however, and literally turned on him near the clock tower outside the central marketplace.

He looked to be alone, but Nicholai scanned the crowd for signs of other agents. It would be almost impossible to tell, he had to admit. They could be mixed among any of the shoppers or merchants in the busy pavilion. But he looked for the overly watchful, the purposefully disinterested, or anyone who made even glancing eye contact with Haverford.

Nicholai eased into the crowd, circled, and came up behind him.

"Don't turn around," Nicholai said. "And walk."

"Easy," Haverford said. But he kept walking. Nevertheless, he took the offensive. "Where have you been? I've been worried about you."

"After setting me up to be killed? I'm touched."

"I don't know what happened in Beijing," Haverford said. "We had an extraction team in place and then you just went off the radar."

"You had an *assassination* team in place."

"What are you talking about?" Haverford asked as they walked past stands selling everything from cold soup to silk parasols. "If something went wrong in Beijing, it had nothing to do with us."

But Haverford had to wonder. Was it possible that stupid bastard Diamond had co-opted the extraction team in an attempt to terminate Hel? What are you thinking? he asked himself. Of course it's possible. And now Hel blames you.

Nicholai herded him out onto the street. Boulevard de la Somme was busy with evening traffic. If Haverford was going to try anything, it would have been in the market. "You can turn around."

Haverford, a look of hurt innocence in his eyes, turned to face him. "You have this all wrong. I don't know what happened back there. Maybe Chinese intelligence made you, somebody flipped, I don't know. How did you get—"

"You owe me money," Nicholai said, "a new passport, and certain addresses in the United States. I'll forgive the monetary debt, but—"

There it is, Haverford thought. Hel had done just what I figured he'd do. Amazing—and characteristic. "Nicholai, did you bring those weapons into—"

"I will require the passport and the addresses."

"Of course," Haverford said, "There's no problem with that. The sooner the better, in fact. You have to go underground, Nick. The whole world is looking for you."

Nicholai suspected that by "underground" Haverford meant "under the ground," but in either case had little choice but to go along. "How soon can you get me the addresses and the papers?"

"Tomorrow," Haverford answered. "Or the next day, at the latest. I'll set up a meeting point—"

"I'll tell you when and where," Nicholai said. Then he asked, "Where is Solange?"

"I don't know. Why—"

"Don't lie to me, I don't like it," Nicholai snapped. "You brought her here, knowing I would come."

"You have it all wrong, Nicholai."

"Yes, I had Beijing all wrong, too, didn't I?"

He saw a *cyclo-pousse* coming down the street, flagged it down, and moved Haverford out to the curb. "Get in."

"I don't—"

"Get in."

Haverford got in.

When he turned back around, Hel had disappeared.

# 111

Yu received the message from Saigon.

Hel had made contact.

You are an interesting man, Nicholai Hel, he thought.

# 112

HAVERFORD SAT in the back of the *cyclo-pousse* and contemplated the state of Nicholai Hel's mind.

Had he come to Saigon for Solange?

Or for other reasons?

And, if so, what were they?

As for Solange, how — and why — had she come to Saigon, and what was she doing? He recalled Singleton's orders back in Washington. *You're clever young men. Lure him in.*

Well, it looks like we both did.

# 113

Nicholai felt at ease in Cholon.

The Chinese quarter of the city, it reminded him of a damper, poorer Shanghai in the old days. The little stands and small shops were the same, the neon signs the same, the smells of cooking over charcoal, the incense wafting from temples, the shouts, the laughter, the crowding — it all reminded him that the Chinese were great wanderers, pilgrims who took their culture with them and replicated their old cities in the new.

He walked along Lao Tu Street, the main thoroughfare, and felt right at home. Cholon was reputed to be dangerous at night, particularly for a *kweilo*, but Nicholai had never felt threatened even in the worst slums of Shanghai and he didn't feel in jeopardy here, even as he turned off the street and walked up narrow alleys into a neighborhood of four-story tenements.

Again, they all looked the same — rectangular wooden structures with tiny balconies from which laundry was hung. Men in sleeveless T-shirts leaned against the railings, smoking cigarettes, women inside yelled domestic questions in an attempt to engage their husbands in at least some form of conversation.

On the street itself, young toughs in brightly colored shirts and tight slacks gathered on the corners watching for opportunities, but didn't see one in the tall *colon* who walked as if he knew where he was going and what he was doing. And he greeted them in Chinese as he walked past. They left him alone.

Nicholai found the address he was looking for.

The tiny lobby reeked of stale opium smoke.

Nicholai walked up the creaking, slanting staircase to the second floor. The hallway was narrow and slanted, as if it was tired and wanted to lie down. A door opened and a woman, clad in the tight red silk dress of a prostitute, looked at him for a moment, then continued down the hall.

Nicholai knocked on the door of Room 211.

No one answered. He knocked twice more, then opened the unlocked door.

Leotov sat dozing in a rattan chair by the small window. The room was sweltering and tight, and Leotov's bare chest was shiny with sweat. He wore a pair of khaki trousers and sandals, his face was sallow, and he hadn't shaved for several days.

The opium pipe was in his lap.

He opened his eyes and saw Nicholai. His eyes were yellow and runny, but wide in the dreamlike state of the opium addict.

"Where the hell have you been?" he muttered in Russian. "I thought you were probably dead."

"There were moments when we shared that opinion."

"I've been here for weeks," Leotov said bitterly, clearly blaming his opium habit on Nicholai's lack of promptness.

"I was detained," Nicholai answered. "I didn't count on being so seriously wounded. It delayed me by weeks. Nevertheless, I apologize — it is good of you to have waited."

Leotov slowly pulled himself up from the chair and shuffled around the room, as if looking for something but unable to remember what or where it was. "You don't know what it's been like," he whined, "being on the run, having to hide in this hovel, never knowing when . . . I took recourse in the local vice."

Nicholai could virtually smell the fear and paranoia coming off him. "I see that."

"Superior bastard," Leotov spat. "You and him, both superior bastards."

The "him," Nicholai supposed, referred to the late Yuri Voroshenin. But he was already bored with Leotov. "Do you have them?"

"I have them," Leotov said.

As arranged in their encounter in Beijing, Leotov had taken Voroshenin's passport and personal papers, including his deposit book at the Banque de l'Indochine in Saigon, where the Russian had not only an account but a safety deposit box.

"So?"

"I'm looking, aren't I?"

He shoved aside some clothes on the floor and came up with a small leather portfolio that he held up in triumph. "Here you go. Here's your precious papers. Bastards, the both of you."

Nicholai took the portfolio and flipped through it. Voroshenin's passport, several bankbooks, scribbled notes.

"Where's my money?"

Nicholai took bills from his pocket and handed them to Leotov.

"Where's the rest of it?" Leotov demanded.

"Our arrangement," Nicholai reminded him, "was one-third now, the rest when I successfully gain access to the safety deposit box."

The documents looked authentic, but there was no telling until they were put to use.

"When will that be?" Leotov asked.

"Tomorrow. I'll meet you somewhere."

"I can barely get organized to make it out of this room."

"You get out to buy opium, don't you?" Nicholai asked.

"A boy comes." Leotov chuckled. "Room service."

I should kill him, Nicholai thought. That would be the smart thing to do, and perhaps the kind thing as well. An opium addict is a loose cannon, a mentally incontinent creature who will open his mouth and tell anything to anyone.

He doubted that Leotov could, in fact, make it across the river to collect the rest of his fee for delivering Voroshenin's documents, but a deal was a deal. "I can wire you funds here if you prefer. A neighborhood bank."

"If I prefer," Leotov mumbled, "if I prefer. Where is that damn boy? Do you happen to have the time? I seem to have misplaced my watch."

Nicholai knew the watch had been "misplaced" at the pawn-shop, or simply taken by the opium delivery boy or any other resident of the flophouse while Leotov was in an opium dream. He looked at his watch and answered, "Eight-thirty."

"Where is that boy?" Leotov asked. "Doesn't he know I need . . . I need that money to get out of this shithole, find a safe place, not looking over my shoulder every second . . ."

"I recommend Costa Rica," Nicholai said.

Leotov wasn't listening. He sank back into his chair and stared out the window. Nicholai took the bills clutched in his hand and stuffed them into his trouser pocket, giving him at least a chance of retaining them.

Then Nicholai took his leave.

He walked past the boy coming up the stairs.

## 114

THE FRENCH SAXOPHONE PLAYER licked her lips, glanced at Nicholai, and then wrapped them around her mouthpiece and blew.

Nicholai, seated at a front-row table at La Croix du Sud, couldn't miss the unsubtle gesture, smiled back, and sipped his brandy and soda, the club specialty. The all-female band — twelve Frenchwomen in high-cut sequined gowns — were quite good at the Glenn Miller and Tommy Dorsey swing tunes.

Then Nicholai saw a gnomelike man, a dwarf with long hair, a red beard, and an enormously corpulent stomach, waddle his way toward the table on short, bowed legs. Sweat poured down his fat cheeks, and he looked like nothing more than a small, hirsute locomotive about to derail.

"No hunting there," he said amiably as he sat down and jutted his chin toward the band. "That's Antonucci's private reserve."

"All twelve?"

"He's a virile little man."

The saxophone player eyed him again.

"She's just being friendly," Nicholai said.

"She'll get a beating if she gets any friendlier," De Lhandes answered. "If you want a woman —"

"I don't."

The dwarf offered his hand. "Bernard De Lhandes, formerly of Brussels, now consigned to this gustatory backwater, where the charm of the women is in direct inverse ratio to the banality of the cuisine. By the salty tears of Saint Timothy, how a refined gourmand is expected to inflict a death from gluttony upon himself in this place I'll never know. Although I try, I try."

"Michel Guibert." Nicholai lifted his glass. "*Santé.*"

"*Santé.*"

"*Comment ça va?*"

"As well as can be expected," the gnome huffed, "considering that I just dined — if one wishes to call it 'dining' — at Le Givral, and all I can say is that whoever conspired to commit the aioli sauce must have been born somewhere in the less enlightened regions of Sicily — presumably in some village whose benighted inhabitants are congenitally deprived of both taste buds and olfactory perception — as the balance, or rather the lack thereof, of the garlic and olive oil smacked of sheer barbarism."

Nicholai laughed, which encouraged De Lhandes to continue his diatribe.

"The fact that I nevertheless managed to consume the entire boiled fish and a leg of lamb," De Lhandes said, "the mediocrity of which would have brought tears of boredom to the eyes of a perpetual shut-in, is a testament to both my tolerance and my gluttony, the latter of which qualities I possess in far greater measure than the former."

De Lhandes was pleasant company. A stringer for several wire services, he was based in Saigon to cover "the damn war." Over drinks, he filled Nicholai in on the *status quo bellum*.

The Viet Minh were strong in the north, and that was where most of the fighting was. They were weak in the south, especially in the Mekong Delta area, but still capable of staging guerrilla assaults in the countryside and terror attacks — bombs, grenades, that sort of thing — in Saigon. The legendary guerrilla leader, Ai Quoc, had gone into hiding, but the rumor was that he was planning a new offensive in the delta.

On the political side, Bao Dai was a French puppet, far more interested in graft, gambling, and high-priced call girls than in attempting to actually govern, much less win independence from France. If you believed the rumors — and De Lhandes believed them — he used the huge subsidies that the Americans paid him to buy real estate in France. He was also partnered with Bay Vien and the Union Corse, getting a profitable cut from the opium that the former sold in Vietnam and the latter shipped to France and then the United States in the form of heroin.

In exchange, the two criminal organizations helped him keep order in Saigon, including Cholon, the Chinese quarter on the other side of the Saigon River.

"Home ground of the Binh Xuyen," De Lhandes said, "but the best food, casinos, and brothels."

"And beyond that?"

"The Rung Sat," De Lhandes replied. "'The Swamp of the Assassins.' There you never go, *mon pote*. Or if you do, you never come back."

The conversation lapsed as they sat back and enjoyed the rather sexy orchestra. They weren't alone in that. At the bar, a large and raucous group of what appeared to be off-duty French soldiers looked on in appreciation, grateful to see European women. At other tables sat men who looked like they might be journalists or government workers. Or spies, Nicholai thought, like De Lhandes.

The "stringer" was subtle, for a European. He had gently tried to sound Nicholai out, find out what he was doing, and Nicholai had given him little or nothing, beyond the fact that he was looking for "business opportunities."

Now De Lhandes said, "Drugs, guns, women, and money."

"I'm sorry?"

"You said you were looking for business opportunities," De Lhandes said. "The best opportunities in Saigon are in running opium, arms, whores, or currency."

He looked for Nicholai's reaction.

There was none.

The music ended and the band took a break. A waiter came over to Nicholai and said, "Monsieur Antonucci would like to see you in the back."

Nicholai got up from his chair.

So did De Lhandes.

The waiter shook his head.

"Him," he said, jutting his chin at Nicholai. "Not you."

De Lhandes shrugged, and then said, "I'm going out for a night in Cholon, if you care to join me. I can be found at L'Arc-en-Ciel. Any cabbie will know it."

"I don't know."

De Lhandes said, "We'll make a night of it. A few drinks, maybe some gambling at Le Grand Monde. My pal Haverford is meeting me. Good man — he says he's some sort of diplomat but of course he's a spy."

"It sounds like fun," Nicholai said, "but I —"

"Oh, come along," De Lhandes said. "Rumor is that Bao Dai himself will be there. Not a bad connection for a man hoping to set himself up in business here."

"I'll try," Nicholai said.

He followed the waiter to the back room.

# 115

Nicholai sat down across the desk from Antonucci.

"You like my place?" the Corsican asked.

"It's quite good, yes," Nicholai answered.

The small backroom office was surprisingly cluttered. Somehow Nicholai had expected a neater, more businesslike atmosphere. The desk was a shambles of documents, letters, old newspapers, and overflowing ashtrays. A lamp, its shade stained with dead bugs, hung over the desk.

One of Antonucci's thugs—a tall, thick man—leaned against the wall, the bulge in his jacket doubtless intentional. Antonucci relit his cigar, rolling it carefully around the flame of his lighter. Satisfied with the even burn, he turned his attention back to Nicholai and said, "You're a young man. Ambitious."

"Is that a problem?"

Antonucci shrugged. "Maybe. Maybe not."

He waited for a response, but Nicholai knew that any response to such a wide opening gambit could only be a mistake. So he sipped his brandy and waited for Antonucci to move the next stone.

"Ambition is good in a young man," Antonucci said, "if he is mature enough to know that with ambition should come respect."

"Youth thinks it invents the world," Nicholai said. "Maturity respects the world that it finds. I didn't come to Saigon to change it or to disrespect its traditions, Monsieur Antonucci."

"I am glad to hear that," Antonucci said. "Tradition is that no one conducts certain kinds of trade in Saigon without paying respect to certain other people."

So, Nicholai thought, the Union Corse already knows about my deal with the Binh Xuyen. Did Bay Vien inform them, or was it their fellow Corsican Signavi? Nicholai would place his money on the latter. "If certain men traditionally control, for example, the armaments trade — 'men of respect,' shall we call them — then that is one tradition that a young man would certainly wish to honor."

"You are wise beyond your years."

"Not to put too fine a point on it," Nicholai said, "what is the percentage on tradition here?"

"I am told that it depends," Antonucci said, "on the particular cargo that is going in and out. But, say, three percent is traditional. So I hear, anyway."

"Three?" Nicholai raised an eyebrow.

"Three."

Nicholai raised his glass. "To tradition, then."

"To tradition," Antonucci said. "*Per tu amicu.*"

Nicholai downed his brandy and stood up. "I've taken too much of your time. Thank you for seeing me and providing me with your wise counsel."

Antonucci nodded.

After Nicholai left, Antonucci told his thug, "Tell Yvette I wish to see her on the next break."

Fifteen minutes later the saxophone player came into the office.

"You make eyes at strangers?" Antonucci asked her.

"No! I was just trying to be hospitable to the customers!"

He slid his belt from its loops and doubled it over.

# 116

So, NICHOLAI THOUGHT as he walked out to find a cab, L'Union Corse wants its cut.

Why not? The cost of doing business.

He got into the back of the blue Renault, which took him down Gallieni Boulevard, across the Dakow Bridge, and back into Cholon.

The cab pulled up on Trun Hung Dao Street by a two-story art deco building with a gaudy mauve-and-green façade. Nicholai went into L'Arc-en-Ciel, through the long grenade-screened terrace into the restaurant, and upstairs to the nightclub. The bar was packed with attractive Chinese prostitutes in skintight *cheong-sams* who struggled to chat up customers over the loud Filipino orchestra's dismemberment of Artie Shaw hits.

De Lhandes was at the bar.

"What are you drinking?" he asked Nicholai.

"What should I be drinking?"

"Well, they have Tiger and Kadling beer," De Lhandes answered, "*cold*, but they make a mean gin fizz."

"I'll have one of those, then," Nicholai said, taking some piastres from his pocket. "May I?"

"You're a gentleman."

Nicholai ordered and paid for two gin fizzes, then, in Chinese, politely declined the invitation of a working girl who tried to perch herself on his lap and offered carnal delights previously unheard of in the mundane world.

"You are a man of iron will," De Lhandes observed. "A veritable fortress of restraint."

"I will admit it is tempting."

"Give in."

"Not tonight."

De Lhandes gave him a long evaluative look, then asked, "Or are you a man in love?"

Nicholai shrugged.

"Ahhh," De Lhandes said, "not only a man of iron will and restraint, a man of fidelity. I am impressed and inspired."

"Glad to be of service."

"But I will doubtless yield to the temptations of the flesh," De Lhandes said, "later tonight. If, that is, I have the cash to do so. It is a mournful state of affairs when the considerable girth of one's masculine member is adversely affected by the regrettable slimness of one's money clip. Alas, the unique nature of the rest of my physiognomy generally precludes amorous arrangements of a less commercial nature. Women find me a charming companion at the table but less desirable for the walk into the boudoir. Suffice it to say, I am therefore limited as to the menus from which I can select. That being the sad case, my sexual future depends on fickle affections of the little wheel at Le Grand Monde — Saigon's finest temple to the gods of chance — in my unceasing attempt to make one vice pay for the other."

"And do you?"

"Rarely," De Lhandes said sadly. "If experience is the best teacher I am an exceedingly poor student. How was your chat with Antonucci?"

"Fine," Nicholai answered. "He just wanted to warn me off the saxophone player."

They both knew it was an evasion.

"He's L'Union Corse, you know," De Lhandes said, watching for Nicholai's reaction.

"What is that?"

"Don't play me for a fool, *mon pote*," De Lhandes said, "and I'll return the favor."

"Tell me, then, do I have in you a friend, or a police informant?"

"I can't be both?"

They laughed, and Nicholai ordered another round of drinks.

"You seem to know what's going on," he said.

"It's my business."

"I'm looking for a group of French film actresses," Nicholai said.

"Who isn't?"

"They arrived last week," Nicholai said. "You wouldn't know which hotel they're at, would you?"

"Would I know?" De Lhandes asked. "I've parked myself across the street like a dog, hoping for a glimpse. The Eden Roc."

Nicholai wanted to set his drink down and go directly to the hotel. She was *so close.* But he curbed his impulse and disciplined himself to take care of business. First things first, he told himself, then you can go and find her.

"Do you have an interest?" De Lhandes asked.

"Same as yours."

"Not the same," De Lhandes observed. "You have a chance, my friend. By the golden pubes of the village virgin, you have a chance."

They finished their drinks and crossed the street to Le Grand Monde.

The casino was in a courtyard protected by a high stucco wall topped with strands of barbed wire. Outside, Binh Xuyen troopers patrolled on foot and in Jeeps with mounted machine guns. Guards at the entry gate stopped and gave them cursory searches for weapons or explosives.

"Saigon these days," De Lhandes observed, his arms raised to shoulder height to allow the guard to pat him down. The guard nodded De Lhandes in, then searched Nicholai and passed him through. That accomplished, they went through broad doors into the enormous white building.

High-ceilinged and lit by chandeliers, the casino was a decent attempt at its progenitors on the Riviera and in Monaco. The thirty-odd gaming tables were covered in rich green felt, the furnishings, mock fin de siècle, were clean and well kept up.

The crowd, save for being predominantly Asians, could have been from the south of France, dressed expensively in the latest styles. The working girls, and there were many, were suitably muted in their nevertheless seductive attire, and the wives, girlfriends, and mistresses of the well-heeled men gracefully ignored their presence. White-jacketed Chinese croupiers worked quickly and efficiently, while larger men, obviously security, stood in the corners keeping watchful eyes.

The large room was filled with excited chatter, shouts of victory and curses of loss, the clatter of dice, the clack of chips, and the spinning of roulette wheels. A cloud of cigarette smoke hovered like protective coverage over the triumphs and disappointments.

Haverford sat at a roulette table. Giving Nicholai only the slightest glance, he pushed some chips onto the table and watched the wheel spin.

He won.

Bay Vien, resplendent in a sharkskin suit and a beautiful Chinese woman on his arm, stood and watched the action.

"Who's that?" Nicholai asked.

"Bay Vien," De Lhandes answered. "Boss of the Binh Xuyen. He and Bao Dai own the joint. Would you like to meet him?"

"Not especially," Nicholai said.

"You will, sooner or later," De Lhandes said, "if you're going to do any business in Saigon."

"Right now," Nicholai said, "the only business I'm going to do in Saigon is at the roulette table."

They went to the cashier's window and purchased chips, then walked back to the table where De Lhandes promptly lost on his first try.

"By the hirsute sack of Saint Anthony!" De Lhandes cursed. "By the inexhaustible appetites of the daughters of the Dordogne! By the unspeakable perversions of the sisters of—"

"Not going well?" Nicholai inquired.

"I am condemned to a chastity born of penury," De Lhandes answered.

Nicholai stepped up to the layout and watched the game. It seemed quite simple—players made bets based on the ball landing on a number from one to thirty-six. They had to choose to make difficult "inside" wagers on a specific number or a cluster of numbers, or more likely yet less remunerative "outside" bets on the even odds of the ball landing on red or black. The combinations of types of wagers seemed infinite, but a child observing the game could readily discern that the odds were always in favor of the house.

"I hope you have better luck than me," Haverford said. He looked a little glum, a dwindling stack of chips on the table in front of him. He offered his hand. "I'm Ellis Haverford, by the way."

"*Un bon ami*," De Lhandes said. "A genial pal, for an American."

"Michel Guibert," Nicholai said, then added, "And what do you do in Saigon, Mr. Haverford?"

"Ellis," Haverford answered. "I'm with the United States Information Service."

"Do you dispense information," Nicholai asked, "or acquire it?"

"First the latter and then the former," Haverford said, enjoying the game. "And you? What brings you to Saigon?"

"The weather."

Haverford laughed. "The ferocious heat or the stultifying humidity?"

"First the latter and then the former."

"Are you going to try your luck?" Haverford asked.

"At..."

"The roulette wheel."

"I might take a spin," Nicholai said.

He started conservatively, placing a modest two-piastre "outside" bet on black, and won. Leaving his winnings on the layout, he added chips and placed three more bets on black, won, and then shifted to red.

The croupier spun the wheel, the ball rattled around and landed on 27.

Red.

Two more reds and a single shift back to black later, Nicholai had acquired a tidy stack of chips. A small crowd, driven by the herd instinct of gamblers toward a "run," had gathered around the table. One of them was Bay Vien himself, who stood at the far end and regarded Nicholai with a look of slightly jaded curiosity.

Nicholai merely glanced back at him, but wondered when, and if, he would make good on his promise of payment.

Nicholai moved his chips onto the square marked 10. "Straight up," he said to the croupier.

"That's a thousand dollars, man," Haverford said.

"*Mon pote*, the odds are —"

"Thirty-seven to one," Nicholai said. "I'm aware."

It seemed obvious.

Several people hastily placed bets on black; a few of the braver ones put money on a split between 9 and 10. The doubters among them laid chips on red.

"*Rien ne va plus*," the croupier said, ending the betting as he spun the wheel.

The ball landed on 10.

"How did you know?" Haverford asked.

"Extraordinary," De Lhandes muttered, "by the pope's wrinkled scrotum..."

Nicholai shifted the pile of his winnings in a square layout on four numbers, 17, 18, 20, and 21.

"Pick them up, by the puckered anal cavity of —"

"Don't be foolish, Michel."

Nicholai looked across the table at Bay, who merely smiled, seemingly unbothered that Guibert was beating the house. Then again, Nicholai thought, he *is* unbothered.

"Corner," Nicholai said. If the ball landed on any one of the four numbers, he would win.

Bets were quickly laid down for and against him.

"*Rien ne va plus*."

The ball landed on 18.

"Cash out."

"Pick them up."

"A feast, I tell you, even in this colonial purgatory...and by the pubic hairs of the Mona Lisa, the *women* you could have tonight, *piles* of them..."

Nicholai pushed the chips back onto 10.

"...tits and asses like Cezanne's hay bales, and —"

Bay looked at Nicholai and nodded, as if to say, *Be my guest*.

"—such a variety, a five-star Michelin sexual buffet, by the boiling hot spunk of—"

Nicholai looked back at Bay. "Straight up."

"That's madness," De Lhandes said.

Haverford just shook his head. The gamblers around the layout scrambled to place counterwagers.

"*Rien ne va plus.*"

The wheel spun. The ball clattered, rattled, and bounced. Nicholai wasn't watching the ball, however—he had his eyes trained on Bay, who met his stare with the same fixed smile. Nicholai heard the wheel slow and stop, and heard the crowd collectively gasp as the croupier announced, "*Dix.*"

Ten.

Nicholai didn't move to pick up his chips or change his bet.

"Michel, you won," he heard De Lhandes say. "Don't be a fool, my new friend. That's a lot of money."

"*Encore,*" Nicholai said. "Straight up."

"*Mon pote*, you are throwing your money away!"

"A fortune!"

Nicholai glanced over at Bay, who shrugged.

The croupier closed the betting.

The ball rolled.

Bounced...

Landed on 12...

And bounced onto...

Ten.

Bay turned away from the table, put his arm around his woman, and walked toward the bar.

Nicholai picked up his chips, worth a little more than $100,000.

Bay had paid in full for the rocket launchers.

*     *     *

The casino was abuzz with the newcomer's amazing run.

Nicholai walked over to the bar and bought a round of drinks.

"Well played," De Lhandes said.

"Indeed," Haverford added dryly.

"By the blue veins on Jane Russell's sainted breasts," De Lhandes enthused, "that was spectacular! For a moment I thought that the admittedly fat-clogged arteries of my overburdencd heart — which more resemble pâté de foie gras than actual blood-bearing vessels — were about to burst! Thor's throbbing member, man, you terrified me! But I am happy, happy — no, overjoyed — for your exemplary good fortune. *Santé*!"

"*Santé*," Nicholai said.

"No one beats this casino," De Lhandes said.

Unless, Nicholai thought, the casino owner owes you a large sum of illicit money and found a clever and entertaining way to pay you.

The roulette wheel was as crooked as a dog's hind leg.

A commotion and a fresh buzz was happening around the entrance to the casino. The security guards made their way toward the noise outside. Through the main door, Nicholai could see a convoy of large, shiny black sedans pull up. Captain Signavi emerged, then a squad of Binh Xuyen troopers, machine pistols in hand, piled out of the lead car as other troopers hastily formed a cordon from the cars to the door.

"Could it be?" De Lhandes asked with some sarcasm in his voice. "A royal visit?"

The third car pulled up, troopers opened the back door, and a middle-aged Vietnamese man in a white dinner jacket emerged from the car as the guards, their heads on swivels, looked anxiously around.

"It's Bao Dai," Haverford explained to Nicholai. "The Playboy Emperor."

He waved his fingers, miming a puppeteer.

Bao Dai turned and reached his arm back into the car, clearly to fetch another passenger in the backseat.

"I hope it's his latest mistress," De Lhandes said. "The rumor is she's *fantastic*."

Nicholai watched as the woman eased gracefully out of the car.

She was fantastic.

Solange.

## 117

SHE WORE A BLACK GOWN with fashionably deep décolletage, and her blonde hair was swept up and off her long neck, with just one tendril carefully disarranged to flow down to her shoulder.

Solange took Bao Dai's offered arm and allowed him to escort her through the cordon of guards, each of whom labored unsuccessfully not to stare at the tall, elegant Frenchwoman who was the emperor's latest love.

"I heard she's a 'film actress,'" De Lhandes said. "At least that's what she calls herself."

"I'd like to be in *that* movie," Haverford said.

Nicholai disciplined himself not to slap his stupid face, but could not prevent the flush he felt burning his own cheeks. When it receded, he let his eyes meet Haverford's, but if the American was ashamed, he didn't show it.

"I had nothing to do with it," he whispered to Nicholai.

If you didn't, Nicholai wondered, who did?

"It's good to be the emperor," De Lhandes observed as Bao Dai and Solange came into the casino.

Nicholai watched as Bao Dai introduced Solange to various important men, watched as she held her hand out to be kissed, as she smiled, made small witticisms, and dazzled. She seemed very much at home in this society, a bit too comfortable for Nicholai's tastes, and he was annoyed with himself that he felt so...

Face it, he told himself, the word is "jealous."

He wanted to walk over and kill Bao Dai with a single strike.

The way the man pawed her, stroked her bare arm, signaling his ownership of her to all in the room. It was disgusting, and he was angry with her for allowing it.

Hypocrite, he accused himself.

You are a whore as much as her, you both sell yourselves, you are both playing roles. If she plays hers well, so do you, "Michel Guibert."

"I don't suppose we'll be introduced," De Lhandes said.

Haverford smiled. "We're not high enough on the pecking order for that."

De Lhandes sighed. "So I can only lust from afar."

"Bad for you, good for Le Parc à Buffles," Haverford said. The casino's courtesans were well beyond De Lhandes's limited means, but Le Parc offered a menu for all budgets.

Then she saw him.

Tall, she looked over her companion's shoulder and spotted Nicholai. Only the most discerning observer could have noticed the small tremor of recognition before her green eyes moved on to a brief glance at Haverford, but Nicholai saw it.

He walked over to them.


Bay Vien looked surprised at the intrusion.

Nicholai glanced at Bao Dai but addressed his words to Solange. "Michel Guibert, formerly of Montpellier and Hong Kong. *Enchanté, mademoiselle.*"

"*Enchantée, monsieur*," Solange said, her eyes warning him away before she turned her look to Bao Dai.

The emperor noticed the *colon*'s rude approach to his mistress but easily hid his annoyance. "Welcome to Vietnam, Monsieur Guibert. What brings you to Saigon?"

"Thank you, Your Excellency," Nicholai said. "I'm starting a business — a manufactury."

"Superb," Bao Dai said. "And what will you manufacture?"

"I was thinking of marionettes," Nicholai said, looking straight at Bao Dai. "You know ... puppets."

It was a deliberate insult and everyone who heard it knew it. But Bao Dai merely smiled and asked, "What sort of puppets?"

"French, I think," Nicholai said. "Or do you think American?"

"I didn't think the Americans were known for such things," Solange said.

"Yes, their ventriloquists use them. They call them, let me think" — Nicholai looked directly at Bao Dai — "yes, 'dummies.' It's quite clever, actually. The dummy appears to be talking but, of course, it's really the ventriloquist. But if you didn't know better, you'd swear that —"

"Yes, I think we understand the concept, monsieur," Solange said, turning slightly to signal Bao Dai that she wished to move on.

"Well, best of luck in your business, Monsieur Guibert," Bao Dai said. "If there is anything that we can do to facilitate your endeavor, I hope you will not hesitate to let us know. We always like to encourage entrepreneurs."

"Yes, I've heard that," Nicholai said. "Even as far away as Laos, they speak highly of your cooperative nature."

Bao Dai's eyelids closed for just a moment and then opened again. When they did, Nicholai saw that his eyes were black with repressed rage. "Do you gamble, Monsieur Guibert?"

"A bit, Your Excellency."

"He just beat the house for a tidy little fortune," Bay Vien said.

"Indeed?" Bao Dai said, raising his eyebrows. "Perhaps, then, you would like to join me in a private game?"

"I'd be honored."

"I prefer games that match player against player."

"As do I."

"Good," Bao Dai said. "Actually, I've become very fond of the American game of poker."

Solange kept the frozen smile on her face, but Nicholai could tell that she was livid. She stared at him with a look that said *Just go away*.

He smiled at her.

"It will be high stakes," Bao Dai said, hoping to embarrass him.

Nicholai looked at Solange and answered, "I like high stakes."

"No limits, actually," Bao Dai added.

"Better."

"I'll get a table together," Bay said, "in the private room."

"Will you be joining us?" Nicholai asked Solange.

Word of the newcomer's insult of Bao Dai and the impending poker game quickly spread through the house.

Bay Vien passed by Nicholai and muttered, "*This* game won't be fixed, you know."

"I trust you to see that it isn't."

He walked over to the bar.

"Christ, man," De Lhandes hissed, "are you out of your mind? Insulting the emperor. He'll have your throat cut. But by the love my mother would have laded upon me had she not been so horrified at what emerged from her womb, you have balls, Guibert. Clanging, great, magnificent balls."

"What are you doing?" Haverford asked.

"Playing poker," Nicholai answered. "What are you doing?"

"Playing poker, I guess," Haverford answered. He walked off to find Bay Vien.

Bay was a popular man. A few moments later, Bao Dai pulled him aside. "I want him broken. Every last piastre to his name."

And De Lhandes said to anyone who would listen, "By the glossy belly of Buddha, would you not love to be in that room?"

# 118

S<small>IX</small> <small>MEN</small> <small>SAT</small> at the round table. Nicholai, Bao Dai, Bay Vien, Haverford, Signavi, and the dealer.

Bay Vien announced the rules — the casino would deal, but a buck would rotate from player to player to determine the order of betting and set the game. That "dealer" could choose between one of two games, seven-card stud or five-card draw, the latter with jacks or better to open. There would be no silliness such as wild cards, and jokers were cut from the deck. Importantly, there were no limits on raises or stakes.

Nicholai sat with a squat glass of single-malt scotch straight up and looked at Solange, who stood over Bao Dai's shoulder like some kind of good-luck fetish. It was demeaning, he thought, demeaning and cheap and far beneath her.

Unless, he thought, she is playing a role that the Americans have cast her in. Just as you are playing a part in their melodrama. But what is her role?

Bao Dai neatly stacked his chips into several piles. Haverford sat to Nicholai's left, Bay to his right.

They cut cards for first deal. Bay won and chose five-card draw.

Nicholai picked up his hand.

Two hours later, the room was full of stale smoke and fresh tension. Haverford was all but out, as was Bay Vien. Signavi had a modest stack of chips in front of him, but Nicholai and Bao Dai were the big winners and headed for a showdown.

Nicholai found the game itself tedious beyond description, as he had for three long years in prison listening to the American guards play endless rounds of the childish game. Poker lacked nuance and creativity and was painfully puerile when compared to Go. It was a simple matter of risk analysis and money management, and basic mathematics dictated that five players over the course of a certain number of deals would basically receive the same hands. In that sense it was remotely similar to Go, as it involved decisions as to when to be aggressive and when to yield.

Nevertheless, he found the one-on-one battle against Bao Dai compelling. He was surprised at how badly he wanted to take the emperor's money and beat him in front of Solange.

Speaking of a lack of nuance, he thought.

He picked up his cards to see that the deal had given him a pair of queens and a pair of tens. It was enough to stay in the betting for the draw, and he threw his chips in as Bao Dai raised the betting.

He got his card, the ten of clubs.

Bao Dai opened and Nicholai saw him and raised him.

Haverford tossed his cards on the table. "Not my night."

Signavi looked hard at Nicholai, whose face was placid and unreadable. He grunted in disdain and pushed his chips in.

Bao Dai smiled across the table. "You're bluffing."

"All right."

The emperor called and raised.

Nicholai and Signavi both saw the bet.

Bao Dai laid his cards out—a red flush.

"Full house," Nicholai said, and swept up the chips.

Signavi swore in disgust.

Bao Dai only smiled, but Nicholai observed the slight flush of anger and frustration on his cheeks. He glanced up to Solange, who quickly turned away, walked to the bar, and fetched Bao Dai a fresh whiskey.

Nicholai looked at his own stack of chips. He had over two thousand piastres' worth—about $120,000.

Bay Vien had the buck, ordered a fresh pack, and called for seven-card stud. The dealer shuffled and Bay Vien cut.

Nicholai looked at his two down cards.

It wasn't promising—a four and five of clubs.

His first up card was a jack of hearts.

Bao Dai showed a queen of diamonds, and bet.

Nicholai stayed in.

The next round brought him the eight of clubs and Bao Dai the queen of spades. The emperor looked up, smiled at him, and raised by three hundred piastres. Nicholai tossed in the chips to see his next card.

A jack of diamonds.

"Pair of jacks showing," the dealer said.

Haverford folded.

Bao Dai drew a deuce. Still the high hand showing, he bet another five hundred piastres, and Nicholai stayed in to get the six of clubs.

The emperor drew the queen of clubs.

"Three of a kind showing. Queen high."

Solange's eyes looked almost sorrowful. Bao Dai bet another five hundred, sat back, and looked at Nicholai. "Do you still prefer games that match player against player?"

Nicholai wasn't sure if he was matched against a player, or against a player *and* the house, but he answered, "Yes, my preferences don't seem to have changed."

"So..."

Bay Vien folded.

Signavi also threw in his cards. "It's not my night, I see." He got up, went to the bar, and poured himself a Pernod.

"So it comes down to you and me," Bao Dai said to Nicholai.

"As it was meant to be," Nicholai said. Insolently, he looked directly at Solange, who turned her face away.

"The lady is tired, I think," Bao Dai said. "Shall we make this the last hand?"

"Fine with me," Haverford said. Bay and Signavi quickly assented.

Bao Dai raised an eyebrow at Nicholai.

"As long as there's a winner and a loser," Nicholai said.

"I think I can assure you of that."

I wonder if you can, Nicholai thought, recalling that the emperor's ally and business partner had ordered the fresh deck, owned the casino and the dealer. I've made a fortune tonight, and still have enough left to purchase a fresh start in life.

The emperor has three of a kind showing. Judging from his aggressive betting, he has another card down. I have only one chance to beat even his up cards—I have to draw a seven of clubs. The odds are overwhelmingly against me.

Bao Dai reached up and brushed the top of Solange's hand.

Nicholai pushed his chips in.

The deal came.

Bao Dai reached for his down card.

Nicholai said, "Let's neither of us look."

"Excuse me?"

"Let's neither of us look, Your Excellency," Nicholai suggested as he pushed all his chips toward the center. "And let's do make this the last hand."

"That's insane," Haverford said.

Solange's green eyes flashed like emeralds.

"He could already have four queens under there and know it," Haverford hissed.

Nicholai was aware of that. He looked at Bay to see if he could discern whether the fix was in.

He couldn't.

Bao Dai took a deep breath and then pushed his chips in.

"I see you," he said. Then he looked to Bay and asked, "Is my credit good here?"

"Of course," Bay said jokingly, but his face looked strained, as if he hoped that the emperor wasn't going to do what he feared.

But he was.

"I see you," Bao Dai repeated, "and I raise you two thousand piastres."

"I don't have it."

"I know," Bao Dai said pleasantly. "I warned you this was no limits. The sad fact is, you had no business being in this game. I played you like a . . . puppet."

Bay looked disgusted. Signavi found a reason to look down at the table as Haverford saw something fascinating on the floor. They were all embarrassed for Bao Dai. He had humiliated himself as a man.

But Solange looked straight at Bao Dai, and her expression was one of contempt. It was ephemeral, it quickly shifted to a mask of indifference, but Nicholai saw it, and it was victory enough.

"Good night, then," Nicholai said, and started to get up.

"Your credit is good here," Bay said to him, glaring at Bao Dai.

"To the limit of two thousand piastres?" Nicholai asked.

"Exactly."

Is Bay's offer sincere, or is the deck stacked and he's setting me up for an even bigger fall? I saved you from a bullet, Nicholai thought, looking at him. Would you set me up now?

Nicholai sat back down.

He looked at Solange, who looked back at him.

"I call your bet," Nicholai said.

Bao Dai turned his down cards and showed his hand.

His first card was the queen of hearts.

Four of a kind.

He looked at Nicholai and his leer said, *I told you that you had no place here. My hand, my pot, my woman.*

Nicholai turned his remaining down card.

The seven of clubs.

# 119

"My God, you're rich," De Lhandes observed.

It was true — Nicholai had taken enough money from Bao Dai to set himself up for life.

To his credit, the puppet emperor had taken his losses with a suave grace. Small wonder, Nicholai thought, he could easily replace the money with the funds he took from the Americans and his percentage of the gambling, prostitution, and drug business.

Still, it took courage to face down the powerful Bao Dai, and Michel Guibert's name was on hundreds of tongues in Cholon before Nicholai even left the casino.

"I will arrange security for you," Bay offered.

All that money, the crime lord thought. While the Cholon criminals were usually afraid to defy the Binh Xuyen by committing robbery on its turf, this amount of money could provoke a rash action. Someone might be willing to risk his life and the lives of his family for such a fortune.

"That won't be necessary," Nicholai answered.

"I suggest," Bay said, "that you allow me to put your chips in the safe. I will arrange an armed escort to the bank for you in the morning."

"That's very kind of you," Nicholai said. "And I accept."

Haverford approached Nicholai and whispered, "That was stupid and dangerous."

"I agree."

"Tomorrow at the Sporting Bar. Five o'clock."

"Very well."

There was a bustle in the main room as Bao Dai prepared to leave. The emperor looked back at Nicholai, waved his hand, and waited for his guard to form.

Solange looked over his shoulder at Nicholai.

"Where shall we go now?" De Lhandes asked.

"To the Parc à Buffles," Nicholai said, loudly enough for Solange to hear.

She turned away.

Momma, the brothel's madam — alerted to this Guibert's new wealth — was waiting for him.

"Monsieur Guibert, *bienvenue*," she warbled, her chins quivering with the effort. "Felicitations on your triumph! Your pleasure is my pleasure."

"Thank you." My pleasure is your *profit*, he thought, but never mind.

"But this establishment is not for a man of your distinction," Momma said, "you must accompany me to the back, which is reserved for our *special* guests."

Nicholai could almost feel De Lhandes's envy. "I assume my friends will be equally welcome, madame."

"Of course," Momma said, broadening her smile to encompass De Lhandes. "Any friends of Monsieur's..."

They followed her out through a courtyard, past armed Binh Xuyen guards who kept an eye on a long line of soldiers waiting patiently for the less exclusive services. The brothel was a model of *assimilation* and Nicholai observed the diverse nature of French forces in Vietnam — paratroopers from the Métropole, Foreign Legion troopers from all over Europe, lanky Senegalese soldiers, and squat Vietnamese.

Momma led them into a separate building, ornately decorated in colonial fin de siècle. Nicholai found it grotesque and tasteless when compared to the spare elegance of Japanese geisha houses.

The House of Mirrors was an establishment so exclusive that only the very rich knew of its existence or could afford the quality of its services. Like the finest of French restaurants, if you had to ask the price, you had no place there.

Momma rang a small handbell and quickly a platoon of girls formed behind her in rank and file, a choice for every taste and predilection. Most of the women were Asians in tight, brightly colored *cheong-sams* or white satin *ao dais*, but a few European women wearing peignoirs stood literally head and shoulders above them. One had blonde shoulder-length hair and heavy breasts, barely concealed under the filmy nightgown.

The madam noticed that Nicholai's eyes rested on her.

"That is Marie," she whispered. "Belgian — like the French . . . but *dirtier.*"

Nicholai selected a Chinese woman instead. Her black, flowered *cheong-sam* was buttoned to her neck, her black hair pulled into a tight bun.

"Ling Ling will please you," Momma said.

"I have no doubt," Nicholai answered. "And please put my friend's selections on my bill."

"You are a good friend."

"I am a man reborn," De Lhandes said, scanning the line of women with the eye of a starving gourmand examining the menu at a four-star Parisian restaurant. He was in a torture of indecision, torn between a zaftig Slav from Belgrade and a Japanese who looked as if she'd been chiseled from alabaster. "One doesn't wish to be perceived as a glutton, Michel, but . . ."

"I don't mind spending Bao Dai's money," Nicholai answered. "Have both."

"By the priapism of a pope, Michel!"

Ling Ling — although Nicholai knew that "Pretty Pretty" was obviously not her name — took Nicholai by the hand and led him to her chamber. He didn't violate her privacy by asking her for her real name. The pseudonym was a small way of keeping what little she had left of herself for herself.

"Should I undress or would you prefer to undress me?" she asked.

"You can undress," Nicholai answered. He was not deluded about the nature of this relationship. He didn't wish the pretense of romance or seduction. This was a simple business transaction.

She unbuttoned her *cheong-sam* and hung it up in the small closet. Nicholai undressed, she hung up his clothes as well, and she then took him in her hand and went to her knees in a gesture of foreplay that Nicholai knew was a subtle health inspection. Satisfied, she pulled him down onto the bed. Nicholai was pleased that her body was thin and spare, what the Chinese describe as a "lean horse," more a Zen garden than the lush, generous hothouse that was Solange.

Is she in bed with Bao Dai now? he wondered. Is she pulling the puppet's strings, making him dance to her charms?

Nicholai was surprised at this flash of sexual jealousy. It was so . . . Western. Unpragmatic and foolish. He turned his attention back to the very lovely naked woman on the bed, looking at him expectantly.

"Let down your hair, please," he said.

She reached behind her head and pulled out a cloisonné pin. Her black hair fell shimmering around her shoulders. Relieved that they could converse in Chinese, she was frank about ascertaining his other preferences.

"Would you like to begin with the Middle Way," she asked, "then perhaps finish by Fetching the Fire from the Far Side of the Mountain?"

"Neither, actually," Nicholai said.

"You do not find me attractive?"

"I find you very attractive," Nicholai said. "But it is so delightful to hear your beautiful Chinese that I would find it most pleasurable to spend our time in conversation."

She looked at him curiously, but chattered away. He made polite listening sounds and the occasional brief contribution to the conversation, but his thoughts were elsewhere.

Your rudeness to Bao Dai *was* stupid, he told himself, your anger at Solange unfair. Deliberately making an enemy of the country's ruler was just courting danger, and as for your attitude toward Solange—did you *want* to drive her into another man's arms?

You'll be lucky if she ever wants to see you again.

He waited in the foyer for De Lhandes to return from his buffet. In a little while, the dwarf came rocking down the hallway on rubbery legs.

"Damn generous of you, Michel," De Lhandes said, "to a fault, if I might say so, but if the indulgence of even recently made friends is a vice of yours, then I say hurrah for vice in all its variegated forms and twisted permutations, speaking of which—"

"You're an information broker?" Nicholai interrupted.

"Yes," De Lhandes said. "Do you have information you wish brokered?"

"I wish to obtain some."

"And a generous discount for you, my friend," De Lhandes

said. "About whom, may I ask, which indeed I may, should, and must, in fact, if I am to be of service to you."

On the taxi ride back to Saigon, Nicholai told De Lhandes what he needed.

"Your luck holds," De Lhandes responded. "By my happily exhausted but cruelly abused male member, your luck holds."

Let's hope so, Nicholai thought.

# 120

SOLANGE PRETENDED that she was lying on the beach at Frontignan and Bao Dai was a small wave that kept washing over her.

The wave — finally — broke.

She waited for a politely appropriate spell of postcoital intimacy and mutual praise, then rolled over for a cigarette.

"He seemed quite interested in you," Bao Dai said, getting up for a smoke of his own and a glass of scotch. "A drink?"

"Thank you, no. Who did?"

Bao Dai smiled indulgently. "Please, my darling, trust me when I say that I've had more than my fill of games tonight. We both know that I'm referring to your handsome fellow countryman."

"That Guibert?"

"That Guibert."

Solange got out of bed, slipped into a white silk robe, and cinched the belt around her waist. Then she sat on the Louis XIV loveseat and looked over at him. "Men do find me attractive. Am I meant to apologize for that?"

"Only if the attraction is mutual," Bao Dai answered. "Was it?"

Solange shrugged. "You said yourself that he is a handsome man. The world is full of them. I suppose you could have me blinded..."

"You're being glib."

"What else should I be," she asked, "when you're being silly? I'm with *you*, darling, not with him. I'm a little hurt—I thought you noticed."

He walked over and put his arms around her neck.

She hated his touch.

"I'm sorry," he said. "Perhaps it's that he took so much from me tonight. I was worried that maybe he took you as well."

"Oh, now you *are* being silly," she answered, turning her neck to kiss his fingers. "*Vous me faites briller.*"

Later he went into his private study, picked up the phone, and ordered, "Kill him."

# 121

Nicholai lay on his back on his bed and forced Solange out of his mind.

Focusing instead on creating a mental *go-kang*, he reviewed the state of play as it stood at the moment.

My position, he decided, is strong but ephemerally so. I have sufficient funds to launch and sustain my next moves, but what should those moves be? The possession of Voroshenin's papers is promising but the promises must be fulfilled — a tricky prospect.

Nor can I rely on Haverford's promise of a new passport. It could just as easily be a setup for another termination attempt, and in any case would still leave a trail that the CIA could follow. Then there are the papers I am due from the Viet Minh, but do I want them and the Chinese to also have a way to track me?

In either case, I would still be in my perpetual peripatetic prison.

But let them both think I need their passports.

Or that *we* do.

Solange had been so difficult to read. She would have made a superb Go player — maybe she will, he thought, if she decides to come with me and we manage it. But she had looked indifferent, icy, and angry in turn — furious, in fact, when I took the money from Bao Dai.

Was it an act? The theatrical skills of a first-class courtesan on display, or is she really with Bao Dai and through with me? Certainly she gave me not the slightest sign otherwise, but then again, given the situation, she had to be circumspect. Or was *I* the one exposed to the "theatrical skills of a first-class courtesan"?

His doubts surprisingly painful, he moved on to scan the position of the white stones that still surrounded him.

They were many and they were in motion.

Start with Haverford and the Americans. Despite his protestations to the contrary, it is still most likely that he intended me to be killed in Beijing and was surprised and dismayed that I survived. Now that I've openly surfaced in Saigon we're both pretending, at least, to be friends and allies.

But will the Americans make another attempt?

If so, *which* Americans? It is most likely that Diamond was responsible for the attempt back in the rock garden in Tokyo (which seemed like another lifetime). Would he now make another attempt in Saigon, with or without Haverford's assent?

Then there are the French, doubtless edgy at the thought of a stranger getting near their opium-smuggling operation. They will be suspicious, perhaps lethally so, and if the army isn't moved to act, the civil authorities might be, considering that a mess will soon land on their desks as soon as it is discovered in Moscow and Beijing that Michel Guibert is alive in Saigon.

And what about L'Union Corse? The opium trade is the wellspring of their wealth, from which they draw to purchase their hotels, clubs, and restaurants. While they appear to be cooperative, soliciting as is their nature their "cut of the action," "Corsican" is virtually synonymous with "treacherous."

On the topic of treachery, he thought, can you really trust Bay Vien, a man who has switched sides before and doubtless will again? Will his albeit temporary alliance with Bao Dai cause him to betray you as well?

And, if so, to whom? Bao Dai is the obvious choice, but it is well to keep in mind that Bay, after all, is Chinese, although many generations removed from the homeland. But Cholon is Chinese, surely swarming with Beijing-controlled operatives, even if Bay himself isn't one of them.

Beijing will certainly be coming for me.

As will Moscow. Even if Leotov has not already lost his nerve and contacted them, they will soon find out—if they haven't already—that Voroshenin's killer is in Saigon. The KGB certainly can't be seen to let that go unavenged. They will be coming. If not here, then somewhere else, and they will be relentless.

"Michel Guibert" needs to disappear, and quickly.

Hopefully, he thought, Solange Picard will disappear with him.

But it all depends on what happens tomorrow.

With delicious irony, my future depends on Yuri Voroshenin.

He put the imaginary board away and went to sleep.

# 122

MICHEL GUIBERT WAS the talk of Rue Catinat.

Even the waiters at breakfast treated him with an increased deference, and Nicholai saw the staff and other guests subtly point to him and whisper.

He found his new status amusing.

So did De Lhandes. He arrived in the dining room looking remarkably fresh from the previous night's excesses, sat down at Nicholai's table, and sniffed disapprovingly at the fare.

"But, my friend," he huffed, "this is shit, especially for a man of your taste and wealth. These Corsicans wouldn't know cuisine if it crept up their anal cavities and warbled Piaf tunes. Look, they can even make a debacle of breakfast. Would you like a real croissant?"

"I suppose."

"Come on then."

De Lhandes led him outside and down to the corner of Rue Catinat and Le Loi to a place called La Pagode, where the outdoor café stubbornly refused to adorn itself with anti-grenade netting.

"The owners act as if there is no war," De Lhandes said. "They consider putting up such vulgarities as the edge of a slippery slope. This, my nouveau riche friend, is how quality is preserved."

Over café au lait, croissant — which were, Nicholai had to

admit, delicious—and apricot preserves, De Lhandes slipped him an envelope. "Exactly what you requested."

"And what do I—"

De Lhandes waved a small, dismissive hand. "On the house, my friend."

"I can't—"

"You can and shall," De Lhandes said curtly. "Am I not allowed to return a gift in my own way, with what means I have at hand, by the ancient bells of St. Germain? I would have cited Notre Dame, but you'll understand that I'm a bit sensitive about the Quasimodo association."

"Thank you," Nicholai said.

"You're welcome."

Nicholai was impressed that De Lhandes never asked why he wanted the contents of the envelope or what he intended to do with them.

It has been a long time, he thought, since I've had a friend.

Later that morning, Bay Vien personally picked Nicholai up to deposit his winnings in the bank. They rode in his personal car, armored, and escorted by machine-gun-wielding guards.

"You are a difficult friend," Bay said on the drive.

"How so?"

"You embarrassed the emperor," Bay said. "In his city, in front of his woman."

*My* woman, Nicholai thought. But he said, "You helped me."

"Everyone saw how you looked at her," Bay said. "For that alone, not to mention the money, he could kill you."

"More likely he would ask you to do it."

"True."

"And would you?"

Bay said, "I'd feel badly about it—you're a good guy, for a

*colon*, and you have balls. But don't kid yourself, Michel — guys like you come and go, I will have to live with Bao Dai for a long time. So if he asks me to get rid of you…"

He didn't need to finish the sentence.

"I would understand," Nicholai said.

"Leave Saigon," Bay said. "Get your money and get out. Tomorrow. Today if you can."

"I have business here."

"The rocket launchers?" Bay asked. "Don't think I've forgotten your offer to procure more of them. But do it from Laos. You don't need to be in Saigon."

"I have other business here."

"What kind of business?"

"*My* business," Nicholai said.

"Please tell me you are not going after this woman," Bay said. "I have a dozen blonde Frenchwomen —"

"As I said," Nicholai snapped. "It's my business."

Bay regarded him for a long moment. "Do it quickly, *xiao*. Do it quickly and get the hell out, before I have to do something that I really don't want to do."

They arrived at the Banque de l'Indochine. The Binh Xuyen guards escorted Nicholai and his cash inside.

# 123

He met with the banker, a *colon* in his mid-fifties, in a private office.

"I wish access to my safety deposit box, please," Nicholai said.

Laval had heard of this Guibert. All of Saigon had. He said, "I'm sorry, monsieur, but I wasn't aware that you had a safety deposit box with us."

"I do," Nicholai answered. "In the name of Yuri Voroshenin."

He slid Voroshenin's passport across the desk. Laval glanced at it and then looked back at Nicholai. "I am informed that Monsieur Voroshenin recently passed away."

"As you can see," Nicholai said, "you were apparently *mis*informed."

"This is most irregular."

"Monsieur Laval," said Nicholai, "the Banque de l'Indochine is most irregular."

Laval looked insulted. He sat back in his chair and then ran his long fingers across his high forehead. "Do you have any additional identification that might authenticate your identity, monsieur...whoever you are?"

Nicholai nodded, removed an envelope from his jacket pocket, and handed it to Laval. The banker took it, opened it, turned ghostly pale, and sputtered, "This is outrageous."

"I agree," Nicholai said. "I imagine Madame Laval would agree as well."

"How did you get these?" Laval asked, stunned by the photographs of him in bed with a young Cambodian girl.

"Does it matter?"

"This is hardly the act of a gentleman."

"Again, we are in perfect harmony. Those copies are for you to keep, I have others safely stored away. However, if this is not adequate identification" — he slid a stack of piastre notes across the desk — "perhaps *these* pictures might suffice."

Laval hesitated. Then he took the stack of bills and stuffed them and the photos inside his jacket pocket.

He grudgingly led him to the vault and handed him the key.

Nicholai opened the steel box.

Bankbooks for accounts in Switzerland and the United States. In addition to the accounts were stocks and securities — a bit ironic for a Communist, Nicholai thought. He knew nothing of such things, but could hope that Voroshenin did, and had invested the Ivanov fortune wisely. Then there were codes to other safety deposit boxes. In Zurich, Bonn, Paris, New York, Buenos Aires.

Of course, Nicholai couldn't know what they contained, but there was already enough money to fund what he wanted to do and for he and Solange to live in reasonable comfort and safety.

And, on the subject of safety, Nicholai was delighted to find what he had hoped to find, and what a man of Voroshenin's profession would surely store in a secure place —

Passports.

One French, another German. With unintentionally exquisite irony, one was Costa Rican — the same nationality that the Americans had promised him. And, speaking of the Americans, Voroshenin had even provided himself with an American passport.

One "Michael Pine," resident of Park Avenue in New York City.

Nicholai took the contents of the box, put them in his brief-case, and walked out of the vault.

Laval was waiting for him.

"Now I wish to open an account, please," Nicholai said, handing him the American passport, "in this name."

The account was opened. Nicholai kept enough for immediate expenses, deposited the rest, and instructed Laval to wire it to their branch in Marseille.

Laval obediently did so.

Nicholai wished him a pleasant day and left.

# 124

THE MEN SAT in Antonucci's office.

Mancini, Antonucci, Guarini, Ribieri, Sarti, Luciani — the whole leadership of L'Union Corse sat around the table and listened to what Captain Signavi's guest, the *amerloque* who called himself "Mr. Gold," had to say.

"The so-called Michel Guibert," Diamond said, "is an asset of an American anti-narcotic unit sent to infiltrate the Indochina–Marseille–New York heroin connection."

The men were silent for a minute.

Finally, Mancini said, "This is what comes of doing business with outsiders."

"He seemed like a respectful young man," Antonucci responded. He took a cigar from its humidor and carefully lit it, not showing his fury at having been deceived by the young Guibert.

"It's the times," Guarini offered consolingly.

"There's more," Diamond said. "His handler is an American working in Saigon under USIS cover."

"Haverford," Mancini said. "I knew it."

More silence ensued, more sipping of espresso, more slow, deliberate smoking. Then Mancini said, "The Haverford thing has to look like something else. A robbery...use some of the local boys."

"What about Guibert?" Antonucci asked.

Signavi interjected, "He's something different. He can handle himself."

The men took this in.

Antonucci said, "I'll give it to the Cobra."

# 125

A DOUR, OVERWEIGHT FRENCHMAN was waiting for Nicholai in the lobby of the Continental. He slowly unfolded himself from his chair and approached Nicholai as he waited for the clerk to retrieve his room key.

"Monsieur Guibert?"

"Yes?"

The man's suit hung off him like laundry. Dark circles under his eyes gave an impression of even greater colonial lassitude.

"Patrice Raynal," he said. "SDECE. I would like a word."

"The bar?" Nicholai suggested.

"Perhaps your room?" Raynal suggested. "For your privacy?"

They repaired to Nicholai's room, where Raynal refused the offered drink, lowered himself into a chair, and got right down to business. "I don't like you, Guibert."

"Ah," Nicholai responded. "Most people wait a day or two until they decide to dislike me."

"They have not had the advantages," Raynal said, "of receiving hostile wires from Moscow and Beijing demanding your immediate arrest and extradition, nor equally strident inquiries from Norodom Palace inquiring about the identity of a Frenchman who insulted the emperor and made improper advances toward his escort. Nor have they received the reports that you sold a cargo of extremely lethal and probably stolen weapons to the Binh Xuyen and that you took an extremely ill-advised airplane ride to Cap St.-Jacques."

"The Binh Xuyen are your allies," Nicholai said pleasantly.

Raynal's voice was tired. "You see, publicly they're not. The French government does not consort with pirates and dope smugglers. And just this morning, Guibert, before I even had a chance to spike my coffee with a fortifying jolt of cognac, I received word that a certain, admittedly minor Soviet functionary, formerly of the Beijing delegation, was dead in a Cholon flophouse, an apparent suicide but, jaded cynic that I am, I can't help but wonder if your presence in the same city is merely coincidental. You do seem to have a habit of being in the vicinity of dead Russians."

Leotov dead? Nicholai wondered, keeping any sign of it off his face. An overdose or the Russians, or the Chinese? "I suppose I have that in common with any number of, say, Germans."

"Witty," Raynal said. "I dislike you more every minute."

"So *are* you arresting me?" Nicholai asked, tired of the jousting. Obviously, extradition to either of the Communist capitals would be the end of the game.

"No," Raynal said. "We don't take our orders from Moscow or Beijing. Not even from Washington, yet. But your business in Saigon is concluded. You managed to make a nice little lagniappe at the casino last night. Leave, Guibert, as soon as possible."

"Bay Vien told me the same thing."

"He was correct," Raynal said. "I really don't care what happens to you, I just don't want it happening in my little garden. Not to put too fine a point on it, get out. *Va t'en.*"

He pushed himself up from the chair, looking even more wrinkled than he did when he arrived.

"One more thing?" he said as he walked to the door. "Leave His Excellency's woman alone."

Nicholai stepped over to the note that was set on his table. If Raynal had noticed it, he hadn't let on.

He opened the envelope.

*Ciné Catinat? À deux heures?*

Unsigned, but in her hand.

He looked at his watch.

He had just enough time to make his rendezvous at Sarreau's and then go meet Solange.

# 126

Nicholai walked up to the counter at Sarreau's and asked for two packets of enterovioform.

"You are sick to your stomach?" the clerk asked.

"Otherwise I would not have asked."

He paid for the pills and then went back onto Rue Catinat and walked down toward the Neptuna Swimming Pool.

The Vietnamese who had followed him from the hotel was still on his tail.

Whoever he works for — the Viet Minh or the French — should be informed of his ineptitude, Nicholai thought. Unless the point is to be discovered, in which case he should be promoted.

Nicholai strolled to the pool.

It was a blistering hot day and the pool was crowded. Children splashed and annoyed the serious swimmers attempting to do disciplined laps in the marked lanes. Nicholai lingered under a plane tree at the edge of the little park, lit a cigarette, and watched.

His tail made a show of "disappearing" into the crowd.

So many games, Nicholai thought, to market the instruments of death.

He waited for fifteen minutes, grew bored and irritated, and decided that enough was enough. As he was walking away from the Neptuna, a Vietnamese fell in at his side. The man was especially short, and clad in khaki shirt, shorts, and rubber sandals.

"You brought the police," the man said.

"They brought themselves," Nicholai answered.

"I could lose him easily," the man scoffed. "But *you* ..."

"I apologize for my stature."

"Buy cigarettes."

"It's a bit late to stunt my growth."

"Buy cigarettes." The man jutted his chin at a tobacco shop and then he melted into the crowd.

Nicholai walked over to the tobacconist's. The owner, an old man, handed him the pack. An address was scrawled on the back.

"Take a *cyclo-pousse*," the old man snapped.

Nicholai went back out on the street to hail one of the bicycle-powered rickshaws. The first one in a long queue hurried to pick him up, Nicholai gave him the address, and the driver pedaled out into the swirling Saigon traffic.

Nicholai noticed the police tail get into the next in line, but the driver argued with him, with much yelling and hand-waving. By the time the police tail found a driver who would take him, Nicholai's rickshaw had disappeared into the current.

The route led across the Dakow Bridge, over the Saigon River into Cholon, and Nicholai recalled the sad joke that there is a Chinese quarter in every city in the world except Shanghai.

This one was no different. Three-story tenement buildings painted in vivid greens, blues, and reds, their tiny railed balconies decorated with drying laundry, leaned over the narrow streets as if they might imminently collapse onto them. Every other block seemed to have a small Buddhist temple or a shrine to a lesser Chinese god.

The driver navigated the vehicle through the clogged, noisy streets and pulled up alongside what appeared to be a tailor's shop, then refused the payment that Nicholai offered as he got out.

Nicholai went into the shop and was immediately hustled through a door into a back room. His proximity sense was on high alert, but discerned no danger. Apparently, the Viet Minh had not brought him there to kill him. Was it possible that they didn't know about his transfer of the weapons to the Binh Xuyen?

The man who had met him near the pool was already there. He did not give a name, but said brusquely, "You did not make the rendezvous in Luang Prabang."

"No," Nicholai answered, "*you* did not make the rendezvous in Luang Prabang."

"Our man was murdered shortly before."

"I can hardly be held responsible for his negligence," Nicholai answered.

"You have no feeling."

"See that you remember it."

The agent frowned at the distasteful necessity of dealing with this mercenary creature. "Where are the weapons?"

So, Nicholai thought, either they do not know or they are not certain. He needed time and space to complete his maneuvers on the board, just a little space to move the stones into position. "Where is my money?"

"When we get the weapons," the Viet Minh agent answered. "Where are they?"

"In a safe place," Nicholai answered.

"We have heard rumors..."

So the Viet Minh had heard about his airplane ride with the Binh Xuyen and the French into Saigon. Yet his making contact through the stamp shop had confused them. Otherwise they would have tried to kill me immediately, he thought. "You shouldn't listen to rumors. It's a morally debilitating habit."

"You are playing a dangerous game," the agent said. "If you have sold the weapons to the Binh Xuyen, you will answer for it."

"I answer only to myself," Nicholai responded. "In addition to the money, I believe there is also the matter of a new passport?"

The agent said, "You will get your money when we get the weapons and your new papers when the weapons reach their destination."

"That would be to this Ai Quoc person?"

The agent didn't answer.

Which is answer enough, Nicholai thought. He knew he had to take the offensive. "You will give me the money *and* the papers when I deliver the weapons to you."

"That is inconceivable."

"Nonsense," Nicholai responded, "as I just conceived of it. You might think it improbable, inconvenient, perhaps impossible, but inconceivable? No."

"I will pass along your request," the agent said stiffly.

"It is not a request," Nicholai said. "It is a nonnegotiable demand."

Nicholai knew that he was acting far too Western — confrontational and direct — but he didn't have the time for elaborate Asian courtesy. And he needed them to believe that the papers were crucial to him.

"Do not contact me again," Nicholai pressed. "I will contact you within two days to tell you where and when we can make the transfer. If you do not have the money, the deal is off. If you do not have the papers, the deal is off. Do we understand each other?"

"I understand you far too well."

"Good," Nicholai said. "Now I have an appointment."

He took a *cyclo-pousse* back into the city and had it drop him off near the Ciné Catinat.

# 127

She was silver in the reflected light of the screen.

Solange sat two rows in front of him, arranged her long legs in the narrow aisle, lit a cigarette, and looked up at the screen.

Simone Signoret starring in *Casque d'or*.

The film was a Belle Epoque crime story that held little interest for Nicholai, and he was glad when, after twenty minutes, Solange got up and left the theater. He waited a few seconds and then followed her out onto Rue Catinat. She walked quickly, with long strides, and didn't look behind her until she came to the Eden Roc Hotel, where she checked her image in the glass doorway and saw his reflection.

Nicholai waited until she went in, then followed her into the small lobby, where he saw the Vietnamese desk clerk smile in recognition and hand Solange her room key. So he knew that this was her official address, although he suspected that she spent most of her nights at the palace.

She went into the elevator and Nicholai stood off and watched the brass arrow above the doors indicate that she went to the second floor. He went over to the small shop, purchased a *Journal*, and perused the headlines before he allowed himself to walk over to the stairway door to make sure that neither the desk clerk nor the concierge were watching, then went in and took the stairs up to the second floor.

He walked the corridor and found that the door to room 231

was ajar. He stood outside for just a moment, allowing his senses to confirm that the perfume was hers.

He went in and shut the door behind him.

Solange stood in the small living room.

"That was foolish," she said, lighting a cigarette. "Foolish and jejune."

"What was?"

"Your behavior last night."

She's beautiful, Nicholai thought. Her golden hair, a *casque d'or* indeed, soft in the muted afternoon light, one hip cocked in anger, her muscled leg set off by the high heels. She turned away from him, pried the bamboo window shades open with her fingers, and looked out onto the street.

"What did you want me to do?" Solange asked. "Starve? Live on the street?"

"I make no judgments."

"How worldly of you," she mocked. "How tolerant you are."

Nicholai knew that this verbal slap was deserved. He asked, "Did Haverford send you here?"

"No," she said, shaking her head. "A different one. He called himself 'Mr. Gold'...he arranged for me to meet Bao Dai. I didn't know what to do. I didn't know if you were alive, or dead..."

Diamond, Nicholai thought, is as unimaginative as he is brutal. He has all the subtlety of a bull. And yet bulls can be very dangerous when they turn, hook, and gore.

"It's all right," he said.

"It isn't," she said. "They sent me here to lure you, didn't they? Even if we get out, they can use me to track you. You should leave me, Nicholai. Walk away now and never come back."

"No."

She looked back again toward the window, and Nicholai realized that she was afraid she'd been followed from the cinema. "I need to get back before the film is over."

"To learn how it ends?" he asked.

She shook her head. "I've seen it three times. The first two times, I cried."

"And this time?"

"I will probably cry again."

He pulled her to him and kissed her. Her lips were soft and warm.

Nicholai brushed the hair away from her neck, kissed her there, and was rewarded with a moan. Encouraged, he unzipped her dress and ran his hand down the warm skin of her back.

"We shouldn't be doing this," she murmured. "This is crazy."

But she shrugged the dress off her shoulders and let it slide down her hips. Then she unsnapped her bra and pressed her breasts against him. "You feel so good."

Nicholai picked her up and carried her into the bedroom.

Setting her on the bed, he peeled the dress down her legs, revealing her black garter and stockings.

Solange opened her legs, nudged her panties to the side, and said, "Quickly."

He unzipped his trousers and fell on top of her. Entered her with one thrust and found her wet and ready. She grabbed his buttocks and pulled him in deeper.

"Come in me."

"What about you?"

"Just come in me. Hard. Please."

She took control of their lovemaking, pulling him into her until she felt him swell and then climax, crying out.

*     *     *

Nicholai lay on the bed, watching her get dressed, elegant even in her postcoital deshabille. She sat on the edge of the bed as she rolled the stockings back up her legs.

"Breakfast tomorrow?" he asked. "I found a place, La Pagode, that serves quite good croissants."

"A date?" she asked wryly.

"We can sit at separate tables," Nicholai said. "Or will the emperor miss you?"

"He'll be busy with affairs of state," she answered. "Trying to decide if he's run by the French or the Americans."

"And what will he decide?"

"He won't," she said, standing up and pulling the dress up over her hips. She frowned, as if she thought her hips were a bit too broad. "The Americans will decide for him. They will decide for everyone."

"Not for us."

"No?" She smiled as a mother might smile at a small boy's heroic fantasy.

"No," he answered.

She leaned down and kissed him. "And what will we decide?"

"To be together."

"Yes?"

"Yes."

He had money now, enough money for them to live happily in a safe place somewhere. He told her all about Voroshenin, the connection to his mother and his family's fortune, about the safety deposit box, the bank accounts, the passports.

"We could go anywhere," he said. "France perhaps."

"I would like that, yes."

"Maybe to the Basque country," he said. "Did you know that I speak Basque?"

She laughed. "That is very odd, Nicholai."

"I learned it in prison."

"Of course you did," she said. "Yes, the Basque country is very pretty. We could buy a château, we could live quietly . . ."

Her face turned more serious than he had ever seen it. "I love you."

"I love you."

She broke from his embrace, went into the living room, found her purse, and took out a lipstick. Coming back into the bedroom, she sat in front of the mirror and redid her lips. "You smeared them."

"I'm glad."

She checked her image in the mirror, then, satisfied, stood up. Nicholai got up, then held her tight. She accepted the embrace, then broke it and held him at arm's length. "I have to get back."

"The film," Nicholai said. "How does it end?"

Her laugh was enchanting.

The heroine watches them kill her lover, she told him.

# 128

NICHOLAI WAS EMBARRASSED about sneaking back down the stairway, but he understood Solange's concern — Bao Dai would not make a complacent cuckold and he would take it out on her, not him.

He walked down the street to the Sporting Bar.

Haverford was already there, sipping on a cold beer. A small paper shopping bag was set on the empty chair beside him.

Nicholai sat down at the next table and both men looked out onto the street.

"You're the talk of the town," Haverford said.

"So I hear."

"Bad idea for a man in your position," Haverford said. "As a general rule, by the way, and understanding that you're relatively new at this sort of thing, a 'secret agent' should try to *avoid* celebrity."

"I'll try to keep that in mind." He turned to look directly into Haverford's eyes. "Diamond brought Solange here."

Haverford didn't know. Surprise — and perhaps anger — showed in his eyes.

"He's tracking you down," Haverford said.

"Because…"

"You went off the radar, Nicholai," Haverford said. "Because you know things that would be extremely —"

"I wasn't intended to survive the Temple of the Green Truth, was I?" Nicholai asked. "Diamond arranged for me to be killed there."

Nicholai would have thought it impossible, but Haverford actually looked ashamed. "It wasn't me, Nicholai."

"But the Chinese rescued me. Why?"

"You tell me," Haverford answered. "You brought the weapons down here, didn't you? You came to Saigon before you even knew that Solange was—"

"But you were here," Nicholai said. "You knew."

"I surmised," Haverford corrected. "I didn't know if you were alive or dead—"

"Odd, you're the second person to say that to me today."

"—but I did my best to enter the very interesting mind of Nicholai Hel," Haverford said. "I sat at the *go-kang* and played your side. This was your only move, Nicholai."

Haverford touched the bag sitting on the empty chair. "It's in the bag, so to speak," he said. "A Costa Rican passport under the name of Francisco Duarte, and the home addresses of your intended victims. Go now, go quickly, forget about Solange—"

"You're full of advice today."

"My parting gift," Haverford said, standing up.

"What about Diamond?"

"I'll take care of him," Haverford said. "I have to fight a little intra-office battle, but I'll win. You have your freedom, Nicholai. Enjoy it. *Sayonara*, Hel-san."

He walked away down the street.

Nicholai picked up the bag and looked inside. As promised, there was the passport and, more important, the home addresses of the men who had tortured him in Tokyo, including Diamond, in what seemed like a lifetime ago.

He ordered a beer and enjoyed it in the oppressive heat. The temperature was in triple digits and it was as humid as a shower.

The air was heavy, and the monsoon would break any day now. He hoped not to see it, that he and Solange would be on a flight out by then. Perhaps to some sunny, dry place.

It was tempting to think that they could go back to Japan. His deck of new identities might allow it, but he knew that the country had sadly changed and would never again be what it was. Japan was Americanized now, and he didn't wish to experience it.

Besides, there was a little matter to settle — three of them, actually — in America itself before he could decide on a place to settle. But Solange would want someplace to be while he was away.

Maybe France, maybe somewhere in the Basque country.

After all, he thought, I speak the language.

Nicholai finished his drink, paid the tab, and walked back out onto the street. He had gone only a couple of blocks when he heard the car come up behind him.

The Renault motor sputtered as the car slowed down to match his pace. Nicholai didn't glance back — he knew they were coming for him and it wouldn't help to signal them that he was aware. A quick glance into a shop window told him that it was a blue Renault with a driver and two passengers.

Nicholai kept walking. Would they really attempt to snatch him here? In the late afternoon on Rue Catinat? And would it be a beating, an assassination, or a kidnapping? He brought the *Paris Match* up to his chest, out of their view, and, flexing his forearms, rolled it into a tight cylinder.

Then he saw the two men coming toward him.

One of them made a crucial mistake — he let his own eyes meet Nicholai's. Then his eyes shifted focus, over Nicholai's shoulders, and Nicholai knew that the men in the Renault were now on the sidewalk behind him.

So either it's going to be knives—if it's an assassination—or it's a kidnapping, because the car was still keeping pace instead of just letting the men out and roaring off. Nicholai didn't wait to find out.

He took care of the men behind him first. Swinging the rolled-up magazine as if he was digging an oar into the water, he struck the first assailant in the crotch, then pivoted and swung the magazine like a cricket bat and struck the second man in the neck. Both went down—the first in agony, the second unconscious before he hit the sidewalk.

Nicholai went into a deep squatting horse-stance and thrust the magazine back over his shoulder, striking the next man in the eye, dislodging the orb from its socket. The fourth man reached out and grabbed him by the shoulder. Nicholai dropped the magazine, trapped the man's hand on top of his own shoulder, and then spun, breaking the arm and spinning him to the ground.

Then he ran.

He sprinted onto a side street that went off to the right from Catinat. The car followed him, bullets zipping as the driver attempted to steer through traffic and shoot at the same time. Pedestrians screamed, fell to the ground, and ducked into doorways, trying to get out of harm's way as bullets flew and Nicholai pushed through the crowd.

Racing ahead of him, the car crashed onto the sidewalk in front of him.

The driver steadied his pistol on the bottom of the open window and lined up his shot. Nicholai dove to the ground and then rolled until he came up under the driver's door. The shooter shifted the gun back and forth, trying to relocate his target.

Nicholai reached up, grabbed the shooter's wrist and yanked it down, breaking the arm at the elbow, then pushed up, slamming the pistol butt into the man's face. Then he sprang up, grabbed the stunned man by the hair, and slammed his face down onto the window ledge. He opened the door, pulled the man out onto the sidewalk, and got in himself.

A second car roared up the street.

A man leaned out the passenger window, blasting a Thompson.

Nicholai flattened out on the seats as the bullets shattered the windshield and sprayed glass all over him. Grabbing the pistol in one hand, he reached out with the other, opened the passenger door, and fell out onto the sidewalk. With the riddled car as a screen, he belly-crawled along the street, then looked up to see a startled messenger on a motor scooter stopped in front of him.

"Sorry," Nicholai said as he lunged and knocked the man off the scooter.

He hopped on and raced off.

The driver saw him and came after him.

Nicholai leaned as low as he could over the scooter's handlebars as the bullets zipped over his head. Police klaxons howled over the shouts and cries of bystanders as he weaved in and out of traffic, the pursuing car hot behind him.

He needed to create some space.

His mind flashed to the Go board, where two ways of creating space existed. The traditional and expected move was to place a stone far from the opponent, which in this case would mean accelerating the scooter to try to gain some ground.

The other was to eliminate the opponent's nearest stone.

Nicholai slowed down to let the car catch up a little and then cranked the handlebars, turned, and charged the car. Firing the pistol with one hand and twisting the throttle with the other, he rode straight at the startled driver like a kamikaze pilot determined to sell his life at high price.

The shooter got off one more burst before he dived out the door. The driver ducked behind the wheel.

At the last second, Nicholai swerved, missed the car by an inch, and drove out into the swirl of traffic on Rue Catinat. Melting into the chaos of rush hour, he made it down to the harbor, across the bridge, and into Cholon.

## 129

THE TIGER GROWLED.

It startled Nicholai at first, because he was in a densely populated city, not a remote jungle. Then he recalled that Bay Vien kept a private zoo on his large villa on the fringe of Cholon. Nicholai froze for a moment, then edged along the high stone wall of Bay Vien's urban fortress.

He had spent the twilight hours hiding in the darkened corners of the Quan Am pagoda on Lao Tu Street in the heart of Cholon. The few pilgrims who came in at dusk to worship the Amithaba Buddha bowed and chanted their Namu Amida Butsu and took no notice of him. When the sun went down and the district was lit only with lamps, Nicholai risked going out. But he stuck to the narrow back streets and avoided the vicinity of Le Grand Monde and Le Parc à Buffles.

He had no way of knowing yet who had tried to kill or kidnap him. It could have been Bao Dai, or Diamond, or Haverford. The attack came ten minutes after Haverford put him in place at the Sporting Bar and then left. Not wasting any time, the ever-efficient Ellis Haverford.

Still, he couldn't be sure.

Perhaps it was the Sûreté or Deuxième Bureau. It might even have been the Viet Minh, if they had decided that he had betrayed them after all.

Nicholai waited until dark, and then made his way toward

Bay Vien's palatial estate. What if it was Bay Vien who decided to have me killed, Nicholai wondered? Then his guards would doubtless have orders to shoot me on sight.

So best to approach him, shall we say, carefully?

At an outdoor kitchen, he swiped a warm piece of charcoal and put it in his pocket. Now, crouched beside the wall of Bay Vien's villa, he took out the charcoal, used it to blacken his face and hands, then tossed it into the bushes.

A double strand of barbed wire fringed the eight-foot-high wall, and shards of glass — mostly from Coca-Cola bottles, Nicholai noticed — had been mortared into the top of the stone. A bulky watchtower stood to the side of the iron gate that guarded the main entrance, and searchlights swung back and forth like a prison yard.

There is no choice, Nicholai thought, but to go over the wall.

It was a shame to sacrifice the tailored jacket, but Nicholai shucked it off, waiting for the searchlight to complete its arc, and then tossed it onto the wire. Then he jumped, grabbed on to the jacket, which the barbs now held in place, and swung himself onto the top. He lay there, balanced precariously, until the spotlight finished its next swoop, and then he dropped.

Something moved beneath him.

Nicholai suppressed a shout as the boa constrictor slithered out from under him, its powerful muscles rippling against his ribs. The snake was a good thirteen feet long, shiny in the moonlight. It turned its head, regarded Nicholai for a moment, and then flicked its tongue out to determine if this creature might make a meal.

"No," Nicholai murmured.

The snake moved off, far more slowly than Nicholai would have preferred. A sensei would have called the snake an omen, a

Chinese *sifu* would have told him to emulate the snake—one of the five model animals of Shaolin kung-fu.

So Nicholai became serpentine as he slithered across the clipped, manicured lawn, the grass, wet with evening dew, soaking his shirt. He kept low to the ground, freezing and pressing his face into the grass when the spotlight swung his way.

Then he saw the tiger.

It was in a cage, perhaps fifty feet off to his left.

It growled a deep, threatening growl, and Nicholai felt a rush of primal fear—an atavistic relic, he thought, from our species' days in the trees. The tiger's eyes were beautiful to behold, enchanting in the true sense of the word, and Nicholai felt himself being pulled into the creature's orbit.

Is that how it happens? he asked himself. Just before your death, are you frozen to the sacrificial altar by sheer awe? Do you realize the magnificence of the world just before you leave it?

He met the tiger's glare.

Two predators, he thought, who meet in the night.

Then he recalled the old Chinese adage: *When tigers fight, one is killed, and the other is mortally wounded.*

Good to keep in mind.

Nodding to the caged tiger, Nicholai resumed his slow crawl.

He stopped a hundred feet from the house and observed the guards patrolling the perimeter. There were four of them, walking interlocking routes around the house. Armed with American rifles, they stepped softly and didn't speak as they passed each other. Just a brief nod to indicate that everything was in order.

The good thing about guards, Nicholai thought, is that they point you toward your target. Each one of them straightened slightly and held his rifle at the ready when he passed outside a certain window on the villa's second floor. A light shone through the curtain. The window itself was open, although barred with an iron grille.

Bay Vien was home, in his bedroom.

With infinite patience—and gratitude toward his Japanese masters who had taught him that virtue—Nicholai made a slow, crawling circle around the entire villa, searching for a weakness.

He found it in the back, by the kitchen.

A white-jacketed cook sat on a stool outside the open door. Head down, elbows on his thighs, he smoked a cigarette.

Crawling a bit closer, Nicholai could smell the distinct odor of *nuoc mom*, the Vietnamese fish soup that was a staple of the peasant diet. Nicholai put all his concentration into his sense of hearing and listened. The cook was having a desultory conversation with someone inside. Luckily, he spoke in Chinese, and Nicholai learned that the boy inside was an underling, a servant, his name was Cho, and that the soup was almost ready so Cho shouldn't disappear to take a nap someplace if he wanted to keep his nuts where they were.

Nicholai waited and timed the guards' orbits until he learned that there was a thirty-second gap at the kitchen door.

Nicholai closed his eyes and ordered his mind to allow him five minutes of rest. Aware that he was fatigued from the battle on the street and his flight to Cholon, he knew that he had to marshal his energies—the next burst would have to be quick and certain.

When he woke up, the cook had finished his smoke and was back in the kitchen.

Nicholai pulled himself up on his forearms and waited for the next guard to come. The sentry came by the kitchen door and then—

—stopped, as the cook came out and handed him what appeared to be a chunk of fish. The guard slung his rifle over his shoulder, thanked the cook, and stood and ate.

Damn the man, Nicholai thought.

He dropped back down and waited.

The guard ate quickly, but it threw the rotation off, and it took another half hour before the guards' circuits were back in order. Then Nicholai waited for a sentry to pass by the kitchen, sprang up, and rushed for the door.

The cook, stirring his soup, was unaware, and Nicholai hit him with a fist to the back of the neck, then caught him before he could fall forward on the stove, dragged him into a corner, and then gently set him down.

It would have been easier to kill him, but the man was an innocent, and Nicholai knew that Bay Vien would not easily forgive the killing of one of his people.

Nicholai stood behind the door that opened into the house and shouted, in Chinese, "Cho, you lazy, useless thing! The soup is ready!"

The young waiter scurried through the door, straight into Nicholai's *shuto* strike, and dropped in a heap.

Nicholai pressed himself against the wall until the next sentry passed outside, then found a slightly longer waiter's jacket on a hook in the pantry, put the waiter's round black cap on his head, put two bowls of the soup on a tray, and headed upstairs.

The guard at the bottom of the stairway nodded brusquely, then blinked when he noticed the waiter's strange height.

It was too late.

Nicholai's leopard paw strike, the fingers folded but not closed into a fist. His second knuckles struck the guard straight in the nose—hard enough to drive the bone into the brain but not forceful enough to kill. Nicholai caught him in one arm and guided him to the floor so the gun wouldn't clatter. Unburdening him of the .45, he slipped the pistol inside his sleeve and walked up the stairs.

His proximity sense told him there was another guard outside Bay Vien's door.

Indeed, the guard heard his footsteps and called, "Cho?"

"I have Master's dinner."

"About time."

As Nicholai feared, the door was at the end of the hallway, which would give the guard ample time to discern that it wasn't Cho. Cursing his large Western frame, he tucked his chin into his chest, hoping to buy a crucial moment.

Looking back up, Nicholai took the spoon off the tray and threw it like a ninja star just as the guard was raising his pistol. The spinning spoon caught the guard in the eye and drove his head back.

His shot fired high.

Nicholai sprang forward, grabbed his gun wrist, and pushed it up. As soon as he felt the guard pull back down, he went with his flow and pulled with him, sweeping the arm in a full circle backward until he heard the shoulder pop. Then he reversed the flow, swept the guard's foot, took him to the ground, and struck him in the throat.

He stepped over the prone guard, pulled his pistol, and kicked the unlocked door open.

# 130

Bay sat up in bed, a pistol of his own pointed straight at Nicholai's chest. A beautiful Asian woman pulled the sheet over herself.

"My friends generally just ring the doorbell," Bay said.

"I didn't know if I was still your friend."

"You know," Bay said, "with one shout from me, my guards will come and they will throw you to my tiger."

"But you won't be alive to see it."

Bay frowned. "I suppose from the clatter that you spilled my soup."

"I'm afraid so."

"You are a bother, Michel."

He elbowed the woman next to him. "Get some clothes on, darling, and get out. I need to have a private talk with my rude guest." The woman leaned out of the bed, grabbed a silk robe from the floor, and put it on. Bay told her, "Go down and tell the cook that we need more soup. The cook is still alive, Michel?"

"Yes."

"Go."

The woman eased past Nicholai and then he heard her trot down the hallway.

"The pistol is getting heavy," Bay complained. "Shall we each put ours down? We're not going to shoot each other, are we?"

"I hope not." Nicholai slowly lowered his gun.

Bay did the same. "You look ridiculous in that jacket."

"I feel ridiculous."

"Do you mind if I get dressed?"

"I'd prefer it, actually."

Bay got out of bed and went into the attached bathroom, emerging a moment later in a black silk robe decorated with a red-and-green embroidered dragon. He tied the knot around his waist and walked past Nicholai as he said, "Let's go to the dining room."

He stepped over the dazed guard who lay on the floor, still rubbing his throat.

"Useless crap eater," Bay said. "I should feed you to Beauty."

"Your tiger?" Nicholai asked.

"Lovely, isn't she?"

Nicholai followed him downstairs.

## 131

THE SOUP WAS delicious.

Served by a cowed Cho and a rather resentful chef ("I told him if he spit in your bowl, I'd cut his balls off," Bay reassured Nicholai), it arrived on the teak dining room table hot and steaming.

Bay skillfully wended his chopsticks to pick out the delicate pieces of fish. "Sleeping with the emperor's woman," he said, shaking his head. "Not good."

She's not his woman, Nicholai thought. She's mine.

"Fifty-seven French whores at my brothel," Bay said, "but you have to have *that* one."

"Does Bao Dai know?"

"I don't know if he knows," Bay answered. "*I* know. He asked me to keep an eye on her. I didn't tell him, if that's what you want to know."

"Who tried to kill me?"

Bay shrugged. "Wasn't me."

"Bao Dai didn't order it?"

"Maybe he did," Bay answered, "just not through me. I guess he's angry that I didn't stack the deck against you. Maybe he doesn't trust me anymore."

"I need to ask a favor," Nicholai said.

Bay shrugged and ate his soup. Finally setting his chopsticks down, he picked up the bowl and slurped down the broth. Then he said, "You break into my home, beat up my staff, scare my evening's companion half to death, point a gun at me and threaten to use it, and then you ask for my help? This after you take my most important partner's money, screw his woman, and then commit mayhem and murder in the streets of Saigon? And *that* after you apparently killed some Russian and have half the world baying for your blood? You have balls of steel, Michel. I should just throw you to Beauty and let her break her teeth on you."

"But you won't," Nicholai said.

"What do you want?"

My life, Nicholai thought. More than that, my honor.

"Sell me my weapons back," he said. "I am prepared to offer you a small profit for your trouble."

"Are you prepared to die as well?"

"Yes."

Bay gazed at him for a long moment. "I believe you. But, tell me, if I sell you back the weapons, what do you intend to do with them?"

"Deliver them to the original client."

Bay looked surprised. "The Viet Minh. Why?"

"I gave my word."

"That's why *you* should do it," Bay said. "Why should I?"

Nicholai answered, "Whatever else you are, or aren't, you are a man of honor and you owe me your life."

"The Viet Minh are the enemy."

"Today," Nicholai agreed. "Four years ago they were your allies. Four years from now, who knows? Bao Dai is going to come after you eventually, and if he doesn't, the Americans will. Besides, the Viet Minh are going to win."

"You think so."

"So do you," Nicholai answered. "But that is all speculation. The only real question is, will you honor your debt?"

"Have I mentioned that you're a difficult friend?"

"Yes."

"I owe you my life," Bay said. "But this is it. We're even."

"Thank you."

"I'll get you out of town," Bay said. "Until we can get you on a ship or something."

Nicholai shook his head. "I need to go back into Saigon."

"Are you nuts?" Bay asked. "Half of Saigon is looking to kill you, the other half is looking to sell you to the people looking to kill you."

"I have to get word to someone."

Bay frowned. "Is it the woman?"

Nicholai didn't answer.

# 132

THE ROOM IN THE BROTHEL was small but adequate.

Whores, after all, Nicholai thought, end up in a whorehouse.

Nicholai's room was down the end of a long, narrow hallway. It contained a four-poster bed, and the walls and ceiling were made of mirrored glass.

"Our guests are narcissists," Momma explained, for she ran this establishment as well as Le Parc. Her silence had been handsomely purchased and guaranteed with the promise of agonizing exfoliation should she as much as whisper of Nicholai's presence. "They like to admire the beauty of their own ecstasy, and from a variety of angles."

Nicholai found the constant inescapable self-reflection somewhat unsettling. Everywhere he looked he saw a slightly distorted view of himself. Nor could he leave — he was imprisoned in the bedroom and the attached (mirrored) bathroom, with its tub, sink, and bidet. His meals would be brought in to him, and fresh air was out of the question.

"As for your other needs," Momma warbled lasciviously, "I have thought of everything."

"I have no other needs," Nicholai said.

"You will."

She shut the door behind her.

# 133

HAVERFORD GAMBLED a few piastres at the roulette table, lost, grew bored, and decided to make a night of it at Le Parc.

He walked out onto the street to hail a taxi and thought about Nicholai Hel.

The dramatic shootout on the street had made all the papers, which printed that the attempted assassination and possible kidnapping of the respected French entrepreneur Michel Guibert had been an act of terror committed by the Viet Minh. The businessman had survived the initial attack but was now nowhere to be found, and French officials were very concerned that he was in the hands of the Communist terrorists.

Haverford knew it was Diamond.

Now Hel was either dead or enduring interrogation in a tiger cage. Or perhaps he was alive and had gone into hiding. If so, he had pulled the earth up over him, because Haverford had all his sources out trying to locate Hel (or alternatively his corpse), and they had turned up nothing.

Nor had Hel tried to contact him, which meant that Nicholai no longer trusted him, perhaps that he thought the Americans were responsible for the murder attempt. Growing fond of an asset was always a mistake, but Haverford had come to like, or at least appreciate, Nicholai Hel.

The blade flashed out of the darkness.

One more second and it would have slashed his throat to the

neck bone, but Haverford saw it and leaned just out of the way. The backslash was already coming at him. He blocked it with his wrist, felt the blade bite in, and yelled in pain and anger.

The Marines had taught him well.

He grabbed the knife hand, turned, and flipped the attacker over his shoulder, onto the sidewalk. The man landed hard on his back and Haverford stomped hard on his throat. Then he pulled his pistol from the inside of his jacket.

One of the other robbers backed off, but the second kept coming and Haverford shot him square in the chest.

By this time, the Binh Xuyen guards had come running out of Le Parc à Buffles.

"Bandits," one of them said.

"You think so?" Haverford asked. He was breathing heavily, blood was running down his sleeve, the adrenaline was already dropping and he knew he would soon feel the pain. He looked at the cut and said, "I'll need to get some stitches."

One of the attackers was dead, the other had run away, and the Binh Xuyen were already taking their bamboo batons to the knife wielder.

"Alive," Haverford snapped. "I want him alive."

"Bandits," bullshit.

No robber in his right mind would try to take a wallet outside Le Parc; only a madman would try to rob one of Bay Vien's customers.

The guards dragged the man away.

# 134

Antonucci watched his girls play.

The club was busy for a Thursday night, full of hard-drinking French paratroopers and Foreign Legionnaires, and Antonucci kept a careful eye lest they decide to brawl in his establishment. So far the soldiers were behaving themselves, and probably would continue to do so, fearful of being banned from the joint and losing the right to stare at the pretty musicians. Later they would doubtless head to a brothel to douse the flame his girls had set alight, and others would profit.

So be it, Antonucci thought, it's a sin to traffic in flesh.

He struck a match and rolled the end of his cigar around the flame.

Cubans, the good stuff.

He glanced at his watch. The whoremongering American should be answering for his sins by now. They had sent three of the best, with instructions to make it look like a robbery. Bay Vien wouldn't like it, but to hell with him too. Sooner or later they would have to deal with that Cholon street rat as well.

And he'll be much harder to kill than the American, Haverford.

*Les amerloques*, Antonucci contemplated as he inhaled the rich smoke, such amateurs at intrigue, so ham-handed, so obvious. It takes centuries to produce a conspiratorial culture, generations of familial connection. America, with its youthful naiveté and mongrel bloodlines, is a blunt tool that no steel can sharpen.

America in Asia? A deaf man at the symphony.

So now Haverford lies in the street, the French police will give their apologies along with their indifferent Gallic shrugs, and "Operation X" will go forward. The opium will flow through the French military instead of the Viet Minh, be shipped to labs in Marseille to be turned into heroin, and will find its way to the streets of New York. We will make our money and life will go on.

For some.

He allowed himself a lingering look at the long legs of the saxophone player. Lucky she can sit in her chair, that one. She'll think three times before making eyes at a handsome stranger again.

And what happened to Guibert? Antonucci wondered. The newspaper story about the Viet Minh was an obvious French fiction. The rumor was that Guibert had made free and easy with Bao Dai's new mistress, compounding the error of embarrassing him at the gaming table and taking his money. Yes, Bao Dai ordered Guibert killed to get his balls back, and then his boys botched it. He should have come to us.

Antonucci turned his attention back to the saxophone player, Yvette. Maybe I'll throw her a fuck tonight, he thought, to show her there are no hard feelings. She's sensitive, gets her feelings hurt so easily. Thin-skinned, that one.

He saw Mancini come through the door and search for him with his eyes. Then the boss of L'Union Corse found him and shook his head.

So subtle a gesture only an old friend would have known what it meant.

Antonucci knew, and it made him angry.

The attempt on the American had failed.

# 135

It had been a good payday for De Lhandes.

So good that he bypassed Le Parc and went straight to the House of Mirrors, where he paid a good portion of his earnings for a Sri Lankan girl of such exquisite skill and beauty that it made him favorably reconsider the possibility of a benevolent deity. He finished dressing, kissed the girl on the cheek, left a generous tip on the night table, and headed out. It was not too late for the pho soup at La Bodega.

But that is me, he thought wistfully as he closed the door behind him. The aspirations of a gourmet with the wallet of a crust-munching peasant.

A large hand clasped itself over his mouth and he felt strong arms lift him and then he was in a room.

"Just be quiet for once," he heard Guibert say.

## 136

HAVERFORD SQUATTED beside the surviving attacker, put a cigarette in his mouth, and lit it for him. "You speak French?"

The terrified man nodded.

"Good," Haverford said. "Look, here's the thing, *mon ami*, I can pull you out of the shit you're in — I have no hard feelings, I know it was only business, yes? Or I can just walk away let these Binh Xuyen boys have you. It's your choice."

"What do I have to do?"

"You don't have to do anything," Haverford said. "Just tell me something."

"What?"

"Who paid you?" Haverford asked.

"The Corsicans," the man rasped.

"Who?" Haverford asked again, because this was a surprise.

"La Corse," the man said.

# 137

"I HAVE PUT MY LIFE in your hands," Nicholai said as he set De Lhandes down.

He knew it was gross and offensive to have lifted the dwarf off his feet that way, but there was no choice.

"By the chancred twat of a Marseille whore..."

"Many people," Nicholai said, "would pay a good price to learn my whereabouts."

"That is true," De Lhandes sputtered, still angry at the rough handling. "Why have you, then, put your life in my hands?"

"I need a useful ally that I can trust," Nicholai answered.

"I agree that I am useful," De Lhandes replied, "extraordinarily so, in fact. But why do you think you can trust me?"

Nicholai knew that everything depended on his answer, so he thought carefully before he spoke. Finally he said, "You and I are the same."

De Lhandes looked up at the tall, broad-shouldered, handsome man, and Nicholai saw his spine stiffen. "I hardly think so."

"Then think further," Nicholai replied. Having started this, he couldn't go back. Both his life and De Lhandes's were on the line, because the dwarf would leave here an ally or not at all. Nicholai would have to either befriend him or kill him. "Look beyond the obvious differences and you will see that we are both outsiders."

Nicholai saw this catch De Lhandes's imagination, so he

continued, "I am a Westerner raised in the East, and in the West you are..."

He knew he had to choose his words carefully, but then De Lhandes finished the thought for him. "A small, ugly man in a world of large, beautiful people."

"We are both forever on the outside looking in," Nicholai said. "So we can either stand on the periphery of their world, always looking in, or we can create our own."

"Create our own world?" De Lhandes scoffed.

But Nicholai could see that he was intrigued. "Of course, if you're happy with the one you currently have, if you are content with the odd turn with a high-class whore, or the occasional fine meal tossed to you like a bone to a dog, very well. But I'm talking about becoming rich, the sort of wealth that allows you to live a dignified life with, how shall I put it, quality."

"How?" De Lhandes asked.

"It's risky."

"What have I to lose?"

Nothing, Nicholai thought. But I have everything to lose, including my life. If I let you walk away from here and am mistaken in you, then I am a dead man. But it's too late for second thoughts now. He said, "I need you to do something."

He gave Voroshenin's papers to De Lhandes and asked him to contact Solange.

# 138

Bernard De Lhandes left the brothel and hailed a *cyclo-pousse* to take him back to the city.

By the bloated buttocks of a bishop, it was a difficult choice.

Guibert's whereabouts would be worth a Sri Lankan girl, perhaps even a woman from the Seychelles, renowned for their abilities and sexual secrets, and a dinner, with wine, at Le Perroquet. His mouth watered at the memory of the wine list that the sommelier had let him peruse that once.

Magnificent.

Of course, one would have to be alive to enjoy it, and from the look on Guibert's face, that seemed far less than a certainty. All of Saigon was jabbering about his escape from the assassins and how he had left several dead on the street.

This was not a man to betray.

Still, he thought, if you broker this particular piece of information, you needn't worry about his revenge. The question, really, is who to approach, and that really depends on who had made the futile attempt.

Oh, the rumors abounded.

Some had it that Bao Dai himself had ordered the assassination in retribution for Guibert's win at the gaming table; better yet, others said that Guibert had succeeded in breaching the long white thighs of the emperor's mistress and the attack was Bao Dai's attempt to remove the horns from his head.

By the absent arms of the Venus de Milo, it would have been worth dying to sample the charms of La Solange.

He returned his thoughts to business. If he were to sell Guibert's location, to whom would it be? Anyone would pay good money, knowing that they could resell the information to the highest bidder. But why should I sell wholesale, when retail would be so much more lucrative? In that sense, Guibert was right. Why should I settle for the crumbs off the table?

He sat back and thought it over.

The *cyclo-pousse* puttered across the bridge back into Saigon.

# 139

ANTONUCCI WATCHED the blonde woman sit on the stool and hook her stockings to her garter belt.

It almost made him hard again.

But he was sated.

The girl had indeed played a good saxophone, then he had bent her over the desk and had his way with her, and now she knew who was boss and didn't feel neglected. Waiting for her to finish dressing and leave, he locked up the office and went out the back way.

Antonucci didn't hear the man.

He did feel the pistol, pressed hard against his back.

"How are the kidneys, old man?" the voice asked in French with a heavily American accent. "You still piss okay? How would they feel if I pulled this trigger?"

"You don't know who you're playing with, *minet*," Antonucci growled. "I eat punks like you for lunch."

The pistol butt came down hard on his back and doubled him over. Then the man pushed him hard into the wall, spun him around, and stuck the pistol barrel in his face.

"Why?" Haverford asked.

"Why what?"

"Why the hit on me?" Haverford pressed. "Was it your idea or did someone come to you?"

Antonucci spat on the ground. "You're a dead man."

"Maybe," Haverford said. "But not before you."

He pulled the hammer back.

Antonucci looked into his eyes and saw that he meant it. Who cared, anyway, what *les amerloques* did to each other? An oath of secrecy to another Corsican? He would die for that. To these people, forget it. And he took some pleasure in answering, "One of your own people."

Haverford knew the answer before he asked the question. "Which one of my own people?"

"He used the name Gold."

Diamond, thought Haverford, is a congenital dolt. "And what did 'Gold' tell you?"

"He said you were going to interfere with our business."

"Your dope business."

"Of course."

Antonucci enjoyed the look of consternation on the American's face. He laughed and said, "Don't you get it, *mimi*? Your man Gold has a piece. Every kilo of heroin that goes into New York, he gets his taste."

Haverford felt a cold rage come over him.

"The Guibert contract," he said. "Cancel it. Stop it."

"Too late."

"What do you mean?"

Antonucci lifted his hand and wiggled it in a waving motion. "The Cobra," he said, "is already loose."

## 140

SOLANGE SAT on a stool in front of the mirror and carefully applied her eyeliner.

Bao Dai liked it a little thicker than she preferred—the emperor went for that smoky, cinema look.

Fair enough, she didn't care.

But in the light of morning she wondered how much longer would he find her intriguing, attractive? What would happen when she had no new tricks to show him and he grew bored with the old ones? The same thing, she knew, that always happened. He would start to find fault, correct her grammar, criticize small things about the way that she dressed, and then he would say he was only teasing. He would stop laughing at her quips, grow impatient with the time she took to get ready, his eye would wander to the next new thing.

*C'est l'amour.*

She didn't really care for Saigon. Too humid, and the air was always thick with intrigue. It was a hothouse, and she found it all rather suffocating. Sometimes it occurred to her to go back to France—not to Montpellier, with its memories, but to Paris or maybe Lyon. The Puppet Prince kept talking about a trip to Paris. Perhaps she could keep him on the hook until they were there, and then let him grow bored with her and leave her.

With a stipend, of course.

Is Nicholai Hel really dead?

The thought struck like a punch to the stomach. Her hand quivered and she had to hold her right wrist with her left hand to steady the pencil.

But is he really dead and is it my fault? Was our indiscretion discovered, did the emperor find out that his crown had horns and order Nicholai killed out of jealousy? No, she thought, if Bao Dai had done that he couldn't have resisted telling me, or at least hinting at it. And his ardor in the bedroom has certainly not diminished.

Solange was familiar with the behavior of men who suspected they'd been cuckolded. They were sullen and ridiculous — wanting sex but not wanting to dip their pens in a contaminated inkwell. They alternately sulked and strutted, and then either went away or came into bed, depending on how she manipulated them, of course. But Bao Dai had been his usual cheerful, unabashedly lustful self.

Tonight she would go with him again, out to dinner somewhere and then doubtless to Le Grand Monde for more gambling. Just as doubtless to bed, where she had better devise some new treat to keep him interested.

That is unless he has found out, and then he could just as well beat me, or take me somewhere to be killed.

If Nicholai isn't dead, where is he?

She was thinking this when there was a soft knock on the door. The maid, finally bringing the hand cloth she had requested an hour ago.

"Come in!" she yelled from the bathroom.

In the mirror she saw the bearded dwarf, De Lhandes.

## 141

"ARREST HER," Diamond said again.

"For what?" Bao Dai asked.

"If for nothing else," Diamond insisted, "disrespecting you."

"That is a shame," Bao Dai agreed, "but hardly a crime."

The argument in Bao Dai's private office in the palace had gone on for quite some time and the emperor was starting to tire of it. He did not like this American. Well, he did not like any Americans, but they were now paying the bills, would soon displace the French, so he was obliged to listen. This "Gold" seemed to have a personal grudge against Solange and Guibert. As to the former it was difficult to feel animosity, as to the latter it was virtually unavoidable.

"She knows where he is," Diamond pressed. "Give me some men, let me take her and get the truth out of her."

"And what if she won't tell you?" Bao Dai asked.

"She will."

Despite his better instinct, Bao Dai had to acknowledge that the idea had some appeal. The woman had, after all, cuckolded him, and he felt it keenly. Worse, his humiliation would soon be the topic for dirty whispers and salacious chuckles all over Saigon. So the thought of Solange under the tender care of the Tiger was not without its pleasures.

There were more practical reasons for seeking her help in locating "Guibert." The flow of opium brought with it a river of gold. When added to the healthy inducements that the Americans were now paying, it all amounted to vast wealth. But the *amerloques* might stop paying if it became public that he was profiting from the heroin that flooded their streets.

His position in the palace was tenuous. The French might seek to replace him; if not, the Americans. Then there was his ally and partner in crime, Bay Vien, who was helping him route money out of the country through L'Union Corse. Already he had massive bank accounts in Switzerland and landholdings in France, Spain, and Morocco, against the time that the Europeans threw him out or, more likely, the Viet Minh won the war.

But his security would be threatened if Operation X were exposed, and it was certainly possible that Solange was in league with Guibert to do just that.

"Pick her up," he said.

Diamond smiled. "Right away, Your Excellency."

"But hurt her as little as possible," Bao Dai said, more to soothe his own conscience than from any hope that this brutal man would calibrate his efforts.

"We'll leave no scars," Diamond assured him. "And her end will look like suicide. An overdose, perhaps. She wouldn't be the first French actress to—"

"I don't want to know," Bao Dai said.

# 142

GETTING INSIDE the House of Mirrors unseen was as nothing, even in the daylight of morning.

Exhausted from the night's exertions, whores sleep in the morning, soundly and sweetly, and the guards around the brothel were equally somnolent in the rising heat. Moisture masks sound as surely as dryness enhances it, and in the wet morning the Cobra was able to slip through the lax security.

It took time and patience, but what didn't?

The prey's room was at the end of the hallway. The Cobra already knew this but didn't need to know, because the faint odor was discernible even behind the closed door. A Westerner simply smells different from an Asian, and there were no other Europeans in the brothel in the early morning.

The Cobra paused in the hallway and listened.

The prey was asleep, so this would be easy.

There were no inside locks on whorehouse doors, in case security needed to get in quickly to aid a beleaguered girl. This would be a simple matter of quietly opening the door, dispatching the deceased in his sleep, and leaving out the window.

The Cobra moved forward and pulled the knife.

# 143

His proximity sense alerted him.

Nicholai was meditating, trying to recover the long-lost tranquil state of his boyhood, when he became aware of the footfalls in the hallway.

So soft as to be almost undetectable.

The light gait of a tiny Asian courtesan? he wondered. Had Momma sent someone, despite his wishes to the contrary? He lay still and listened, allowed his proximity sense to focus on the target. As he did so, the steps stopped.

Perfect silence.

But Nicholai knew.

It wasn't a whore, but a predator.

Nicholai slid off the bed to the side opposite the door. He flattened himself on the wooden floor and waited. The slightest trace of a scent came from the hallway.

But the door never opened.

The hunter had sensed the prey's awareness and backed off, and Nicholai realized that this was no ordinary hunter.

# 144

THE COBRA COILED in the bushes outside the window.

The prey had been flushed, and if it fled, would come this way.

But the prey didn't come.

The Cobra waited for a while, then sneaked away.

## 145

"You wished to see me, monsieur?" Momma asked.

"I wish to see Bay Vien," Nicholai answered.

"He is hardly your butler," Momma said, a tad annoyed, "and besides, he has asked *me* to see to your every need."

"Very well," Nicholai answered. "I need to leave. I have been discovered here."

"Impossible!" Momma thundered, deeply offended. "No one in my establishment would breathe a word, I assure you!"

More likely it was De Lhandes, Nicholai thought, and I played the wrong stone and misjudged his character. I will deal with him another time, but for now this place has been compromised and I have to find another. "Madame, I must depart."

"It is not safe for you out there!"

"It is not safe for me in here," Nicholai said. "Did you send a girl to me a little while ago?"

"No, monsieur, you said—"

"Quite so," Nicholai answered. "Did you send anyone?"

"No."

"Well, someone came," Nicholai said, "with the intent, I believe, of killing me."

Whoever had come was a professional, Nicholai knew, who realized that he had been discovered and then laid a trap outside the window. He could sense him out there, and later, when Nicholai sensed that he had withdrawn, he had looked out the window to see that the bushes were bent down and the slightest trace of footprints were still extant.

There was something else lingering...something that his proximity sense warned him of...

Momma drew in a breath of apparent shock. "I am devastated, monsieur! Devastated! *Désolée!*"

"Apologies are unnecessary, madame," Nicholai answered, "but I need to leave right away."

"I will telephone—"

"By the frothing jism of Jove, let me pass, sir!"

Nicholai heard De Lhandes's indignant voice echo down the hallway.

"I will have him—"

"Let him through," Nicholai said.

A few moments later, an even more than usually tousled De Lhandes came into his room.

"I thought you betrayed me," Nicholai said.

"I thought about it, believe me," De Lhandes answered.

"Why didn't you?"

"I'm not entirely certain," De Lhandes responded, "and were I you—a tantalizing concept now that I think on it—I wouldn't advance that query too much further less it impel me to change my mind—a great flaw of mind, by the way, this dithering to and fro—and market you like a hung hog in a *boucherie*. But what made you suspect that I had played the Judas?"

Nicholai told him about what he had sensed in the hallway.

De Lhandes frowned. "The Cobra."

"While I usually find your non sequiturs charming—"

"There is a rumor," De Lhandes said, "more of a legend, really, although the distinction between those two qualities is vague at best when one considers—"

"For God's sake, man."

"—of someone they call 'the Cobra,'" De Lhandes said. "Supposed to be absolutely deadly with a blade, and . . . this is not good news, I'm afraid . . . it is whispered in certain circles that the Corsicans are, collectively, the Cobra's chief employer."

"L'Union Corse."

"Just so, by the cursed blood of Bonaparte, may it boil in hell," De Lhandes said.

So it's the Corsicans, Nicholai thought. Their first attempt turned into a bloody burlesque, so they decided to hire their best talent for the next attempt.

But why?

Realizing that this wasn't the time to ponder that question, he asked, "Did you see her?"

"She said she will come to you."

"And the papers?"

"Safely stored, Michel."

# 146

Diamond left the hotel frustrated and angry.

The blonde bitch that had cuckolded the emperor wasn't in her room.

He put men out on the Saigon streets.

Himself, he went to lead the search for Nicholai Hel.

Bay Vien walked into Nicholai's room at the brothel and said, "You have to leave now."

"Not until I hear from her."

"The Sûreté are coming," Bay argued. "Don't just think of yourself. You're endangering everyone in this house. We'll keep looking for her, we'll bring her to you."

It's true, Nicholai thought. He had no right to do that. "Where are we going?"

Bay told him.

"What about Solange?" Nicholai asked. "She thinks I will be here."

"I'll get word to her," De Lhandes offered.

"And my men will bring her to you," Bay said.

Appropriately, Nicholai thought, to my hiding place — the Swamp of the Assassins.

THE RUNG SAT LAY southeast of Saigon, east of the mouth of the Soirap River where it drained into the South China Sea. A wilderness of swamps, mangrove forests, bamboo, and countless little tributaries formed an impenetrable maze to all who didn't know it well.

The Binh Xuyen knew it well.

This was their birthplace and sanctuary, where their old pirate raids had originated and returned, the place from which their famed assassins emerged to slip into the city, kill, and then slip back again.

Nicholai lay in the bottom of the skiff as it came downriver then turned east on a small channel in the dense swamp. The terrain was surprisingly varied — now a flat, sun-drenched stretch of low vegetation and algae, then a dark, dense stand of mangroves, then a wall of bamboo. This pattern repeated itself for an hour, and then the boat slowed onto narrower channels, pressed hard by the mangroves that loomed beside and above and at times shut out the sky, casting the boat into a diurnal darkness.

A man could get lost in here, Nicholai thought.

Get lost and never find his way out.

Finally the skiff pulled up alongside a houseboat anchored against a line of mangroves. The boat was squat and wide, with open decks fore and aft and a cabin in the center. Binh Xuyen troopers, machine pistols slung over their shoulders, stood on guard. Bay Vien emerged from the aft cabin door and stood on the deck as Nicholai stood up.

"You are nothing but trouble, Michel," he said, helping him onto the boat.

"Is she here yet?" Nicholai asked.

"No," Bay said impatiently.

He led Nicholai into the cabin, which had a small kitchen with a gas cooker, a table, and a couple of chairs. A narrow set of stairs led down into the hull where there was a small hold and sleeping quarters.

"You'll be safe here," Bay said, "until we can get you on a ship out."

That was the plan — hide him and Solange here in the swamp until the next night, then take them by boat to a freighter coming out of the Saigon docks.

"Have you heard from her?" Nicholai asked.

"You're monotonous," Bay said.

"Answer my question."

"No," Bay Vien said.

"I'm going back to look for her."

"In the first place," Bay said, "no one will take you back; in the second place, you can't get back on your own; in the third place, even if you did, you would only be killed. Her karma is her karma now."

Nicholai knew that he was right.

"You want tea?" Bay asked.

He shook his head, lit a cigarette instead, and sat down in the bamboo chair at the small table.

"Relax," Bay said.

"*You* relax."

"A man in love," Bay said, shaking his head. He jutted his chin toward the hatchway. "Go get some sleep."

"I'm not tired."

"I said go get some sleep."

Nicholai went down the hatchway into the hold.

The crates were there.

Crates of rocket launchers.

Bay nodded. "I'll go back to Saigon and see what's happening. Besides, there are pursers to bribe."

"I'll pay it."

"Yes, you will." He called for the skiff and left.

Nicholai went down into the hold, lay down on one of the beds, and tried to rest.

His promise to Yu was almost fulfilled, he had money and papers.

Now there was only one thing left to do.

Get Solange to safety.

# 149

DE LHANDES WADDLED down the aisle of the cinema.

Michel had said that Solange loved the films. The screen was dim, some film noir, he thought, of the type that he couldn't bear. De Lhandes preferred comedies or period pieces, with low bodices and heaving bosoms.

Then a daylight scene brightened the screen and he saw her in the third row. He slipped into a seat behind her. She was staring up at the screen and weeping as she dabbed a tissue to her eyes.

"Mademoiselle," De Lhandes whispered. "Michel is waiting for you. Go out the back. There are men to take you to him."

He saw her neck stiffen with doubt.

"You have no reason to trust me," he said. "Only that I am an admirer of beauty and, like all cynics, a disappointed romantic. And I am his friend. Go now, Mademoiselle Solange, before it is too late."

He waited as she decided what to do.

Then she got up, slid down the aisle, and walked out the back door of the theater.

# 150

GUIBERT WASN'T at the House of Mirrors.

Nor at Le Parc, nor the Continental, nor Le Grand Monde. He wasn't on Rue Catinat, the Central Market.

He was gone.

Diamond cruised the streets. If he couldn't find Hel, he'd find someone who would tell him where he could.

# 151

HAVERFORD WALKED the narrow alleys of Cholon.

If the Corsicans had sent another killer, it meant that Nicholai was still alive, and he figured that Hel would most likely run to a neighborhood where he spoke the language and knew the customs.

But no one had seen a tall *kweilo* who fit Hel's description, or at least no one was talking.

# 152

BERNARD DE LHANDES was looking for a decent meal, reading the sidewalk boards that listed the evening's fixed-price menus when the men jumped out of the car, grabbed him, and shoved him onto the floor of the backseat.

"Where is your friend?" Diamond asked.

"I-I-I don't know."

"Tell me before I hurt you very badly."

But De Lhandes did make them hurt him very badly. He made them bruise organs and break bones but, in the end, he couldn't stand the pain.

"Forgive me, Michel," he wept. "By the sacred blood of Saint Joan, forgive me."

He told them what they wanted to know.

## 153

"THE RUNG SAT?" Signavi questioned.

"That's what the little bastard said," Diamond answered. "Believe me, he was telling the truth."

The French paratrooper found the information troubling. "The Rung Sat is Binh Xuyen country."

Diamond didn't want to hear it. He'd already gotten the word that La Corse had botched the hit on Haverford, and that the smart-mouthed son of a bitch now knew about his connection to Operation X and the heroin trade. And now Hel had made it out of Saigon, into the so-called Swamp of the Assassins, which could only mean that he was under the protection of Bay Vien.

"I don't care if he's in the pope's living room!" Diamond yelled. "You have troops, send them!"

Signavi shook his head. Americans were so clumsy—they would always use an axe when a stiletto would do. "The Cobra will track him down. We don't want to get in the way."

"Yeah? Is the Cobra as good as the guys you sent to kill Haverford?" Diamond asked. "Listen to me—if 'Guibert' gets away he takes Operation X with him. It's over! We're finished! You think Bao Dai is going to sit around and watch all his money go down the chute?"

He could see Signavi wavering and pressed, "We know that the woman is on her way to Guibert. Send a team, get it done."

Signavi nodded.

# 154

JOHN SINGLETON SAT and contemplated the Go board.

He had acquired an appreciation for the game during his days in China, but could find no one in Washington who could give him a decent match, so he preferred to be alone and play both sides.

It was a good mental exercise, disciplining him to see a situation from all perspectives.

Now he looked at the *go-kang* and pondered the whole Nicholai Hel scenario. He reviewed it from all angles, considering Hel's origins, his killing of Kang Sheng as well as Voroshenin, the arms connection to Liu, Haverford's Beijing network of spies, Hel's escape from China into Laos, his liaison with the Binh Xuyen.

He changed his perspective to consider the situation in Vietnam—the intense Viet Minh activity in the north, the relative quiescence in the south since the last failed Communist offensive, the fact that the very dangerous Ai Quoc had been in hiding, that Hel had delivered the weapons to Bay Vien instead of to Ai Quoc, the fact that Haverford had served in Vietnam during the war...

Then there was Diamond, the allegedly secret Operation X, his connection to the Corsican heroin trade, and his visceral hatred for, and fear of, Nicholai Hel...

Now both his agents were on the ground in Saigon, and it

would be fascinating to see which of them emerged victorious. He found it amusing that each stone on the *go-kang* thought that it determined its own moves and never saw the hand that moved them toward their fates.

This Hel, on the other hand...

He did seem to move himself.

# 155

Nicholai heard her footsteps on the hatchway steps.

"Solange?"

"Nicholai."

Her perfume was intoxicating.

Nicholai rolled out of the bed and came to her.

"Thank God," she said. "I was so afraid . . ."

Solange pressed herself tight against his chest. He wrapped his arms around her, trapped the knife against her back, and whispered, *"Per tu amicu."*

She stiffened, ever so slightly, and he knew.

And felt his heart break.

"It's you," he whispered into her hair. "You're the Cobra."

Then he let her go and took a step back. The light in the cabin was dim, but he could see in her eyes that it was true. Lying in the bed, waiting for her, he had seen it, and realized that he should have known sooner.

*The Cobra is deadly with a blade.*

La Corse had recruited her all the way back in Montpellier to kill the German colonel. They had taught her to use a knife and she slashed his throat. They took her to their base in Marseille and used her for other missions.

She kept her association with La Corse, but started to freelance, both her sexuality and her other skills. That night in

Tokyo, after the attack in the garden, she came in with a knife in her hand and murder in her eyes.

*Were you going to use that?*

*If I had to.*

And you knew how, didn't you, he thought.

She might have killed him during their romantic rendezvous at the hotel, but she knew that she was under observation and would be a suspect. But, the next day, De Lhandes had told her about the House of Mirrors and she had come, as the Cobra, to kill him. His proximity sense had told him it was someone he had encountered before, but now he truly realized it.

Life as it really is.

*Satori.*

"Is it Picard," he asked, "or Picardi?"

"Picardi," she said.

*The Corsicans are the best assassins.*

"The story you told me," Nicholai asked, "how much of it was true?"

"Most of it," she replied. "The hurtful parts, if it's any consolation."

It wasn't.

"How many men have you killed?" Nicholai asked.

"More than you, perhaps," she said. The knife slid out from behind her back. She held it low at her waist, slightly back, out of his reach. "I make money as I can — as a courtesan, as a killer. Tell me the difference."

"In the latter case, people die."

"You are hardly in a position to look down at me from a position of moral superiority, *mon cher*," Solange answered.

So very true, he thought.

So very true.

"You must have amassed quite a fortune," he said.

"I save it," she acknowledged. "The lives of both my professions are quite short. Beauty and swiftness fade quickly when they fade. I will need to retire young, I'm afraid."

Nicholai doubted that her beauty would ever fade. Not in his eyes, at least. Nor for *her* eyes, those amazing, beautiful green eyes. He saw her shift her right hip ever so slightly forward. The muscles in her calf tightened.

"La Corse hired you to kill me," he said.

"I told you to walk away from me and not come back."

"Was that my unforgivable sin?" he asked. "Loving you?"

"It's the one thing a whore cannot abide."

The tendons in her right wrist tensed.

It was subtle, but he saw it.

Could he stop the lightning lunge he knew was coming? Perhaps, perhaps not. If he did block it, could he counter with *hoda korosu* and kill the Cobra?

Again — perhaps, perhaps not.

Nicholai stepped back. "Then kill me."

Her eyes flickered with doubt and suspicion. He understood it — her past gave her no reason to trust a man. He said, "I would live for you and kill for you, so dying for you..."

She shook her head, her golden hair shimmering in the lamplight.

"Please, Solange," he said, "free me from my prison."

Just as I freed Kishikawa-sama.

He closed his eyes, both to assure her and to summon his tranquility, and breathed deeply. This life was as a dream and when the dream ended there would be another and then another in an endless cycle until he realized perfect enlightenment.

*Satori.*

He heard her foot turn on the wooden deck, the preparatory move for the thrust, and readied himself for death.

She burst forward.

Into his arms.

"I can't," she cried. "God help me, *je t'aime, je t'aime, je t'aime.*"

"*Je t'aime aussi.*"

Over her sobs, they heard footsteps crash heavily onto the deck.

# 156

THERE WERE EIGHT OF THEM and they were coming for the guns.

The black-clad troopers from Signavi's Vietnamese special forces piled onto the deck and came down the hatchway.

Solange whirled out of Nicholai's arms, spun again, and slashed the first trooper's throat. She yanked his body clear and then stabbed the second one in the stomach. The third went to shoot his pistol, but she slashed downward, severing his wrist tendons, and the pistol clattered down the stairs. The shocked trooper grabbed his dangling wrist and stared at her. She used the moment to plunge the knife into his throat. Another trooper vaulted the railing over him and went for her.

Nicholai hit him in midair, their momentum sending them crashing into the bulkhead. Grabbing him by the shirt, he threw him, scooped up the pistol, shot him, and pulled Solange aside just before a burst of machine-gun fire came down the stairs. The bullets bounced crazily around the hold as he shoved her into the bulkhead and shielded her as he reached back with his gun hand and fired up the hatchway.

He could hear the survivors regrouping on the deck, and then heard the metallic rattle and saw the grenade bounce down the hatchway. Pushing Solange down, he dove, grabbed the grenade, and tossed it back up.

The sharp crack of the explosion preceded the screams of gutted men.

Then it was quiet.

"Stay here," he ordered.

She shook her head. "Claustrophobia. I don't care for closed spaces. Ever since Marseille, they frighten me. Badly."

"Stay here anyway."

He went up onto the deck and saw the dead men. A flat-bottomed swamp boat bobbed alongside. Hearing footsteps behind him, he whirled and saw Solange, the knife caked with dark, congealing blood still in her hand.

"I told you to —"

"You don't tell me what to do," she said, picking up one of the machine pistols from a dead trooper and slinging it over her shoulder. "Now or in the Basque country."

She stopped as they heard boat motors and the slaps of hulls on the water.

They were coming and coming fast.

"Stay low at least," he said.

Then he scrambled down the hatchway.

Nicholai cracked open a crate, took one of the rocket launchers, found the solvent, and quickly wiped the weapon clean of the protective grease.

Even from the hold, he could hear the motors getting closer.

He found a tripod, took it and the launcher in either hand, and hurried back up the hatchway.

"*Mon dieu*," Solange said, "and what do you intend to do with that?"

"Screw the tripod into the barrel," he said. "*S'il te plaît.*"

He trotted back down to the hold, found the ammunition, and came back up with two of the rockets. "Eight-pound high-explosive antitank rockets with a velocity of 340 feet per second, capable of penetrating eleven inches of armor plating at an effective range of a hundred yards. Or so I'm told."

"Men."

Now he could make out the running lights of the first boat, and troopers standing in the bow. The boat looked loaded with men.

Nicholai shoved the rocket down the back of the tube, then lay down, adjusted the tripod, and sighted in. Waiting until the boat came inside the hundred-yard range, he took a deep breath and pulled the trigger on the exhale.

The rocket shot out, whooshed through the night air, and plunged into the water behind the speeding boat.

Solange flipped the machine pistol onto full automatic.

Nicholai sat up, reloaded, and settled back in again. He adjusted the sight, waited, and fired.

The boat exploded in scarlet flame.

Men on fire shrieked and leaped into the water.

Solange winced.

The next boat was coming hard.

Nicholai went for more ammunition, came back, and sighted in. The boat was so close he could hardly miss now.

So close he could make out the face of Bay Vien.

# 157

BAY'S MEN LOADED the crates onto the swamp boat as he examined the carnage on and below the deck.

"You killed these eight men?" he asked.

Nicholai nodded.

"The two of you?"

Nicholai nodded again.

"Mmmph."

"How did they find us here?" Nicholai asked.

"De Lhandes gave in, under torture."

"Is he dead?"

"He'll recover," Bay answered.

"That's good," Nicholai answered. He didn't begrudge his friend the betrayal under torture.

Bay shouted for his men to hurry.

"We don't have much time," he explained. "They'll be coming with more men. Getting you on the freighter is out now. Police and soldiers are checking every boat. They're all over the harbor. Maybe we can get her on board, but not you."

"I won't leave without him," Solange said.

"Where are we going?" Nicholai asked.

"Up the river," Bay said, "into the delta. Deliver the guns to the Viet Minh and then find a way to get you out of the country. It might take some time."

"We have time," Nicholai said.

But he wasn't entirely sure.

# 158

"Rocket launchers?" Diamond asked.

Signavi confirmed that rockets had sunk two boatloads of his men and sent them plunging into the Swamp of the Assassins.

God damn Nicholai Hel to a fiery death of his own, Diamond thought.

And God damn that traitor Haverford, who had to have had a hand in this.

"Do you know where he might be headed?" Signavi asked.

"He's taking them to the Viet Minh," Diamond said. "Guibert is a Chinese agent."

"You told me he was an American narcotics agent."

"Grow up," Diamond said. "I lied."

Either way the man had to be found and killed. Signavi took command of the military operation to sweep the delta and find Guibert and the weapons. A shipment of those weapons to the Viet Minh could change the course of the war.

"I'm going with you," Diamond said.

He hated battles, but this was his best chance to kill Nicholai Hel.

# 159

HAVERFORD LOOKED at De Lhandes in the hospital bed.

"Who did this to you?" he asked.

"One of yours," De Lhandes murmured through the painkilling drugs. "That's why I asked to see you. I'm hoping you're better than that."

He told Haverford about giving up "Michel" and Solange's whereabouts, then fell back into unconsciousness.

Haverford left the hospital in a cold white rage.

He went back to his office, checked out a service .45, and went hunting for Diamond.

# 160

THEY MADE IT safely up the river, navigating without running lights past naval patrols, hiding in channels, mangrove swamps, and stands of bamboo. Then they took a tiny tributary, little more than a stream, north through the swamp until they came out on the Dengnai River south of Saigon. Safely crossing the stream, they landed near a small village, where the people helped them transfer the cargo to a canvas-covered truck.

"What's the name of this place?" Nicholai asked.

"Binh Xuyen." Bay Vien chuckled. "We're pretty safe here."

They took some tea and rice with pickled vegetables, then got into the truck and drove the roadway inland, then left the truck and the main road and set off on foot. Daylight found them carrying the crates along dikes built above the rice paddies, steaming now in the cloying humidity that came just before the monsoon season.

Nicholai and Solange, dressed unconvincingly in the black shirt and trousers and conical hats of Vietnamese farmers, walked in the center of the small column—just enough Binh Xuyen to carry the load, a handful of armed guards, with Bay Vien in the lead. It was treacherous country, flat and open, observable by French aerial surveillance, vulnerable to the watchtowers and blockhouses that punctuated the landscape.

It was too risky, so they decided to abandon the dikes for the low rice paddies. Trudging through sometimes waist-high water was exhausting, progress was excruciatingly slow, and they had to stop and flatten themselves in the water every time they heard an airplane engine.

At this pace, Nicholai thought, they would never make it to the rendezvous with the Viet Minh. Solange, although stoic and uncomplaining, was clearly played out. Her calves and ankles were cut from blade grass, and her eyes showed a dunning fatigue.

"Are you all right?" he asked her.

"Splendid," she said. "I've always enjoyed a stroll in the country."

She pushed ahead of him.

Just before midday, Bay walked back to them.

"It's too dangerous," he said. "We have to stop for the day."

Nicholai agreed, but asked, "Where?"

"There's a *bled* just a kilometer or so from here," Bay answered. "The villagers owe their allegiance to me."

Nicholai knew exactly what that meant — if the people of the tiny hamlet betrayed them, the Binh Xuyen would come back and kill them all. It saddened him but he understood. Collective responsibility was an Asian tradition.

When they made it to the *bled*, Nicholai and Solange lay on the floor of a dark hut and tried to get a little sleep. There wasn't much time to rest — they would move out again as soon as it was dark and hope to make some progress before the moon rose.

Solange fell asleep, but Nicholai lay awake, listening to the sound of airplanes circling above them. The tension in the village was palpable, especially when in the late afternoon he heard whispers that a Foreign Legion patrol was just a half kilometer away.

The village collectively held its breath.

Nicholai laid his hand on the warm metal of the machine

pistol and waited. He wasn't going to be captured—he had seen all he wanted of the interrogation room and the cell. If they took him, they would take him as a corpse.

Then he decided that was selfish. If it looks as if we're going to be discovered, I will hand her the Ivanov bankbooks, then hold a gun on her and let them think we took her as a hostage. Then I will find a way to kill myself on the way to the prison. That resolved, Nicholai watched through the bottom slats as a Legion officer stood on the edge of the village and questioned its elder.

The man shrugged his shoulders and waved his finger in an arc, indicating that the foreigners could be anywhere, in any one of the dozens of villages nestled among the rice paddies. The young lieutenant looked at him skeptically.

Nicholai noticed that his finger had tightened on the trigger.

The lieutenant stared at the old man for a second, the old man stared back, and then the lieutenant ordered his men to move on. Nicholai lay back and looked at Solange sleeping. He drifted off himself, and when he woke up it was dusk. A few minutes later Bay came in, followed by a woman with bowls of rice and steamed fish. Solange woke up and they ate, then got ready to resume the march.

They walked the dikes now, shielded by the neat rows of mulberry trees. Staying in tight formation, they literally walked in each other's footsteps and made reasonably good time until the moon rose and lit them. Then they stretched apart and moved by twos and threes, the scouts going ahead and whistling signals that it was safe for the next group to move.

The local militias were out, walking the dikes themselves, going from village to village. Several times, its patrols came within eyesight, and Nicholai's party flattened themselves to the ground and belly-crawled, if they moved at all.

It was a deadly game of hide-and-seek in the moonlight, a

match of stealth and wits. To Nicholai's surprise, Solange was very good at it — she moved with a quicksilver grace and silence, and he laughed at himself when he remembered that she was not only Solange but the Cobra.

She is more experienced at this, he thought, than I am.

The night seemed to go forever, but they made about ten miles before the sky started to turn to the stony gray of predawn and they came to a long line of mulberries a half mile from a small hamlet.

Bay signaled them to lie and wait.

A few minutes later, Nicholai heard the single sharp whistle to come ahead and he quick-stepped in a slouch along the dike until he reached the relative safety of the tree line. There was a small clearing among the trees and there he saw Xue Xin.

# 161

"IT'S GOOD TO SEE YOU again," Nicholai said.

"And you," Xue Xin answered.

He looked so different now, in the light khaki jacket of a Viet Minh officer with a holstered pistol on his hip.

"You knew we'd meet again," said Nicholai.

"I always knew it," Xue Xin said. "I knew your true nature."

More than I did, Nicholai thought.

His name wasn't Xue Xin, of course, but Ai Quoc.

Nicholai saw it clearly now.

Quoc had controlled the operation and had counted on Nicholai to honor his deal with Colonel Yu.

"I knew," Quoc continued, "that you would realize the truth and see things for what they are."

"And now I want a life," Nicholai said.

Quoc looked past him to see Solange and smiled. "We will do our best to get you out. It might require some patience on your part."

"I have become the personification of patience."

"Why do I have my doubts?"

"It must be your monklike wisdom," Nicholai answered. "All that clipping of vines and deep breathing."

The sky was turning a coral pink.

Quoc said, "We should be going."

Nicholai walked up to Bay Vien. "Where are you going now?"

"Back to Saigon," Bay answered, "to curse your name to the heavens for stealing my weapons and getting away with it."

"Will they believe you?"

"Yes, or they'll pretend to," Bay said, "for a while longer, anyway. Then..."

He left it unfinished. It was obvious — no one knew the future, no man could say what his karma held in store for him.

"Goodbye," Nicholai said. "I hope we see each other again in better times."

"We will," Bay answered.

Bay gathered his men and headed out.

"We need to go," Quoc said. His soldiers, thirty-odd veterans, started to heft the crates on bamboo poles and were already walking north.

Quoc began to limp after them.

The airplane came out of the east.

# 162

WING GUNS BLAZING, strafing the tree line, it came in low and out of the sun.

Three Viet Minh went down like toy soldiers knocked off a shelf.

The shells splintered trees, spraying shards of wood like shrapnel.

Nicholai tackled Solange and lay on top of her. The ground shook under them from the vibrations of the low-flying plane.

"Go now!" Quoc yelled as the plane rose to come around for another strafing run.

Nicholai got to his feet and pulled Solange up behind him and, hand in hand, they ran for the next rice paddy, racing to get over the exposed dike before the plane completed its turn. Its wings shone in the rising sun as it banked, came back, and dove, a hawk on the hunt.

They made it over the dike, but two more Viet Minh behind them weren't as lucky and were picked off easily. Nicholai and Solange slid down the slope into the muck of the rice paddy and plunged under the surface.

Holding her hand as he held his breath, Nicholai tried to listen for the now muted popping of the guns and the sound of the plane's engines as it climbed again. When he heard a higher-pitched whine he pushed up, and together he and Solange sloshed across the rice paddy.

Looking around, Nicholai saw that Quoc had survived the

last attack and was waving them toward a copse of trees on the far side of the paddy. Ahead of them, the men carrying one of the crates made it over the top of the dike and disappeared from sight. Another Viet Minh lay down on his back on the dike and started to fire his machine gun up at the plane, which was now coming in behind them.

Solange jerked him down, and again they held their breath and felt the rounds zip into the water around them. When they came back up, the plane was climbing in front of them. It waggled its wings and kept flying away, apparently out of ammunition or low on fuel.

Nicholai and Solange made it across the paddy, over the dike, and into the copse of trees, where the Viet Minh were regrouping. Wounded porters fell out as other men took their place. Loads were shifted, weapons exchanged. A soldier who was apparently a medic gave rudimentary aid with the scant supplies at hand. Other men were beyond help, and lay dead or dying.

Nicholai found a rifle and picked it up. Solange draped the sling of a burp gun around her neck. They walked to the far edge of the trees. In front of them stretched a long rectangle of tall sword grass bordered on the right and left by paddy dikes. Beyond the grass rose another stand of trees.

"We'll be safe once we get there," Quoc said, pointing to the trees.

"Why is that?" Nicholai asked.

"We disappear."

Nicholai had no patience for Zen metaphysics. If Quoc, whether he was really a monk or not, thought they were going to meditate themselves into thin air, Nicholai wanted a more mundane plan. The plane had flown off, but the pilot had certainly radioed their position to the patrols that were thick on the ground.

It wouldn't be long before troops arrived, and they would run out of neither bullets nor fuel. The French troops and native militia that had been crisscrossing the countryside would converge in a neat, organized pattern and surround them. The sheltering trees would become a death trap, unless Quoc had an actual plan for escape.

"Our motherland will swallow us," Quoc said.

Poetic, Nicholai thought, but hardly practical.

Of course his mind went to a different metaphor, the *go-kang*, and he saw it all too clearly. Their little pool of black stones would soon stretch into a thin line and progress toward Quoc's apparently magic trees, there to group into a pool again. The white stones—and there were many more of them—were even now gathering around them.

Go players had a term for such an isolated, surrounded group.

Dead stones.

And, Nicholai recognized, the flat *go-kang* surface had become an anachronism. The ancients never anticipated modern airpower, which literally added another dimension to the game. They couldn't have imagined stones floating above the board, delivering death and destruction below.

Nor, he had to admit, was Go a model for battle. The *go-kang* was serene, quiet, perfect in its organization and form. The modern battlefield was chaotic, noisy, hellish in the anarchy of its blood, carnage, and agony.

Modernity, he thought, has destroyed so much.

He forced his mind back to the reality on the ground. Trap or no, the copse on the far side of the grass was a better position than the one they now occupied, its size created a larger defensive perimeter from which to make a last stand. He made it to be a little less than a half mile away, so it should take only minutes to reach.

But the sword grass would be a painful impediment, although doubtless narrow foot and game trails had been cut through the chest-high blades. The burden of the weapons, especially now that there were fewer porters, would slow them down further.

Perhaps...

No, Quoc would never think of abandoning the weapons, and when Nicholai looked at it honestly, neither would he.

They had come at too high a cost.

The quiet behind told him that the Viet Minh were ready to move out.

He turned and saw that they would leave their dead comrades. Everything useful had been removed from their bodies.

"It comes at a high cost, your freedom," Nicholai said.

"For every enemy we kill," Quoc answered, "they will kill ten of us. And in the end, it won't matter."

"Save, perhaps, to the ten."

"The individual is nothing when compared to the whole," Quoc answered.

Nicholai stared at him.

Seeing his true nature.

And, perhaps, a bit of his own.

"You're wrong," he said.

"You will come to see."

"I hope not," Nicholai said. "I hope never."

If each individual became only part of the machine, at the end of the day there would be only the machine. The inexorable, impersonal, grinding machinery of the modern. He turned away from Quoc, took Solange by the arm, and walked her away, out of hearing.

"I was thinking," he said, "about the first meal we'll have when we get to wherever we're going."

"Oh yes?" she said. "And what were you thinking?"

"You made a dish back in Tokyo..."

"I made a number of dishes back in Tokyo," Solange said, her wide mouth opening into a smile.

Nothing can dim the light in those green eyes, he thought. "The coq au vin, perhaps."

"Simple French country cooking."

"Simplicity sounds wonderful," Nicholai said. "With what wine, then?"

She speculated on a number of choices, narrowing it down to a handful and then finding it impossible to choose. Then they discussed which vegetables they would have as side dishes, how they should be prepared, and then which dessert would be best, a *tarte tatin* or perhaps a *marquise au chocolat*.

"Should we invite De Lhandes?" Nicholai asked.

"Yes, of course," Solange answered, "but he must leave straight after coffee so we can make love."

"Out he goes, then."

She kissed him, long and lovingly.

# 163

THEY WERE ONLY fifty yards into the sword grass when the shooting started.

Turning to his left, Nicholai saw the line of Legionnaires come onto the dike, and to the far right of the troops he thought he saw a soldier with a vermilion beret directing their fire.

Signavi.

Nicholai lifted his rifle to his shoulder and returned fire, shooting to his left but moving ahead. The copse of trees was their only faint hope and they had to keep moving, for getting bogged down in the grass was certain death.

Quoc saw it and ordered a dozen men to form a screening line to their left to try to slow up the French advance and buy enough time to get the weapons into the trees. The porters were amazingly disciplined, not pausing to shoot, or drop to the ground, or even duck. They just kept shouldering their loads and moving ahead at a slow trot.

Signavi saw what they were doing, directed fire on them, and several of the porters dropped. The others strained to carry the weight, and a couple of Viet Minh lowered their rifles and took their places on the bamboo poles.

Two Legionnaires fell as the screening line came into action, and Nicholai saw Signavi direct a squad to his left, toward the copse, to cut off the Viet Minh. If the French got into the trees first, it was over.

He shouted to Solange, "Can you run?"

She nodded.

They took off, the saw grass slicing their faces and chests as they ran toward the copse, angling off to the left to block the French. Several Viet Minh joined them, and they ran through the grass as bullets zipped around their heads. One man dropped, and then another, and then it was as if they had disturbed an angry nest of hornets and the air buzzed around them.

But most of them made it to a tiny rise above a ripple of ground, and from there they could lay down fire on the flanking Legionnaires, forcing them to stop, drop to the ground, and engage in a firefight.

Behind him, the porters moved toward the trees.

Nicholai looked back to the dike and saw Signavi talk into a radio attached to the backpack of one of his soldiers.

No, Nicholai thought, please no.

He raised his rifle, sighted in, took a deep breath, and fired. The bullet hit Signavi in the high spine, and he clutched at his back and then fell.

But it was too late.

Only a minute later, Nicholai heard the plane engine, and then he saw it, but this time it didn't drop low to strafe, but stayed high until it was directly above the rectangle of grass, and then it dropped its load.

Napalm.

The grass caught fire immediately, and a wall of flame rolled toward them.

Men ignited like torches and spun madly around, shrieking. Others seemed to simply melt.

Nicholai took Solange's hand and ran.

The wave of flame rolled behind them like a fiery red tsunami from a nightmare. Nicholai felt it scorch his back and singe his hair as the intense heat seemed to suck the air from his lungs.

He pushed Solange into the trees.

Quoc was thirty yards ahead of them, waving them forward.

But leaves above him were inexplicably dropping. Leaves don't fall in the springtime, Nicholai thought weirdly, then he saw that bullets were clipping them off the branches and at the far end of the copse he saw Vietnamese militia coming toward them.

We are dead stones, he thought.

The flames were fast coming up behind, the French rapidly working their way to the left, and the militia was in front and on the right. If we run to the front, right or left, Nicholai saw, we will only run straight into the guns. If we stay here, we will burn.

Surviving was not an option.

They had only a choice of death.

Quoc waved violently. "Here! Here!"

Nicholai looked more closely and saw a Viet Minh crouch at Quoc's feet and then —

— disappear.

Into the earth.

Tunnels, he thought.

*Our motherland will swallow us.*

Sure enough, when he reached the middle of the copse, Nicholai saw small square openings. The Viet Minh were taking the rocket launchers out of the crates and handing them down the tunnel entrances.

"Come on," Quoc said, pointing to the little square hole at his feet.

It was narrow.

Solange could squeeze through it, *maybe* Nicholai could.

"You first," he said.

She balked. "I told you — I'm claustrophobic. I can't."

"You have to."

He helped Solange get down into the square hole and watched as she wiggled her shoulder and made her way down. Then he looked forward to the far end of the copse. He could make out individual soldiers. They were advancing too quickly for the Viet Minh to get the rest of the weapons down the tunnel. Even if they did, they wouldn't have time to cover up the entrances again, or escape in what could only be a vast and complicated maze of tunnels.

They would be trapped and caught.

Solange with them.

Quoc misapprehended his hesitation. "You are also afraid of tight spaces?"

Nicholai smiled, thinking of his blissful days exploring caves with his Japanese friends. "No."

He pointed toward the advancing troops. "We need more time."

"Yes."

"Take care of her," Nicholai said. "She isn't one of your 'ten.'"

"You have my word."

Quoc quickly chose five of his best men and Nicholai went with them toward the edge of the copse. The gunfire increased, branches dropped on them, men fell. When they got to the edge of the trees, one of the Viet Minh bent over and opened a square of earth.

Then they lay down and started to fire across the open ground.

Nicholai felt a body fall beside him, then he was face-to-face with the blazing green eyes of angry Solange. "I said I wasn't leaving without you."

"I'm sorry."

"Don't ever do that again."

She laid the stock of the machine pistol against her cheek and started shooting.

Diamond flattened himself onto the ground and peered through the grass at the copse of trees.

Nicholai Hel was trapped between the approaching flames and the rifles.

He hoped Hel chose the fire.

A harsh roar came up as the fire hit the trees.

Nicholai turned and saw them go, the flames climbing up the trunks and then igniting in the leafy branches with a hideous *whoosh*.

A Viet Minh ran from the center of the trees and signaled.

The weapons were in the tunnels.

"Time to disappear," Nicholai said.

They crawled back to the tunnel entrance.

Solange balked, but Nicholai helped her and she squeezed down. When she was clear, Nicholai lowered himself into the hole, his wide shoulders snug against the entrance. It was a very tight fit, and for a few seconds he thought he might not make it at all. But his caving experience had taught him how to narrow his shoulders, and he felt Solange tug at his legs, and then he slid down the entrance shaft.

Four Viet Minh came behind them, and the last one pulled the tunnel entrance shut behind him. Another one gave his life to replace the camouflage on top.

Nicholai found himself in a small oval chamber that opened to a narrow horizontal shaft, just high enough to crawl into on all fours. Lanterns, apparently run off a generator, were hung every twenty feet, and although the light was dim they could see to move. He eased Solange into the next tunnel and crawled behind her.

A minute later, Nicholai heard the flames erupt above them.

It would have been a bad death.

"Are you all right?" he asked Solange.

"I hate this."

"I know."

He paused, then followed Solange into the next chamber.

This one was larger, high enough to stand up in. Three horizontal shafts came off it in different directions. They rested for a moment, then one of the Viet Minh led them into another shaft, reached behind him, and ripped a plug from a cable, plunging the tunnels behind them into darkness.

Diamond cursed when the tunnel went black.

He had found the hastily camouflaged entrance and led several of the Vietnamese down the shaft into the first chamber. They crawled until they came to the chamber with the three shafts, then split up. Diamond took one of the men with him and was sure that he had the right tunnel as he could see recent scrape marks in the dirt below and could swear he heard the sound of movement, like rodents, ahead of him.

He was on the track and then darkness hit.

Fighting off a momentary panic, he felt for the flashlight on his belt, turned it on, and shone it in front of him. The light in his left hand, his .45 in his right, he crawled forward.

They crawled until they came to what seemed to be a dead end. But another shaft ran sharply to the right, and they took it, and then repeated this process of seeming dead ends until this maze zigzagged at least three hundred yards and Nicholai roughly reckoned that they must be literally out of the woods. They came to a chamber that had a vertical shaft and they descended a wooden ladder another twenty feet down to a much larger chamber.

"Your home for the next couple of days," Quoc said.

It was an underground barracks of sorts. Wooden-framed bunk beds lined the walls, rudely constructed wooden chairs were placed about, some medical supplies, bottles of water, and canned foods were neatly stacked and organized. There was even a small shelf of books, and relatively fresh air was being pumped from a narrow ventilator shaft.

"It's quite good," Nicholai said, "but I prefer the Continental."

"I'm sure Mancini would be pleased to welcome you," Quoc answered. "Shall I call for a reservation?"

"That's all right."

"Or the Beijing Hotel?"

"I'm growing fonder of this establishment by the second," Nicholai said, "assuming, of course, that the price is reasonable."

"Your bill has already been taken care of," Quoc said.

"It's a small city down here," Nicholai said. "How far does this complex go?"

"Now?" Quoc said, "Almost all the way to the outreaches of Saigon. Eventually, all the way to the suburbs."

"And then you pop out of the ground with rocket launchers and take the city," Nicholai said.

"When the time is right," Quoc said, "hopefully before the Americans blunder in. You will stay down here for a few days, then we will get you out, I think through Cambodia, if that suits you."

"That will be fine," Solange said.

She took a bottle of water, sipped from it, and handed it to Nicholai.

"We will leave you alone," Ai Quoc said.

He and his men left the chamber to see to the rocket launchers.

Diamond crawled to a dead end and realized that he must have chosen one of the false tunnels. They were clever, these Communist rats. He started to back out, then paused and felt a small waft of air. He shone the flashlight to his right, saw the concealed shaft, and headed into it.

Soon he came to another dead end.

Damn these bastards to hell, he thought.

Then he saw the next shaft.

He was halfway through the maze of zigzags when he heard a dull throb above him.

Nicholai looked up.

So did Solange.

They stared at the ceiling as if they actually thought that they could see what they were hearing.

A low-pitched hum and then a whining sound, and then the bombs hit.

The bombers came in directly over the tunnel complex and laid their ordnance in a spread pattern over a rectangle of a thousand square yards.

The chamber shook.

Dirt fell from the ceiling.

It all held for a moment and then there was a horrific bass thud and the bunk beds came down, and the neat stacks of supplies, and the walls quivered and more dirt came down and then the lights went out.

Nicholai heard Solange moan, "*Mon dieu, mon dieu.*"

He reached for her hand, found it, and pulled her forward, his mind reconstructing the chamber and locating the shaft. He found it with his hand, reached up for the rungs, and pulled her behind him.

"We have to get up!" he yelled, and then he felt her find her feet and they climbed up the ladder to the next chamber. They had to get up and out quickly or they would be buried alive.

A slow, suffocating death in the dark.

"Nicholai…"

"We're all right," he said. "We're all right. Stay with me."

He pulled her up into the next chamber. It was pitch dark now, a tight cloying blackness as he forced himself to remember the layout. It was difficult in the noise of the explosions above them, the falling dirt, the concussive force of the blasts.

You have been here many times before, he told himself, in many caves, in tighter spots than this, so *think*. He found the tunnel entrance first with his mind and then with his hands. Then he took off his shirt, tied one sleeve to his belt and the other to Solange's.

"Come on," he said. "We're going to be fine."

He led them into the entrance and they started back.


Diamond spat the dirt out of his mouth and rubbed it from his eyes.

God damn the Frogs, he thought. Didn't they know he was down here? Or did they know and didn't care?

"Come on," he said to the soldier behind him.

There was no answer.

The man was dead.

He plunged ahead.

* * *

The tunnel was fast coming in around them as Nicholai pulled Solange along. They came to one false wall after another, but Nicholai had the route firmly in his head and he crawled quickly, encouraging Solange all the way.

"Almost there."

"That's good."

"Oh, that's very good."

Diamond heard voices.

Speaking French.

He stopped, lay flat, and held the pistol out in front of him.

Nicholai's proximity sense warned him.

Someone was around the sharp right angle in front of them.

He stopped.

"What—"

"Ssshh."

A bomb blast rattled the walls. Dirt slid, narrowing the tunnel. His ears ringing, Nicholai couldn't hear. He slid forward on his stomach, and then a muzzle flash lit the tunnel and he saw Diamond.

Diamond crawled forward, shooting in front of him.

Nicholai reached his right hand as far as it would go, clutched at the air, and grabbed Diamond's wrist. "Solange, your knife!"

Diamond ripped his arm backward and freed his hand.

He lowered the pistol again, toward Nicholai's face.

Nicholai felt the powder blast burn his cheek.

He reached again in the dark, lunging out with a punch. "Your knife!"

\*    \*    \*

Solange coiled as much as she could in the narrowing confine of the tunnel. She pushed out with her long legs and squeezed past Nicholai, her knife in front of her.

Diamond pulled the trigger.

The muzzle flash blinded Nicholai. He crawled past Solange, and heard Diamond crawling away. He started to go after him, but then he heard Solange moan.

Diamond would have to wait.

He stopped and turned to Solange.

"Are you all right?" he asked her.

"Yes."

But then he felt the warm stickiness of her blood.

She was bleeding badly from the side. He couldn't see in the stygian darkness but he could feel.

So could she. "Please don't let me die down here."

"I won't let you die anywhere," he said.

Another blast rocked the tunnel. Dirt fell into their faces, their eyes, their noses, their mouths. He felt for her face, brushed the dirt away, then turned onto his back and started to pull himself along the tunnel shaft, pulling her behind him.

It was excruciatingly slow and he knew she was losing blood fast. The tunnel was collapsing, they were half buried, and he could only feel his way along, turn his head, and try to smell the way to open air.

He had to do it. He couldn't let her die.

After an eternity he turned, saw a faint beam of sunlight, and sensed a fleeting breath of fresh air. He pulled until they reached the bottom of the tunnel entrance.

"We're there," he gasped.

Now he clawed his way up the shaft with one hand and pulled her with the other. He climbed and fell four times before his hand gripped the surface with enough purchase to pull her weight up behind him.

He collapsed on the surface and pulled her into his arms.

"We're here, my love," he said. "We made it."

But Solange was still.

Limp and lifeless in his arms. He wiped a strand of her golden hair from her green eyes, and closed them.

Then the next bomb hit.

## 164

HE AWOKE in a bed.

Clean, crisp sheets tight around his legs.

Haverford looked down at him.

"Good morning."

"Where…"

"You're in a Saigon hospital," Haverford said. "A Foreign Legion patrol found you staggering around out in the delta. You were severely concussed, had some second-degree burns, shrapnel wounds, and three broken ribs."

"Solange?"

"I'm sorry," Haverford said.

Then Nicholai remembered.

A deep sorrow came over him.

"Why aren't I in a cell?" he asked, looking around the room. It was impossibly white and clean.

"Ah," Haverford said. "Your name is René Dazin. You're a French merchant that the Viet Minh kidnapped. You were very lucky that the bombing raid happened to set you free, my friend, the same bombing raid that killed Michel Guibert."

"Who made up that story?"

"I did, of course," Haverford said. "But you might want to get out of the country as soon as you can walk."

"Which should be when?"

"Might be another month or so," Haverford answered.

"I have a clean passport for you. You recuperate, then you disappear."

Nicholai nodded, and even that small move made his head throb. But he was heartened that Haverford thought he needed the passport, even though he had Voroshenin's multiple identities safely stashed with De Lhandes. The American agent, Nicholai thought, will believe he has me on a leash, and he will be wrong. Then he asked, "Diamond?"

"He made it out," Haverford said. "Rats usually do."

"Good," Nicholai answered, relieved that Diamond hadn't been killed by an impersonal bomb. He would visit Diamond personally and hold him to account. Not only for himself, but for Solange.

Haverford leaned closer and whispered, "Ai Quoc made it too. So did the weapons."

"You were working with him all the time," Nicholai said. He saw it now, all of it. Haverford had played a very deep game of Go, and played it well.

"Since we fought the Japanese together," Haverford answered. "It's a triple for me—the Soviets and the Chinese at knifepoint, Mao weakened, and a chance for Quoc to take Saigon and end this war before we can get into it."

"Do your bosses know?"

"I think so," Haverford answered. "My boss respects victory. I get promoted, Diamond gets put out to graze. Who knows, maybe you and I will get together again sometime for tea."

"I'd like that."

"Me too, chum," Haverford said. "*Sayonora*, Hel-san."

"*Sayonara*, Haverford-san."

Nicholai lay back and looked out the window at the pretty garden in the courtyard outside. Slashes of silver rain started to fall, the beginning of the wet season.

The beginning of a lot of things.

He had a new identity, the means to effect his revenge, access to the Ivanov fortune, not to mention the money he won from Bao Dai. After settling matters with Diamond and his cohorts, he could start a new life.

If indeed, he thought, there is such a thing as a new life without Solange.

There is, he thought, there must be, because you are alive and that is your karma. And it is your karma also that you are free now, truly free.

But to do what? he asked himself. How do you use your freedom? You are a killer, a warrior, a samurai — no, not a samurai, for you are not attached to any master. You are a *ronin*, a wanderer, an individual. So what does the *ronin* do now? How do you spend this life that has been restored to you?

You begin by killing Diamond, he decided, and then you go on to rid the world of as many Diamonds as you can. The men who kill the innocent — who torture, intimidate, brutalize and terrorize in the name of some "cause" that they believe in more than their own humanity.

He heard Kishikawa's voice.

*Hai, Nikko-san, it is a good way to spend a life.*

He looked out the window and saw the hard rain shear a leaf from a branch. The leaf fluttered to the ground, shimmering gold and green in the rain.

*Satori.*

# Acknowledgments

First, to Richard Pine and Michael Carlisle, for e-mailing to ask if I knew the meaning of the word *shibumi*, and for all their enthusiasm, counsel, and support; to Alexandra Whitaker, for her gracious cooperation and generosity; to Graham Greene, for writing the great Saigon novel; to Howard R. Simpson, whose *Tiger in the Barbed Wire* was essential reading; to Mitch Hoffman for being such a kind, patient, and perceptive editor.

Most of all, of course, to Rodney William Whitaker, a.k.a. Trevanian—I hope I did you proud, sir.

# Author's Note

Three summers ago I was sitting in my room at Oxford University (I was there to speak to a group of international students) when I received an e-mail from my agent, Richard Pine, that said, "Does the word *shibumi* mean anything to you?"

I thought, What are these guys doing back in New York, crossword puzzles?

But I wrote back helpfully, "It means 'understated elegance' in Japanese."

Richard responded, "How did you know that?"

I answered with what I thought was obvious: Back in the day there had been a famous book called *Shibumi,* which a bunch of my friends and I just gobbled up. It featured an assassin named Nicholai Hel who was, inter alia, an expert in the Japanese game of Go. We all took up the game (I was terrible at it) and played it well into many nights. I also recalled that Hel had a villa in the Basque country that he tried to imbue with the spirit of *shibumi.* The book, I needlessly typed to Richard, was written by an author whose pen name was Trevanian.

Figuring that I had put this curious correspondence to bed, I turned on the electric kettle to make myself a cup of Nescafé. It was a typical English summer day with the rain pelting against the window like the clacking of an old typewriter, and I was looking to the coffee to keep the chill off as I searched for a pair of dry socks and a snorkel with which to venture out for my next lecture. So, in truth, I was a little annoyed when I heard the *bong* of another e-mail summons and thought that, prominent literary agents that they are, Richard and his cohort Michael Carlisle at Inkwell could probably figure out a ten-letter word for "total destruction" without my help.

Richard's message read, "How would you like to be the next Trevanian?"

Well, I'm not, and nobody will be.

Rodney Whitaker, aka Trevanian, had such a unique and powerful voice that an attempt to imitate him would leave any writer looking like the second runner-up at a third-rate comedy club's open mike night.

So I approached the possibility of writing a prequel to *Shibumi* with great trepidation. First of all, what would the Whitaker family think? And how would his legion of devoted fans respond to a pretender to the throne? But more importantly, could I find a way to be true to the substance and style of the man's work without falling into the trap of offensive—and ultimately futile—mimicry?

But the temptation to try was overwhelming. How could you not seize the opportunity to work with a character as complex and fascinating as Nicholai Hel? How could you not accept the challenge to create within the parameters of the fascinating plot that Trevanian merely hinted at in *Shibumi*—a story that begins in Japan, proceeds to China, and then finds its way to Vietnam? Not only did I admire Trevanian's work, but I also have a great love of Asia, its culture, and history, so the chance to combine those enthusiasms was irresistible.

I sat down and wrote a letter of introduction to the Whitaker family.

They have been nothing short of wonderful.

Alexandra Whitaker has been pitch-perfect in safeguarding

her father's legacy without coming even close to suffocating this nervous writer during his efforts to do the same. She has offered discreet, invaluable counsel, and I truly hope that I have repaid her kindness with quality.

I usually work very much alone—in almost reclusive solitude—but this was a very different experience. In writing *Satori,* I quickly became aware that I was representing a group of people who were passionately excited and invested in the Hel saga. The aforementioned Messrs. Pine and Carlisle offered crucial critiques and suggestions. Mitch Hoffman, the editor at Grand Central, was an amazingly thoughtful and perceptive contributor. At first I was concerned that I would find all this close attention a bit much. In fact, the opposite was true—conspiring with this team to create a work worthy of Trevanian has been more fun than a writer should be allowed to have.

The work was nevertheless daunting. I had to re-create the Asia of 1951 and '52, a research task that was as rewarding as it was enormous. More complex was the challenge of styling a Nicholai Hel that the reader would recognize as the fully formed man of *Shibumi* while at the same time writing a character who was twenty-six years old—and a neophyte in the world of espionage—at the time of the story. Then there was the task of trying to blend my own voice into that of Trevanian's, as well as writing to the "corners" of the story that he had left in place.

All of which is to say that I had a *wonderful* time writing this book. What a gift I was given from a very brief e-mail on a rainy day in Oxford. I hope that I've passed even a small part of that on to the reader.

Don Winslow